LOOKING FOR MR. RIGHT

"Are you cured?" CeeCee asked.

"Cured?"

"Of bad relationships," Daphne stated impatiently.

"That's the point, isn't it?" Jill put in. "You seem about to swear off men forever."

"Really?"

They all nodded in unison. The three of them acted as if they'd been talking this out behind my back. I could gain a serious complex. I swear, sometimes I think it's a conspiracy: Fix Ginny Blue.

Why is it that I think *they're* the ones with the problems?

"Swear off men forever?" I repeated.

Jackson Wright's face swam in front of my vision. My inner eyes focused on the curve of his lips, the strength of his jaw. His humor. His intelligence.

I knew I was going to sleep with him . . .

Don't Miss These Jane Kelly Mysteries by Nancy Bush!

CANDY APPLE RED

ELECTRIC BLUE

ULTRAVIOLET

Published by Kensington Publishing Corporation

Ginny Blue's Boyfriends

NANCY KELLY

KENSINGTON BOOKS
http://www.kensingtonbooks.com

KENSINGTON BOOKS are published by

Kensington Publishing Corp.
850 Third Avenue
New York, NY 10022

Copyright © 2005 by Nancy Bush

All rights reserved. No part of this book may be reproduced
in any form or by any means without the prior written con-
sent of the Publisher, excepting brief quotes used in reviews.

All Kensington titles, imprints and distributed lines are available at special quantity discounts for bulk purchases for sales
promotion, premiums, fund-raising, educational or institu-
tional use.

Special book excerpts or customized printings can also be
created to fit specific needs. For details, write or phone the office of the Kensington Special Sales Manager: Kensington
Publishing Corp., 850 Third Avenue, New York, NY, 10022.
Attn. Special Sales Department. Phone: 1-800-221-2647.

Strapless and the Strapless logo are trademarks of Kensington
Publishing Corp.
Kensington and the K logo Reg. U.S. Pat. & TM Off.

ISBN-13: 978-0-7582-0371-7
ISBN-10: 0-7582-0371-3

First Kensington Trade Paperback Printing: September 2005
First Kensington Mass Market Printing: August 2007
10 9 8 7 6 5 4 3 2 1

Printed in the United States of America

Chapter

1

Was it George Strait who crooned, *All My Exes Live in Texas*? I think so. It's certainly one of those country western singers. I'm envious of George. Truly. He only has one state to worry about. All my exes reside in varying parts of California, Oregon, Washington, and Arizona, and since I have no desire to leave the great state of California myself, I'm constantly surrounded by them. Worse, they all live on and on in my mind. The Ex-Files—currently weighing in at seven—take up way too much of my brain matter. I've got to find a way to expunge them. I swear, it's the only answer to the funk I find myself in these days. Past romances really put the pressure on my relationship with Nate the Nearly Normal, lover and roommate. In fact, I had this worrisome, itchy feeling that Nate was about to become Ex-File Number 8.

Let me back up . . . .

I have this penchant for nicknames. I can't help myself. As soon as I learn someone's name—especially if that someone could be a potential boyfriend—my brain starts churning out rhymes and allusions and ironic twists. It's like I go into a zone until I've come up with some clever name. I blame my mother. It's the curse she wrought when she had the lunacy to name me Virginia November Bluebell. Could I make a whole lotta names outta that one! As it is I've shortened "Virginia" to "Ginny" and my close friends call me "Blue." I asked Mom once, "Why November?" and she answered, "Because I love the sound of it." The look on my face must've reflected my desperation to understand, so she added, "And November 11th is Veteran's Day," as if that explained it all. Since my deadbeat father had never been a veteran and no one in my family seemed attached to this particular holiday, this made even less sense. My mother is nothing if not obscure. However, she's one hell of a real estate agent and I love her dearly. Lorraine Bluebell could sell ice cubes to Eskimos and probably does on the side.

Anyway, I woke up this particular morning with Nate the Nearly Normal's arm wrapped possessively around my stomach and realized I couldn't stand his flesh touching mine another nanosecond. This feeling of repulsion had been coming on for a while; a niggling thought I'd kept buried way down deep. Nate was the proverbial nice guy and there had been so few of them during the past few dating years that I had hung onto him for dear life. I'd made myself believe I liked—loved—him, as much as I could love—like—anyone. I told myself I was happy in the relationship.

And there were benefits to being with Nate. He didn't completely embarrass me in public by doing any of those disgusting male things that seem to be tacitly okayed by other males, such as scratching his ass, farting, or adjusting his balls. And whenever I peered out at the competition, I literally shuddered. Conclusion: It was easier to stay in my current position as Nate the Nearly Normal's girlfriend than to throw myself into the dating pit again.

But this particular morning was different. As I plucked his arm from around my waist, sliding cautiously from our bed, cringing at the movement, afraid even the slightest quiver of the mattress might wake him, I knew it was time to get out while the getting was good. I dropped one foot to the hardwood floor and Nate's breathing kind of stuttered and stopped for a moment. I froze. He expelled air in a long, morning-breath sigh, then started up again, more lightly. I waited in this immobile limbo, counting my heartbeats. Finally I slipped out of the bed and tiptoed to the bathroom.

In a rush of joy I did a little dance of freedom on the other side of the door. I actually had the audacity to turn the lock. Privacy. Aloneness. I craved them like chocolate in the midst of a particularly heavy period. With my own exhalation of breath—a deep sigh of contentment—I stepped into the shower and turned the taps.

The door knob rattled. "Ginny? Gin? You taking a shower?"

Nate: Master of stating the obvious. I turned my face to the hot spray and pretended to be deaf.

How had this happened? How come all his traits suddenly bothered me so much? What had once been endearing were flat-out irritating, and what had once been irritating now was beyond bearing. The thought of him turning over in bed and kissing me was flat-out repellent, yet it hadn't been that many months ago that I'd looked forward to our lovemaking, had daydreamed about it while on the job, had planned for it, yearned for it, lived for it.

I must have made some sound because he called through the panels, "Did you say something, honey?"

"Can't hear you!" I hollered back, then scrubbed at my hair with masochistic energy and force. Mentally, I listed all the reasons that Nate had to get out of my life. First and foremost, he liked to cuddle. Now, I know many women find this behavior something to put in the plus column, but for me it was like being surrounded by a boa constrictor whose radiant heat sent my internal temperature into thermonuclear levels. I'd wake up only to find myself ready to pass out again from the suffocating BTUs. Who would have guessed such a seemingly mild-mannered man could turn me into a device able to melt the polar ice cap?

Okay, to be truthful, this cuddling thing had once been

lodged in the "endearing" column. But after six months—
oh, God, was it almost seven?—I'd had to shift it into "beyond bearing."

But his body temperature was only part of the problem.
There were just so many things about him that bothered me,
I marveled that we'd ever gotten together in the first place.
Let me elucidate:

I don't like the food he eats. Too healthy. Enough alfalfa
sprouts and tofu to open a southern California bistro. There
are just those days I crave an Oki dog as if it were life-giving
elixir. Oki dogs are from that little spot on Fairfax of the
same name. It's a hot dog, sliced flat and smothered in
sauces and onions and all kinds of stuff guaranteed to make
your heart seize up but good. It smells and tastes so fabulous
you want to roll up in fetal position and moan. Sometimes I
wonder if I was born in the wrong generation. I know I'm
definitely in the wrong decade. I like red meat with nitrates
and potato chips—the real kind, none of that no-fat shit—and
gravy and angel food cake. Yes, I can get off on lattes and
macchiatos, too, and sure, I like salads with radicchio and wal-
nuts, so I'm not completely out of it yet. But Nate is sooooo
early-twenty-first-century Californian it makes me want to
scream. And he flirts with vegetarianism. He really does. If he
goes over to the other side once and for all, let me tell you:
it's over for good.

What am I saying? It's already over. No one can suffer
these feelings without recognizing that it's over.

I closed my eyes and shuddered. There had been a time
that we'd talked about the "M" word, at least jokingly. Marriage, though somewhere in the distant future, had been a
perceived, possible goal. Our relationship had changed from
gentle interest, to friendship, to romance, to thinking about a
future together, to . . . disenchantment. Did Nate feel it? I
wondered. At all? Or, was he as blissfully happy as he'd been
at the beginning?

I soaped my hair for the third time and stuck my head

under the shower head. The hot water was not quite as hot as it had been. If I stayed here long enough I'd use it up completely and then Nate would be faced with a cold shower. *Not only am I heartless, I'm mean,* I thought. Unable to believe myself that low, I turned off the taps.

It's because he's a native Californian, I decided suddenly. That would explain it. I'm an Oregonian, and we have this basic snobbery about our neighbors to the south. They're too self-indulgent, too flaky, too shallow, too politically correct (not that we aren't, too, but I'm just saying . . .). There are also about a billion of them compared to us. Okay, that's an exaggeration. But statistically there are something like ten million people in Los Angeles alone and only three million in the entire state of Oregon, so hey, if we've got a bit of an inferiority complex we come by it naturally. Oregonians and Californians don't mix. They can't. It's a law of nature, or something.

Okay, okay . . . I know everything I've said is a total crock. My problems with Nate had nothing to do with where I'm from versus where he's from. I was just. Done With. The. Relationship. It had come to this and now I had to address it and I really didn't want to.

Sighing, I stood dripping for a few moments in the shower, not quite ready to step into my morning world. Nate the Nearly Normal . . . Mr. Wonderful . . . ideal husband and sweet lover. When I first met him I thought his only flaw was that he worked in finance as some kind of low-level manager who oversaw clients' pension plans or IRAs or whatever. I knew next to nothing about what he did, and it was just as well, because anytime he talked about it I began to yawn. This wasn't intentional on my part, but it was an equal and opposite reaction to his business talk. It couldn't be helped.

"When our clients lost faith in stocks and even mutual funds, we transferred a lot of money into bonds," he said the other morning over breakfast. I was grabbing a piece of peanut-butter toast and listening with half an ear. "I did some of that myself, but the market's come back. I'm not really sure I like the percentages of my own investment portfolio. I never like to 'overweight' any one kind of investment."

What I heard was "overweight." I've never had a serious weight problem and at 5 feet 9 inches I can hide a lot of bad nutritional decisions. But I was feeling at my top end, scale-wise, and the word ran around my skull like the ball in a spinning roulette wheel. I didn't hear the rest of what he said as I dropped the toast crusts into the disposal as if they were hot coals. Then, I yawned. I could feel the droop of my eyelids mixed with an anxious churning deep inside my gut that reminded me I'd eaten three mini-Snickers bars from the bag of Halloween candy we were saving for trick-or-treaters.

This was two nights ago and I'd steered clear of those little bastards ever since. A very difficult task since as my interest in Nate waned, my interest in chocolate waxed. Snickers bars were a perennial favorite no matter what man was in my life. Sometimes I consider them a breakfast food.

Rubbing my face, I finger-combed my hair and un-snapped the shower door.

"Hey! You locked the door!" Nate called from the bed-room.

"Oh . . . sorry."

Wrapping one towel around my wet hair and another around my torso, I took a breath and turned the knob. The lock opened with a distinctive *click*. Nate pushed the door inward and looked at me with a furrowed brow.

"You okay?" he asked, sounding slightly wounded.

"Never better."

He took that on face value and squeezed past me, dropping his dark green boxers along the way as he stepped into the shower. I stared down at them and listened to the taps turn on. I had to stifle the urge to slingshot the underwear over the top of the shower door.

I'm a bitch. I am. There's no way I should be feeling this way about Nate.

"Jesus!" he hollered. "Did you have to use all the hot water?"

I closed the bathroom door behind me and beelined for the closet. Nate the Nearly Normal. I'd labeled him fairly early on, giddily thrilled that yes, I'd finally met someone nice and yes, he was nearly normal. My mother—who refuses to take any kind of blame herself—says my penchant for giving all my boyfriends nicknames is my way of distancing myself from both them and the invariably ugly breakup that will relegate them to the "Ex-Files." This is undoubtedly true. Besides Nate there are, in my steadily growing Ex-Files: Don the Devout, Hairy Larry, Black Mark, Brad Knowles-It-All, and I suppose, Dr. Dick, if you count my shrink as an ex, which he isn't, but he ought to be, to name just a few. There are several others I'd prefer to just forget.

Sinking onto the end of the bed, I thought, *I've hit the relationship quagmire. That yawning pit surrounding my feet where men fall into the abyss and are never heard or seen again . . . thank God.*

Thinking about my mother had me gnawing on my fingernails before I could stop myself. My mother thinks my problems all stem from one man, Jackson Wright, with whom she caught me in bed at a very early age. Actually nothing was going on between us. Well, nothing serious, anyway. A little bit of early high school exploration was all, but it nearly sent my mother around the bend. She does have that streak of white hair now, but I like to think that's an affectation, a nod to style and fashion, though it did first appear shortly after the incident. I tell her it's becoming and she has a tendency to respond to this buttering-up with a Bronx cheer. Once or twice she's even whacked me on the backside with one of her big-ass purses. This is affection, not abuse.

But she's right about Jackson Wright in one regard: he blighted my youth. Though I try not to think about him—I mean, seriously, a high school affair?—he definitely contributed to my cautiousness and distrust when it comes to men. Oh, and let's not forget my father's contributions in that area. He managed about ten months of child support before disappearing completely. Bully for Dad. He almost helped pay my keep for a year. My mother supported me my entire life.

But I digress . . .

Cradling my chin in my hands, I sighed and thought about Jackson. I didn't know if he really even counted as a boyfriend, ergo, how could he really be an ex? We never officially dated. We just sort of always knew each other and so our relationship fell somewhere between acquaintanceship and friendship. He moved to SoCal about the same time I did and he works peripherally in the entertainment biz, as I do. Jackson's a financial manager to the rich and famous, and an investor in projects and productions. I recognize him when I see him and he recognizes me. I'm not sure if he feels that same little jolt of remembrance that I do, but we are certainly courteous to one another. I suppose it's telling that I don't have a nickname for Jackson, but then, as I said, he's doesn't truly belong in the Ex-Files.

Still, he's the guy I tend to use as a yardstick to rate other men. For instance, when I first kissed Eric Digby in seventh grade outside the mall behind one of the garbage bins, my mind was on Jackson Wright, the hottest guy in junior high. I wondered what his tongue was like. Was it as wet and wiggly as Eric's? Impossible! At least I hoped not. And then Kevin McNally, with his wandering hands and moaning kisses. There was no way Jackson could ever be accused of the same kind of uncool moves, I was sure. And later I was proved right, for when Jackson and I had our own bed *tête-à-tête,* I learned his style was just about perfect. Ever after that night all the guys I've known have faced the Wright Standard Test. Not one has made it into the top ten percent, more's the pity.

Luckily, in high school I never let myself have any real

feelings for Jackson. I knew better than that. Other girls fell for him but I always sensed he was unattainable and steered clear. It simply wasn't worth the heartache. I made it my practice to keep my emotions under tight control, and I've managed fairly well all these years, thank you very much.

But, Jackson does infiltrate my life, even to this day. Did I mention that every single one of my friends has fallen for him on sight? And these aren't high school girls. I'm talking about my college friends: Jill, CeeCee, and Daphne. I warned them. I truly did, but I guess you have to experience Jackson Wright personally to really appreciate and understand. Luckily, their easily won hearts are also fairly fickle, so Jackson simply moved through them like a wave, leaving only minor jetsam and flotsam damage, as near as I can tell. Of course we all hate him.

"Hey, Blue!" Nate the Nearly Normal hollered above the hissing spray of the shower. Yanking the towel off my head I scurried around, quickly sticking one leg through the pants of my jeans, hopping on one foot, then managing to thrust the other leg through before I fell back on the bed. I refused to answer him. Screaming at someone over running water never works and, let's face it, I didn't want to talk to him anyway. Dragging my black turtleneck sweater over my head, I caught sight of my black leather jacket but even though it was nearly Halloween, this is LA, my friend. Chances were I'd bake as it was.

Apparently Nate forgot whatever he wanted from me because moments later I could hear his off-key singing permeate the air. Heading downstairs I wandered into the tiny U-shaped kitchen of my two-bedroom rented condo and popped some bread in the toaster. Thinking about Nate depressed me, so instead I concentrated on Jackson Wright. Transference of anger is a good thing, I often think.

So . . . yeah . . . Jackson. As I've said, he's an old classmate with whom I snuggled naked but didn't actually consummate anything worth noting. Of course it consumed me at the time, though I hid my feelings, and once or twice I felt kind of melancholy over the whole damn thing, but I was a kid. It was really nothing. I moved to California and attended a junior college while Jackson headed to Eugene and the University of Oregon. When I was back in the Portland area for vacations and the like, and he was home, we would often run into each other. We have always been kind of on again/off again friends. Nothing earth-shattering.

But then Jackson moved to California and, through me, was introduced to my circle of friends. Jill was particularly smitten with Jackson until he paid her absolutely no attention and/or made some clever, albeit slightly cruel comment about an issue tender to her psyche, which pissed her off. I've never quite heard the full extent of it. He's actually managed this with all my friends. Daphne can't say his name without curling her lip. None of them got all that involved, as far as I can tell, although there was talk of actual thumping bedsprings with CeeCee before the disillusionment. It's amazing how Jackson keeps cropping up like the proverbial bad penny. When my friends and I meet at Sammy's on Saturday mornings—a loosely formed complaint club—someone invariably makes a comment on Jackson. Reliving the Jackson fallout every week would be excruciating, except that our Saturday morning meetings often have a tendency to be postponed. If someone can't make the Saturday meeting, which is almost always, things fall apart. I made a silent vow to be better about seeing my friends. Jill, Daphne, and CeeCee were sometimes all that stood between me and despair over the male sex.

My roommate, bedmate, and what currently felt like cellmate, whose footsteps I'd heard on the stairs, suddenly joined me in the kitchen. Nate's dark hair was damp and he was wrapped in a white terrycloth bathrobe.

"Hey," he said, heading to the refrigerator as I buttered my toast.

"Hey," I answered.

We're known for our scintillating conversation.

"I'm heading to work," he added.

"Me, too."

"What are you doing today?"

I swallowed a piece of toast with difficulty and murmured, "Nothing much. Gotta check with the caterer for that Waterstone Iced Tea job."

He grunted acknowledgment. Nate has about as much interest in my career as I have in his. I left without another word. I was in my Explorer and scooting east on the 10 freeway before he'd picked up—hopefully—his shorts and begun to dress.

It was an exceptionally brilliant late October morning in sunny southern California. You could actually see the Hollywood hills and almost make out the Hollywood sign. I was heading toward the downtown business district and suddenly remembered how Jackson had once said that he wouldn't be able to stand Los Angeles if it weren't for the rare, bright morning of clear air that surprised Angelinos and tourists alike. He was right on that one. He's been right on a lot of things. *Probably why "Wright" is his last name,* I thought sourly. It's infuriating how right he is and, because he's a man, you just have to be careful how many times you point out this fact. I never would tell Jackson he's right, but then, luckily, I hadn't seen him in a long while so it was a moot point. I never told Nate he's right either, although that's because I wondered if he truly ever was.

I nearly slapped both of my faces right there. Good grief. Nate was a good guy. A great guy. I was the one having the problem.

Better not to dwell on that and send my self-esteem into a tailspin. Instead I soaked in the pretty day. LA is something else. People either love it or hate it. Weather's good, weather's better, weather's sometimes too smoggy. Big deal. I've spent the last ten years living in Santa Monica after my final anemic semester. Currently, I'm debating on signing up for a film editing class at USC. Don't ask me why because I have no

answer for that. I'm a production manager for film and television, which sounds a lot more glamorous than it is since
I'm basically the person who keeps the job moving forward
and who gets screamed at by the actual producer if something goes wrong. I am *not* the producer, therefore I am not
the person in command. Nor am I the director, who is the
person with attitude and therefore the real power behind the
throne. I guess you'd say I'm midlevel management; top-
level stress. This puts me about two levels above a PA, that
is, a production assistant, which is synonymous with "the person everybody else shits on." I've been that person. I know
of what I speak.

The caterer I was meeting was one everyone raved about,
but also one I'd never actually met. The meeting wasn't all
that important, but I'd wanted to escape from Nate and I figured I might as well get it over with.

Cars tore along on all sides of me. We were moving at a
nice clip. The 10 can back up but it's not as bad as the 405,
which is a nightmare at damn near all hours and I avoid it
like the plague. I've actually been stopped cold on the 405
more times than I'd like to count. Once, the only thing that
kept me sane was watching the couple in the Nissan next to
me screaming at each other in fury one moment, making out
the next, and then having sex, she on his lap, her head thrown
back and screaming in ecstasy while he bounced around beneath her. All before we moved forward. Afterwards I wished
I'd had a cigarette. The hell of it is, I don't smoke.

Maybe I should take it up, I mused now, throwing a
glance to the silver BMW convertible on my right. The girl
behind the wheel wore sunglasses and that bored "you can't
impress me" look refined by southern Californians. A cigarette dangled from her lips. Very sexy, really. My eyes water
from smoke, though, so I don't think I could pull that one
off. And let's be honest, smoking is bound to take up too
much time. When I think about all the smokers I've witnessed searching for lighters and matches, or cupping their

hands around the ends of their cigarettes to keep the breeze from blowing them out, it actually raises my anxiety level. I *worry* for them. What if they don't get it lit? What if they break out into some kind of nicotine-deprived fit? What if they turn their frustration on me? No, it's really not worth it. And I'm basically cheap anyway, so I would never be able to stand the expense. Oh, and if I were called back to set, just as soon as I lit one and then had to stub out the end before I even took two drags . . . That would just plain hurt.

I do so need a vice, however, and alcohol consumption is not cutting it. I'd love to indulge in wild, illicit sex, but I seem to be totally disinterested in nearly every man who crosses my path these days. This worries me slightly.

My cell phone chirped. I snatched it up in mid-tweet. "Talk to me," I said.

Jill stated flatly, "Goddamn men."

"Is it Ian?"

"The *fucking* asshole!"

The *fucking* asshole was Ian Cooper, Jill's boyfriend. He used to be the man she cooed over while she walked six inches above the floor, stars in her eyes, little red hearts zinging rapturously from that beating, lovestruck muscle in her chest as she floated along in a haze of drunken joy. During this time they were inseparable, so we collectively named them "Jill-Ian," which unfortunately may now be difficult to completely eradicate. But Ian had, as it turned out, made a grave error in the game of love. He had *lied*. Deliberately and with malice aforethought, at least according to Jill. He had taken another girl to Belize exactly one week before he started sleeping with Jill. Ian had patiently pointed out that this shady event had occurred while he and Jill were still technically friends, and he had also added that he and said girl had not actually had sex on that trip. It was, again according to Ian, one of those unforeseen disasters in the making: a vacation planned and prepaid while the romance was still hot and heavy, only to then loom over them like some

Sword of Damocles as the relationship sped rapidly down, down, down. The two ex-lovebirds had, of course, gone on the trip anyway and had enjoyed a perfectly terrible time.

Here's the lie: Ian told Jill that he took this jaunt with a guy-friend named Worth rather than risking the fallout from Jill. Unfortunately, she learned of the lie six months later when Worth, who did not live in LA, came for a surprise visit and was not properly cued by Ian. When asked by Jill, "How was the trip to Belize?" Worth answered with a snotty, "I hate foreign countries. And I especially hate South American countries. I wouldn't go there if I was flaccid as a cooked noodle and it was the only place on earth selling Viagra. If I'm going to leave the country I'm going to Hawaii!"

If I'd been there when this conversation took place, I would have pointed out that Hawaii wasn't exactly leaving the country. Jill, however, was too incensed to pick up on this nuance, and from all accounts, Worth is a snobbish moron who, luckily for him, possesses enough money to make up for his horrifyingly midget pea brain—a harsh but true fact of social life in greater Los Angeles, which is undoubtedly where Worth is from. In my opinion he is simply Worth Less. I do not know his last name and do not plan to learn it. My mother would point out that I was nicknaming outside of the Ex-Files, but the name just begged to be used. Besides, I don't strictly follow my own rules.

Jill, outraged by Ian's deception, accused him of lying about the trip straightaway. Trapped, he shrugged his shoulders and admitted it. He's been the *fucking* asshole ever since.

But they still sleep together.

I said, "What's he done now?"

"He's bought me a ring. A diamond ring," she added significantly.

My jaw dropped. "An engagement ring?" The subject of marriage turns my palms clammy. I have this conviction that it will never, ever happen to me, and though I'm fairly certain I will never want it, one never knows. . . .

"I think so." She inhaled and exhaled shakily. "I just—want to strangle him."

"That doesn't sound like a 'yes.' "

"What the hell is he doing? I can't marry anyone. He knows that. He's just doing this because he wants to make a point."

"Pretty dangerous point to make if you don't mean it."

"Stop being so sane. You know how I hate that."

"Do I sound sane? I don't feel sane. And everything you're saying is insane." I shook my head and tried to concentrate on traffic. The girl in the BMW lackadaisically stubbed out her cigarette in the ash tray as we hurtled merrily along at an easy 75 miles per hour. You had to love the 10 when there was no traffic. "What do you want to do?"

"Blue?"

"Yeah?"

"Blue, are you there? Blue?"

The phone went dead in my ear. There are mysterious blank zones on the 10 that cut off cell phones with a distinct click. It's as if there's this roguish god, watching, chuckling, touching a magic finger into cell-phone-space and breaking the connection. I glanced upward, expecting a grinning Cheshire cat face to emerge from the puffy clouds, high in the sky. *God, it's a nice day,* I thought, and I'm sure my mind would have drifted to Jackson again if the cell phone hadn't gone through a series of aborted half-rings. Jill was trying to call back and unable to get through.

Good. I really didn't feel like talking any longer. Jill has already received two previous marriage proposals. She's clocking them in at about one per year. The last time I came close to that, if you discount my current live-in relationship with Nate, was when I was dating Dave the Devout, and I was so afraid he would somehow suck me into his obsessive

God thing that it makes me shudder to even remember those days.

Jill is about thirty pounds lighter than I am. She is thin, thin, thin, and would never believe it if you told her she needs to gain weight. The hell of it is: she looks pretty good by today's unhealthy standards. She's a few inches shorter than I am and a whole lot narrower. She's cute and smart and pugnacious and when I'm standing next to her I feel like a water buffalo. We definitely attract different types of men, but hers always seem to be ready to tie the knot.

The phone was still in my hand. I fiddled with it. Maybe I should call Daphne for moral support. She'd been going through a romantic dry spell recently and needed tons of reassurance. Her problem is she always hankers after the wrong kind of guy. She's like a magnet for losers. Currently she's hankering after some guy she works with at Starbucks. Both Daphne and Mr. Starbucks are aspiring actors. Bad karma, I say. Never date an actor. Period. I suppose you can turn that around and make it sound as if I don't want anyone to date Daphne either, but that's not entirely true. Daphne is better than most actors. Less egocentric. Less needy. But then, I've done the dating-the-actor thing. I've even dated a so-called "famous" actor. It just doesn't work. Too weird. I was at a party once, not long after Mr. Famous Actor and I broke up, and all I had to do was mention that I'd had a relationship with him and the guy I was speaking to suddenly started choking on his shrimp roll and was outta there faster than you can say Chinese Take Out. No one, but NO ONE, wanted to be the guy directly after Mr. Famous Actor. I've had to eighty-six that relationship from my personal history just to get guys to talk to me. As far as I'm concerned, Mr. Famous Actor is not a member of the Ex-Files.

I punched out Daphne's number then hit the "send" button. A moment later I cut the connection. What was I thinking? I didn't want to hear her moan about the Starbucks/would-be-actor guy again, did I?

I set the phone down.

The girl in the convertible removed her shades for a moment, then studiously put them back on. I did the proverbial double take. *It's Carmen Watkins*, I thought, shaken. Carmen and I had met in college and she'd always been wealthy and snobby and gorgeous, apart from a rather prominent nose that she'd clearly had fixed in the intervening years. I'd truly thought the girl in the car was much younger than I was. It was a terrible shock to realize she was thirty-two as well. No way! She looked twenty-two.

How *could* she?

I'm not normally affected by the southern California overindulgence in plastic surgery but seeing the effects on Carmen got to me way down deep. Wondering if I needed therapy, I called Dr. Dick's number.

His receptionist answered on the third ring. "Offices of Dr. Richard Malcolm," she said smoothly.

"Hi, it's Ginny Bluebell," I said. Hearing my own name is easier now. For years I'd wondered if my mother had saddled me with this moniker from some primal need, maybe fueled by the same urge animals feel when they're about to eat their young. But then, her last name is also Bluebell, so she was stuck, too. But *Virgin*-ia? No wonder her hair went when she caught me in bed with Jackson.

"Is he in?" I asked.

"He's with someone right now," she said. Was her tone as smug as I imagined? She's never liked me. Probably because I, like many of Dr. Dick's screwed up patients, I'm sure, tend to lose myself in a fantasy while on his couch. He's just so great to look at. Tall, with long legs and pressed, light-blue denim jeans, a white shirt rolled up the forearms, serious blue eyes, dark, slightly wavy hair . . . he's gorgeous. Movie-star gorgeous in fact, but, well . . . normal. Or as normal as any therapist can truly be, I suppose. I've tried for months to reveal my deepest, darkest secrets, but in his office I confess that all I manage to do is devise truly convoluted plots to get him into bed with me. He's the guy with whom I'd really love to indulge in wild, illicit sex, but he appears to have scruples. He doesn't want to screw around with one of his clients/patients. I've thought of quitting him, but that wouldn't guarantee I'd ever see him again. Though I secretly and lustily drool over him, he seems genuinely disinterested in me.

A true conundrum. One that could send me straight to the Zoloft if I had any around, which I don't, because Dr. Dick won't prescribe it to someone as "frightfully well adjusted" as I am. Go figure.

"Would you like to make an appointment?" the receptionist asked briskly.

"Umm . . . no, not now. I'll call back later."

She didn't even respond. Just hung up. A true bitch, but she gets high marks for style.

The caterer—and restauranteur—I was supposed to be meeting was named Liam Engleston. I knew him by his reputation: wonderful food, but high maintenance to the point of ionospheric. I was really doing this as a favor to the crew members who regarded him as some kind of gastronomical deity, but it worried me slightly because I'm not good at stroking egos, and even worse at frozen-smile groveling. Plus, we have a minimal budget on the job for feeding the production crew. Craft Services provides Red Vines and candy bars, and those are available all day. Gourmet/schmourmet. Chances were the lunch and possibly breakfast would be too rich for our budget, but at least I could say I'd tried.

I strode into the building that housed Engleston's restaurant, my fatalistic attitude all over my face. The restaurant was in the heart of the business district which meant it catered to the Suits. Spying several Suits twirling through the revolving door and riding the escalators to the mezzanine/restaurant level, I did a quick mental check of my own outfit. Not good. The business people were all as buttoned down as Wall Street bankers in this part of town while I was dressed in my jeans and turtleneck. I rode the escalator to the restaurant with an underlying feeling of anxiety. It was a rather stark atmosphere of black leather booths and ultracool, high-tech lighting. Glassware sparkled over the bar. Nothing about the place read "cheap," so when Liam Engleston appeared I was already ready to say thanks, but no thanks, and vamoose.

He shook my hand and passed a quick look over my getup. His nostrils flared ever so slightly.

"Ms. Bluebell," he greeted me with a stiff English accent, offering a handshake as warm and welcoming as an Alaskan cod. His lips had a way of curling around his words that had me somewhat mesmerized. I had to force myself not to stare. He wasn't attractive in the *least* but I was fascinated anyway. It was kind of like stopping to watch a car wreck.

I didn't waste time. "We're shooting a Waterstone Iced Tea commercial at Venice beach at the end of the month. I've heard nothing but raves about your hors d'oeuvres and sandwiches. I just need to know the total price for lunches for a three-day shoot."

He stroked his moustache. Did I mention that he had this kind of Fu Manchu thing going? Not quite the real thing, but close enough to send my mind wandering down red-lit hallways decorated with Chinese lanterns. I really try not to mind facial hair but it is such a turnoff. I can dislike a man on sight if he's bearded. I hate to admit it. I truly do. But it's one of those things I just can't seem to get past. Don the Devout had a close-cropped beard, and I kind of associate facial hair with head-bowing over the dinner table amidst murmurs of Jesus and God and all that is holy. Don's favorite meal was lamb and tiny roasted potatoes with mint jelly and I can't face a menu with that combination listed without getting all reverent and nostalgic. (Actually, that's a lie. Don's devotion to his religion has left me a bit of an atheist, I'm afraid. Except that I believe in God. Sort of. Don certainly does. Many's the time I remember him screaming, "Oh, God, oh, God, oh, oh, my GAWD . . ." which was my cue that orgasm was imminent. Kind of like playing the *Star Spangled Banner* and then hearing, "Play ball!" I still meld the two events upon occasion.)

"What are the exact dates?" Liam Engleston said stiffly.

I pulled out my organizer. A Kate Spade rendition. I've thought about Palm Pilots or Visors, but hey, one step at a time. E-mail is great, buying airline tickets online even better. The cell phone's a wonder, but I tread lightly into the full-blown electronic age. I do love my iMac.

I gave Liam the information and he rubbed his mustache a few more times. I pasted a polite, "I don't have anywhere to go right now, you just take your time, honey, don't mind me one little bit" look on my face and tried to imagine him without the scraggly hair around his mouth. Better. Not good enough though. He still possessed the weird lips and overall nebbishness and priggery. He'd sure as hell better be able to whip up something good in the kitchen. And it better not be traditional English food, I concluded with a slight shudder, contemplating boiled cabbage and potatoes. My California work crew would revolt. But, then, they were the ones who'd recommended this guy in the first place, so who was I to argue?

"What is your job, exactly?" he asked.

"Mine? I'm the production manager."

He waited.

"My job is getting everything lined up and ready to go," I added patiently.

"Do you have—a superior?"

I stared. "You mean a superior attitude?" I said it with a smile, though, because I wasn't sure whether to completely piss him off yet.

He stiffened. "Do you have the authority to make the final decision, Ms. Bluebell?"

I said evenly, "We're asking you if you would like to cater the shoot. If it doesn't work into your plans, or if you don't think you can meet the budget, I won't waste any more of your time. I've been given a list of names. Yours was at the top."

He was mollified by my little flattery. The faintest of smiles touched those snarly lips. He reached up for another petting of the mustache and then muttered something about getting in touch. I gave him my card, half-inclined to tell him where he could stuff his British bangers. I left without knowing whether he intended to do the job, but I doubted it would matter. I could just tell we were going to get stuck on the price. I decided to call my own favorite caterer—Jill—and tell the crew I'd done my best with Liam. Let 'em howl and complain and blame me for not having Liam. My job isn't about being popular; it's about being underbudget.

I couldn't quite get Liam Engleston out of my thoughts on my way back to Santa Monica. He seemed like a jerk-off to me, but at least he had a business going, which is saying a lot in a town where out-of-work actors are thick on the ground. Of course there are thousands of men with decent jobs in a city the size of Los Angeles—Nate being one of them—but when I'm on the dating scene I don't seem to meet anyone with serious career aspirations. Not that a healthy bank balance is the absolute top of my criteria list for dating, but I sure as hell get tired of always paying at the end of the meal.

The thought made me wonder if I was being too hasty in throwing away a relationship that was working—or *had been* working—at several levels.

I sighed and asked aloud, "What's the answer?" as I drove into my underground parking space in my condo complex. The gate moved slowly backward. There's a schematic, black-and-white depiction of a person getting crushed by the gate with the words: *Beware of Gate!* underlined dramatically. This warning makes it sound as if the gate is hunched down, lying in wait, ready to sever your spine. Schematic Man has sharp lines jutting from all sides meant to indicate pain. His body is bent in half. I'm sure he's in terrible, twisting agony. But as slow as the lumbering gate moves, you'd have to be in a coma to actually get squished.

I let myself inside and tossed my keys on the hall table, catching a glimpse of myself in the mirror directly above. My dishwater blond-to-brown hair was tousled in a ragged way that was almost sexy. Or, it could be considered unkempt, depending on how you looked at it. It hung to just below my chin. My eyes are gray; my nose is straight and just a tad longer than I would like. I wish I were two inches shorter.

I thought of Carmen Watkins. Leaning forward, I examined the crow's feet around my eyes. Practically nonexistent unless I smiled, but then they radiated out like bicycle spokes. Maybe I should give up smiling. Carmen had, by all appearances. I took out a pen and dangled it from my lips and tried to adopt her look. Then I thought of all the hands that had touched that pen and I yanked it from my mouth. I'm not normally so Jerry Seinfeldish about these kind of things, but I didn't like the image in the mirror anyway. Smiling was still in. Crow's feet were just a side effect I was going to have to cope with.

I cocked my head and listened. No one home. Nate and I currently have a part-time roommate, Kristl, who's staying in the spare bedroom. She's a friend from Oregon and when she's in town she stays with me. She had arrived three weeks ago and I was initially thrilled at the diversion, but honestly I hadn't seen a lot of her. I was just glad to catch her between marriages. Three, so far, and she's only thirty-two. She graduated in finance, I believe, but as yet she's never fashioned a career out of it. Currently she's working as a bartender at a place on Sunset Strip. Can't remember the name of it either. I've only been there once. It's not Skybar, where all the staff wears white, and it's not the Viper Room, where River Phoenix OD'd on the street outside. It's got some funky, kooky name, I think. I don't believe there's a sign outside, which is the LA way.

My cell phone chirped. Jill again. She said, "We're meeting at the Standard for drinks around six."

"Okay." No need to check my calendar. I was determinedly free. Mentally reminding myself to leave Nate a note, I said, "I'll try to catch Kristl on her cell, too."

"Good." She hung up.

When Jill said "we," she meant herself, Daphne, CeeCee, and me. Kristl was someone they'd met and knew of, and if I wanted to bring her along, no problem, but she's my friend and therefore one tier outside of our group. Once in a while Jill brings Ian along, the *fucking* asshole. Why he wants to come has always been a mystery to me, but now that a marriage proposal is on the line, maybe that mystery's solved. When "Jill-Ian" are together, no matter how pissed they are at each other, they're just *sooooo* together. With a proposal on the table, I feared things might worsen.

Putting that aside, I changed into a short, black skirt and a sleeveless top with a plunging neckline. Not that I have a huge chest to show off; it's just one of my better outfits. I gave another critical glance at my hair. Sometimes I doll it up with blond streaks. It was probably time for another appointment, I thought, though I shudder at the cost of a trip to the salon. Grabbing my keys, I headed for the door.

My hand on the knob, I suddenly heard the metallic jingle of a key inserted in the lock. I stepped back just as Nate the Nearly Normal swung open the door and stepped across the threshold. To my surprise he was accompanied by a girl at least fifteen years younger than his thirty-five years. My first impression was that she was just out of puberty.

"Ginny!" Nate said in surprise, though why it should surprise him to find me home didn't make much sense. It was four o'clock. Cocktail hour, for sure.

"Hey," I said, gazing pointedly at his little friend.

She smoothed her cap of jet-black hair and smiled shyly, her lashes fluttering.

"This is . . . Tara." He closed the door gently. "She works in the office."

"Great."

We all stood there.

Nate finally seemed to notice the way I was dressed. "Going out?"

"I'm meeting the girls at the Standard."

"Were you going to leave me a note?"

"Of course," I lied. I'd already forgotten.

Nate looked past me, his expression tired. "No, you weren't," he said. "That's why I came home early. To pack."

"To pack?"

"I'm moving in with Tara for a while. Don't fake surprise, Ginny. I know you don't want me here any more. I've already talked to the leasing agent. Surprise, surprise. My name isn't even on the lease."

"I always meant to put it there." My head was reeling.

"I know." His tone was short. "We both meant to do a lot of things. You were here first. You stay."

I couldn't catch my breath. There was no faking involved, no matter what Nate thought.

He peered closely at me. "This is what you want, right?"

Well, yeah . . . yeah . . . I'm pretty sure . . . yeah . . .

We stood there for a moment more, then Nate and Tara headed upstairs to the bedrooms. I heard drawers opening and murmured conversation as they apparently gathered his belongings. Numbness settled over me. This was too fast. I *didn't* want him to leave. Not like this.

And I was suddenly furious. I wanted to kick Nate in the balls and drag Tara around the hardwood floor by her hair.

I did neither. Gritting my teeth I slammed out of the door.

I headed to the Standard and my friends.

Chapter

2

The Standard Hotel on Sunset is the best. A large, coffin-shaped glass case sits behind the reception desk where a girl in a bathing suit or something skimpy or sexy reposes, reading a book or half-sleeping, or something. It's the human equivalent to a terrarium. Sometimes there's a guy inside. Tossed around the lobby are pieces of contemporary furniture of the strange-looking, brightly colored and comfortably foamy type. The rug is thick and whitish, reminiscent of Walt Disney's *The Shaggy Dog*. Globe chairs of hard, clear plastic hang from thick silver chains. There are two bars. The one on the west side is generally quiet but full and opens to the pool area which, before midnight, is available for anyone to wander by. In the northeast corner is the second bar, which doubles as a coffee shop during the day and therefore has an actual door accessing it from the main lobby. Go in the morning and you can order breakfast at one of the booths, but a look toward the bar and you'll encounter your friends Johnny Walker, Jim Beam, and Jack Daniels. I've never asked for a highball with my omelet, but the day may come.

I was early, so I grabbed a place to sit by the pool and settled in to wait in the surprisingly hot, late-October evening air. Traffic had been light for rush hour, which normally puts a smile on my face, but tonight my mood was still dark. Nate's defection hurt; there was no escaping that fact. My anger had deflated like a leaky balloon and now I felt dispirited. I could scarcely concentrate on my surroundings because of the churning in my gut.

Spying Jill and Daphne arriving together, I tried to pull myself out of my funk as I walked to meet them. We turned as one toward the breakfast-bar—a term which has new meaning at The Standard—and seated ourselves in one of the booths. CeeCee wasn't here yet, which was typical. CeeCee moved to her own time.

I said, by way of greeting, "Check out the booze. If it's got a guy's name on it, it starts with a letter J."

Jill considered this as she took a seat opposite me. She wore dark, teal green—a kind of a flowing ensemble that washed out her face but made her look like a butterfly about to take flight. She's small and dark, with liquid brown eyes and a nice, albeit way too thin, figure. No wonder she gets proposed to, although her pugnacious jaw does have a tendency to put people off from time to time, especially men. Daphne, also brunette, is tinier and rounder, more voluptuous in a long-gone Marilyn Monroe style, and she possesses the whitest teeth, white even by blue-light-zapped southern California standards, in a heart-shaped face. In personality the two of them are as unlike as they can be: Jill's a bulldog; Daphne's a peacemaker.

And CeeCee never looks the same twice so you can't even go there.

I pointed out Jim, Johnny, and Jack.

"And José," Jill added, gesturing to José Cuervo tequila.

Daphne sighed and said, "I don't really care, as long as somebody brings me something to drink soon. I've had a terrible day."

No shit, I thought, but I kept my lips sealed tightly.

Though these are my closest friends, I wasn't ready to spill what had happened with Nate. I couldn't quite process it yet. *He* left *me*? I was supposed to be the leaver, not the leavee.

"What happened?" I asked Daphne.

"No, no, no," Jill interrupted, shaking her finger at both of us. "Me first." She turned to Daphne. "Ian bought me a ring."

Daphne stared. "An *engagement* ring?"

"Yep. Can you believe it? The *fucking* asshole!"

Dazed, she turned to me for verification. "He bought her a ring?"

I pointed out practically, "I don't see it."

"That's because I'm not wearing it," Jill snapped. "I can't wear it. Jesus, Blue. You, of all people, know how I feel."

"Do I?"

"You can't stand the idea of getting married, either," she declared.

"Whoa," I said. "That's not exactly true."

"Yes, it is." She glared at me.

Jill and I tend to argue a lot. I don't know why. Astrologers would probably blame it on the fact that we're both Aries, although I've known a lot of other Aries with whom I've gotten along famously. They are, in fact, my favorite Zodiac sign, with Aquarians running a close second. Not that I pay much attention to that kind of thing, unless my daily horoscope mentions falling in love with a particular sign. This gives me lots to ponder, especially when I'm chatting up some new prospect—something I was going to have to start doing sooner than expected, I thought glumly. Why, now, did Nate's bad habits recede into the distance? I should be concentrating on them and working up a judicious anger instead of bemoaning the ending. This was what I'd wanted. It galled me that he'd apparently known it all along.

"I can't believe you're engaged," Daphne murmured to Jill.

"Did I say I was engaged?"

Daphne shrank into her seat, away from Jill, then lifted her brows at me.

"Jill, why don't you tell us how to feel about your ring?" I suggested. "Then we won't have to get the answer wrong, which is apparently what you think we're doing."

"I don't know how I want you to feel," she said tersely.

"Sleep on it," I suggested. "And get back to us."

CeeCee entered at that moment. Like me, her true hair color lies somewhere between blond and brown, but she's currently cropped her hair really, really short and bleached it platinum with hot pink tips. Tonight she looked exotically trendy/punk with ripped jeans, a black tee shirt, and buff arms. She didn't ask what was happening, just sat down and waited to catch up.

"I'm not engaged," Jill said after a tense moment. "Ian just bought the ring to annoy me."

"What ring?" asked CeeCee.

"Maybe you should call his bluff," I said, waving down a cocktail waiter who finally came to take our order. "I want a stinger."

The waiter, Latino and smoldering, looked at me askance. Daphne was the one who voiced, "What's a stinger?" after he'd taken our orders and moved off.

"Not sure. One of those cool drinks from the fifties."

"What happened to Ketel One vodka martinis?" Jill asked, naming my usual drink.

"I just want something else," I said.

"It's got milk and crème de menthe," CeeCee informed me, glancing around the room.

"The stinger?" I made a face. Crème de menthe? Milk?

"You ordered it," CeeCee pointed out unnecessarily.

I held my tongue, mainly because she was right. I'm leery of those creamy drinks. I always avoid white Russians or your basic Kahlua and cream. And coupled with crème de menthe . . . ? Why had I veered from my usual? What was I trying to prove? I wanted to call the waiter back but he was busy taking another order.

"What am I supposed to do?" Jill demanded. "How do I call his bluff?"

Daphne sighed and looked at me.

"Say yes," I suggested. At Jill's look of horror, I added, "Then, what do you want?"

We all waited. Jill opened her mouth and closed it several times. "I don't know," she finally admitted, which was as close to winning an argument with her as anything I've experienced. Daphne looked at me with awe and even CeeCee seemed impressed.

Kristl breezed into the bar, looking distracted. Kristl's a redhead—the dark-haired kind with an overall red hue so popular in Clairol and Nutrisse ads, but Kristl's color is real. She's Irish, with tiny little freckles and a mercurial temper that puts Jill's bullishness to shame. Kristl's too new to the scene for my friends to have seen this aspect of her personality, which is just as well. I don't think I could take any more drama right now. Kristl also possesses one of those Barbie-doll type bodies with big boobs and a tiny waist that you'd swear couldn't be real, but of course, it is. No wonder she's been married three times. Jill may be adding up the proposals, but Kristl's taking it to the mat, so to speak.

"Jill's boyfriend bought her an engagement ring," I greeted her. "Thought you'd appreciate that."

Kristl snorted, plunked down in the open seat next to me and said a desultory hello to the table at large, finishing with, "God, I hate men."

This was so un-Kristl-like that I thought I'd heard wrong. No one else realized the magnitude of the statement. In fact, Daphne took offense.

"I don't," she declared. "I want a man. I want a relationship. I'm not afraid to say it, even if it's unpopular."

Jill sniffed. "Give me a break."

"Why do you hate men?" I asked Kristl. From the number

of trips she'd made down the aisle you'd think she'd have felt a tad differently.

"Because they're thick-skulled, limited, and can't keep their eyes on you when a pretty girl walks through the door even if they try, which they don't."

"This isn't news," CeeCee drawled.

"Yeah, but it sucks every time it happens," Kristl observed, burying her nose in her just-arrived drink, a mohito—lime, rum, sugar, etcetera. I envied her as my stinger was placed in front of me.

Daphne asked, "Doesn't anybody want to hear about my bad day?"

The table's silence was answer enough, though none of us meant to be so obvious. It hurt Daphne's feelings, however, so she subsided into silence for a while. Kristl, involved in her own world, ignored Daphne and launched into her own tale of woe, "I've been seeing this guy for a while. Brandon."

I nodded. I'd heard her speaking to him on the phone.

"And we've been sleeping together. It was more than three dates," she added as an explanation.

That brought Daphne out of her funk. "You don't have to sleep with someone just because you've been on more than three dates with them."

"One date's enough if it's right," CeeCee inserted. "Even half a date."

"But three dates you have to fish or cut bait," Kristl pointed out. "And Blue, you know how I feel about cutting bait." My other friends' eyes swung toward me, and I could read the question marks forming above their heads. I hadn't really brought them up to speed on Kristl.

"You don't have to sleep with them ever," Daphne argued.

"Shut up and let her finish," Jill ordered.

Daphne straightened. "Well . . . sorr–eee . . ."

Kristl tried to light up a cigarette and we all stopped her at once. Even though she works in a bar she can't seem to remember that in California—there is no indoor smoking, period. It's the law. Kristl's from Oregon and hasn't quite woken up yet.

She swore without any real heat, put the cigarette away and picked up the thread of her story. "So, we've been having sex for a while, Brandon and I."

CeeCee asked, "Good sex, bad sex, or okay sex? Most sex is just okay sex. We know that. Don't feel bad. Go on."

"It was pretty good sex," Kristl related. "I was really getting into it. And I started thinking, you know, about marriage . . ."

"No," I stated flatly.

"And I can't get married again. I mean, the ink's barely dry on the last divorce settlement."

"The last?" Jill asked.

"She's been married *trés* times," I said, adding, "Get anything good out of that one?"

"No."

I grunted an acknowledgment. Three marriages and she always got screwed. One could not say Kristl was in it for the money.

"So, to get my head straight, I went right out and tried to meet another guy," Kristl finished, fiddling with her pack of cigarettes. "Just to be safe."

Daphne and Jill looked to me for elucidation and CeeCee asked the obvious question, "Safe from what?"

Kristl didn't immediately explain, so I said, "If she sleeps with a guy, she marries him. She slept with Brandon, ergo she's worried she might be heading for the aisle again soon."

"They do have to ask, though," Jill pointed out, as if Kristl were getting ahead of herself.

"They ask," I said.

"Wow," Daphne said, faintly admiring.

CeeCee regarded Kristl with pity. "You've only slept with three guys?"

"Oh, there were a few I managed to get away from after a quick night, but not many. Not enough," Kristl admitted. "Basically, yes. I only count sleeping with three of them, and they're the ones I married. Only now I really have to count Brandon, so it's four."

"You can't not count times," Daphne said.

"Oh, yes, you can," I said. "I don't count Charlie."

Jill snorted. "Who would?"

"Why don't you count him?" Daphne asked.

"Because he was so godawful in bed." It wasn't completely the truth but close enough to count.

"Who's Charlie?" Kristl asked.

"My first relationship of any consequence. Don't make me think about him. It was my last year of high school." Though we were from the same area, Kristl and I had attended different high schools and I'd managed to keep some things to myself. Not so with my college friends. They'd squeezed almost every bit of worthwhile, or even mildly interesting, information on my life out of me.

"High school. All right, I stand corrected," Daphne said. "High school doesn't really count."

CeeCee said, " I want to hear the rest of this."

Kristl settled in. "About a week ago this fabulous-looking guy comes to the Pink Elephant and we strike up a conversation and I end up telling him my dilemma."

I was interested. "You really told this new guy about Brandon? And all the ex-husbands?"

"Okay, okay," Daphne interrupted. "All right. I was wrong. This is when you *definitely* don't count them all! Never say how many men you've slept with to another man. It doesn't matter if it's only four. They can't hear about *anybody* else. It makes them insane."

CeeCee agreed tiredly, "It's a male thing." She shrank further into her chair. A guy wearing chains hanging from his pockets cruised by and they locked eyes but neither made a move. "So, what happened?"

I was intrigued and worried at the same time. Kristl wasn't known for her plodding, thoughtful nature. She was rash, impulsive, and swept away at the least provocation.

"I really liked this guy," she continued. "He was so amazing. Just kind of straightforward and smart and listening to me. Not like most guys, y'know? And being with him practically knocked Brandon out of my head, which is amazing that it could happen that quickly."

"I once fell in love over a bowl of edamame," CeeCee revealed. "He was a poet."

We all paused for a moment, visualizing. With effort, I pulled my attention back to Kristl. "So, it sounds like Brandon's out."

"That's what I thought. So what if he possesses this big dick and knows just how to use it? So what if he whispers all the right things—words of love and what I do to him in bed . . . and how amazing I am. You know the kind."

We all remained silent, collectively wondering if we did.

"Go on," Jill insisted, intent on the story.

Mr. Chains strolled by again and CeeCee climbed out of her chair to meet him. They went outside for a cigarette. I briefly thought of Nate and felt a pang.

Kristl inhaled and exhaled. Leaning closer, she said, "All of a sudden I just wanted this other guy. Right there. It was wild. I couldn't think about anything else. I swear, if he'd asked, I'd have stripped naked and gone for it on the bar."

"Isn't Pink Elephant really crowded?" I asked.

"Blue." Jill closed her eyes, long-suffering.

"And all these thoughts were just running around in my brain and I felt like Jell-O and I walked around the bar and sat beside him and I think I might have even slipped my hand onto his crotch."

"Bold," I observed.

Jill gazed hard at Kristl. She was hanging on every word. I was, too, for that matter.

"Were you drunk?" Daphne asked.

Kristl said deliberately, "I'm a bartender there."

"Oh. Sorry."

"Yeah?" I pushed. I'd been at the Pink Elephant a time or

two. When things got rocking, the rules got bent from time to time.

"I *was* a little buzzed," she admitted. "He kept buying me drinks."

"You were working?" Daphne asked, scandalized.

Kristl gave her a look.

"Then what happened?" Jill asked a bit breathlessly.

Kristl's lips tightened. "Then this beautiful—I mean *beautiful*—blonde sits down beside him. Long hair, you know, with those streaks and just so California-perfect and she said, 'Hi, Jackson. Long time no see,' and he looked at her and it was all over."

A prickle ran over my skin. "Jackson?"

"Jackson Wright," Kristl elucidated, shaking a gasp out of the rest of us.

I couldn't believe it! The universe is just full of these nasty little surprises! Jackson Wright seemed to be floating around on the air waves, hovering over me at all times. My friends looked shell-shocked. I know my lips curled in an imitation of Liam Engleston's. Wouldn't you know it. Wouldn't you just *know* it!

But Kristl was momentarily oblivious. "So, I took my sorry self back to Brandon and now he's talking about moving to Seattle—he's been offered a position at some Microsoft subsidiary in the area—and he wants me to go with him and you know what that means."

A funereal rendition of *Here Comes the Bride* circled inside my brain. "You're not thinking of going, are you?"

"I don't know . . . I think I hate him," she answered, reaching for her raspberry Cosmo and dropping it down her throat.

"Brandon?" Daphne asked.

Jill groaned. "No. Pay attention. *Jackson Wright*. She hates Jackson Wright."

"We all do," I pointed out, tipping up the remains of my

stinger—which hadn't been half-bad and gently shaking the last, reluctant drops of alcohol into my mouth.

I am so very classy.

It was strange coming home to an empty apartment. Kristl had gone off to her job at Pink Elephant, and Nate had packed up enough items for his temporary move-in with Tara to make me feel forgotten and discarded despite my earlier resolve to sweep him from my life. Oh, there were still a lot of his belongings lying around, and I knew his chair—my favorite chair—would be one of the first things to go once he got permanently resettled. I sat down in it and leaned my head back.

I felt . . . well, blue. Endings aren't fun. I wondered how long it would take before I experienced what I'd briefly felt this morning in the bathroom: the euphoria of being alone. Now that I'd had solitude thrust on me, it didn't seem quite so great.

I sighed and considered having a glass of wine, but I was about drinked-out at this point. The cocktail hour had started deteriorating the instant Jackson Wright's name was invoked. Kristl had looked around perplexed, waiting for an explanation. None of us jumped in to tell her, so she turned to me.

"You know him? Jackson Wright?" she demanded.

"Jackson and I went to high school together," I explained. Someone else I had neglected to mention from good old Carriage Hill High.

"We *all* know him," Jill added repressively.

Daphne sighed. "Blue tried to warn us about him, but we didn't listen. CeeCee actually slept with him."

"So she says." Jill wasn't about to let that one go by without a challenge. "But CeeCee isn't totally honest when it comes to men."

"Yes, she is," Daphne disagreed. "She's just . . ."

"Skewed in her perception," I finished. CeeCee didn't look at relationships, sex, or even friendship quite the same way the rest of us did. Someone had once asked her if she was from a different planet and I swear she's made a point of proving that theory correct ever since.

Kristl looked in the direction CeeCee had gone, and I could tell she really wanted to quiz her about Jackson. I set my empty glass down and glanced around for our waiter.

"You're probably lucky Jackson took off with the blonde," Jill stated. "You could be in a worse mess than with Brandon."

"I don't want to move to Seattle," Kristl said.

"Don't," I said. Then I asked, because I had a feeling she might be heading north despite her words, "When's he leaving?"

"Soon." She twisted her fingers around the stem of her glass.

"Why not try a long-distance relationship?" Daphne suggested. "Seattle's not that far. A quick two-hour plane ride or so."

"Two of my marriages ended because they became long-distance relationships," Kristl revealed. "I'm not good at 'absence makes the heart grow fonder.' It's more like 'out of sight, out of mind.' "

We collectively nodded. Who among us hadn't cheated on an out-of-town boyfriend? No one at our table.

"Brandon was out of sight for ten minutes and look what happened. Now I can't get Jackson out of my head."

"Jackson Daniels and Coke," Jill called to the waiter as he cruised by. Kristl gave her a sharp look. I yelled my own order, "Ketel One vodka martini!"

"Think he heard us?" Jill asked.

"Doubtful," I said.

Daphne asked, "What happened to the third marriage?"

Kristl made that "bombs-away" explosion noise, the kind

young boys seem to learn through osmosis but which I've never been able to master, no matter how hard I try. I regarded Kristl with true admiration. "It blew up," she added unnecessarily. "One day we just lost it with each other and neither of us looked back."

I nodded sagely, but inside I was asking myself why things never worked that way for me. I *always* looked back. To my detriment, to be sure. I was half-looking back at Nate already and somehow a pair of rose-colored glasses were perched on my nose. I would have to be careful or I'd be begging for a second chance before the week was out.

"Leo started dating someone else at work," Daphne blurted out. "We'd barely kissed goodbye and he was flirting and making goo-goo eyes and it was all I could do to keep from crying. That's my bad day. That's what I've been waiting to say!"

"Goo-goo eyes?" I asked. "What does that mean?"

"Don't get all semantic on us, Blue," Jill said. "Don't tell me Leo was goo-gooing that mousy-looking blonde."

Daphne looked miserable. "How'd you guess?"

Jill made a strangled noise in her throat. "Don't you wish they'd go for brains over beauty just once?"

"Thanks a bunch."

"You have a brain," Jill pointed out. "That's all I meant."

"Maybe he's an equal opportunity dater and he's already filled his quota for cute brunettes," I said.

"Nice try." Daphne wasn't about to be consoled.

We lapsed into silence.

Kristl dug through her purse, pulled out some money and laid a few bills on the table before climbing to her feet. "I need a cigarette," she explained, exiting quickly. I watched her hunt down CeeCee, who was deep into conversation with Mr. Chains. CeeCee accepted Kristl's arrival, but I could see her expression cloud over at whatever Kristl was saying. Had to be about Jackson.

After that, everything kind of broke up. I had wanted to

tell them about Nate, but the words stuck in my throat like a fish bone. Now, as I climbed out of Nate's chair and looked around the empty apartment I felt like I might do something rash, like throw things or cry or call him on his cell phone and demand, "Why? Why? *Why?*" when I knew I didn't want to be with him. I just wanted the last word.

"And Dr. Dick thinks I'm frightfully well adjusted," I said aloud. My voice echoed throughout the empty condo. I didn't like it one bit. Switching off the lights, I locked the door and determinedly marched up to bed and to the suddenly wide-open spaces of the king-size mattress.

I lay in the darkness, staring at the ceiling. The jacaranda tree outside my window was dancing in a stiff breeze. Bathed by the riot light from the building next door, its leaves flittered across my ceiling in tiny, darting shadows between the stripes made by my jalousie blinds.

I drifted into a troubled sleep.

I would have expected to dream about Nate, or Jackson, but instead I found myself back in high school with Charlie Carruthers. Only it was kind of like college in the dream, as I was living on my own. I was freaked out the whole time because I'd missed the cutoff date to drop chemistry, the reason being I was banging Charlie under a blanket in a little garret-style attic room while his roommates smoked dope in the corner and totally ignored us. Charlie and I were trying to keep things quiet, as if his stoned friends would even notice. Between fretting about chemistry class and keeping quiet during sex, I worked myself into an all-out nightmare, and I woke suddenly at the sound of my own hoarse yell—which had been me crying out in the dream when Dr. Dick suddenly entered the room and caught me in the sex act.

My heart was pounding wildly in fear. Half asleep, I searched my feelings for what had scared me so badly and was surprised and a bit worried to realize it was Dr. Dick's disappointment in me. Frightfully well adjusted? I feared it was all an act that he, as my shrink, might well discover some day.

I punched my pillow and buried my face in it.

Sleep eluded me. Charlie hung in my thoughts. Persistent. I wondered if his sexual technique had improved with age. He was the quickest, most self-centered lover I'd ever encountered—and that's saying a lot. But it was high school, after all, and the jury was out on whether that counted or not.

My vote was for not . . . because otherwise Charlie was Ex-File Number One.

Chapter

3

Daphne called the next morning from work and woke me from a deep sleep. When I'm not on a job I tend to sleep in, and after a night of roiling about Charlie, I could have used some more. But I tried to be coherent, offering ums, and uh-huhs, and ohs where appropriate. She didn't seem to notice. She was on the Starbucks early shift, which conflicted today with an audition for a chewing gum commercial, and she was bummed.

"Last time I went on a chewing gum commercial I got a callback," she revealed. "This guy and I were in this fake car and we kissed and kissed, passing the gum back and forth."

In the background I could hear people ordering coffee and the whir of one of those machines that pulverizes coffee beans to grounds. I squinted one eye open in the morning light. "And you're sorry you're missing that?"

"We weren't actually supposed to pass the gum, just make it look like it. But he was really, really cute."

I tried to look beyond that, but my Seinfeldish self reared its ugly head and all I could see were myriads and myriads of germs settling in all the little folds of the chewed gum. "He'd have to be really, really cute."

"He was." She sighed. "I'm hoping to reschedule for this afternoon." Her voice shifted to a tone of accusation, "I hardly got to tell you about my bad day yesterday. I couldn't get a word in edgewise with your friend Kristl and then Jill's engagement."

Is Jill engaged? I wondered briefly, but then decided I didn't want to revisit that conversation. Carefully opening both eyes, I was momentarily dazzled by the sunlight coming through my blinds. I took a moment to admire them. Wood overlaid with a white plastic coat of some kind of fabulous product that looked like paint and wore like iron. Really cool. I'd paid a small fortune for them but it made my bedroom seem far, far better than it was. And no Nate . . .

I cleared my throat, trying to get my voice to work. Half the time I can't talk at all before—I checked the blue numbers on my clock's LCD—nine A.M., especially if I've been out. And although I'd gotten home early last night, it felt like I was suffering a hangover. Nate's doing. Breakups are pure shit.

I wondered if Kristl had come back in the wee hours after work. Even with my restless night I hadn't heard her. If she was with Brandon it was a bad sign.

"Leo is just so distant. Like he doesn't even know me. God, it's awful. I feel just like a teenager who's been dumped after sex!"

"You had sex with him?"

"Didn't I just say so? Oh, God. There he is." I heard her rustle with the phone, then apparently she was in a safe nook because I could make out every syllable even though she was whispering. "He hasn't even looked at me once today," she moaned.

"Which date was it? The third?" I stretched my mouth. I didn't want to think about what it tasted like.

"Does it matter?"

"No, it's just we were talking last night and—"

"It was the first date, okay? I know what I said, but it was

the first date." For a moment I really did think she was going
to break down and cry, so I jumped in quickly.

"It's okay. No big deal."

"Then why is he doing this! He's with her now!"

"The mousy-looking girl?"

"Oh, God, Blue."

"Maybe Leo's just—just . . ." *An asshole, like Ian,* I
wanted to say.

"Just what?"

"Not ready—for someone like you."

"Well, he was certainly ready when we were in bed," she
reminded me as if I were extremely dense.

"I mean he's unformed. Most men are unformed. Their
brains don't work the same way. They're more prehistoric.
I'm not kidding. I read that somewhere."

"So, because he has a prehistoric brain he can't be nice to
me after having sex?"

I paused. "Yes," I said.

"Well, that's crap."

I grimaced in commiseration. I knew how much she liked
this guy even though I'd met him once and thought he was a
Huge Waste of Time. Leo possessed that shaggy California
blondish hair that looks suspiciously as if it's been forgotten
to be combed after a day out surfing. This is a disguise, however, because I've known guys who spent too much of their
hard-earned, or ill-gotten, disposable income on this "do."
It boggles the mind.

"*I* thought it was a potential boyfriend evening," Daphne
said, sounding choked up.

"How was the sex?"

"I can't answer that."

"Sure you can. Was it bad sex?"

"No."

"Okay sex?"

"It was GREAT sex! Great sex. Totally, totally GREAT
SEX!"

I wondered how much of that hit the coffee drinkers' ears as I had to yank the receiver away from mine. "And now he doesn't even look at me!" her faraway, tinny voice accused. "For God's sake, Blue, what is *with* men? Are they all just moronic juveniles who only want us for a roll in the sheets?"

I actually debated answering that one, but then realized it was probably meant to be rhetorical. Instead, I mumbled something about giving him some time, not dwelling on it too much, how she was better than he was, and how it was always best to be the bigger person. A whole bunch of platitudes that had the effect of reducing her to tears. "Can I come over later?" she asked in a small voice. "I really need to talk."

"Sure," I said, just managing to hide the inner groan. I needed coffee. I could practically smell it wafting over the line, but it was as far away as the moon. I didn't, in fact, have any coffee in the house, I remembered.

"And you can tell me about Charlie," Daphne slapped on. "I know it was high school and I said that didn't count, but maybe in your case it does."

"I don't want to talk about Charlie."

"Well, you brought him up last night."

"I didn't mean to, believe me. I don't know what I was thinking. I don't count him."

"You don't count that actor guy, either. Really, Blue. They either exist or they don't."

"They don't!"

"Oh, God, there's Leo! And he's still talking to Heather!! What am I gonna do?" she wailed and hung up.

Dropping the receiver, I covered my eyes with my palms and took several deep, cleansing breaths. I didn't want to think about Daphne and Leo. And I sure as hell didn't want to talk about Charlie. What gave her the idea I wanted to talk about him? Just because she was feeling low, vulnerable and miserable in her pseudorelationship didn't mean I wanted to talk about any of mine. Okay, so Charlie's a member of the

Ex-Files. Fine. I'll accept that. Charlie's the founding member. Okay.

But I sure as hell didn't want to talk about him or anyone else in that not-so-illustrious list.

Throwing back the covers, I padded to the bathroom. I brushed my teeth with alacrity, then splashed water on my face. I stared at my reflection. The grim set of my jaw reflected my thoughts.

Charlie . . . Charlie Carruthers. His name was wedged into one of my brain tracks and I was going to take a ride down that path whether I wanted to or not.

I'd originally given him the nickname C.C. But now that I had a friend of the same name, I couldn't go there anymore. He was simply Charlie. My first, and worst, lover.

We had gotten together the night of the Homecoming game, a rivalry between Carriage Hill High and Western that bordered on lunacy. I was bored out of my skull and wondering if I was the last virgin left in Clackamas County. I was seventeen and I'd read enough *True Sex Stories* and watched enough R-rated movies to be convinced that I was missing something truly spectacular. All the secrecy. All the whispered gossip. Pammy Gracefield had been caught doing it in the back of her parents' minivan and Mr. Gracefield had yanked the offender—what was his name? Oh, yeah, Richie Moltano—by his leg right out and onto the cement driveway. Richie's pants encircled his ankles and Mr. Gracefield was so infuriated he bellowed at Pammy to get the hell out of the minivan loud enough that their nearest three neighbors turned their lights on. Or so the story went. To add to the tale, Pammy got pregnant and was sent away. The Gracefields moved out of the area the end of that year and Carriage Hill High settled back down to soccer, football, a dance team that went all the way to the state finals, and, of course, the requisite schoolwork. I was deep into SATs and wondering why I didn't have this incredible urge for higher education that everyone, kids and parents alike, seemed infected with.

At the time Mom was really working on becoming the real estate maven she is today, so I was kind of left to my own devices. Not that she wasn't there when it counted, but I had plenty of time to get into trouble, especially since I'd been pretty much a dream child up until my senior year. It was like I woke up one day and thought, "What the hell am I doing?" I really worried I was going to miss the whole "I was a teenage terror" thing, so I set out to drink, have sex, smoke, whatever.

I decided to start with sex, because I had the most interest in it. I wanted to get laid and get it over with. I know this isn't the most romantic view of the whole thing, but it was becoming such a BIG DEAL that I could hardly stand it. I wanted to KNOW. As Joel Goodson said in *Risky Business,* "College girls have knowledge." Well, I wanted that knowledge and I wanted it before my first days of college, so I was sort of obsessed with the whole thing when Charlie Carruthers threw a wadded up test at me and gaily yelled, "Flunked another!" to the room at large. Everyone laughed, myself included. I'd managed a C. Terrible class, chemistry. Couldn't imagine why I was taking it. Something about it looking good on a college resume. All it's done for me is given me bad dreams.

I picked up his test and surreptitiously stuck it in my book bag. Later, I smoothed it out to realize the reason Charlie had flunked was because he hadn't bothered to answer half the questions. The ones he had answered were all correct. This prompted the question: had he simply choked? Been unable to answer them? Or, had this been some sort of Machiavellian way to undermine his own chances of getting into a good school? Maybe he was an iconoclast, breaking down established barriers.

I immediately decided to fall in love with Charlie. He was my kind of guy. Never mind that I hadn't been able to stomach him the year before because of all his gross, crude jokes and stupid, juvenile teen-guy ways. Sure, he was no Jackson

Wright, but after my bedtime tête-à-tête with Jackson that had resulted in my Mom's shock of white hair and no real sex—okay, I hadn't been *perfect*—I was glad Charlie was simply who he was. I decided he would be the one to de-flower me.

This sounds a lot easier than it turned out to be. I mean, where were all the guys with raging hormones? Whose moral compasses couldn't find magnetic north if they were standing at the pole itself? Here I was, ready, willing, and able and possessed of decent-sized breasts—all right, fine, they're a bit on the small side but they've got a nice shape, okay?—and the only viable deflowerer in my sight was Charlie. This was skewed logic, but I was seventeen and not inclined to second-guess myself.

Anyway, I decided to fall in love with him. At seventeen these kinds of decisions seemed to just pop into my head randomly. Like the time I was temporarily a vegetarian, a state I announced loudly to all and sundry at any given op-portunity for about three and a half days until the smell of a sausage dog at a stand outside Costco—one inch in diameter and just shy of a foot long, grilling and sizzling away—did me in. I smothered the thing in mustard, ketchup, sauerkraut and a mound of rather suspect chopped onions—how long *had* they been sitting there?—and dug in as if I'd been starved for a month. It tasted so mouth-wateringly good I still mentally flip back to that moment upon occasion.

But I digress. Falling in love was easy. Once the idea took root I simply had to make my plan. There are rules to this kind of thing. A nice girl, even one who's hellbent on losing her virginity, can't go up to a guy and say, "Hey, there, I just realized I love you, and so therefore it's okay that we have sex, so let's just skip the preliminaries and start thumping." Even my teenaged logic knew that wasn't going to fly. Sure, I might get sex out of it, but I would definitely be labeled a total wacko-hot-pants-slut-ho, so I had to run through a mod-icum of courtship to convince Charlie that he was the love of my life and then, and only then, could we have sex. As it turned out this courtship played out mostly in my mind because when my chance arrived, it came down to a do (me) or die kind of thing.

There were, as it turned out, several drawbacks to my plan. Obstacles to this path of romantic bliss. Drawback one: Charlie had a girlfriend. Drawback two: She was someone I actually liked.

How could that be? I had moaned to myself. How come I didn't know? But I was utterly determined to have Charlie for myself, so I devised a series of plots to break up the happy couple and worm my way in.

This is the lowest kind of behavior, I know. But to be honest, there was just no one else at Carriage Hill High worthy of my attention. As I've said before, I wouldn't have Jackson Wright on a dare. Not that he seemed to want me after our aborted fumbling, but hey, I liked believing I was in the driver's seat.

But back to Charlie and Serena. They were absolutely wrong for each other. It was all so painfully obvious to me and my friends that we concluded something must be done. I confess that I obsessed about breaking them up and having Charlie for myself. When I think back on how much energy this cost me it makes me feel weary, but at the time it was all that mattered. Lucky for me, none of my plans had to be put into action.

Believe it or not, Charlie was a football player. Don't ask me what position because even if I knew I wouldn't care. I know what a quarterback is, though why they're called that still isn't clear. They can pass the ball and somebody else catches it and everybody tries to push everybody out of the way and when someone breaks away and runs for the goal it creates mass cheering or booing. Football has never interested me, although at least I understand it better now. In high school, it was just an event to attend. I have always liked the uniforms, though.

Charlie was on the team by default; his father, who owned a string of Quickie Marts around town was a huge supporter of high school sports in general and football in particular. Charlie wasn't the best player. He wasn't even a good player. He treated football kind of like he treated school: with an utter lack of direction, attention, and determination. He likely wouldn't have played at all, regardless of Daddy's financial support, but Charlie was blessed with one enviable asset: speed. He could run down almost anyone. I learned later that he started out on defense, but he was so awful at actually tackling anyone that they moved him to offense. So, once in a while, when the second or third string was in, Charlie would play wide receiver—this is a term I've actually since learned and somewhat understand—which meant that he would race away from the pack, wait for the quarterback to throw him a pass, and leap into the air, reaching for this spiraling bullet. If Charlie had possessed any ability to catch the ball at all, he might have made it to first string, but hey, you can't have everything.

I came to the Homecoming game dressed all in black because I thought it was moody and sexy. It was November in Oregon and I'd already lost all of my summer tan, such as it was. I'm sure the black looked just great with my lovely, pasty white skin. I certainly felt I was hot shit. My look, coupled with the fact that November is my middle name, made it seem as if I might actually get lucky that night. With romance in mind, I'd darkened my eyes with heavy liner and mascara—very 60's which I thought was the height of cool— but then, when I looked over the playing field, my spirits sank. Charlie and Serena seemed as tight as ever, and when I glanced down at the cheerleading squad my depression grew. There she was, jumping and screaming and shaking her pompons with the best of them. I had a secret yearning to be a cheerleader, but it would have been a tough sell with my pseudo-intellectual crowd, so I contented myself with looking sulky and bored, all the while scouring the field for a glimpse of Charlie.

He was number eighty-eight. I spotted him on the sidelines, goofing off with another player. Watching him, then glancing at Serena, I finally began to doubt the wisdom of my plan. They were football people. They were meant to be together. And I was playing at personae, trying to figure out who the hell I was and devising schemes that were born to fail.

I probably would have left the game right there and gone home to soul-search and eat Snickers bars when two things happened, almost simultaneously. One: our team's best wide receiver was jerked out of the sky by the opposing team, came down with broken ribs and Charlie ran in to replace him, and two: Serena got so excited she slipped, fell, and twisted her knee big time. Actually a third thing happened as well, which was really the kicker: Serena's ex-boyfriend, who was a soccer player and disdained football, stepped up to help take Serena to the emergency room. She was last seen squeezing his hand as she was helped toward his car. Whether they actually made it to the hospital was a source of speculation for weeks to come, but the resulting aftermath was that against all odds Charlie scored the winning touchdown, Serena wasn't around to congratulate him, he decided to celebrate by drinking about a hundred beers, and yes, he ended up with me.

Lucky for Charlie he didn't attend the postgame dance or he would have been caught drunk and thrown off the team and suspended from school. I ran into him at the local hangout, Louie's Burgers. His friends were as drunk as he was; the designated driver might be eschewing alcohol but it sure as hell looked as if his cigarette was the funny kind, if you know what I mean. I took this in at a glance.

"Hey," I greeted Charlie. (My dialogue hasn't improved with age.)

"Yo, there, Ginny Blue," he said, wearing the biggest shit-eating grin in the state of Oregon. "Where's the kooky makeup?"

I touched a hand to my face. I'd scrubbed off the 60's-raccoon eyes in the stadium washroom in a fit of "I will never get laid" angst. "I'm changing my style."

"Really? Cool." He struggled to stand up unaided and light a cigarette at the same time. His friends had all straggled back to the car, tumbling inside in a heap. The designated driver stood about three feet away, aloof and smoking weed with a devil-may-care, I-don't-give-a-shit attitude that I instantly admired.

"Wanna go somewhere?" I asked. At the time I was driving my mother's car, a ten-year-old Ford sedan. She hadn't yet moved up to the nearly new Mercedes she now sports. It bothered me, how uncool I must look, but Charlie was drunk enough not to notice.

"The football field," he said. "Where that bitch missed my touchdown, Goddammit."

Who was I to argue? My heart was all aflutter. Charlie sank into the passenger seat and I pulled away from Louie's Burgers and headed back to the stadium. No one was there by now, not even the cleanup crew. The concession stands were locked up and only the faint scent of popcorn reminded anyone of the mad activity that had transpired mere hours before. The lights were out, and apart from a distant street lamp, which cast a bluish glow to the north, and a silvery moon competing with rapidly scudding clouds, the place was dark, dark, dark.

Charlie stumbled out onto the field, long-necked beer bottle in hand. He threw back his head and howled at the moon. I remember thinking how terribly romantic it all was. I had reality issues, for sure, but I was seventeen, okay? I followed him onto the field, wishing to high heaven that I could have scored some booze, too. I was freezing to death. It was damn near December after all, and we were just lucky Oregon's infamous rain wasn't beating down in torrents.

And then Charlie stripped, right down to his skin. He grinned at me. "Ah, fuck her," he said. "You wanna do it?"

Now, here's where it gets a little weird. Charlie was drunk, eager, and the object of my desire, sort of. You'd think I would have thrown myself into his arms and said, "Let's go, baby," but instead I got all rational and clinical. I guess I wanted to remember every aspect of the evening, so instead of stripping off my own clothes, I furrowed my brow and considered. As an opening salvo to lovemaking, I said, "I've been kind of planning this. I thought you should know."

"Planning this?"

"I decided awhile ago that I wanted to have sex with you, if that's all right."

"Hell, yes! Why didn't you speak up sooner?"

"Serena."

"Oh, yeah, her. Well, she's with Erickson, isn't she? She left all hot and panting with him." He stumbled and fell onto his clothes, spreadeagle, on the ground. I strolled forward and looked down at him.

"I just want to know," I said. "You know . . . about it . . . ?"

"'Bout what?" He was struggling to pull on his beer without pouring it all over his face.

"Sex."

"Well, c'mon over and let me show you."

"I've been thinking it's time for me. I don't want to go off to college and not know anything. I don't even want to go off to college."

He patted the cold ground beside him.

"But I wanted it to be with someone I really care about. That's why I want it to be you."

"You care about . . . me?" He squinted. Definitely having trouble with the concept.

Well, of course I did! I reminded myself. You can't have

sex unless you're in love! I didn't actually say this, luckily, deciding instead that I'd better get on with it if I were going to have any chance of getting back before curfew.

Sex without love . . . are you kidding? That was not part of the "first time" mythology.

So, there I was on the fifty-yard line, struggling out of my draping black clothes, shivering, and hoping Charlie didn't completely pass out before we had a chance to do the deed. He didn't. Although he did right afterwards. Then he woke up and puked, but I'd fortunately redressed by that point, as I'd been turning bluer than the gleam off the streetlight.

I've got to say, it was really, really disappointing. One moment he was kind of fumbling with my clothes, the next I was lying in the pile of them, and the next he'd jumped on me and wasting no time with preliminaries. I remember trying to kiss him, but Charlie, for all his drunkeness, was an eager beaver, and apart from clutching my breasts and gasping, he pretty much got to it. Wham, bam, thank you, ma'am. I tried to squeak out words of love, but they fell kind of flat, given the situation. It was cold outside and mostly painful inside, so to speak, and I'm sure my face was contorted into a deep wince throughout the whole lovely moment.

To give Charlie credit, he did try to have a relationship with me. Afterwards he would walk with me down the hall at school, and he even bought me a Christmas gift that year: a small bear—our mascot—dressed in a football jersey with number eighty-eight on its teensy little jersey. Very romantic. We had sex a couple more times, but those episodes were disappointing replays. At least I got the experience I craved and I didn't end up pregnant, which, given we were into the *coitus interruptus* method, was a very real possibility. I was much, much smarter the second time I got involved sexually, and I've remained that way to this day—at least about birth control. My choice of partners is up for debate.

A footnote: Charlie and Serena got back together, got married, had a couple of kids, then split up. I heard Serena moved to Tucson and married a college football player. Don't know what happened to Charlie.

Why had I brought him up last night? I asked myself as I began placing calls to set up the Waterstone Iced Tea shoot. Where had that come from? Had Kristl's Jackson Wright sighting dredged up Charlie?

I thought about Charlie for a solid fifteen seconds. I don't know why, but I suddenly felt the need to know more about him, so I went online and checked the listings for Portland, Oregon. There was only one Charlie Carruthers listed, and I dialed the number before I thought.

"Hullo?"

It was Charlie all right. Sounding kind of drunk.

"Charlie? It's Ginny Bluebell. What're you doing?"

"Hey, Ginny! God! Haven't talked to you in ages. I'm hung over bad, what about yourself?"

"Oh, I'm working," I said, the desire to get off the phone suddenly so intense that I had to scold myself severely to remain on the line. I'd been the one to reconnect. I'd done it to myself. No need to feel such distaste. So he hadn't moved past high school. So what? I certainly could get drunk with the best of them.

"I'm on disability. Screwed up my back working at a brewery here. Those kegs are goddamn heavy. Hey, you in town?"

"No, no. No . . . still in Los Angeles."

"Well, get up here. Let's have some fun."

"Yeah, I was thinking about it," I lied. "Maybe over Christmas."

"Your mom still here?"

"Yeah."

"Maybe I'll stop by and see her."

"You do that, Charlie," I said, glancing at the clock. I'd been on the phone less than five minutes. "I gotta go. I'll be in touch."

"You were the best!" he suddenly blurted out happily. "Weren't we great?"

"Yeah . . ."

"Hey, what's your number? I could be comin' down your way. Friend of mine's takin' a trip to Tijuana."

"Wow."

"Hey, maybe we can crash at your place? Wha'd'ya think?"

"Call me," I said.

"What's your number?"

I didn't want to give it to him. I really didn't. I wondered if I could get away with just hanging up. A true cheat. My finger hovered over the receiver, but then he said, "Hey, it's on the caller ID!"

Fucking technology.

He promised to call me when he arrived in L.A. and I squeaked out a, "That'll be great," before gently cradling the phone. I took a step back, staring at the machine. Charlie Carruthers. Ex-File Number One.

Holy shit.

Chapter

4

As soon as I was dressed I made my way to Wyatt Productions, the company I mostly work for. Wyatt's offices are a couple of blocks off Sunset on Robertson. My restless-night-hangover was still, well, hanging over, and I couldn't shake that overall sense of badness that permeates everything whenever there are uncomfortable, unresolved issues floating around in your brain. I was feeling really bad about my breakup with Nate and trying to rationalize it at the same time. There is just no good way to end a relationship easily. It's like that perma-goo used for do-it-yourself projects that you can purchase at Home Depot or Lowes: its sticky, its nagging, and only time really gets rid of it.

As soon as I stepped across the threshold, Holly, my producer, started barking orders at me. She glanced up mid-directive and did a classic double take. "Jesus, Ginny," she said, eyeing me from head to toe, a hard line etched between her brows. "You look like death warmed over."

"I guess that's better than death served cold."

Holly gave me a long-suffering look. She never finds me funny. She's an emaciated forty-year-old who thrives on power and all the schmoozing of old-time Hollywood. I'm the workhorse. Generally uncomplaining, I definitely still have a problem with authority and so once in a while I just kind of blow up. So far, I've managed to hold things together around Holly, and therefore we have a grudging respect for one another. She, also, can look tough with a cigarette hanging from her mouth, although those sharp little incision-type lines radiating from her lips have deepened with age and should soon match the one between her eyes. I swear they etch a little bit further with each hard drag on the cigarette, and as she began to rant about the cost of the crane we were going to need for the shoot, I swear I saw them draw deeper yet. She calls me Ginny; I call her the Holy Terror—although not to her face. I do need to keep working, and I try to keep my forays into self-destruction to a minimum.

"God *damn* it. What the hell happened to it?" she demanded. "I thought you ordered the crane!"

"I did. Let me call the company and see—"

"Fuck! No! Just change everything."

"Change everything?" I asked cautiously.

"Yes! Everything!"

"You mean, you don't want the crane, now? I thought our guy was supposed to be flying, or something, above the ocean. Like iced tea had him soaring."

"We'll do it in front of a blue screen or something. Too expensive. And it's a stupid commercial anyway."

No argument there. Like any liquid short of 151 proof rum could really give you that flying feeling. (Please note that she said this solely to me, someone who does not matter, not in front of the advertising company—known simply as "Agency"—and/or the client, who would have taken offense.) I thought about asking Holly if she had run this new scenario past either of them. This was, after all, their commercial and therefore their concept. But noting the glower on her face, I decided I really didn't need to know. Holly probably knew what she could get away with anyway, otherwise she never would have lasted this long as a producer.

After her burst of fury things sort of settled down. Called away, Holly left the office for a while so the rest of the staff made phone calls and arrangements and ordered in lunch. We had a new PA working the job; one I'd never met before. His name was Sean and he was definitely a cutie. He looked about twenty-three, and he was obviously into bodybuilding. I was momentarily horrified to learn he was a wannabe actor, but he was clearly interested in the production side of the business so there was hope for him after all. I can't stress how much I distrust actors. And it isn't all Mr. Famous Actor's fault, although he carries a lot of the burden. It's because all the actors I've met are such a freaky combination of charm and pure neediness, the kind of neediness that reaches black-hole levels—reaching into your soul and twisting your guts, then turning you upside down and shaking you hard before dropping you on your head. I steer clear of the whole lot of them. I swear, getting involved with Mr. Famous Actor was like scuba diving and having my arm grabbed by a Moray eel just as the oxygen tank registers empty. Pretty much a death. Bad enough that I halfway wanted to drown. I'm just too much into self-preservation to give up without a fight, though cutting off one's arm to get free is a particularly tough choice. Moray eels are right near the top of my "must avoid" list. I've seen them on the Discovery Channel. They live in holes in undersea rock formations and just lie in wait until you get too close. Then suddenly they dart out, grab an unsuspecting limb, retract into their cave-like holes and drag you back as far as they can get you. This horrific fate befell Jacqueline Bisset in the film *The Deep*. Luckily she was saved by a partner, but who counts on that? Mostly you're trapped and you run out of air and suffocate. That's how it felt with Mr. Famous Actor: John Langdon. (I'm sure I don't have to add that I've never been scuba diving and I don't intend to start.)

As these thoughts crossed my brain I regaled the production group with my feelings about the Moray eel, starting up a lively conversation about all of our particular fears. Tom, my favorite production coordinator, a man who loved rumors, hard liquor, and a good dirty story, said he suffered severe vertigo and could scarcely walk up a flight of stairs unless there were walls on either side. Sean literally scratched his head—not exactly inspiring me with confidence about his set of smarts, if you know what I mean—and mumbled, "Ummm . . . I guess it's those dolls, y'know? The kind that're serious and they wink and blink when you pick them up or move them. I always think they're gonna laugh."

"I saw that episode of the *Twilight Zone,* too," I said.

"Twilight Zone?" he repeated blankly.

"With Telly Savales. Where his wife trips over the doll and falls down the stairs and he picks up the doll and it opens its eyes and says something like, 'I'm Talking Tina and you'd better be nice to me.' "

Sean stared at me, eyes wide. "Fuckin' A," he breathed.

"You've never seen that episode."

He slowly shook his head from side to side, then headed out the door to go pick up lunch. Tom said, "Way to give the kid nightmares."

"You've seen that episode." It was a directive, not a question.

He nodded. "But Talking Tina's got nothing on a stepladder."

I decided not to point out that my Moray eel tale was merely a parable for how I felt about actors. It seemed kind of an unpopular phobia to have, especially in LA, where every third person has secret aspirations in that direction.

Half an hour later Sean brought in lunch. We'd ordered from In-N-Out Burger, a California franchise from the fifties that's flat-out terrific. I'd ordered a protein burger—a hamburger patty in a lettuce cup, no bun—my nod to salad-crazed Californians. It was so good I wanted to lick the little paper wrapper it arrived in but I managed to keep myself reined in.

Sean said, "I could eat three more of these."

I glanced over. He'd had a double-double—two patties of meat. He was so fit and hard-looking that I figured he probably could handle the mucho-thousand extra calories. Probably would just work it off. I said, "I'd like to take a half-dozen of these to the beach with a six-pack of Bud and a disc player with good 80's music."

Sean's lips parted as he stared at me. I outwardly smiled, but inside I was a little annoyed at myself for popping that out. Sometimes I know just the right thing to say. It's a gift, this ability to read people without them realizing I'm reading them, then giving them what they want. It's a sort of odd flirting technique that makes me want to kick myself. I mean, why? Why do I do it? It's like I think life's a popularity contest and I can't compete in the 5% bracket of perfect looks, brains, and body, so I reach for this strange attribute and toss it out.

I had hooked Sean in one heartbeat. He wheeled his office chair closer to mine, looked at my protein burger and asked, "Did you get fries?"

"Nah. I'm trying to keep my girlish figure."

He said intensely, "Let's do it. Let's get some burgers and Buds and go to the beach. I've got the music."

Somehow I knew he would. But I could feel Tom's searing interest and that of several other production people, men and women closer to my own age of thirty-something, and I had to take a pass. "After the job's over, let's make it a production wrap party."

"Bullshit," Tom said. "We're going somewhere that serves vodka."

There was a general consensus that the beach idea wasn't on. Sean was a little crushed but accepted defeat gracefully. I kept surreptitious surveillance of him the rest of the afternoon but by the time I'd finished my day's work he was out on a production run and I left without seeing him again.

I placed three calls to Liam Engleston over the course of

the day and he never got back to me. Jill has her own fledgling catering business since she quit the snooty catering company she was working for—the same catering company where she'd met Ian. But Ian went off to some equally snooty restaurant and dived into the purchasing and business end of the biz. Jill stuck with the food itself, which is weird, weird since she's basically an anorexic and/or bulimic. She seems drawn to food—her enemy—and she can make the most delicious meals from the strangest assortment of items, but she rarely eats them. She shudders over my penchant for fast food, but I don't really get why. Let's face it: when it's coming back up, it looks bad no matter what it is. I guess for Jill, choosing to be a caterer is a lot like a policeman swearing if he didn't go into law enforcement, he would have become a criminal. The yin and yang of obsession. Whatever the case, I determined that Liam was out and Jill was in, and the rest of the production staff could just whine and moan.

Just before I took off for the day the phone rang and one of Liam Engleston's assistants, who was equally as fussy as the man himself, said Mr. Engleston would be phoning me the next day as he was too busy to talk to me today. I rolled my eyes but murmured, "That'll be fine," then made retching noises as I dropped the phone into the receiver. I figured I'd kill the assignment directly with Liam. I'd tried every way I knew to make it clear that we would be eating SANDWICHES and SALAD if we were lucky, but the man still acted as if he were catering to the royal family.

Around three P.M. I let myself into my condo, suffering a slight headache, the kind that feels like it could work its way into a full-blown clanger if not properly taken care of. It's sad to say, but I'm not as good at drinking into the night then getting up in the morning as I used to be.

Noticing the deep silence I thought of Nate and that bad feeling stole over me once more. Grinding my teeth, I refused to go down the "poor me" road. Instead I kicked off

my shoes and threw myself into Nate's chair—was that a ripping sound from the leather?—when my doorbell rang.
Swearing softly beneath my breath, I pulled myself back out
of the chair and silently asked the gods why they couldn't
make sure everyone left me the hell alone until I felt better.
Peering through the peephole I viewed Daphne standing dejectedly on the porch. Shit. That's right. She wanted to stop
by and talk.

"Could this day get any better?" I muttered to myself as I
threw open the door. "Hi," I greeted her with a lot more enthusiasm than I felt.

"Hi," she answered dully as she entered. *Uh oh*, I thought
as I closed the door behind her. This looked like real depression. The most frightening thing of all was that Daphne's
arms were flat to her sides, the fingers of one hand lackadaisically holding an open bottle of Chardonnay by the
neck. It didn't appear she remembered the bottle. Before I
could remind her, she hiccupped twice and stumbled into the
kitchen, throwing open one of my cupboard doors until it
banged hard against its neighbor. I cringed. She stared inside
as if the interior held all life's mysteries. I actually craned my
neck to peer past her but all I could see was a box of Honey
Nut Cheerios. I wondered about the pull date. Might've been
before this millennium.

"Doesn't appear that things improved at work," I noted
gingerly, checking my watch. Theoretically I was done for
the day, but production work can be round the clock when a
job gets going. I could certainly *pretend* I had somewhere to
go.

"I can't STAND it one more MINUTE! God DAMN it,
Blue! Don't you have any wine glasses?"

I reached across her and flipped open a different cupboard door than the one she'd opened and slammed shut five
times. "Are you drunk?" I asked.

"Not near enough. I left work early because Leo just ig-

nored me! *Ignored me!* I mean, scream and yell at me, okay.
I can deal. And if you look my way a time or two, well,
howdy-doody, I might be looking back. But *ignoring . . .* !"
She seemed to collapse on herself as she grabbed a fluted
wine glass. One of my favorites. My hand fluttered forward
protectively as she slammed it onto the counter so hard the
fragile stem snapped off. She looked at me and burst into
tears.

"Hey, hey," I said, taking the wine bottle and remains of
the glass from her unresisting fingers. "It's okay. Leo's not
worth all this. You know that."

"I'm sorry. Oh, God, I'm sorry. I'm so sorry. I'll pay for
it. Don't tell Nate, if it's his. I'll get another one."

"Forget about it. They're mine and therefore cheap. Sit
down." I steered her toward the couch, then returned to the
cupboard for two fresh glasses and grabbed a bottle of white
from the refrigerator as I put Daphne's in to chill. Like my
wine glasses, my bottle was cheap, but not too bad. I returned to Daphne (slumped on the sofa . . . or some other
descriptor) and handed her a glass. As I twisted the cork-
screw I realized I was going to have to tell all my friends
about Nate soon. I wasn't trying to be deceptive, but sometimes it takes a while for the right time to admit you've
maybe made a mistake. And I was really thinking I may have
made one with Nate. I don't know. . . .

"Why do I pick such losers?" Daphne moaned. She lifted
up her empty glass and I attempted to pour about an inch
into its depths. Her wrist was limp as a noodle and the glass
waved in front of me. Wine sloshed over the rim of her glass
and onto her hand but she appeared not to notice.

I was beginning to think I was the one who needed a
drink. Might even cure my headache.

"I'm not going to make it to my chewing gum audition at
four," she said on a desperate sigh.

No shit, I thought, unless the commercial was hawking
the benefits of wine-flavored gum. To Daphne, I said, "This

is a new look for you. Part soused chic, part dewey-eyed desolation."

"Don't make fun," she said. "Could I have more wine?" she asked in a tear-choked voice, holding out her glass.

I took a long, hard swallow from my glass. "We both will."

We spent about an hour finishing off my bottle and working our way through hers. Wonder of wonders, my headache disappeared. *A little hair of the dog,* I thought happily, then momentarily worried that maybe all I did was drink. A moment later I shrugged that off. At this point, I didn't much care. Drinking comes in waves for me. My social drinking is rather sporadic, as I have a tendency to sometimes hole up and insist on being alone. Occasionally I'll have a glass of wine by myself, though to me, it never tastes as good when you're alone. But with Daphne dropping by in her current state of depression, this would qualify as commiseration drinking and, if you're any kind of friend, commiseration drinking is a total must. I couldn't let her down. Yes, I could have made the phone calls I'd been planning when I'd schlepped into the condo, but after enough Chardonnay I found I had no interest in doing much of anything. In a replete, half-drunken voice, I stated, "Why do today, what you can put off till tomorrow!"

"I did Leo yesterday." She hiccupped.

I gave her a penetrating look. At least I thought it was penetrating. I sometimes fantasize that I'm more interesting than I am. "You must forget about Leo. He's a Huge Waste of Time."

Daphne closed her eyes and inhaled deeply. I remembered, faintly, that drinking this early is generally a very bad thing. I had another moment of clarity: I was going to feel really rotten about eight o'clock this evening. More hangover. Hangover on top of hangover.

Daphne said, "I want . . . *someone.* It doesn't have to be forever. But I want to be half of a couple, like Jill and Ian."

"Jill-Ian is—are—unworthy of envy."

"I just want a good guy."

"You're going to have to get away from actors, then."

"They're not all bad."

"No . . ." I faded off. I didn't want to argue with her. Daphne's problem had always been men. We all had our Ex-Files, I guess. Mine were just more noted, for some reason. I tried to concentrate on this but my wine-addled mind couldn't take the pressure. I started thinking about food.

Daphne planted her face into a pillow on the couch, sprawling out. I was once again seated in Nate's chair. In a muffled voice, Daphne said, "Tell me about Charlie."

"I'd rather have a root canal."

"Tell me, Blue."

"We had sex on the fifty-yard line after a high school football game."

For a moment nothing happened, then she started laughing. Her whole body shook. She looked up, flat out howling now. She couldn't get her breath. Tears of hilarity ran down her cheeks.

I started laughing, too. Why we both found this so hysterical was a mystery later on, but we totally cracked up for a good five minutes. When we ran down, we were both out of breath.

"Anything else?" I asked, which sent her into renewed peals of mirth.

"I think that about covers it," she finally gasped. "Can I tell you about Leo, now?"

I waved a languid hand. "Fire away."

By dinnertime I'd heard the entire story of the Huge Waste of Time several times over. I must confess that my mind wandered. I mean, what was so compelling about this guy, anyway? He was a sometime actor who worked at a coffee shop and constantly hit on all the female employees. Not my dream date by a long shot. He hurt Daphne over and over with his awe-inspiring self-interest. There wasn't room for anyone but Leo in the room. Ever. I couldn't understand what Daphne saw in him, but then, love is strange.

That "really rotten" feeling I'd worried about began to set in about seven (I was an hour off), so we ordered in Chinese food to combat it. The order came on a wave of mouthwatering scents, tucked into a half a dozen little white boxes. What is it about those Chinese boxes that makes it feel like a surprise every time you open one? I scooped a heapin' helpin' of Szechuan chicken onto a plate and decided it was time for my standard anti-actor speech.

"Y'see," I mumbled over a mouthful, stabbing my chopsticks into the air for punctuation, "Actors are always a problem for one obvious reason, they're always acting."

"The guy you dated was FAMOUS," Daphne declared. "That's totally different. Leo's not—"

"Doesn't matter," I cut her off. "They're all the same. Successful, struggling, working, not working . . . they're actors. They act. That's the common denominator. I've dated some struggling ones, too. You have to stay away from *all* of them."

"I don't think so."

"This is something I know, Daphne. They're self-absorbed and always need to be the center of attention."

"I'm an actor," she reminded.

"You're not a male actor," I pointed out. "And besides, you're not like that."

"Well, that kind of goes against your whole theory, doesn't it? Wow, my head hurts. And this Chinese food isn't making me feel good."

"Don't puke. We're not in college anymore."

"I'm not going to puke. I'm just going to feel bad."

I eyed her carefully. "You're going to puke."

"Shit . . ."

She ran for the bathroom, barely made it. I cringed at the urping noises that followed. Made me a little queasy inside as well. I had a fleeting thought of teenage boys who find this kind of thing the height of hilarity and wondered if I was turning into an old stodge at age thirty-two.

At that moment the key turned in the lock. Shocked, I raced to the door and called out, "Nate?" before I realized it was Kristl. I was disappointed, then felt terrible when I realized she looked like hell.

I said, "You were with Brandon last night."

"And most of today," she said on a long sigh. "What's the matter with you?"

"Me?"

"You look like hell."

I was annoyed, vaguely, that I hadn't got to be the one to say that to her first. And I was getting pretty damn tired of people telling me I looked awful. Nevertheless, I turned immediately to the hallway mirror to see. I would have shrieked if I trusted my eyes. Why hadn't Daphne told me my makeup had run all over my face? "I was laughing," I said lamely.

"Looks like you've been crying."

"I was crying I was laughing so hard."

"About what?"

When I didn't immediately answer she stood there and stared at me, somewhat impatiently. There was no way I could relate the whole story and expect her to find it as amusing as Daphne and I had, so I just kind of shrugged. "Nothing, really."

Luckily, she'd already lost interest. "We had sex again, but don't worry. We're not engaged."

"Yet," I said ominously as she headed for the stairs.

"I'm trying really hard to break my bad habits, so don't lecture me, okay."

"I wasn't lecturing."

"I've got to take a shower and get to work." At the sound of renewed vomiting, she froze, then glanced in the direction of the bathroom door. "Who's bulimic?"

I almost said, "Jill—sometimes," but decided to answer the obvious question instead. "Daphne mixed Szechuan chicken with cheap Chardonnay and bad romance."

"Hmmm . . ." Kristl was distracted. "I think I'm going to quit bartending."

"And do what?" I called after her as she disappeared around the upstairs landing. "Bartending jobs are hard to come by these days. One of the places on Wilshire put out an ad and got 400 applicants. You're lucky to be at Pink Elephant."

"I have years of experience, Blue," she called back.

"This isn't about Jackson Wright, is it?" I yelled. "Because he came into your bar and made you feel like there was something more out there?" My voice grew louder with each word but Kristl didn't respond.

Daphne stumbled from the downstairs bathroom looking green around the gills. I had just enough time to squeeze in and wash my face before the doorbell rang again.

"Geez, Louise," I muttered.

Daphne, now on the couch, waved a limp hand at me, as she pressed a damp washcloth to her forehead with the other. I answered the door, acutely aware my face was scrubbed clean of all makeup and I was not looking my best. Of course, this time it was Nate.

We stared at each other a moment. Finally, he shrugged, a bit awkwardly. For my part, I managed a crooked smile of welcome.

"I came for . . . my chair," he said, glancing behind him toward the street where a truck sat tucked up to the curb, its engine idling. "I'll get my table and lamps later." He gestured around the room.

"Good thing the bed's mine," I said lightly. "Guess this means you're not sticking around for a goodbye chat." I worried I sounded pathetic and cleared my throat.

Another shrug.

I watched him head into the room. Daphne gave him a

desultory, "Hey, Nate," to which he smiled quickly, sheepishly, and darted me a look. He hefted the chair and I noticed the strong muscles in his arms.

"You don't waste any time," I said.

"We wasted a lot already." He looked me up and down. "Didn't we?"

I nodded, aware that Daphne's head had swivelled my way in surprise. He carried the chair through the front door, then set it down on the cement walkway outside. We stood there for a few uncomfortable minutes longer. For one terrible second I thought he might actually kiss me good-bye, but he thought better of it and hefted the chair once again. I waved at his disappearing back and my headache returned with a crash.

"What was that all about?" Daphne asked when I returned. This time I stretched out on the area rug in front of the couch. She turned her head and gazed down at me.

"Nate and I broke up. I should've probably mentioned it last night."

"Oh, my God." Daphne declared, surprised. "When did it happen?"

"Yesterday," I said, and suddenly, irresistibly, I wanted to cry. I struggled. Managed to hang on. Just barely.

"Fucking bastards," she said softly.

"Yep."

That effectively ended our conversation for the night. We watched a little TV together, then Daphne pronounced herself well enough to go home. I didn't try to stop her, and I didn't have the energy to walk her to the door. It was several hours before I felt like I had enough strength to haul myself to my feet, lock the door, and head upstairs to my bedroom.

I heard Kristl's tread on the stairs as she left for work. Much later, somewhere around 3 A.M., I woke from a fitful sleep to the sound of her clattering around in the kitchen, which is directly below my bedroom. I wondered if she'd really put in her notice at work. I wondered also, despite her words to the contrary, whether she would keep to her pattern and marry Brandon, or if Jackson Wright had somehow derailed her.

That sent my thoughts spinning toward Jackson and I actually pulled the pillow over my head and fought valiantly for a few hours of blessed sleep. It was over with Nate, and that was okay. It was going to have to be.

Chapter

5

I headed to work sporting another hangover; this one more emotional than the first. Luckily, we put in an uneventful day. Still, I felt weary by the time I was off work, and it took me a moment or two to recognize that it was Friday night, the beginning of the weekend. Two full days of leisure time stretching out in front of me. Normally this filled me with expectation, but tonight my first thought was a kind of panicked: what the hell am I going to do? Without Nate I had a lot of hours to fill.

For most of Friday night I watched TV. Nameless, flickering programs crossing the screen that I couldn't remember as soon as they ended. Saturday morning was better. I got ready for our group's usual Saturday morning get-together at Sammy's. Jill had called and said she couldn't make it; something to do with Ian, naturally, the *fucking* asshole.

"Figures," Daphne muttered as she slid into her seat and I relayed this information.

"I asked Kristl to join us," I said. "But she was sleeping in. Last night she threatened to quit her job," I mentioned, remembering that Daphne had been in the bathroom during my discussion with Kristl. "But I don't think she's had time to go through with it."

"She's planning to stick around LA permanently?" Daphne asked. "I thought it was just an extended visit."

"She took that job at Pink Elephant." I shrugged. "But she could be engaged by tonight for all I know."

"Oh. Right." A pause. "Ya think?"

"She says not. But it's early in the game."

"She really marries every guy she sleeps with?"

"Damn close."

At that moment CeeCee strolled in, pink-tipped platinum hair more spiky than usual. She wore a pair of painter's pants and had a bottle of Arrowhead water tucked into the loop at her left thigh. She sat on the chair next to Daphne's, across from me. "California omelet," she said to the waiter.

I grunted an agreement. The California omelets were wonderful, full of avocado and tomato and goat cheese and delivered with a small bowl of salsa and another of black beans. CeeCee and I never varied our Saturday morning meal. Daphne, however, pored over the menu. I said, not trying to be bitchy, but for expedience, "You know you're going to order granola with yogurt, so just do it."

"Don't push me," Daphne muttered.

CeeCee pulled out a cigarette and played with it, turning it over and over again against the white formica tabletop. One of the waiters swooped by, opened his mouth to give the State of California no smoking rule, felt the power of CeeCee's baleful look, and skittered away in silence.

"You'd think they'd know us by now," CeeCee complained, incensed. If she'd actually been allowed to smoke, disdainful twin streams of smoke would have issued from her nose at this.

Daphne, in a non sequitur that left me mildly shell-shocked, asked, "Did you ever sleep with Jackson Wright?"

CeeCee leaned forward. "Why?"

Slightly intimidated, Daphne said, "It's just that we've always wanted to know."

"We?"

"Hell, yes, *we*," I declared when CeeCee turned her lethal gaze on me

She casually lit the cigarette, said, "No," rather flatly, and strolled out of the restaurant. Our waiter fluttered around her heels until she and her smoke were safely outside.

After that, the waiter wouldn't serve us. Just goes to show you. Regular customer or no, you don't screw around with the state antismoking laws. Everyone's a policeman at heart.

Daphne said, "Sometimes I don't think CeeCee likes me."

"CeeCee doesn't like anybody. She just puts up with us because she hates us less than others."

"Oh, I don't believe that, and neither do you. She just likes to be tough."

"She is tough," I pointed out.

"So, what happened with Nate?" she asked.

"I told you the other night."

"You just said you broke up."

I shrugged. "That's about all there is. I was really toying with the idea of ending things, and then he beat me to the punch. Not fun," I added.

A different waiter finally came to take our order and we lapsed into silence. CeeCee deigned to return and demanded her California omelet before our new server escaped. Our original waiter looked down his nose at her from across the room. CeeCee stared right back at him, slid her sunglasses on her nose, then pushed them upward with her middle finger. She capped this off by pulling her still skyward-pointing middle finger away from her face, holding it out to him in case he wasn't into subtlety. His nose twitched and his cheeks reddened.

"Gay," Daphne decreed, having watched the whole incident.

"Nah," I said. "If he were gay, he'd be more fun."

"No, he's that really non-fun, judgmental type," she insisted.

"He's straight," CeeCee said. "I know him. God, this town is just too small."

We both stared.

"The fucker worked at the radio station as an intern. Hates me because I got the job. It pisses me off that he took a job here. Makes coming to Sammy's a chore sometimes."

CeeCee had worked at KULA for six months. She was a fill-in DJ for the afternoon guy who specialized in techno songs and pop psychology. I loved it when she was on the air, because sometimes the "bleep" machine went nonstop. On her off-air hours she was a whatever-you-wanted-her-to-be around the station. Sort of like being a PA on one of our commercials.

"How do you know he's straight?" Daphne asked.

"Because he grabbed my ass hard when I was on air one afternoon."

I gave the ex-waiter an admiring look. "Didn't know he had it in him."

"He only did it once," CeeCee revealed, pulling out another cigarette and turning it over and over on the table again. She held it up for inspection and added, "Because afterwards I ground one of these out on the back of his hand. Did you notice the scar?"

We turned collectively, as if pulled by a string, and the ex-waiter strode stiffly out of the room and into the kitchen. "What's his name?" I asked.

"Who-The-Fuck-Cares."

"Couldn't he, like, sue you, or something?" Daphne asked.

I was a little horrified by CeeCee's casual account of physical violence, but then, serious ass-grabbing wasn't something anyone should have to put up with. I would have probably found some more peaceful means of dealing with the situation, but it might not have been as effective as her choice of retaliation.

"I don't care what he does as long as he stops ass-grabbing."
CeeCee was unrepentant. "He still comes around the station."

"Oh." Daphne looked in the direction he'd gone. "Maybe
he likes that kind of thing."

"Maybe he does," CeeCee said, her voice a challenge.

"Maybe you do . . . too?" Daphne suggested carefully.

"This sounds like a dangerous relationship." I wasn't sure
what to make of it.

"He wants to grab my ass, he's gotta ask first. That's all."

I started laughing. I couldn't help myself. As our food came,
delivered by waiter number two, my amusement scared a
small smile out of CeeCee. I told her that Nate and I broke
up and she said he wasn't right for me. Daphne shot me a
look and we both wondered what kind of guy was right for
CeeCee.

I was glad she hadn't slept with Jackson.

That night I drove Daphne and Jill to Pink Elephant to see
Kristl tend bar. CeeCee was filling in on the night shift at the
station, although she wouldn't be on the air, but we tuned in
anyway, on the off chance the DJ of the hour would engage
her in some kind of lively conversation. No such luck. He
was one of those guys who hovers between reality and that
land of music only true afficionados or crazies seem to have
a pass to. We were subjected to alternative rock, and though
I like most of it, tonight's selections just seemed blaring and
tuneless.

So I wasn't in the best frame of mind as I entered Pink
Elephant, a kitschy, retro kind of place that actually had
some class. Kristl, her hair pulled back into a ponytail, red
highlights catching the overhead lights, was busy lining up
martini glasses and filling them with blue curaçao. The row
of them, electric blue and shining like liquid aquamarines,
was a visual feast. I love looking at martinis. They're so geo-

metrically . . . triangular, and in today's world, infinitely colored: Red, gold, green, blue . . . utterly inviting. But personally, I can't bear the taste of blue curacao. It's too . . . metallic, or something. I ordered my old standard: a Ketel One vodka martini.

"Hey," Kristl greeted us with a nod. She was too busy to do more. The colorful martinis were dispersed to a sleek group of women sitting at the bar. They all wore short skirts and showed trim thighs, toned by 24-Hour Fitness or Bally's or maybe even a personal trainer. They clinked their glasses and drank. I noticed there was a fifty-cent tip on the bar.

"Oh, shit . . ." Daphne whispered and I turned from a view of the pretty cheapos to the direction of her gaze. My heart sank as Nate walked in with Tara, whose ID was examined very, very closely by the bouncer. She was allowed in, however. Must be one helluva good fake. These bouncers generally know what they're doing.

I smiled at Nate, though my lips felt stretched and frozen. Through the smile, I muttered in an aside to my friends, "He knows Kristl works here. He knows it's on my list of places to go."

"It's on *your* list," Daphne agreed indignantly. "He shouldn't use it now that you're broken up."

Jill, who'd been brought up to speed about my breakup on the drive over, said in disgust, "He doesn't have his own list, so he has to poach on yours."

Daphne snorted. "The bastard."

"I should feel sorry for him," I said.

"Not on your life! The *fucking* asshole," Jill spat.

"I thought only Ian was the fucking asshole," Daphne said.

"They're all *fucking* assholes. Sicko, fucko, shits."

She managed to steal my attention from Nate and Tara, which was something. "What's wrong with you?" I asked her.

"Nothing." Jill clammed up tight.

"Give," I demanded.

"Where's Ian tonight?" Daphne put in.

Our dual attack broke open Jill's reserve. "Don't talk to me about him. He's totally pissed me off and all I want to do is drink and swear." She glanced predatorily around the room. "And flirt. Are there any decent males here?"

A cluster of three attractive men was holding up a section of Pink Elephant's pink bar. They didn't look over at us when we gave them the eye. Male bonding was on the menu du jour, apparently.

"What happened with Ian?" Daphne insisted.

My gaze wandered toward Nate and Tara. Having seen me, they were acting very circumspect. I did an inward check of my feelings, prepared to thicken the wall of insulation around my heart, if necessary. I'd gotten myself all worked up about him, but seeing him there, the curve of his back, his wrinkly pants, the way he kind of hunched when he sat at the bar stool . . . I felt surprisingly disengaged. Not thrilled for my freedom as I had fantasized in the shower, and not angry or melancholy as I'd definitely been feeling the last few days . . . now I just felt distanced.

This made me happy. I'd been right after all. The breakup with Nate was the smart thing to do.

"Which Ex-File is Nate?" Daphne asked, reading my thoughts.

"Ummmm . . . I guess he's number six. Seven, if you count Charlie."

"Did you count Mr. Famous Actor?"

"I never count him."

"Then Nate's really number eight," Jill declared. "You have eight Ex-Files."

I shook my head, feeling depressed all over again. "Jesus. Eight failed relationships. And that doesn't even count the near misses."

"I'm glad you recognized Charlie on the list," Daphne said.

"He was my first," I said. "No matter how hard I try to forget."

"Who was number two?"

When I didn't immediately reply, Jill said, "Come on, Blue. Get it all out there. Consider it therapy. And count them all."

"Kane Reynolds was number two," I finally admitted. "Right before graduation. I think we all agreed the other night that high school does count, so Kane's on the list." In an attempt to get off my Ex-Files, I added philosophically, "Sick as it is, those relationships shape how we feel about the men the rest of our lives."

"We don't meet *men*," Jill said. "We meet *fucking* assholes."

"If you're not going to talk about what happened with Ian, don't make comments like that," I said reasonably. "We have no criteria to base your opinions on."

She snorted. "You've all been dating for years. Think back on those guys. There's your criteria."

"My relationships may have ultimately failed, but I had some good times," I defended.

"Me, too," Daphne chimed in staunchly.

"Just because you and Ian are fighting is no reason to make it out like all men are useless bastards," I added.

Jill lapsed into injured silence. To be honest, that was about the extent of our evening fun. Jill wouldn't cough up what had transpired between her and Ian, and frankly, Daphne and I were pretty sick of asking. On the way home, KULA's DJ rhapsodized about some weird, new group whose music, which he played for our listening enjoyment, was produced using guitar and something concocted with Pringles cans. I said, "I heard somewhere that Pringles cans are the perfect conduit for catching wireless electronic information. Like your cell phone numbers and your bank accounts. All kinds of stuff. And just about anyone on the street can use one and maybe get your computer password, empty out your accounts or something."

"I like this group. That's what their music's about," Daphne said. "That's why they use Pringles cans. To protest our lack of privacy through technology."

I thought about Charlie picking up my number from caller ID.

Jill, who'd been silent for the entire ride, said flatly, "Ian loves Pringles."

Neither Daphne nor I felt like going there—or trying to go there—so I just drove them both home.

Sunday was a bust. Nobody was around. None of my friends. By Sunday night I'd once again done a 180 on the breakup idea. I was sorely missing Nate. Or at least the "idea" of Nate. My brief moment of emancipation and epiphany at Pink Elephant was superseded by an ugly female neediness. Once or twice I almost called his cell phone, but reason prevailed. Also, I feared Tara might be with him. She looked like the type who would move in to stay.

I was heading to bed Sunday night, looking desperately forward to work the next day, when Kristl appeared in my bedroom doorway looking flushed and kind of pent-up, as if she had a secret just bursting to come out.

"What?" I asked.

With a little shudder of delight, she held out a tremulous left hand. A diamond ring sparkled.

"Oh . . . God." My heart sank.

"I—I didn't know how to say no." If she'd been a little girl she would have clapped her hands and giggled. Instead, she just drew me close to her for an intense "Please don't be mad at me" hug. Her whole body was quaking.

As well it should be, I decided. I made appropriate noises to show how happy I was for her, but I couldn't believe she'd done it again. I'd joked about it; I just hadn't truly believed it would happen.

Though I sometimes like to lie, sometimes the truth just

needs to be told. I said, with real sincerity, "I'm worried about you. Really. Nobody gets married like you do. It's like you're trying to fill up some inner void. It's not going to work."

For a moment she held my gaze, then she looked away, her mouth trembling. "I really hoped you'd understand, Blue. You of all people."

"Why me of all people?"

"Because I need you to," she said in a small voice, and then she walked toward the stairs, totally beaten down. I called after her, but she ignored me and a few moments later I heard her bedroom door close, sounding oddly final.

Way to put the period to one stellar weekend, I thought miserably. I looked at myself in the hallway mirror and really resented that I seemed so normal. I was evil incarnate. Which reminded me of Ex-File Number Four, Don the Devout, who believed in his own goodness and rightness in a way that defied description.

But I get ahead of myself. Before I can think of Don, I really should consider Kane Reynolds, Ex-File Number 2, then Larry Stoddard, Ex-File Number Three, and probably Mr. Famous Actor, although I still resist counting him. However, thinking of my exes all at one time made my head hurt. Delving into my own problems isn't my strong suit.

For now I would just have to accept that I was evil. Eeeeville.

I'm not sure I like me without a boyfriend.

At work Monday afternoon I walked into the men's room by mistake. "Oops, sorry," I said as soon as I saw the telltale urinal hanging on the wall. Men's rooms make me close my nose. An automatic reaction brought on by experience: they always smell bad. But before my nostrils could retract I sniffed an aroma that I usually don't associate with bathrooms, and as I hesitated, Sean appeared from one of the stalls, grinning like an idiot. Pinched between his thumb and index finger was, as my mother would say, "one of those funny cigarettes." He inhaled deeply, said, tightly, "Wanna hit?" and offered the joint to me. I shook my head as he held his breath to ensure every pneumatic sac absorbed the smoke. Alas, this is another reason I can't smoke. I just visualize my lungs dragging in all kinds of noxious gases, irritants, and chemicals and I can't do it. LA smog is bad enough.

"I'm not good with marijuana," I said.

He cocked his head and lifted his brows, still unwilling to release the smoke.

"Smoking dope makes me salivate," I explained. He expelled with a rush and a gasp, his starved lungs sucking in the wonderful bathroom air.

"Salivate?" he questioned. "Haven't heard that one before. It's s'posed to make your mouth dry."

"I hope you're going to tell me you're through working for the day," I said. I could just picture him driving around under the influence and having it somehow be the production company's fault.

"Yeah, totally!" he assured me emphatically. "I'm done here. Just on my way out." Seeing my look, he said, "Well . . . not *immediately*. Wouldn't want to get a DUI or anything. It really makes you salivate?"

"Yep."

I didn't feel like going through my brief attempt at smoking dope. It had been another of those decisions made for popularity and acceptance during high school. Not long after the Charlie Carruthers episode, I briefly turned my attention to my grades and caught the fever of needing those last semester GPAs to get into the "right" school. Well, it was way too late for that. I mean, you wanna impress some college you gotta start freshman year. But I was suddenly convinced I could do it, and I started hanging out with the nerds. That's where I met Kane. He was the nerdiest of the nerdy, pocket protector and all, but he had this fantastic baritone speaking voice, and he sounded so incredibly smart that I went into some kind of fugue state, I swear, and my last high school semester I followed him around and listened to him like an acolyte.

It was during the Kane phase that I had my one excursion into dope smoking. A group of the nerds hung out at Kane's. He lived in this tract house that was surprisingly nicely done. His mother had flirted with interior design, more as a hobby than a career, but her decorating sense made the place seem like a Better Homes and Gardens article: "How to make your dwelling sparkle on a limited budget."

I was mildly shocked to learn the nerds were deep into dope smoking. When they passed the joint around, I attempted a quick puff, was told I needed to inhale, did, then coughed until my stomach hurt. Embarrassed, I tried again, and finally managed to take that terrible, smelly smoke into my lungs. Immediately my salivary glands went on overload. I was flooded with saliva, struggling to swallow, wipe my mouth, not cough, and be cool all at one time. Nobody else seemed to suffer this malady, I noticed, as I looked around the room. Kane smiled at me. I was never sure later if it was the dope, or just a sincere need to reestablish that I was cool, but I smiled back and actually went over and sat next to him. "Cool," he said, and that pretty much won my heart.

Just before I graduated from Carriage Hill High, Kane and I engaged in some sexual gymnastics that helped a lot after the disappointing Charlie Carruthers episode. Kane was one of those talkers, whispering all kinds of things in my ear that honestly, I found very distracting. Between that and worrying I might get caught screwing Kane in his parents' basement—or that one time in my parents' powder room—I could never get to the Zen mode his voice promised that might allow me an actual orgasm. Still, it was exciting and his voice was one deep purr.

Kane Reynolds became Ex-File Number Two. I've heard he's a motivational speaker these days. Garnering national attention, no less.

"I gotta get to the right restroom," I said to Sean.

"Hey, maybe later . . . you and I could do that Bud thing on the beach?"

"Sure," I said lightly. *Later* was unspecific enough to mean *never* in my book, if I so decreed. Sean was cute, but twenty-three. There was no getting around the age difference. And I really wasn't into dope smokers. Or wannabe actors.

I left him to his joint, wondering what it says about my character that I wasn't having a shit-fit that he was smoking dope at the office. I'm pathologically nonjudgmental, which isn't necessarily a good thing, but since the rest of the world seems to run on passing judgment as if it were fossil fuel, I figure somebody has to take another tack. If it had been Holly who'd discovered Sean's extracurricular activities, his ass would be on the street.

My conscience chose to recall my conversation with Kristl the night before and I realized I might be wrong about myself about the judgment thing. But honestly, the words I spoke to her came right from my heart: *she was worrying me sick.*

Jill called and asked if I could take time out for a long lunch at the Farm of Beverly Hills. Much as I love In-N-OUT burgers, the Farm has this fantastic apple and brie sandwich on wheat bread that could drop you to your knees. It's as close to health food as I dare, but at the mere mention of the Farm my mouth started salivating as if I'd taken Sean up on his earlier offer.

"I'm there," I said, and headed out to meet her with some vague excuse to the Holy Terror who eyed me with intense suspicion. When you're working with Holly she feels she owns your time. Production can be one of those slave-labor-type-jobs—hour upon hour, sometimes sixteen hour days, but it pays well. Still, I figured I deserved a lunch hour . . . or two.

Jill was already seated when I arrived, which was just as well because the place was packed. People were standing around the bar waiting for tables that hadn't cleared yet. She was at an outside table in front, under the awning, a great spot for watching the world pass by.

The Farm is on Beverly Boulevard and it's chic/country. Inside, the pitched ceiling is supported by exposed, stained rafters; the entire place reminiscent of a really clean barn. The tables are cute and clustered, but the prices on the menu are not for the faint-hearted. I squeezed by the other diners to join Jill who had ordered a bottle of wine. I eyed it with some reluctance. "I don't think I can drink," I said. "It's Monday and I've got tons of pre-pro before next week's shoot."

"That's okay. I'll drink. You listen." She'd also ordered a salad, which had arrived before I did and she stirred the lettuce leaves around with her fork. None of them made it to her mouth.

"You're going to finally spill about Ian?"

"Sit down. It's long."

I groaned as I took my chair. "Then you're going to have to buy me lunch."

"Done," she said flatly, topping off her glass with more Chardonnay. The waiter came by and I ordered my sandwich before she could launch into her tale of woe. I was pretty sure I was going to need sustenance. As soon as he left Jill drew a breath and said, "I'm breaking up with Ian."

Jill-Ian? Turning to just *Jill* and just *Ian*? Unheard of.

"You know what he did, the *fucking* asshole? He started putting restrictions on the marriage offer.'"

"What kind of restrictions?"

"Dos and Don'ts or no nuptials. Those kind of restrictions."

"I thought that happened after the wedding."

"I'm not marrying him."

"I know. You said so."

She gave me an assessing look, as if deciding how much to tell. I wasn't really certain what my role was here. Did she want me to probe and pry? I gave it one try. "Was there a particular do or don't that pissed you off?"

Her eyes were directly to the barely touched salad, but she muttered, "He said if I wasn't keen on getting married, then the offer was off the table. Asked for the ring back, for God's sake."

"I thought you didn't take the ring."

"I didn't *wear* the ring. But I took it. Now he wants it back." She swirled her glass of Chardonnay, frowning down at it. "I should have said yes." She fell into a morose silence and I wondered if I'd been too hasty about turning down the wine. I saw our waiter heading our way with my sandwich and my mouth watered. He put it in front of me and I grabbed it with gusto. Melted brie dripped over the edges of the crust. I stuck out my tongue and caught some.

Jill swirled her wine and frowned. "Did I make a mistake?"

I shook my head. "Kristl just got engaged . . . again . . . and there's something almost pathological about her need to be married."

"That's not the way it is with Ian and me."

"Yeah? Well, last week you thought it was all some strange plot on his part. I thought you might even break up with him."

"Never," she murmured, nose in her glass.

"You're nuts," I decreed. Okay, okay. I *am* judgmental sometimes. Just not most of the time.

"I love him, Blue."

I gave her a look. "Is that any reason to get married?"

She snorted on a laugh.

"I think arranged marriages might be the way to go," I said. "This searching for the right partner takes too much effort, and the results aren't any better than having someone say, 'Hey, you. You're with him now. Congratulations.'" I paused, intrigued by my own idea. "I need a yenta."

"If you were in love right now, you'd think differently."

I shook my head. "Love only lasts two years, three at the most. That's when the endorphins, or whatever the hell, wear off. And your serotonin levels go up, I think. Those levels are depressed when you're in love, and that's why you can't think about anything but this wonderful other person. It's kind of like obsession. Obsessive people have depressed serotonin levels."

"I'm not depressed," she pointed out, annoyed by my tangent.

But I was on a roll. "So, when you're all obsessed and in love, it's a chemical imbalance. And you know stalkers, the really, really obsessed people? Their serotonin levels are *way* down. They must be terribly depressed." I paused. "Or, is it way up? No, I think it's down. So, they focus on someone and really think they're in love. So being in love is kind of like being a stalker. Luckily, if you both feel the same way, it doesn't really matter. You can stalk each other."

The look on Jill's face caught me up short. It was fear mixed with realization. "What?" I asked, wondering what I'd said that had actually gotten to her.

She put her mouth over the edge of her wine glass and mumbled, "I guess you could say I kind of stalked Ian last weekend."

"You mean . . . what? You drove by his house a few times?"

She drew a breath and said, "You know after we went to see Kristl? And then you went home because we saw Nate with that girl?"

"Tara, yes. The teenager."

"Well, I took the long way home and drove by Ian's place and there was someone there. I'm pretty sure. I think I saw her. He had the blinds down but there was someone there."

I thought that over. If Ian were really with someone else, I was going to have to totally rethink my opinion of him. Frankly, I'd never felt he possessed the balls. It's not that he's a wimp. It's just that he's so serious and careful and truly in love with Jill. "Are you sure?" I asked.

"I heard them, Blue. The window was open and she was laughing. And it was that kind of flirty laughing. She was into him."

I slid past the issue. "I wouldn't call that stalking. That's wanting information. There's a difference."

"It gets better," she warned.

"Oh, goody." I braced myself.

"The next day I went over early. I was going to talk to him, but then this girl came out."

"Of his apartment?"

"I think so. It was one of 'em. Maybe it was his neighbor's. I don't know. But I just wanted to kill him, y'know? So . . . I followed him."

"You followed him in your car?"

"Yeah. Only it was CeeCee's car. We'd switched."

I finished the last bit of my sandwich and chased crumbs around on the plate with my licked index finger. "I know I'm going to hate myself for asking, but why did you switch?"

"Because I didn't want him to see me following him, okay?" She stirred her salad with renewed vigor. The motion was as if she were cooling off a bowl of soup, except the bits of salad were getting mangled, crushed, and pulverized.

"And CeeCee went for this?"

"Stop sounding so judgmental."

Momentarily I was stopped. Am I going to have to *completely* rethink my own vision of myself? I put that aside for the moment. "Following Ian around sounds kind of boring to me. Where'd he go? The gym?"

"He went over to his friend's place and they just hung out for a couple of hours."

"You didn't wait the whole time."

"No." She shook her head. Something about her body language bothered me.

"How long did you wait?"

"Okay, fine! I waited the whole goddamn time. Happy now?"

I lifted my hands in surrender and noticed a bit of brie stuck to my wrist. I debated licking it off, but I do occasionally try to have some class so I wiped it off with my napkin instead. "You wanted me to listen. I'm listening. I'm just not sure what I'm hearing. Last week you were pissed off because he asked you to marry him, and now you're following him around like a jilted girlfriend. But just because he took the ring back doesn't mean you're completely through. You guys are still Jill-Ian," I said with more conviction than I felt. I watched her carefully. Her head jerked in a nod. Then to my surprise her eyes filled with sudden tears. She seemed not to know what to do about them, so I awkwardly handed her an unused cloth napkin I filched from the just-set nearby table. The waiter gave me a dirty look, but didn't complain when he saw Jill press the cloth to both eyes.

"He called last night and broke up with me," she choked out. "The *fucking* asshole."

"Oh . . . ."

"I should have told you. I know. I just can't believe it." Her face contorted in an effort to stem more tears.

Jill and Ian had been Jill-Ian for so long that this sudden switch was difficult to process. Okay, she'd had a brief delusional moment when she'd been starry-eyed over Jackson, but she and Ian had never fully separated, even then. From a purely selfish standpoint I liked the idea of Jill being free. Ian seemed to just always be so *there*. But her pain distressed me. She's usually so good at hiding her feelings. This really hurt.

I tried to come up with something sage and truthful and helpful, but my mind was a blank. And fresh off how badly I'd wounded Kristl, I didn't think any militant feminist stuff from me about how she was lucky to be rid of the *fucking* asshole was going to be the answer.

I said, "You need something stronger than Chardonnay."

She blinked at me. "What exactly are you suggesting? Straight vodka?"

"Not a bad idea . . ."

Her gaze sharpened on me. "Something even stronger? Something . . . illegal?"

"No. Well, I don't think so." I was surprised by the way she jumped to that conclusion.

"Well, what then? You sounded so . . . nefarious."

Had I? I really had only meant to comfort. But seeing the interested look on her face—the only glimpse of hope that she might actually ascend from the depths of wallowing grief—made me suddenly want to help her out chemically. I said, off the top, "I caught one of our PAs smoking dope in the men's room at work. I didn't tell Holly. I don't know exactly why."

" 'Cause you hate being a rat. You're almost pathological about it."

"I like the guy, and he likes me. I could probably score you some, if you're interested."

She sank back into her chair, defeated. "I fear I need more than marijuana to kill this pain," she said.

"That's about as far into controlled substance procuring as I go."

She thought it over, shrugged, and said, "Okay, why not?"

I hesitated a moment, not certain quite how I'd suddenly become the pusher. This was not a role I'd ever been in before. It was definitely outside of the Ginny Blue boundaries for okay behavior.

Then I looked over at Jill. Her unhappiness was huge, practically a living thing. Medical marijuana helps glaucoma and is helpful in controlling pain in cancer patients. Maybe this would do some good. And dope was a notorious trigger for the munchies. Jill might actually *eat* something.

I'm all about rationalization sometimes.

I said, "We'll talk again at 2100 hours."

"Oh, Blue."

"Get the check and let's skedaddle."

Chapter

6

Sean came back to the office in the afternoon for a delivery and pick up. I followed him outside and caught him at his car, a Jeep, as he was just about to leave on another run. He looked at me expectantly. For a moment I was tongue-tied. What had sounded like "help for a friend" at the restaurant now didn't seem like such a hot idea. Was I really going to ask this kid for some dope?

"I've got this friend . . ." I started lamely.

"Yeah? A guy friend?" He gave me a look and a smile, the kind that says he finds you attractive.

I suddenly worried about my hair, my clothes, my lack of discernible makeup. I was on a job for pete's sake. In jeans and a green T-shirt. He couldn't expect me to look like a model, could he? As soon as these thoughts crossed my mind I wanted to slap myself. I was not, not, not interested in Sean. "No, it's my friend Jill. Rough time with the guy she's been with."

He waited patiently for the point. My mind wandered, briefly, as I considered what he would look like without his shirt. Like me, he was working, and you never knew when that could involve lifting or minor carpentry or, in my case, a six-page document on cost analysis. You had to be ready for anything. Still, I catalogued his denim jeans and shirt and work boots and wondered what his real wardrobe was like. I pegged him for rumpled, like Nate.

"She's incredibly depressed. I think she needs medication."

"Prozac? That stuff'll dead'n ya."

"I was thinking more like—dope. Could I buy a joint from you?"

He laughed. "Hell, no. Man, that's commerce, y'know? Bein' a dealer? Forget it . . . here." He dug into one of his pockets and pulled out two rather beaten-up joints. "They're yours. Have fun with your friend."

I felt a warm feeling for Sean as he handed over the contraband. And that's when I said it, just off the top of my head. "My friend—another friend—is having a birthday next Saturday. We're celebrating. Having a party."

"You inviting me?"

I nodded.

"Cool," he said, and the lifted brow he sent me was decidedly flirty.

I gave him a long look over my shoulder as he left and he did the same. For the rest of the afternoon and into the rest of the week we caught each other's eyes and smiled. It was so high school it made me giddy. I didn't ask myself what I was doing because I was pretty sure I wouldn't want to know the answer.

As luck would have it, I didn't connect with Jill until the weekend. By that time I'd nearly forgotten about the dope and CeeCee's birthday party. Sean, however, had entered a new space in my mind. I listened for his return and took extra effort on my appearance. I even found myself plucking my eyebrows Thursday night, a bit of personal grooming I'd let slide those last months with Nate. It was curious how unable I was to conjure up Nate's face. I was shocked one morning when I realized I hadn't required tons and tons of

counseling from my friends. My God! It was highly possible
they didn't even all know yet. Had I told CeeCee? Kristl?

Liam Engleston himself called on Tuesday. I was surprised not to speak to an underling, but upon hearing his su-
percilious voice I made an executive decision and said,
tersely and sharply, "I'm sorry, Mr. Engleston. We have hired
a different catering firm." I hoped Jill was up for the job. I
should have nailed this down earlier. I had a memory of the
defeated slump of her shoulders at the Farm and worried that
I should have made a greater effort to contact her over the
course of the week.

There was silence on Engleston's end. When he finally
spoke, I could tell he was trying extremely hard not to
scream. He asked for my superior, one of his favorite lines,
apparently, and I waved at Holly who just happened to be
walking by at that moment. She silently queried me with furrowed brow as she took the receiver. I mimed that I was eating.

"Hello?" she said in a cool voice, glaring at me. She ex-
pects me to handle all problems. I lifted my palms in surrender, but then whatever Liam was saying snapped her
attention to the matter at hand. She listened for a solid ten
seconds and then said crisply, "I don't give a rat's ass about
anything you're saying. Either deal with Ginny or get off the
phone." She handed the receiver back to me without a word
and kept walking.

Tom started choking on one of the Jolly Ranchers he
likes to consume by the truckload. I could tell he was about
to burst as I gingerly put the receiver to my ear. "Mr. Engleston?"

There was only dead air. I hung up and Tom hooted with
laughter and gave me a high five. I grinned. I decided I liked
Holly. I really, really liked her. Okay, I knew that would last
a New York minute, but I love it when someone steps up and
takes care of things just the way you'd like them to be done.

Friday morning I was driving west on the 10 at breakneck

speed when my cell phone started singing. It was Jill. She needed to see me right away. She and Ian truly were split up, apparently. I found this notion so hard to wrap my brain around that I couldn't quite process it as truth.

"I'm late," I told her. "The Holy Terror is waiting for me and she's not good at waiting."

"Am I catering your job, or not?" she asked.

"Yep. Liam Engleston is out. Too expensive, too gourmet. A bad idea right from the start. Remind me never to listen to my crew again."

"Shoot days are Wednesday through Saturday?"

"Sunday, too, if necessary."

"Sandwiches, salads, desserts, beverages," she said.

"Nonalcoholic beverages," I reminded her, to which she snorted.

"I know my job, Blue," she said in an acid voice.

"Well, ex-cu-uuu-se me."

"Did you talk to that PA guy? Y'know . . . ?"

"Got it handled," I assured her.

We agreed to stop by her place, which was in Venice, on the way to CeeCee's party at the trendy bar called Someplace Else. The bar was someone's brainchild and that same someone had also opened The Other Place across the street. This way you could go from The Other Place to Someplace Else without ever getting behind the wheel. My plan was to deliver Jill the contraband, then head out to Someplace Else. But nobody was smokin' nothin' until after the party.

On this, as it turned out, I was wrong. I'd barely turned off my ignition in front of Jill's bungalow when Sean, whom I'd invited to our prefunction plans, drove his Jeep into the curb and stopped with a screech of brakes. Jill, who'd stepped outside upon spying my Explorer, eyed his car suspiciously. As Sean stumbled out and slammed the door, she demanded, "Who are you?" in a withering voice meant to intimidate lesser mortals.

Sean, however, was impervious, unaware, and uncaring. He

said, "Sean," sticking out his hand. Jill carefully shook it, her eyes sliding my way.

I explained, "Sean is the procurer of our devil weed."

"Uh-huh." Jill looked annoyed. "So, what are you doing here?"

"I invited him," I answered.

"Hope it's okay," he said, though his tone suggested he couldn't have cared less.

Jill glared at him and then me. "This birthday party is for close friends."

He shrugged his shoulders, grinning like a goof. "I'm friendly."

Jill slowly turned to me, her face frozen. Taking my cue from Sean, I shrugged, too. "We might as well get going."

Jill stiffly climbed into the passenger seat of the Explorer and Sean jumped in the back. I knew I would pay for bringing him along, but truthfully, there was something annoyingly wonderful about Sean that alternately irked and amused me. I'd begun to feel jaded about men, I'd realized, and it was time I got over that.

Someplace Else was down Abbott-Kinney, toward the beach. Jill sulked sullenly while Sean, already high and in that doofus-like, surfer-boy mode so popular in B-comedies these days, prattled on and on about the most inane Tolkien minutiae, his current obsession, apparently. I finally realized in surprise that he'd actually read the books.

"You've read the whole trilogy?" I said in disbelief. "All of the *Lord of the Rings?*"

"Totally, man."

Jill snorted and pointed out, "Blue is a woman."

"It's okay," I said, shooting Jill a quelling look. She just turned her head to the window and Sean leaned forward, breathing his pot-laced breath near my ear.

"Like, I loved the films. Wow. Went back like eleven times." He chortled. "Couldn't wait for the third one, so I started readin' it, y'know? But shit, man, there are a lotta names!

So, I went back to the first one and kept on readin' till I was done. Read *The Hobbit,* too." He turned to Jill. "It's the prequel."

"I'm aware," she managed tightly.

"You're kinda uptight, aren't ya? Good thing I brought the good stuff. Want some now." He fished in a pocket, but I quelled this fast.

"We've still got the two you gave me. And I don't want to do anything in the car. Or at the party. Got it?"

"Got it."

Jill, who normally wasn't quite such a prig about things, couldn't seem to shake her mood. But once started, Sean could not be stopped. He talked about Middle-Earth as if it were more real than Los Angeles. Thinking of the endless traffic and generally ugly commercial storefronts lining the streets, I wondered if he might be on to something.

"I am GinBlue-san of the shire," I said.

Jill snorted. "What are you? Japanese-hobbit?"

"Cool," said Sean.

"Okay, I'll drop the 'san' part."

"Hell, no." Sean threw Jill a thoughtful look. "I like Gin-Blue-san. Sounds like Bombay Sapphire gin and saki, or something. Hey, maybe we should stop and have some saki bombs? Just to get started."

"Someplace Else'll have some, probably," I said, sure Jill was about to erupt.

To my surprise she seemed to think over Sean's suggestion. "Ian and I had saki bombs at the Paper Door a couple of weeks ago."

Her wistful tone surprised Sean who'd only seen Jill in vicious mode thus far. "Who's Ian?"

"The *fucking* asshole," Jill answered as the words crossed my mind at the exact same moment.

I recalled those saki bombs; Nate and I had met up with Jill and Ian and imbibed. Not that I'm much for saki, but when in Rome—or Tokyo—so to speak. A saki bomb is a jigger of saki balanced on two chopsticks above a pint of beer. You pound the table with your fists until the jigger falls into the beer then you chug the beer. At least that's the theory. In my case I go through the pounding ritual then sip at the beer because I'm neither a saki nor a huge beer lover. Okay, I like beer, but I can't ever drink a brewsky without thinking of all the calories. Don't ask me why, as I can swill other alcohol without a second thought. Anyway, Jill and Ian were having a wonderful time that night, but Nate and I weren't, so I couldn't view the evening through the same set of rose-colored glasses as Jill apparently did.

We arrived at Someplace Else and were forced to valet park. I always worry that some guy wearing a pair of black pants and carrying a tag-notepad will jump into my car and take off, never to be seen again. I'm fond of my Explorer and as I watched it being driven off I felt a pang of worry, which I did not communicate to Jill or Sean as they would've undoubtedly derided me for my fears.

We walked inside and the bouncer checked our IDs through a computer setup of some kind. I swear, it's getting harder and harder to cheat and/or talk your way into a bar if you're not of age—unless maybe you're Nate's Tara. I guess I should be glad they still bother to check my ID, but truthfully they check anyone no matter what their age.

I looked around for CeeCee, worried maybe she was at The Other Place, and I'd screwed up. Suddenly I zeroed in on the one person I really did not want to see: Jackson Wright! *Oh. My. God.* What the hell was he doing here? And why did he look so damn good, with hair grown a tad long over the collar of a blue silk shirt?

He was seated at the bar, his back to me. For an immature moment I thought about turning and running, but then I shored up my confidence and sauntered over. I mean, what was the big deal? It's not like we'd ever slept together or anything. He was just a guy I was bound to run into from time to

time since we both lived, and apparently played, around
Santa Monica, west LA and Venice.

I said as an opening gambit, "And here I thought you'd be
at The Other Place."

He turned to look at me. I was hit afresh by his dark, attractive looks. Not a good sign. He's got that swarthy complexion and lean, muscular body that gets to me right in the
core. I was flummoxed when he smiled widely as if he were
truly thrilled to see me.

"Ginny Blue," he said, gathering me in a deep hug.

This was more physical contact than I was prepared for
and I immediately tightened up. If he noticed, he had the
good graces not to mention it. Instead he released me and
said, "CeeCee called me about the party. I thought I might
see you here." His smile was of friendship, nothing more,
but it hit me in the gut. Or, maybe it was just learning that
CeeCee had specifically invited him. That she had his phone
number. It was a good thing Kristl wasn't coming.

"Is CeeCee here?" I forced out, holding onto my cool
with an effort.

"Don't think so."

"Hey!" Sean said, having finally gotten past the bouncer
and coming up on my right. Jackson gave him an assessing
look, not unfriendly, just curious. I introduced them, feeling
like I was playing a part in some play as Jill joined us, her
head swiveling around in search of CeeCee's party.

"You know Jill," I said to Jackson.

"Of course." He actually rose from the barstool and gave
Jill a quick hug, too, which turned her to stone. Over his
shoulder her eyes reached out to me in askance. I shook my
head, still bemused that CeeCee had invited Jackson.

And she hadn't slept with him, either.

Jill wasn't a fan of Jackson. She'd suffered an unrequited
crush which had never seriously gotten off the ground. They'd
managed some of those almost dates—meet-me-here, we'll-

see-what-happens kinds of things—but as far as I knew it had never progressed much further. For one thing, Ian was always in the background. For another, Jackson Wright never committed. It wasn't his way. Like me, I think Jill saw that for what it was right away and she veered away from him. Like all of us, she badmouthed him whenever possible.

As I considered this, I wondered why we all acted so strangely toward him. But I knew. We were all half in love/lust with him and all our nose-in-the-air disdain was merely to hide our own insecurities. The thought made me squirm. I didn't want to like Jackson. At all.

"What have you been doing?" Jackson asked the both of us.

"Production," I said.

"I'm a PA on her job," Sean said, making it sound far more intimate than it was.

"Catering," Jill said.

"That's right. You've got your own business now."

"If you can call it that," Jill said. "It's feast or famine. I love weddings," she added with a catch in her voice. "They're great gigs."

"What about you?" I asked, though I already knew.

"I'm still a glutton for punishment. Financial management," he added for Sean's benefit.

Sean pretended interest. "Yeah? Cool."

"You still taking care of actors, directors, etcetera?"

"Mostly I'm investing for myself," Jackson admitted. "And I'm getting involved in some other projects."

"What kind of projects?"

"Film projects."

"Really?" I said, totally intrigued.

He shrugged lightly, dismissing it. "Nothing's together yet. You know."

I nodded. Until the day it happened, one never knew if a project was really going to happen. In the commercial business we were always waiting to see when the job awarded.

No use counting one's chickens until they hatched, because if you did, those chickens would definitely stay in the shell forever.

"We'll have to talk," Jackson said to me.

"Sure." Whatever that meant.

The bartender came and Jackson insisted on buying us all drinks. Jill and Sean ordered saki bombs and squeezed up to the bar beside Jackson to down them, drawing dark looks from the group of girls who'd staked claim to the bar stools on either side. I passed on Ketel One for a gin and tonic. Bombay Sapphire gin martini in honor of 'Ginny Blue.' I was actually toying with adding the moniker as a nickname. I could see myself telling everyone I met that my name was Ginny Sapphire Blue, but it sounded sort of pretentious.

Jackson continued, "When the market went down I lost some clients and had to rethink what I wanted to do."

"Taking care of other people's money wasn't what it was cracked up to be?" I carefully sipped at my martini. Gin is a little tricky, I always think. Especially basically straight gin.

"As soon as I decided to get out of the financial management business, some of my clients came back. Go figure."

"So, you're a little of this now, and a little of that."

He nodded. "Your friend John stayed with me the whole time, though."

"John?"

"John Langdon."

The blood drained from my face. I could feel it. Luckily, the place was dark and hopefully my voice didn't sound as strangled as it felt when I said, "Oh, yeah, sure. Lang."

"You know John Langdon?" Sean breathed, impressed.

Jackson grimaced, clearly aware that he'd put me in a tough position. I could have kicked him.

"They had a thing," Jill decided to reveal, "but she doesn't like to talk about it."

John Langdon. Ex-File Number . . . Four. Okay, he's the real number four. Mr. Famous Actor.

"It was a short thing," I said through my teeth.

"How short?" Jill asked, picking up on the double entendre.

Jackson's brows had lifted and he was looking amused. When I didn't respond he drawled, "According to Lang, that isn't the case. He can't keep his mouth shut about its size and where it's been and with whom." I must have looked stricken because he added kindly, "Although he refers to you as the 'one who got away.' "

"Bullshit," I said.

"Just the truth," he assured.

Sean was staring at me. "Un-be-fuckin'-lievable!"

To my relief CeeCee and Daphne entered at that moment, followed by a couple of guys and girls I didn't know. The party swarmed around us and we were carried off to a reserved table. Somehow I'd thought CeeCee's party was going to be small, but it grew as the evening wore on until we were spilling onto other people's tables, stealing chairs and tables and absorbing others into our group.

I stayed sober, being a designated driver and finding that I had no desire whatsoever to have another drink. Maybe it was seeing Jackson, maybe it was learning the disturbing news that he was Lang's financial manager, maybe it was the phase of the moon. Whatever the case, I had become the least happy person around, and I tried desperately to keep my eyes off Jackson until he had the bad judgment to actually come over and engage me in further conversation.

I was not interested with a capital *not*.

I tried to fob him off, but Jackson can be damn entertaining when he wants to be. For reasons I didn't want to explore, he seemed to want to be now.

"Someone ought to watch the candles on the cake," he observed dryly, "or hair, ribbon, packages are going to catch fire."

I was at the far end of the table from CeeCee who was less interested in the usual birthday accouterments than she was in the long-haired guy to her right. People kept thrusting packages and little birthday bags with huge ribbons in her hands, but her eyes and thoughts and ears were bent toward the guy. Jill had told me he was with the radio station. For a brief moment I'd thought it might be the guy with the cigarette burn, but the backs of both hands were unscarred. This was somebody else, apparently. I was relieved to think the ass-grabber could be history.

Someone said, "What is that? It smells like wet dog."

Everyone glanced toward CeeCee. The cake, illuminated by twenty-eight tiny candles, was close to a pile of bags and gifts, but nothing was aflame. CeeCee's hair, which had been growing out a bit, still wasn't long enough to catch fire but her male companion's was. I could see the filaments of his mane curl up and singe.

Then suddenly tissue paper went up in a bright yellow *whoosh*.

"CeeCee!" I yelled.

Screams echoed through the room. Everyone jumped from their seats. I had to fight to stay where I was. Jackson pushed forward and calmly beat out the flames with a table napkin. Daphne snatched up the cake and held it aloft. The cake teetered for a moment on its cardboard platter and the party collectively screamed as Daphne quickly did a wild balancing act, managing to steady the dessert and miraculously keep the candles flickering merrily away.

"Geez, Louise," I muttered and sat down heavily. Mr. Mane was examining the blackened ends of his hair as Daphne set down the cake and collapsed with relief into a chair. CeeCee looked amused by the spectacle.

Jill said, "I could use another saki bomb," which Sean eagerly seconded.

Jackson shot me a look. I shrugged my shoulders and started laughing. Disaster had been averted. Jackson smiled.

Before we could settle back into the party, the grim, white-faced manager came over and asked us all to leave.

CeeCee's answer was to blow the candles completely out, then give the manager the finger. Luckily, he'd turned away for just a brief moment, enough to miss her act of insurgence. Jackson took him aside and talked to him and we were all grudgingly allowed to stay.

I moved toward Jackson as the guests settled back into their seats, a little more alert, a little more sober.

"You can hardly blame them," said Jackson. "A fire in a public place . . . it's deadly."

"I see the future and it's a cold, cold place without birthday candles on cakes." I glanced to the guy with the burned hair. He was desperately trying to laugh it all off while being totally pissed. "What is it with CeeCee and fire around men?"

"Has this happened before?"

"Not exactly." I broke down and told him about the cigarette incident. He wasn't surprised in the least, as it turns out, which made me give him a long look.

He admitted, "I knew about what happened with Richter."

"What do you mean *you knew*?"

"CeeCee and I go out for drinks sometimes. She told me about him. It happened about six months ago."

Richter? I was hurt. CeeCee hadn't revealed this information—this *serious* information, no less—to her girlfriends but she'd managed to blab the story to Jackson Wright, thank you very much.

As if reading my thoughts, Jackson said, "She was kind of embarrassed about it. Felt maybe she'd overreacted. She thought he might actually file charges against her and wanted to know what I thought. Jace Richter's a real asshole, but he's also a coward. He didn't want to have to go to court and explain what had provoked CeeCee."

"You know him?"

He shook his head. "CeeCee's station manager is a client. I kind of got in the middle of it without meaning to. I did talk to Richter, though. That's why I'm qualified in calling him an asshole."

"Well, he likes to grab asses."

"Specifically CeeCee's. He's got a thing for her."

I thought again how CeeCee seemed interested in him as well. My revulsion must have showed because Jackson asked, "What?"

"I'm worried there might be a reciprocal 'thing' going."

Jackson didn't immediately answer. I could tell he was holding out on me. It was my turn to ask, "What?"

"My client. The station manager. He's got a thing for CeeCee, too. It's a real mess. I told CeeCee she might be better off quitting."

"No way! She loves that job."

"She's got two men interested in her. One of them wants her job."

"And her ass," I pointed out.

"They both want that, Ginny. It's unfortunate, because she really hasn't asked for any of this."

I looked over at the partiers. CeeCee was making her way through her gifts. Mr. Mane was nursing his anger in a corner away from the crowd. CeeCee shot him a look but I could tell she was turned off by his little-boy behavior.

I was stung by how much information had passed between Jackson and CeeCee. "You're really in the know, aren't you?"

"In this case."

"Do you know who that guy is?" I inclined my head toward Mr. Mane.

He shook his head.

The evening wore on. I stayed near Jackson, but that was about the extent of our conversation. Sean had somehow managed to get stuck beside a gay couple on one side and Jill on the other. His voice had grown louder and louder with his consumption of alcohol but no one was listening. I thought I should rescue him, as technically he was my date. He finally managed to extricate himself from his chair and I helped him get around the chairs that stood in his way. He half-tripped, then finally got clear. Instantly he slung an arm over my shoulder, his beer teetering somewhere above my right breast. I kept a wary eye on it, expecting it to drop to the floor and drench me on its way down.

He managed to hang onto it until jostled by one of the other drunks. I jumped away and avoided most of the beer spill. CeeCee opened the last of her gifts: some kind of rude sex-shop item, which turned out to be licorice crotchless panties. Yep. Love that kind of good taste in gifts. Turned out it was from Mr. Mane. What a guy.

At the end of the evening I watched as Jackson kissed CeeCee goodbye on the cheek. He scared a smile out of her. It was all very big-brotherly but it depressed me nonetheless. I was definitely going to have to take this up with Dr. Dick.

Jill caught me looking and I shrugged. She left it alone. We all headed outside with Sean totally drunk and stumbling after me. He gave my shoe a flat tire before dropping like a stone into the passenger seat. As I righted my shoe, Jill climbed in the back.

"Nice," she remarked as Sean's chin dropped to his chest and he passed out.

At Jill's place I determined I could not let Sean get behind the wheel of his own car. Although he'd roused himself out of my car, he couldn't seem to insert key into keyhole of his car. Looking at him, weaving slightly on his feet and giving me a shit-eating grin, I sighed and piled him back into the Explorer. I was taking a guy home with me, but it was the last thing I wanted to do.

I told Jill goodbye and that if she wanted help smoking her weed, I was going to have to take a rain check. "You wouldn't smoke it anyway," she said on a sigh. "And truthfully, I just want to go to bed." Her cell phone rang and she examined the caller ID. "It's Ian," she said, sounding suddenly tense.

"Call me and tell me about it," I said. She nodded, click-

ing on the receiver and said a tentative, "Hello?" sounding
very unlike herself as she walked toward her front door.

I climbed in the driver's seat and Sean roused himself
enough to mumble, "Thanks for driving" in between a spate
of hiccups.

"I'm taking you to my place. You can have the couch."

"It was a good party. Thanks for invit—inviting me." He
finished this off with a huge belch, laughed, threw me a
drunken, partially sheepish look and sank against the head-
rest. "Nice upholstery," he added dreamily and promptly
passed out again.

MADD and the LA police were lucky I was around to
drive Sean, I decided as we pulled into the bunker—my
name for my underground parking. Schematic Man was still
bent over in supreme pain, but my brain had moved ahead to
bed, rest and a chance to bury my head under the covers and
hide from the world for a few hours. I didn't want to examine too closely why I felt the need for this burrowing. Jackson Wright was the only answer and I just didn't want him to
matter this much.

Fifteen minutes later I had thrown a pillow and blanket on
the couch and pointed out Sean's bed to him as he stood head
down, in a walking coma. Then I opened the sliding door and
stepped onto my postage-stamp sized patio. I've got a great
view of the street and the noise level is loud enough to make
me certain I'm deaf sometimes. Several large pine trees block
the worst of the view but they drop these long, deadly brown
needles all over the place, covering my concrete patio. It's hell
being outdoor gardening-challenged.

But it was a beautiful evening. I stood in the cool breeze
with my face turned skyward, eyes closed. I felt weary beyond my years and the realization totally depressed me. It's
not often that I spend much time with dark inward thoughts,
but I can be as down as anybody now and again. However, as
soon as I reach my own depths—which I have to admit are

fairly shallow anyway—I tend to bounce back fast. I was almost waiting for this to happen when I sensed Sean coming up behind me. My first thought was impatience, especially when his arms circled my waist from behind, but then he pressed his forehead to my back, just below my nape, and there was something so intimate and almost forlorn about it that part of me responded in spite of myself. I couldn't tell if I wanted to cry. It felt like I might. A moment later, sexual desire awoke, stretched, and lifted its interested head. Nate had been gone for several weeks now, and I couldn't recall the last time I'd actually wanted sex with him before that. It felt, suddenly, like I was on the brink of something I desperately wanted. It was invigorating and scary.

"Whoa. My head's killin' me," Sean mumbled, still bent against me as if in prayer.

"Don't talk," I said.

"Okay."

We stayed like that a few tense moments longer. Sean, picking up something on his masculine radar, sensed my shift in mood. He might be barely into adulthood, but he had all the necessary antennae to appreciate female emotions, apparently. I concentrated on his masculinity, as well. My thoughts touched on taut muscles, thickly lashed blue eyes, and a sensual mouth, even though I wasn't looking at him. Truth to tell, I wouldn't have been able to tell you exactly what color Sean's eyes were or what shape his lips were or anything else. I was suddenly looking at a fantasy man, my inner vision narrowed as if through a funnel toward him and something just out of reach. I didn't want Sean to do *any-thing* lest he somehow destroy this tension-filled moment. But suddenly Sean did move, and it was to slide his hands beneath my shirt and under my bra to cup my breasts.

With an effort I pictured "fantasy man" doing the same thing. I imagined him ripping off my shirt and raining a scorching line of kisses down my shoulders. No, make that a hot, wet tongue. I would have moaned with desire but then it all went to hell when Sean started panting and humping against my buttocks.

"Oh, baby . . . oh, baby . . . oh, baby . . ."

"Sean."

"Oh, baby . . . c'mon . . ."

"Sean—"

"Shhhh . . . ." His hands, which began massaging my breasts so hard I wondered if he'd been a mammogram operator in a previous life, suddenly dropped to my jeans, ripping down the zipper and snap in one quick move. I was momentarily diverted, impressed at his efficiency. But then he was grinding against my buttocks again, my cheeks now only encased in a pair of flimsy black underpants, my favorites, as a matter of fact. (I know they're often referred to as 'panties' but there's something so pornographic about that word I struggle with it. Which is interesting when I realize I have no trouble saying, thinking, and hearing 'fuck.' Some day I'll have to take this issue to Dr. Dick.)

"Sean," I said again, twisting in his arms. I was worried he might suddenly lose control and spray sperm before either of us was truly ready.

He took the moment to rip off his own jeans and boxers and his penis just popped out, strong, straight, and eager. The cartoon sound *boing* went through my mind. I half chuckled. A difficult move on my part, as Sean's mouth and tongue were all over me while his fingers pulled down my underpants and Mr. Happy took up residence between my thighs: ready, willing, and able for complete entry.

I laughed aloud, choking in amusement. I couldn't help myself. Luckily, Sean didn't suffer from self-confidence issues and he started grinning in the midst of his "lovemaking." It was with real regret that I pushed him away.

"You know," I said matter-of-factly. "I wish I could do this with you, but I can't. Don't ask me why, because I couldn't explain it in a month of Sundays."

"Could you just suck me off, then?" Sean asked.

I looked down at Mr. Happy. Oral sex is something I struggle with. Usually takes a bottle and a half of Chardonnay or more.

"How about a hand job?" I suggested, to which he wrapped my fingers around his shaft and away we went.

Later, sitting beside Sean on the couch, with his head drooped onto my shoulder and his arms around me in a thoroughly sweet, childlike way, I gave myself a stern talking to. I was too old for this stuff, wasn't I? Where was romance? Did I even care for romance? Why couldn't I just have sex with Sean? What kind of skewed sense of propriety had steered my decision making tonight?

I made a noise of true annoyance. Sean stirred sleepily and asked on a yawn, "What's a month of Sundays?"

"Lots of 'em, I guess."

"Why Sundays? Why not Mondays?"

"Beats me."

"You wanna smoke a joint? I got some more in my car."

"Your car's at Jill's."

"Oh."

Stymied, Sean ended our conversation. He fell asleep within thirty seconds, and as I got to my feet he flopped onto the couch. He was still wearing his shirt and a pair of socks. The boxers and jeans lay in a pile by the sliding glass door. I thought about Kristl coming home, if she even would as she'd been working and/or with Brandon almost exclusively, and decided she might think my life was more interesting than it is if she caught Sean bare-assed on my couch.

I left him where he was, locked the patio door and headed upstairs.

Chapter
7

An impromptu meeting for Waterstone Iced Tea took place at 4 P.M. at our offices. As production manager, I wasn't always required to sit at the table with all the players: the director, our producer, Holly, the advertising agency producer, the art director, the client, and various and sundry others. This made me happy as a clam as these meetings are notoriously boring from a production point of view; they were more a means to lay out everything in two-year-old's terms to the client and ad agency. I was glad to be "below the line." Above the line is top management: well-paid, well-heeled and well-on-their-way-to-ulcers. Below the line are the production manager (me), the production coordinator (Tom), the production assistants (Sean et al.), and other office gofers. We below-liners sat at our desks and rechecked all the to do lists we'd already checked. It's amazing what can be forgotten or overlooked that may rise up and bite us in the ass later on.

Sean was not around and hadn't been all week, mainly because we hadn't needed him. Actual filming started tomorrow and I knew he was slated to be onsite in Venice at six-thirty A.M. I have to admit: I had a certain trepidation about seeing him again. My romantic encounter with him—if you could call it that—had left me feeling faintly embarrassed and ashamed. We'd hardly spoken the morning after as I'd driven him to his car. The kid was just too young for me, in every way. I needed to steer clear of him.

I hurriedly counted out the forty-nine pages of the final production manual we'd assembled for the job; the above-liners needed them in the production meeting *tout suite*. But my thoughts were traveling down different pathways. Truth to tell, I was kind of down. Running into Jackson at CeeCee's party hadn't been the height of my month. Seeing him had put a fine point on the fact that I—and all my friends—couldn't seem to find a decent man anywhere. Currently Jill and Ian were in serious trouble, Daphne and Leo weren't even an item, CeeCee seemed particularly hostile toward all males these days, and Kristl . . . well, Brandon might actually be her knight in shining armor, but based on her track record, I wasn't betting on it.

We were all definitely in a dating decline. The dearth of datable men boggled the mind. In fact—

"Ginny!"

I jumped about a foot out of my chair, my heart pounding. The harsh whisper had come from Holly, who was frantically signaling me from the doorway to the meeting room.

"The book's almost done," I mouthed, which only earned me more signaling.

I realized they wanted me in the meeting, with or without the preproduction book. Damn it. I was so not ready to suck up and make nice. Steeling myself, I tried on a smile and ran a mental inventory of my wardrobe: jeans, black-ribbed cotton shirt, black boots. Adequate.

They were all seated around the rectangular table as I entered. Everyone greeted me, some even by name. I glanced at the director, a sour-faced man whose thoughts always seemed to be floating somewhere in the ionosphere. He gave

me a faint nod. The client, two young Waterstone Iced Tea
men, did seem happy to see me. I couldn't read the agency
people, as they appeared to all be jockeying for some kind of
political position within their group that I couldn't immediately identify. I always get the feeling they're in fear for their
jobs. Tough work, advertising. I'd take production any day. I
sat down and put an interested expression on my face.

The discussion concerned the talent who had been chosen for their commercial. It was all about heat, the beach, the
waves, ice cubes, and sweating glasses of iced tea, which
made you "high." Personally, I thought it was dumb, but production is not to reason why. That's for the agency.

The storyboards had all been approved and there was
nothing really left to do but shoot. My gaze stole toward the
plate of cheeses, deli meats, fruit, and crackers artfully
arranged in the center of the table. I'd sent one of the PAs out
for groceries and we'd put the centerpiece together in short
order. Nobody ever ate anything at these meetings, from
what I could tell, but food always had to be available and
look inviting. If it wasn't there, production would be seen as
skimping and maybe the next job would be awarded to a different company.

The meeting broke up without me saying a word. Truthfully, nobody appeared to have said anything of import. I
wasn't sure why I'd been invited in. Probably just to break
the momentary tension. The political infighting that accom-
panies these jobs is always a mysterious wrangle. When we
scraped back our chairs I murmured some polite words and
hurried back to my desk.

When I got there I realized the production book was
missing. Before I started swearing I politely asked Tom and
a couple of others if they'd seen it. No one had. Since the
book had taken me hours to compile, I was ready to blow,
but then Sean breezed in with the original and five extra
copies of it.

He saw my face. "There was a note on it to make five copies," he explained. "I just thought I'd do it while you were in the meeting."

"Thanks." The possibility of losing all my work had elevated my heart rate with real fear and made it difficult for me to be nice. I said stiffly, "What are you doing here? I thought you weren't working today."

"I'm not. I just came to see you."

I sensed Tom's ears perking up as he reached nonchalantly into his Jolly Rancher bowl. All business, I said, "Well, I'm kinda busy right now. What time are you scheduled at the shoot tomorrow?"

"Six-thirty."

"Then I'll see you bright and early," I said, turning away.

I did manage to catch the hurt look on his face, but I ignored it, mentally flogging myself. I felt like a heel. I wasn't sure what the hell to do with Sean. I'd really stepped in it this time.

Sean departed and Daphne called, sounding decidedly chipper. She wanted to meet for lunch but when I'm deep into a job it's like I fall into another dimension. I'm simply unavailable.

But Daphne's not one to give up. I'd barely walked in my door late that night, my mind still running over the myriad details of getting ready for the shoot—had I forgotten anything?—when she appeared on my doorstep, insistently ringing my bell. I swore succinctly and pungently, then flung open the door. "I can't. You know I can't. Whatever it is. I've got a huge day ahead of me. After the shoot and post-production, I'm free, but not before."

"You always say that, and it's never true. There's always another job," Daphne complained, barreling past me into the living room.

"Yeah . . . well . . ." That was as clever a response as I could come up with.

Surfacing from my own funk, I belatedly realized she was

practically bursting with news. I did a mental check of the time—nine-thirty—calculating how many hours of sleep I would actually get if I relented and let her tell me all. With a sigh of annoyance directed solely at myself, I asked, "Okay, what is it?"

"Do you have any wine?"

"No. None. Not a drop. I'm working tomorrow. Early."

"Okay . . ." She hesitated, waiting for me to relinquish the hard-ass attitude. I crossed my arms. I couldn't afford to. "I just wanted to celebrate because Leo and I are together!"

She uttered this last triumphantly, as if it were a *coup* beyond *coups*. I tried to be supportive; I really did. I didn't call him a Huge Waste of Time. But my answer of, "Well . . . that's . . . great" must've sounded pretty anemic because Daphne's face fell.

"I *knew* you'd be this way."

"I'm just not his biggest fan, Daph. Sorry." I spread my hands. "I wish I could be more supportive. I'm just tired."

"He stopped seeing Heather, just like that." She snapped her fingers. "We had a few drinks after work the other night and it was like we'd been together forever. It was so great. I can really talk to him."

I wanted to say, "He's an actor!" but I bit my lip. Hard. She knew the score. If she wanted to live in a world of unreality, who was I to be the voice of sanity? Relenting, I said, "Let's walk down to the Love Shack, and I'll buy you an amethyst. One amethyst. Then I'm in bed."

Daphne was thrilled. She hugged me and babbled on about Leo as we headed the few blocks toward Wilshire and then a few blocks west to the Love Shack, a little bar whose name implied it was a lot more fun than it really was. But it was nearby, and their amethyst martinis, so named for a touch of black-currant liqueur which turned it a faint lavender shade, were rather fine. The last thing I wanted before a shoot date was a drink of any kind, so I settled for club soda while Daphne sipped her drink and raved about Leo.

It was nice to see her so deliriously starry-eyed, I decided a bit enviously. None of us had been in a long time. Even Kristl didn't appear as happy with Brandon as Daphne currently was with surfer-dude Leo.

"So, what happened?" I asked. "Why did he suddenly decide that you were the one?"

"I don't know. I kind of ignored him for a while. I was really just trying not to let it all get to me, y'know? The way he was with Heather? I felt like an idiot for sleeping with him. I know lots of people are doing that 'fuck buddy' thing, but I just can't. What's the point? I want something more, something to build on."

I thought of Sean, felt a twinge of uncomfortableness, nodded. I knew exactly what she meant. What I didn't add was that I didn't believe she'd found it with Leo. He wasn't the "build a future with" kind of guy.

"I know you don't like him," she said. "Maybe when you get to know him . . . ?"

"It's not that I don't like him. I just don't like what's happened so far, that's all. It doesn't bode well."

"Lots of guys make mistakes."

"Yeah. You just have to decide how many is too many. When the mistake list starts outweighing the 'things done right' list, it's a problem."

Daphne quickly rose to Leo's defense. "That's not the case here."

"No. Okay. Fine." I was not in the mood for a debate. "It's too early to tell."

"You're being really negative," she complained.

"You're right. I am. I'm sorry. To be honest, my mind's on work. I'm really glad you've gotten what you want, Daphne. Seriously. And I want it to work out," I said, putting everything I had into it, meaning it. I really did want Daphne to be happy.

"But . . . ?" She crossed her arms.

"No buts. No qualifications. None." I tapped the rim of my glass against hers. "I hope Leo brings you happiness."

She smiled, and I silently vowed to keep further comments about Leo trapped firmly inside my head.

Wind proved a total problem on the job. Shooting stalled, started up again, stalled. The beach tossed up sand in front of the camera lenses and into everyone's eyes. I was in the production trailer and relatively sand-free, but the delays only meant I would be putting in longer and longer hours along with everyone else.

Sean came in and stood behind my right shoulder. I was on the phone and he was distracting me, which pissed me off. To counteract his effect, I gave him a job. "Go pick up the talent at LAX."

"They're not coming in for another two hours," he said.

"We all need coffees here. Run to Starbucks, okay? And ask Tom and Joe what they want. Oh, and get Holly a Tazo-chai latte. Do you still have enough petty cash?"

"Got it," Sean said with a nod and left. Momentarily I felt like an ogre, but I didn't have time to dwell on it.

Some of the talent arrived in their own cars and one of our cube truck drivers swiped the side of one of the actor's cars. It left a minuscule scratch, but the guy was incensed. We offered to settle right then, but he wanted to go to the insurance company which meant more paperwork. What started out as an accident became an all-consuming fiasco for me, and I was so annoyed at the guy I called up Joe, the video guy, and asked how big the actor's part was and if he could be scratched.

Joe hooks up video equipment to the film cameras while the commercial is being filmed. We can then watch what's being shot through the camera on televisions. It's easy to get a feel for the whole thing this way. He assured me that he would talk to the film editors and direction and make sure said actor would hit the cutting room floor.

I know it sounds like I hate actors. I don't hate them. They're attractive and charismatic, and hate is way too strong a word and implies a depth of feeling I'm not sure I possess. I do think they're all a pain in the ass, however. They're just not good for my health.

I think it's past time I explained about Mr. Famous Actor.

I met him at a commercial shoot when I was still a production assistant. As the lowest minions on set, the PAs were warned to stay far, far away from the talent and the director. And don't wear anything to draw attention: too much perfume, makeup, distracting Britney Spears-like outfits. Directors hate to be distracted. This all worked for me because basically I'm a blue jeans and overshirt type. If the weather's too hot, I'll switch to a basic black T-shirt, baggy capris and flip-flops. There is absolutely nothing sexy about my wardrobe.

Which is why it was so funny when Lang did the classic double take on me. I can't say I wasn't flattered. Who wouldn't be? He was famous enough to have people on the street recognize him even if they didn't know his name. He'd been on a television show that ran four years, then had segued to commercials and even small parts in feature films. Since my time with Lang, he'd actually become more famous. I wasn't sure how to feel about this as it was weird to see some fantastically huge poster or magazine cover of his face. I wondered how Cris Judd felt while J.Lo was living large on Ben Affleck's arm. Bennifer had been everywhere and he'd been the one left in the lurch. During that time I felt such a kinship toward him it made me forget we didn't know each other. For instance, once I actually saw Cris at a trendy Hollywood bar, and it was all I could do not to run over, clap him on the back, shake my head in commiseration and say, "I feel your pain." (I suspect this is just the kind of thing celebrities get from stalkers; it's just as well I curbed my impulse.)

But then, I'd never married Lang so maybe I didn't really know what Cris felt about being dumped or about having been Mr. Jennifer Lopez. And when I look back on my affair with Lang I still didn't know how I felt about that glimpse into the surreal world of Hollywood stardom.

What I do know is that John Langdon took a hard look at me and smiled, so I smiled back, kind of thrilled. I wanted to glance around and see who'd noticed. I wanted to shout, "Hey, everybody! Somebody famous noticed me!" as if this would somehow validate my existence on the planet. (My shallowness shocks me sometimes.)

After the smile, Lang strode over to me on his next break and started up a conversation. I was still working, however, and didn't have a lot of time to do anything. Also, my producer at the time was such a ravenous bitch that I really had to mind my p's and q's. Hence, I scarcely glanced up when Lang started in.

"You're all in black," he observed, "and it's eighty-five degrees."

We were on location near Joshua Tree, east of LA. I was baking and so was everyone else. Shading my eyes against a very hot late-August sun, I said, "This is standard-issue production assistant attire. Besides, sweating is good for you. Exudes the poisons."

His brows lifted. "You're into that stuff? Mud baths and hot steam? Pulling out the poisons?"

"Not really," I admitted. "I just kind of like the word 'exude.' Ecks—oooood."

He smiled lazily, then repeated, "Exudes the poisons."

I nodded.

Okay, it wasn't exactly poetry, but it served the purpose in catching Lang's attention. He seemed to think I'd said something really, really smart, which should have clued me in right there that he wasn't exactly brain-surgeon material and maybe ought to be left well enough alone.

My producer snapped at me then and I hurried to do her bidding. But Lang's appreciation of my designed insouciance left me with a good feeling all day.

Late that night, I was one of the last people working. A PA's job is never done. Dog-tired, I climbed in my car for the hour's drive back to our rented rooms. The production staff's rooms were not located at the same place as the talent; we were motel, they were spa/resort. After I'd changed and showered I found I had a second wind. There was this little excitement buzzing beneath my skin. I drove back to the spa/resort and caught up with some of the above-liners. They invited me into the resort bar and I sat down just as Lang walked in.

I'd taken the time to wash and dry my hair and change into a clean set of clothes. Unfortunately, I'd brought nothing outstanding to wear, so I was relegated to another pair of jeans and a slightly wrinkled white shirt. I'd pulled my hair into a ponytail, worked studiously on my makeup for a good three minutes, then sworn at my vanity and headed out.

When Lang strolled into the room, all heads turned. He said something to the man he was with—the spot's director—then beelined toward my table. I decided to make a pre-emptive strike, so I stood up at that very moment and turned toward the bar. "Would you like something?" I asked.

I'd definitely caught his attention. "What are you having?"

I wasn't a master of the drink list at that time. I glanced toward the bar and my eye fell on the Ketel One bottle. "A Ketel One vodka martini," I said, as if I drank them all the time. In actuality, it was my first. Impressed, he asked for the same.

And then . . . one thing led to another and Lang and I ended up back at my not-so-high-grade motel room. I tried not to be mortified at the scattered clothes I'd strewn around the room in my frenzy to get ready. Lang didn't care. He flopped down on my bed fully clothed, still wearing a pair of worn westernish boots that he proudly told me he'd possessed for a good ten years. I lay down gingerly beside him, my head swimming a bit from my three martinis. Lang had managed about five. I'd lost count. He kissed me once, hard, on the lips. I remember thinking my lips felt numb, but I suspect that was more from the effects of the vodka than the pressure of his lips.

The next thing I knew my phone was shrilling in my ear. Fumbling in the dark, I snatched up the receiver, "Hullo?"

"Goddamnit, Ginny! Where the fuck are you?"

My eyes flew open. It was the production manager. "What time is it?" I croaked.

"Eight o'clock! You were supposed to be on set at seven-thirty."

"I'm on my way," I mumbled, leaping off the bed and switching on the light. It was then I realized I was still dressed from the night before, even to my shoes. Lang, too. He was lying on his back, snoring, still wearing his boots.

I hesitated, torn, wondering if I should wake him up, too.

"John," I whispered. "John? What time do you have to be on set?"

He opened one eye. "Today? Shit. I don't know. Noon, maybe."

"You're in my room. I just—thought you should know."

"Oh . . . yeah . . . hmmm . . ." He turned over onto his shoulder.

"And I'm taking the car, so . . . how will you get back?"

"Eh," he muttered dismissively.

I had no choice. I had to leave. I scrambled around and ran for the door, driving like a maniac to the set where my duties included standing at one side of the shoot and making sure no extraneous outsiders got past me and stumbled into the shot. This included the costumer's dog, who somehow had escaped earlier and frolicked amongst the equipment, much to the roaring fury of the director. While I worked I ignored the worried comments the crew made about the missing John Langdon, then I ignored John when he sauntered in, looking rather refreshed, as he'd slept till late afternoon.

My producer came over to me, eyeing me suspiciously. She mentioned that Lang had arrived by taxi and someone had thought they'd seen me leave with him. I answered that we were all at the bar and that's all I knew about it.

I survived the rest of that shoot by becoming a blank slate. Vapid vacantness was my salvation. After a while, everyone believed I knew nothing. A noteworthy acting job on my part; actually better than anything Lang was offering up for the commercial.

I was worked way too hard by my suspicious producer for anything further to develop on the job site, and though Lang had my cell phone number, I didn't expect to hear from him. Therefore, I was shocked and thrilled when he called. I was living in West Hollywood at the time, in a true dive, sharing with a gay couple who somehow managed to make the bedroom they shared liveable and inviting while mine was pretty much unopened boxes, a twin bed, and a beat-up dresser I'd inherited from the person who'd lived in the room before me.

When Lang called I instantly said I would meet him somewhere. I didn't want to have to make any explanations. We met at a small Thai restaurant where no one noticed him. He was a vegetarian, I soon learned, and though he encouraged me to order whatever I wanted, I went for the tofu. I'm glad the Thai can make it edible because it's terrible stuff, in my opinion. White, spongy, tasteless. Forget the bean curd; give me the whole bean.

Anyway, my relationship with Lang developed from there. We stayed at his place—a condo in West LA—ate our meals in bed, watched TV. Somehow, because I didn't have sex with Lang that first night it made me special to him. At least that's how I explain his fascination with me. It lasted a whole four months, which believe me, was a tour of duty that left me wishing for reassignment with anyone else. At that point

I think I might have even been willing to switch genders. Lesbianism never looked so good.

Why was it so exhausting? Because after a brief wooing period, and some fair-to-middling sex, I learned that my function was to make John Langdon feel good about John Langdon. This included constant reassurance. Let me say that again: *constant* reassurance. And sick puppy that I am, I was right there, cheerleading away, telling him how great he was, how misunderstood he was, if he didn't get the part he was after, how fantastic-looking he was, how amusing, intelligent, all-around terrific he was, how he was the best lover I'd ever had, bar none. If I'd had pompons and a bright cheerleading outfit, I couldn't have been more the part. Again, better acting than anything Lang was putting out at the time.

And still . . . we would go someplace and he would be recognized. A gaggle of girls would interrupt our meal, drinks, whatever. He would pretend that the attention bothered him but he ate it up. He insisted that he only had eyes for me, that he didn't find them attractive, though I never acted as if I believed he did. His hollow excuses, however, convinced me that he was lying. He could lie with a smile, kiss me, and still be looking, winking, at someone else.

I began to feel anxious. Suddenly it seemed superimperative that I break up with him before he had the chance to do the deed himself. (This is a flaw of mine, as you can probably tell, since I tend to feel this way about every impending breakup though it can't possibly matter in the grand scheme of things.)

But . . . he beat me to the punch anyway. Like Nate. Things had slowed down between us. Lang was doing a series of guest spots on one of the most inane sitcoms on the air, and he just couldn't be reached anymore. Finally, I got all huffy and hostile and demanded a Saturday lunch out of him. We went back to the original Thai place and he yawned and yawned. He'd hung out with a couple of the actors from the show the night before. They'd hit some Hollywood hot spots. These "actors" happened to be a pair of voluptuous babes who played total bimbos on the show. Lang assured me they were both really, really smart.

My answer to this was, "They'd have to be smart to be able to play so dumb."

He gave me a sharp look, trying to see if I was kidding or not. He couldn't. He said, "What's the matter with you? You look like shit."

Stunned by this unexpected attack, I said, "Sorry. Guess I forgot my false eyelashes and haute couture."

"You've just been bitching me out."

This was so blatantly untrue that I stared. "I don't think so."

He glanced away from me, jaw set, glowering at the reader board of today's specials. "I think this is it, Ginny."

I sat there numbly. Later, I read in the tabloids that he and one of the really, really smart bimbos were shacking up. It hurt like hell.

He called me once, about a year later, just to check in. We talked for a while, but I'd definitely learned my lesson and when he suggested we go back to "our spot," the Thai place, I made up some excuse even though I truly, truly wanted to see him again.

I told all this to Dr. Dick, who listened patiently and said I'd made the intelligent, adult choice. This was when he'd made that comment about me being so frightfully well adjusted. I don't know why I've resented it so much, but I have.

As time's marched on, I've been gladder and gladder that my time with Lang was so limited. I've watched actors on set, talked and flirted with them, even met one or two for a drink here and there. The ones I've met are all the same; I'm not kidding. Peel back a layer and there's nothing underneath. This isn't to say I don't like them, I do. But they're bad for me. Like refined sugar. Empty calories that taste so good, but at the end of the day, you would have been better off with the—tofu.

Anyway, by the time we were wrapping it up for today's Waterstone shoot, I was feeling less hostile toward the actor whose car had been accidentally sideswiped. It wasn't his fault, specifically, that I distrusted actors. I told Joe the video guy to leave the actor in, but Joe said it was too late. He'd already talked to the film editors and the guy was going to be on the cutting room floor, period. Joe didn't like him, either.

As I headed for my car I chastised myself for being so petty.

Holly was leaving at the same time. I said, "I've been meaning to ask you. Why was I at the pre-pro meeting?"

"Isn't it obvious? Owen likes you."

Owen was our scowling director. I said, "Really? How could you tell?"

"He asked you to the pre-pro meeting," Holly responded with perfect logic.

I did a quick mental review of my feelings for Owen. He liked me. Did that mean he *liked* me? If so, could I *like* him?

Thinking of his angry, black brows and snapping, snarling commands, I shook off that idea before it could take root. I've fallen for directors before, too. I haven't written them off as completely as actors, but the next time I plan to step a toe into that pond again, I want it to be with someone a whole lot more worthwhile than Owen the Ornery.

Chapter

8

My head was so far into the Waterstone Iced Tea commercial that I didn't keep up with my friends for over a week though they left me a series of cryptic phone calls, reminding me of their current fates. Daphne was now over the moon about Leo, who seemed to be managing to keep himself *mano y woman-o*, at least for the time being. Kristl was either working or spending her time with Brandon. She'd made no comment on Sean, so I've had to assume she missed seeing his bare ass. Since her birthday party, CeeCee had had her nose to the grindstone at work, much like myself, only reporting on my voice mail that she'd been on a date with a coworker and it had gone all right. I wondered if the coworker was Mr. Mane. Then she startled me with the bad news: the guy she'd nailed with her cigarette, Richter, had obtained a permanent position at the radio station. CeeCee sounded mildly contrite about it all, but she rallied back at the end by adding, "At least he's no longer working at Sammy's, but I wonder whose dick he's been sucking at the radio station?" to which I called her back and left my own voice message: "Your boss's, obviously."

"No way," she said, phoning me back almost instantly.

"My boss can't stand him. It's the owner he's in tight with. He hired him in the first place, but he's not around. He just swoops in and creates havoc from time to time. Trust me. It's not my immediate boss."

"Okay."

"And Cheese-Dick's going to be heading right back out the door if he even looks at me funny. My boss is with me on this."

"Good." It all sounded weird, but hey, I don't know what goes on over there. It was CeeCee's gig. "So, who was your date at the party? The guy with the singed hair?"

She snorted in disgust.

"You're not dating him?"

"He's a total waste. Works mornings bringing coffee. He just heard about my party when I was inviting Gerald, so I invited him, too."

"Who's Gerald?"

"My boss. He couldn't come."

She jumped off the phone after that. I was left with the impression there might be something percolating between CeeCee and the boss. Cheese-Dick looked like he was a political hire, someone no one wanted but who knew people at the top, but he was going to have a tough time if CeeCee and Gerald became partners.

My thoughts turned to Jill, who of all my friends was worrying me the most. She'd catered the shoot as if in a fog. For all anyone knew, Jill and I could have been strangers, that's how little she'd talked to me. But she caught me after work one night and I quickly learned that what had started out as Jill merely dogging Ian's heels appeared to be turning into something far more serious. I'd cautioned CeeCee about loaning Jill her car, and that was a huge betrayal in Jill's eyes; she thought I'd torpedoed her, somehow. I'd just been trying to keep things from going over the edge, but Jill hadn't seen it that way. Two days ago she'd chewed me out, big-time.

"You think I'm a sicko, don't you?"

"You're the one who told me what you'd been doing."

"And you kind of brushed me off!"

"You're mad at me?" I said, a bit hurt.

We'd met for a quick drink at the teensy wine bar across the street from my condo and not far from the garishly lit Sav-On store, which was where I bought everything from Tide to Beringer's Founder's Estate Chardonnay, my current favorite white wine. I was tired and just wanted to go to bed, otherwise Jill and I might have trekked the couple of blocks to the Love Shack and indulged in an Amethyst. We were through filming and heading into post-production, but this had been Jill's last day. I had wrap ahead of me, which meant nearly a week of balancing and closing the books on this job. I had to make sure that all monies were accounted for, that all rental equipment was returned, that every penny was coded and marked and logged where it belonged. My head was working out a knotty conundrum all the while Jill was yammering at me, so, okay, maybe I wasn't as empathetic and attentive as I could have been.

Still, I didn't expect her to suddenly scrape her chair back and march out of the place, leaving me with staring eyes all around and the bill.

I threw down some money and charged after her. "I don't deserve these histrionics," I told her in short order. "You've got a problem. I don't know what you expect me to say."

She stopped short in the parking lot and rounded on me. "Can't you just be on my side?"

"Your side?" I questioned.

"You told CeeCee to stop loaning me her car. How do you think that made me feel?"

"I guess I was hoping you'd realize what you were doing before things got out of hand." I was getting hot under the collar.

"That is so unfair," she said, wounded.

"He called you the night of CeeCee's birthday party. You told me you were meeting with him, but you never told me about it. I gotta tell you: I got the impression it did not go well."

"It went okay."

"Yeah? Then, why are you—" I stopped.

She gazed at me. "Stalking him?"

I spread my hands. We were talking in circles.

She hesitated, looking oddly uncertain for someone usually so bullheaded. Then she burst out, "It's all such crap! It's so silly. I *know* him, but he acts like we're strangers. How can he do that, after everything?"

"I don't know."

"I don't know either. I mean . . ." She sighed and her lips trembled slightly. Pressing them together, she drew a deep breath. "He wants me to stop by tonight."

"Well . . . good."

She shook her head. "I have that stuff your friend Sean gave you. Maybe I should try some."

"Before you see Ian?"

"I'm nervous as hell. I feel like everything's fallen apart. I don't think I can see him stone-cold sober."

It had scarcely been three weeks since he'd offered up the diamond engagement ring. "Sometimes," I said, picking through my words, "there's a point in a relationship when a decision has to be made."

"What does that mean?"

"It *means* that you've probably hit that point."

"No." Jill shook her head in utter denial. "Why does it have to be all or nothing? It doesn't have to be all or nothing."

I shrugged by way of an answer, effectively ending our conversation, and Jill went to her car without another word. She hadn't called me since her meeting with Ian, and I'd been reluctant to phone her. We'd entered that weird zone of friendship where nothing was safe. I had this mental picture of myself jumping from one floating piece of ice to another, all the while afraid I would miss my footing and fall into frigid water and go into hypothermia and drown. I was afraid Jill wouldn't talk to me again. I was afraid she'd transfer her upset and anger from Ian to me.

This had bothered me more than I cared to admit. My answer was to make an appointment with Dr. Dick. His receptionist smugly told me that he was booked up till the following month. I really felt I needed some serious counseling a bit sooner, but I scheduled the future appointment anyway. I had a moment of pure bliss when the receptionist called back, clearly on Dr. Dick's orders, as she would never go out of her way to do anything to help me, and asked in a clipped voice if I could make it for the following Wednesday, as they'd had a cancellation. Grinning, I told her I was delighted and would be there with bells on. She hung up without a goodbye.

Today was that Wednesday. Thinking about Dr. Dick, I glanced at the clock. I'd just gotten off the phone with one of our PAs and now had a throbbing headache. All the PAs had been given several hundred dollars of petty cash at the start of the shoot. This was money they needed to either a) bring back if unused, or b) bring back receipts for proof of purchases. However, a group of them had been running errands and had apparently passed around the cash to each other as if they were dealing cards. So, Mike had ended up with five hundred dollars whereas Carlos only counted $60.00. Sean was short about a hundred and ten, and someone named Bettina, whom I'd never even seen, was supposed to come back with a pile of receipts and straighten it all out. I'd screamed at all of them about the dangers of passing money around, how they were ultimately responsible, how they might not be offered future jobs because of their negligence and to a one they'd responded with hurt and apology and loaded silence that meant, "What a hysterical bitch."

Holly appeared in the midst of my search for some aspirin, or whatever available painkiller I could get my hands on. I would have settled for Sean's/Jill's devil weed if it had been nearby. "What's up?" I asked, as her role in the job was basically over.

"We've been hired on for another job. In Sedona."

"Arizona?" I asked, though I knew full well where Sedona was.

"Uh-huh. Pre-prop next week. Can you do it?"

I'd really wanted a week off between jobs. I hesitated. Working with the Holy Terror again so soon might be bad for my health.

"Well?" Holly demanded impatiently.

But it was good for my financial health. "Yeah, let's go. Who's the client?"

"House About You? Will Torrance is directing."

She left and I sat back a moment. I'd heard of Torrance. I'd heard he was kind of a player. Attractive as hell. Dangerous . . .

"Anyone's better than Owen the Scowler," I said to the room at large, just as a young woman who looked like a flower child in a long flowing skirt and mane, peeked tentatively into the room and dropped a cascade of receipts onto my desk, which had been crumpled in her grimy little fist.

"I'm Bettina," she said with a sweet smile. "Sean's friend."

I looked at the messy, crumpled pile. I should have been nicer to Sean.

Settling myself into one of the uncomfortable blue office chairs in Dr. Dick's waiting room, I picked up a magazine and studiously ignored Janice, as her name tag read, the snooty receptionist. She shot me a superior look and, without bothering to hide her delight, told me Dr. Dick had been called away on an emergency and that I would have to wait. If I hadn't traversed the Greater Los Angeles area to get here—and been desperate for the appointment—I might have turned on my heel and left right then and there. But that would have been admitting defeat in our cold war, so I smiled instead and said brightly, "That's great. I've got phone calls to return," and promptly started dialing merrily away, leaving messages and talking to my friends—even some mere acquaintances—as a means to while away the time. There was no one else in the waiting room at this time, as, I supposed, the receptionist had managed to actually phone Dr. Dick's other appointments and warn them of his absence. This left me to chat, chat, chat away. I had the satisfaction of seeing the snoot's generally pissy expression become downright black with suppressed fury. Life is full of unexpected pleasures.

Dr. Dick breezed in, looking decidedly unwound from his usual appearance. He shot me a surprised look, said, "You waited? I'm sorry. Janice should have rescheduled you."

This instant blaming of Janice—rightly so—warmed the cockles of my heart and caused her expression to change from disgruntled glower to ashy horror. I became the "bigger person" and said, "Oh, no problem. Actually gave me some time to get some stuff done." I lifted my cell phone.

Dr. Dick came back to his usual in-control self with a bang, picking up the nuances very quickly. He ushered me into his inner office and said he'd be right in. I chuckled to myself and settled into a squooshy mocha suede chair. The outer office was all clinical chic, but inside the furniture was made to melt inhibitions. It sure as hell worked with me.

Apparently it was taking a few minutes for Dr. Dick to switch gears from his emergency. However, by the time he entered he was once again calm, competent, and pressed: his usual demeanor. He'd also changed clothes, and was now wearing a different pair of jeans and a white shirt. I could see the crease. I've got to admit, I envy people who actually iron their jeans. They look fantastic. Not that I would ever bother.

He said again, "Sorry about the delay."

"What happened?" I asked.

"I was called in on an emergency."

"One of your patients flipped out?"

He shook his head. "One of Dr. Drenmill's."

"Psychotic break?" I'm nothing if not nosy.

"Interruption of meds," he explained, then gave me that straightforward look that means it's time to get to the matter at hand. I find this look very sexy, actually, and I felt an odd twinge of guilt for a moment before searching around in my head to find the cause: Sean. A rush of disbelief followed. Sean? I felt guilty about lusting after Dr. Dick because I felt somehow beholden to *Sean*?

"So, what's happened since we last met?" Dr. Dick asked.

"Nate and I broke up. He took up with a junior-high student and now they're living together."

"How old is she?" He was used to my hyperbole, which is really just a fancy word for exaggeration which basically means lying. I'm into hyperbole, as Dr. Dick well knows.

"Nineteen? Twenty?"

"And he started seeing her while you and he were still roommates?"

"They worked together, I guess. Things . . . were falling apart between us anyway."

Dr. Dick considered. Without pulling out my file, which sometimes he does just to remind me of the tale I told the last time I was in his office—since I like to "hyberbole" a lot—he said, "You mentioned feeling suffocated and trapped in the relationship."

"Did I?" That gave me pause. "Sometimes I really piss myself off."

"In what way?"

"It would be nice if just once I could keep things to myself."

Dr. Dick managed a faint smile. "That's not exactly the point of therapy, is it?"

"Do you talk to all your patients this way?"

"No." He gazed at me, clearly calculating how forthright he should be. He took the Dr. Phil 'no holds barred' approach and said, "Some people need to be gently introduced to the truth or they can't assimilate it. But you want it bold and unvarnished and right between the eyes."

I blinked, feeling he might have actually hit me in that spot. "Who says?"

"You do. Every time I talk to you."

"All right. I woke up one morning wanting to lock Nate out of my life. I did manage to lock him out of the bathroom. Then that night he showed up with Tara. He said he knew how I felt about him and was moving out. It—surprised me. And I didn't like it."

"So, now you're living alone?"

I nodded. "Well, no. My friend Kristl, who's been married three times, is temporarily living with me. She just got engaged again, though, so having a roommate will be short-lived. I should bring her to see you. There's something really wrong with her."

He paused for a very long time. I had the feeling I'd touched on something in his own life, but I knew he'd been married only once. The divorce had been civil and discreet, and I'd only heard about it after the fact. Dr. Dick had been single for over a year, which had only increased my fantasies where he was concerned.

"Have you thought about how you feel about Nate? Since he moved out?"

"Sure. Lots." I snorted. "I'm not that sorry, actually. It *is* what I wanted," I admitted. "It's just that having it taken out of my hands kind of . . . deflated me, I guess."

"You've moved on."

I nodded. I looked around the office and resisted the urge to play with my cuticles, an old habit I can't quite break. "I've been thinking a lot about my Ex-Files lately. All the members. I even called Charlie. Ex-file Number One," I clarified. "Hearing his voice was like fingernails on a blackboard. He said he might stop by and see me when he's in LA. It scared the liver out of me."

"Charlie was your first real boyfriend."

"My first sexual encounter, if you can call it that," I said. "He wasn't really a boyfriend. Then after Charlie I thought about Ex-File *Numero Dos*—Kane Reynolds. You know him? The motivational speaker?"

Dr. Dick looked interested. "Sure do. He's going to be in LA next month."

I stopped short, not sure how I felt about this news. "You're into that stuff?"

"More like I saw his name listed in the paper," he said with a smile.

I love it when Dr. Dick smiles. It's just so . . . cool. The curve of his lips briefly derailed me from my trip through the Hall of Exes, which is how I envision all those in my past. Like they're standing behind the doors in a long hallway. If I could get past them all to the end of the hallway and step outside, I might learn something valuable. But it's a long, long way . . . .

"Then I skipped ahead to Ex-File Number Four," I said. "I don't usually count him, but I've been warned by my friends that I can't just skip over him. I haven't told you this before, but number four is John Langdon, the actor."

Dr. Dick hesitated momentarily, then blew my mind when he said, "He came to see me once."

"Who? *Lang?*" I sat bolt upright.

"He came to ask me about psychology. He was researching a role."

"Oh." I should have known Dr. Dick wouldn't spill any of his real patients' names, especially famous patients. "*Las Vegas Blues?*"

"I think that was it."

"I knew him after that," I said.

"Why are you thinking about your past relationships?"

I shrugged. "Because of Nate, I guess. It's like giving myself a history lesson. If we don't examine the mistakes of the past, we're doomed to make them again. There's a quote like that, isn't there?"

"Has examining the past helped?"

"Not so far. The way I look at it . . . it's their fault, not mine."

He fought another smile.

I left Dr. Dick's office feeling better. Feeling surprised, in fact, that I'd spent less time actually fantasizing about him and more time in serious conversation. Well, pseudoserious, anyway. It's hard for me to equate my failed romances with anything of true value.

That night I met Daphne and Leo at the Standard. Leo has wild, curly hair and a full beard, and when people ask about the beard he pretends it's for a role. This gets the conversation centered squarely on himself for a while, which I suspect is his game plan, but at least it gave me a chance to talk to Daphne. It was a tad nauseating how thrilled she was to be seen with him.

"Be honest, Blue," she said. "He's cute, isn't he? People just respond to him."

Because I was trying to be nice, and because Leo wasn't terrible, I said, "He's definitely cute." I bit back the urge to ask about the so-called "role" and instead ordered my usual Ketel One vodka martini. No more stingers. I wanted familiarity and stability.

Leo was trying harder than he had been the first time I'd met him. To be fair, he'd been working the Starbucks counter during that introduction and hadn't given me more than a passing glance. He'd also been disinterested in Daphne, however; the only time he'd been able to brighten was when a young, heavily tattooed pal entered the place. I'd labeled Leo a Huge Waste of Time without really getting to know him. Maybe there was more to him than met the eye.

"Leo," I said. "What's the role?"

He slid me a look out of the corners of his eyes, his lips tightening a bit. "It's for Spielberg."

"Steven Spielberg?"

"Blue . . ." Daphne's eyes warned me.

"A film?" I asked, shrugging.

"Yes, a film," Leo stated flatly, then moved across the room to seat himself deliberately in one of the clear, swinging plastic chairs.

Daphne shot me a hurt look. "The part's down to Leo and four other guys. It's very stressful for him. I can't believe you said that."

She scurried toward him, taking the only other plastic chair. I found myself sitting alone on one of the leather couches until a young couple sat down beside me. So much for trying to get to know Leo.

Not long afterwards they decided to take a cab home rather than ride with me, the designated driver. I drove home lonely and annoyed with myself. Though I'm no fan of Leo's, I envied their relationship—in the early days as it was—and wished I had someone to hug and kiss and make love to.

I didn't realize my prayers were going to be answered until I unlocked my front door and a shadow emerged from behind the jasmine bush that separated my small stoop from the condo facing toward the alley.

I screamed bloody murder.

"Jesus fucking Christ," a slightly familiar voice declared, sounding as shaken as I felt.

"Charlie?" I asked, peering into the darkness.

"You could wake the dead. Jesus. My heart's pounding."

"You scared me."

"No shit."

My neighbor's porch light came on. I unlocked my door and practically yanked Charlie inside. That particular neighbor is what a few generations back they called a "nosey parker." We get along fine, but I absolutely hate having to explain anything.

I sat on one of my rickety bar stools at the kitchen counter. The stools are usually tucked beneath the breakfast

bar, which is part of the piece of counter that also houses my
sink. No one ever sits on either of the stools because they're
uncomfortable and dangerous. Since Nate took his chair,
and then later his lamps and coffee table and a few other
things, now my living room consists of, well . . . a couch. A
few end tables. The television, inside my only expensive piece
of furniture—a Pottery Barn armoire that I'm still paying
off. One nice table lamp and a convoluted sculptured piece
of plastic and metal that Daphne gave me for my birthday a
few years back. Art, she'd called it. I'm pretty sure it's a
bong.

The reason I was sitting on a stool was that Charlie had
draped himself over the sofa. He had that aging hippie, well
used look. His hair was long and suspect; it may have seen
soap and water in the last decade but a hair brush was something else again. His clothes were wrinkled and all in
shades of cream—or what once was cream—and army
green. He wore sandals; the strap was broken on his right
one. I had a picture of him in Eugene, at the University
of Oregon, fitting in with a kind of bohemian lifestyle,
but I don't think he ever really made it to college.

He still had a boyish look, but it was spoiled somewhat
when he smiled and revealed a space about three teeth back
on the left side of his jaw. His blue eyes were innocent and
joyful, however. I kept my gaze on them and tried hard not to
think about the hair. One of my true inner fears is lice. I can
hear a whole news story about death, disease, and despair
and feel bad, but mention lice and my skin crawls and I instantly have to do an intense check of my own scalp. Phobias. What can you say. They're not rational.

Kristl appeared from upstairs, surprising me, as she'd
been missing in action for an untold number of days. She regarded Charlie curiously after I introduced him as someone
from Carriage Hill High. I was so glad to have her with me
that I forgot to finish the introductions. I never mentioned her
name to him. She ended up doing that herself, leaning for-

ward and shaking Charlie's hand. I watched surreptitiously and noticed that she frowned a bit and stealthily examined her palm when she thought Charlie wouldn't notice. He didn't. I did, however, and I wondered what she thought she'd picked up from him. Another frisson down my back.

"How'd you find my place?" I asked, belatedly, having initially been too bemused to pop out with the most important question. He had my number, yes, but the address?

"Your mom," he said. "After you called, I checked in with her. She said she's gonna come down this way sometime, too. I always liked her. She's cool."

Charlie had never known my mother except by sight, as Mom was a sometime real estate agent whose picture smiled from the card she handed out to my friends right and left. As if any of them could buy property. Mom had carefully woven the white streak into a purposely bleached, more blondish mane before the photographer got hold of her.

"Why do I feel like I know you?" Kristl mused to Charlie, turning to give me a puzzled look.

Ex-File Number One, I silently telegraphed, but she didn't pick up the message.

Charlie said, "Me and a buddy are heading down to Tijuana. I just wanted to stop in."

"Where's your buddy, now?" I asked.

"At the Sav-On. Buying some beer. Good thing it's open 24/7. Roadies, y'know." He winked at us both.

I damn near opened my mouth to give him the old "don't drink and drive" caution, but I managed to contain myself at the last moment. If he didn't know it by now, my blathering wasn't going to help.

Kristl, however, had no such compunction. "I hope you don't really mean that you'd drink and drive."

He looked offended. "Hell, no. I'm the passenger!"

That was it for Kristl. She gave me a hard look, made some excuse and headed for the stairs. Panicked, I said, "Where're you going?"

"I'm meeting Brandon," she said, and I thought I detected a whiff of true relief in the fact that she had an excuse for departure. Charlie had clearly not made the best impression. Given that she got married every time someone said "boo," I didn't see that she had anything to feel so superior about.

I was also extremely annoyed with my mother for being such a blabbermouth. Note to self: Call Mom and lie to her about where I live.

The phone rang and I snatched it up like a lifeline. It was Holly. I've never been so delighted to talk business in my life.

She said flatly, "We got a bill here. That Liam Engleston person. Charged us twenty-five percent of his catering fee for canceling with him."

"*What?*" I screamed.

"He can go fuck himself," Holly said. "Take care of it."

She hung up.

"Bad news?" Charlie asked.

The guy was quick.

Before I could react, Charlie's buddy—someone Charlie introduced as Hog for obvious reasons—returned, carrying two sacks from Sav-On. Hog must have weighed three-fifty and he had short, stubby hair covering his pink scalp. I thought I saw screw-tops on the wine.

"I've got something to take care of," I said, glancing at the clock.

"No problemo." Charlie grinned and he and Hog started digging through their Sav-On sacks.

I headed out the door, hoping my condo would still be standing when I returned and that my neighbor wouldn't call the cops.

Chapter

9

Liam Engleston's restaurant was closed by the time I got there. It was nearly midnight. I guess I'd hoped the bar would at least still be open, but as the place was centered in the business district, everything was shut tight. Nobody hangs around this section of LA for late-night partying.

I was going to have to wait to confront Liam the next day, which was too bad, as I was spoiling for a fight tonight. I'd probably known this at some level but I was so infuriated with the rat that I'd run out of my condo like a madwoman. Anger still coursed through me. I wanted to spit and rant and throw myself at the door. General-usage swear words could not cover how I felt.

And I sure as hell didn't want to go home to Charlie and Hog.

As I drove away from Liam's restaurant, I castigated myself for listening to the crew about Liam and even meeting with the man in the first place. How *could* he send that bill?

Gnashing my teeth, I hit the gas and tore down the 10 back toward Santa Monica. I was not in a logical frame of mind, to say the least. This is my explanation and excuse for what happened next.

I veered off to see Sean.

I had not made the colossal mistake of stopping in at his place earlier, though I'd been invited. Nobody, but nobody, drops in on a guy as young as Sean. (Let's just start with the decorating motif of most straight males under thirty, if you get my drift.) And then there's the whole, "what does this mean?" thing. I did not want a sexual relationship with Sean, and with that in mind, I had decided early on that I didn't want to get myself into any place/scene/abode that was "too comfortable."

But here I was, parking the car, yanking on the brake, and walking up to Sean's front door. It was no surprise he resided in a tired-looking apartment building south of Pico and on the eastern border of Santa Monica. I immediately realized my fears about getting too comfortable were unfounded. Nothing about his place could remotely get me in the mood for a sexual romp. Peeking through the windows I saw the front room was a place where pizza boxes came to die.

I would have turned right there, tiptoeing back to my car, but his door flew open and there he was—in boxer shorts and a blue cloud of marijuana smoke.

"Hey, Blue!" He was delighted to see me.

"Hey, yourself. Thought I'd stop by and say hello, but y'know, it wasn't such a good idea. I'm beat. Maybe we can get together tomorrow."

My words tumbled from my lips in rapid succession but Sean was deaf and heedless as he ushered me inside the tiny, messy room. "My roommate's gone 'til Saturday. Death in the family. He lives in some place in Minnesota. Here, have a seat." He swept pizza boxes and crusts out of the way and patted a worn-looking pad with his hand. Dust, or maybe flour—or, God forbid, dog dander—poofed upward. I struggled with my phobias and managed to perch on the edge.

"Do you have pets?" I asked.

"Nah . . . hey, I haven't seen you at all lately," Sean said.

"You've been in that office and on the shoot you were just . . . whew . . . really a bitch!" He laughed. "God. I thought you were like somebody new. Like a pod-person, or something, y'know. Like *Invasion of the Body Snatchers*."

"I just had a job to do. Bettina brought in the rest of your petty cash receipts."

"Ah, yeah . . . kind of a mess, huh?" He rubbed a hand through his hair, yawned, then patted his bare stomach. The guy did have nice pecs and abs. He was young enough to have a firm body with minimal ritualistic workouts. I instantly imagined what it would be like to be naked with him, his taut body pressed against mine. But the pizza boxes stayed in my peripheral vision . . .

"I shouldn't have come over here this late." I tried to rise, but he waved me back down, accidentally slapping my arm in the process. I lost my balance and fell, half sprawling onto the sofa. Instantly I thought of cooties. All kinds. With an effort I tried to crush these traitorous thoughts, but I suddenly felt itchy all over.

"Y'wanna smoke?" He searched through a pile of stuff on one of the end tables—matching scarred garage sale rejects.

"No, thanks." I made myself sit back. Sean smoked another joint and babbled happily away about—oh, hell, I have no idea. I wasn't there any longer. Not in spirit, anyway. I'd jumped back to my anger at Liam Engleston. What an asshole. I'd never hired him and he knew it. No contract had been signed. His ploy was just meant to infuriate me and it was working.

In an effort to stop roiling about it, I pulled my thoughts from Liam to Charlie and Hog. I wasn't exactly horrified that they were at my condo, although that was pretty close. I was also bemused—no *astounded*—that I'd ever had anything in common with Charlie. High school is like this cult we live in for a few years then drift away from because—

luckily—we graduate. The binding factor for members is merely locality, at least for public schools . . . a proximity to each other on the planet.

And some people, like Charlie, seem to stay there, happily cocooned in the cult.

I inhaled, and definitely took in some secondhand smoke. Well, fine. I could probably use some self-medication. I grimaced. Who was I to judge Charlie, anyway? I'd found my way over to Sean's tonight, hadn't I? This wasn't exactly something to be proud of.

"Sean . . ."

"Shhh," he said, a finger over his lips. "Y'hear that?"

"No."

"Y'don't?"

"No," I reiterated.

"Oh. Yeah. It's the washing machine. The coin-ops are directly beneath my unit. Sometimes I can hear 'em."

"Romantic," I said, and Sean nodded. He was not a man for sarcasm.

"Hey, I hear we might be going to Sedona," he said with return of animation.

I was surprised. "Holly talked to you about it already?"

"Uh-huh. I'm driving a cube truck over."

I had a sudden vision of Sean driving, weaving and sucking on a joint. I imagined a wrecked rental truck and the ensuing insurance woes and expense to the production company. Already it felt like my fault. I hadn't frowned on his extracurricular activities. Hell, I'd been egging him on, buying dope off him, encouraging his behavior. Good god.

I fretted, wondering if I was going to have to get in the middle of this, too. If I'd just left Sean alone I wouldn't be embroiled in this.

"Jesus," I muttered, getting to my feet.

"Where ya goin'?"

"Home, Sean. I'll talk to you later." I patted him on the shoulder. He climbed onto a pair of wobbly legs, but couldn't seem to find the energy to see me to the door. I practically ran outside and gulped clean, LA air—such as it is.

I drove home and into the bunker, parking in my spot. My feet were leaden as they approached my front door. I could hear music and loud conversation. Wincing, I put the key in the lock and entered.

Charlie and Hog were sitting on the two rickety bar stools, drinking and shouting at each other. Kristl stood to one side in silent disgust, clearly trying to figure out what to do. She turned to me. "My one night off where I can get some sleep and look."

"Sorry," I said.

"Blue, I've decided to move in with Brandon. I was going to tell you, but . . ." She shrugged.

I shrugged right back. "You're getting married anyway, right? It was just a matter of time."

She clamped her lips shut. What more was there to say?

Our conversation was set against a loud backdrop of male voices as Charlie and Hog downed their brewskies. Luckily, they seemed to be pretty happy drunks. I told them they could sleep on the couch and/or the floor and mentioned the blankets in the entry closet. Whether they heard me I couldn't say. I followed Kristl upstairs, aware that her back was inordinately stiff; she was pissed.

"What are you going to do with them?" she asked at the corner landing.

"Sleep on it."

"Blue . . ."

She was getting ready to blow. Kristl's Irish temper is generally kept well under rein—a result of her Libra rising, she'd once told me—but my snappish remark about her upcoming nuptials had gotten to her. I could see the flush gather beneath her skin.

I cut her off at the pass. "I don't know what I'm going to do with them. I'll figure it out. And look, moving in with Brandon is okay."

My capitulation took all the fight out of her. "We're moving to Seattle," she said. "I don't want to go."

I eyed her. The guys downstairs were bellowing with laughter. I hoped my walls were thicker than I believed. "Then don't."

"I have to. I'm getting married."

"Why, Kristl?"

I hadn't meant to sound so imploring, but my words had the effect of straightening her spine once more. "Because I love him," she said.

I turned toward my bedroom.

Yeah. Sure.

I was a lot more clear-headed with the dawn. I got up, did a quick jog up to Bundy and around, showered, and was actually taking the time to blow my hair dry rather than let it dry naturally when I heard a light tapping on my bedroom door. I opened it cautiously, afraid of confronting either Charlie or Hog, though it was probably way too early in the morning for either of them.

It was Kristl. "I packed my stuff last night," she said. "I'll probably be out of here by this afternoon."

"Okay."

She seemed to want me to say something more. I couldn't think of what that might be, so I simply folded her into my arms for a quick good-bye hug. When I released her, she stepped back quickly. I could swear she had tears in her eyes, but truthfully, I wasn't feeling the same sentiment. Though I wanted her to know there were no hard feelings, I definitely felt impatient with her and her need—compulsion, really—to be married. Everybody has a certain amount of weirdness, and I guess this is hers.

I realized I was going to be living totally alone very soon, which momentarily made me feel sad . . . and worried. Rent was going to be a factor. I needed a roommate to help with the bills.

I reached the lower floor and smelled the beery, stale scent of Charlie and Hog's "good time." Hog was asleep on the couch; a beached whale in a white T-shirt and red boxers. Charlie was snoozing on the carpet, lying on his back, mouth open, face clear of worry and concern. I flashed back to the 50-yard line and involuntarily shuddered.

"So, what do you guys do for a living?" I asked as an opening salvo into their alcohol-fueled, coma-like slumber.

Hog, who'd been softly snoring, jerked awake. "Huh?"

"When you're not on vacation?" I asked. I, myself, was mentally preparing for my upcoming conversation with Liam Engleston. Now that my ire had cooled somewhat, I was even beginning to think the telephone might be a better instrument than a face-to-face encounter.

"We're going to Tijuana," Hog said, herding his bulk into a sitting position. He pronounced Tijuana in a "tee-yuh-wahn-ah" drawl.

That information I already possessed. "But what do you do for a living?"

"Oh." He rubbed the half-inch stubble on his head. "Yeah. We do computers."

Charlie lifted his head at this last and said, "Fix hardware."

I was pleased and a little surprised that they were actually employed. "You always were a fat brain," I told Charlie.

He grinned. "Yeah?"

"Got bad grades on purpose."

"Just didn't give a shit, Ginny."

"I know." We smiled at each other. Feeling a bit more comradery than I'd expected, I asked, "What would you like for breakfast? I could whip up some scrambled eggs. I think I have some bread that hasn't turned to penicillin yet." I turned to Charlie's heavyset friend and delicately asked, "Hog?" as he didn't appear to be paying attention to me.

Hog said, "Fuck, I think I left my wallet at Sav-On."

Immediately they both scrambled into their pants and shoes before I could even turn toward the refrigerator and crack an egg. The front door slammed behind them. I was still frozen in space, undecided, when the door reopened.

"Blue?"

It was Jill's voice. "Come on in," I called.

She appeared, still looking back over her shoulder as if viewing a tag-along ghost. "Who were those guys?"

"Ex-File Number One and his sidekick, Hog."

"Oh," she said, seating herself at one of the bar stools. Then, "Oh, God," more sympathetically, as I guess she realized I'd lost my virginity to the leaner of the scruffy twosome. I started cooking eggs, figuring we would eat them if Charlie and Hog failed to return in a timely fashion. While I cooked, I told her about Liam Engleston.

"I'm going with you," she declared. "The rat bastard! You didn't book him. He can't charge you!"

"I was thinking of phoning him. I made a trip out there last night."

"No way." She shook her head determinedly. "We're going to make him face us. I'm a caterer. I've been shut out by the best of them. Until you get the contract signed, it's not a done deal. I want to tell him so myself!"

I smiled. This was her way of apologizing, of letting me know all was forgiven between us. I love it when she gets all bossy. Well, sometimes . . .

Charlie and Hog returned with, lo and behold, Hog's wallet. Someone had turned it in, and wonder of all wonders, had not taken the thirty-three dollars inside. Also, they hadn't touched Hog's ten percent discount coupon at the Sex-It-Up, an erotic specialty store where Charlie and Hog swore they only bought gag gifts for friends. Like, oh sure. But if they wanted me to believe, no problem. What I did care about was that they were going to be on their way, and, after scarfing down my scrambled eggs and politely leaving a small amount for me and Jill—well, okay, for me; Jill wouldn't have touched it on a dare—they climbed into Charlie's SUV, a newer model than my own by a long shot, and charged off on their adventure. Silly me. Once they were gone I almost mourned their departure. It's not that I wanted them back . . . just that I wanted company.

But Jill was with me and we took off in my Explorer. When we arrived at Liam's restaurant we were approached by the man himself, and I was struck by the same quasi-Asian hit. That mustache . . . But then he spoke in his clipped-off British-way. "Ms. Bluebell." He flicked a disinterested glance to Jill, who was looking him up and down.

"You remember me." I said. "Do you remember how I didn't give you a contract to sign?"

He inhaled through pinched nostrils, as if I were a particularly noxious smell. Pissed me off to no end. I was going to say as much, but Jill broke in tensely, "I have a catering business, Mr. Engleston. Wyatt Productions doesn't owe you anything. What were you trying to do?"

"Am I to understand you have some stake in my dealings with Wyatt Productions?" he flared back.

Again I attempted to interject, but Jill held up her hand. "No, I want to hear this. Really. Did you think you were going to get paid? Did you think you'd weasel a few bucks out of them? That no one would notice?"

"We had a gentlemen's agreement," Liam stated, rubbing his Fu Manchu with his thumb and forefinger.

"What the fuck is that?" Jill asked, to which I quickly intervened.

"Your price was too high, Mr. Engleston. My producer told you as much. There was no gentlemen's agreement."

"No shit," said Jill.

Liam breathed noisily. "I was led to believe in good faith that I had the job. I made the menu and sent it to you. I asked you to sign and return it. If you did not want my services, you were requested to let me know, otherwise I would go ahead as planned. Your negligence cost me money. I went to the job site with my food and was turned away."

I said carefully, holding my temper in check, "You sent a menu to my producer that made her laugh. Sandwiches, Mr. Engleston. That's all we needed. And I was at that job site. No one showed up with food."

"My assistant did."

"Who the fuck's your assistant?" Jill demanded.

"Her name's Bettina."

My head swam. Bettina? Sean's friend? "Bettina was not on the call list," I said, crossing my fingers and hoping it was true. Everyone involved with a commercial shoot is on the call list, from the director and executive producer down to the production assistants. But if there'd been some error . . . ? "If she showed up, she had no right to be there."

Liam's mustache quivered. "If you do not pay the bill, I have no choice but to sue you and report you to the Better Business Bureau."

Jill snorted. "They'll laugh you out of court. What part of NO SIGNED CONTRACT are you missing?"

"I would prefer to speak to your superior," he said to me. "Certainly not to people who swear."

"Are you fuckin' talking about me?" Jill demanded.

"Just a second," I said, holding up my hands.

"Well, FUCK YOU!"

Liam snarled, "This meeting has ended."

He turned on his heel and glided away. I swear, there's something not quite real about that guy.

Jill watched him go. "Is he like—the living dead, or something? He's a fucking weirdo."

"Since when is the 'F' word all you say?"

She gave me a look. "Like you never say it."

"I always say it. But this was supposed to be a business meeting."

We headed out to my car and climbed inside. Jill had somehow transferred all the turmoil and unrest in her life to Liam Engleston.

"So, you're blaming me now?" she asked.

"You don't think we could have handled it better?"

"Would the results have been any different?"

"Probably not," I conceded. "But that's not the point. This was my battle, and I would have rather done it without saying fuck a dozen times."

"Sorry." She lapsed into silence as I concentrated on the traffic zooming past us on the 10.

"As much as I appreciate your support," I said with what I felt was incredible patience. "This is my job, not yours. You catered the shoot. That's all. It's my ass in a wringer if things get ugly. Uglier."

We hurtled down the road in further silence. I suspected she was thinking about Ian and her penchant for following his movements. She might not like the term 'stalker,' but I couldn't think of a better word to describe her behavior.

"Who's this Bettina?" she asked, blowing my theory about her thoughts.

"A friend of Sean's," I said.

"Oh, God."

"She wasn't hired by me, so therefore she wasn't hired. But she was around."

"Liam Engleston's an ass."

"Ya got that right."

"I'll talk to Holly . . . make sure she knows it was me with the potty mouth."

I shrugged. "It all just pisses me off."

"So, what are you going to do?" Jill asked seriously.

"I'm going to tell Engleston to fuck himself and the horse he came in on."

Jill said, "If you'd just given me time, I could have probably handled that one for you, too."

* * *

As it turned out, it was all a tempest in a teapot. Engleston called Holly and actually caught her at work during wrap. He threatened her with the same action, and also complained about my professionalism and language. Holly, who has no serious love for me but can't handle being told what to do by anyone—especially anyone male—blistered his ears with her own language, making it clear she was going to broadcast to anyone and everyone she knew that he was a "chiseling, slimy, small, little man." Not an "F" word in sight, but enough to have him slamming down the phone on one of those "or else" threats. *You'd better do a, b, or c, OR ELSE!*

Nothing infuriates Holly faster than a superior attitude—which is the only area my producer and I could be said to be truly *sympatico*. Doesn't matter. It's a big common denominator. When I heard her short, bitten fury blasting into the receiver I grinned in delight. Tom popped a Jolly Rancher and gave me puzzled eyebrows. I waved him aside. We could do the postmortem later, when Holly was out of the room. For the moment I wanted to just savor the win.

With Charlie and Hog off in Tee-yuh-wahn-ah I was all alone, Kristl having packed up the rest of her belongings and shifting them to Brandon's. But she realized she'd forgotten her cell phone charger—doesn't everybody?—and she and Brandon stopped by on their way out of town to retrieve it.

I got my first look at Brandon on my doorstep. Attractive, pleasant, kind of nondescript in a really nice way. Kristl seemed lit up around him, so I tried to discard my cynicism and hope for the best. Maybe he *was* the one. Why shouldn't he be? She'd failed three times. Fourth time's the charm . . . right?

Then I remembered her reaction to Jackson Wright. She could be a four-time loser, I thought, annoyed with myself for letting the traitorous thought creep in.

"You'll come to the wedding, I hope," Brandon said as I handed Kristl her charger.

"Will it be in Seattle?"

Kristl and Brandan looked at each other, neither one of them sure how to answer.

"Why don't you get back to me on that," I suggested magnanimously.

"Thanks, Blue." Kristl half-hugged me.

Brandon shook my hand. "Nice meeting you."

"You, too," I said and watched them walk away from my front door.

It was depressing seeing other couples when I wasn't half of one myself. I was going to have to work on it.

Chapter
10

On Saturday morning I showed up at Sammy's and was pleased and a little surprised to see Jill, CeeCee, and Daphne already seated. "You all made it," I said.

"It's been weeks since we got together." Daphne glanced around as if expecting someone else.

I looked around too and CeeCee drawled, "Cheese-Dick may have quit Sammy's, but Daphne's expecting Leo."

"I invited him," Daphne quickly inserted.

Leo? Heretofore Ian had been the only male who ever was allowed and then only because none of us knew how to tell Jill no. I gazed at Jill accusingly, making my feelings clear about who was really to blame.

Jill snorted. Her arms were crossed over her chest in classic, "so sue me" style, but her brown eyes were filled with pain. Uh-oh. More trouble there.

Daphne began waving frantically and Leo, who'd just sauntered through the door, stopped short, finger-combed his tousled tresses, then strolled to our table, sucking up as much attention from the other diners as possible. He grabbed a chair and reversed it, straddling it.

CeeCee watched his approach with a stern face. Her pink-tipped hair had grown longer over the last few weeks and her roots were dark. I thought she might remark on Leo's backwards chair choice as he gave her a somewhat challenging look. Apart from a faint smile, she kept her own counsel.

Daphne said brightly, "Leo's got a callback for a recurring guest spot on *Losers, Inc.*, that new comedy on the WB."

"It's not on the WB," said Leo.

I looked away, certain my face was going to give me away. But catching sight of CeeCee's expression, then Jill's, a shit-eating grin spread across my mouth. Even CeeCee's cool started to desert her.

"Well, that about sums it up," Jill said and we all broke out laughing.

"Oh, yeah, that's just real funny," muttered Leo, truly smarting. He nearly knocked the chair over, jumping from the seat. I thought he might stride off in a huff, but he caught himself up and managed to saunter out as he'd sauntered in.

"Thanks a lot, you guys!" Daphne cried, scraping her own chair back. "I knew it was a bad idea to bring him. It's okay for Ian, but nobody else, right?"

"Daphne, wait . . ." I protested between fits of laughter, but she was already at the door, scurrying after him.

"*Losers, Inc.*?" CeeCee repeated in a tone of wonder.

"Oh. My. God." Jill shook her head.

"Incorporated, no less," I pointed out, which sent us into new heights of hilarity. Daphne's sudden return bumped us back to earth and with an effort our amusement finally wore down. She sat in her chair, clearly unamused.

"I'm sorry," I said. "Really. I didn't mean to crack up. It was just so damn funny."

"Come on, Daphne," said Jill. "It *is* funny."

"It is not," she said.

"He'll get the part," CeeCee assured. "He's perfect for it." This time we were able to keep our amusement reigned in. Barely.

Daphne said, "I think I might love him."

We sobered up instantly. I wanted to say, "Really? *Really?*" but just managed to keep my mouth shut.

"You're in love with Leo?" CeeCee clarified, sounding as full of disbelief as the rest of us felt.

"We've been having such a great time. He told me he was only pretending to be interested in Heather to make me a little jealous. He wasn't sure how I felt, so he played a little game."

I could have pointed out his kind of game playing wasn't exactly a sign of maturity. I could have also told her how I felt about said game playing, but I sensed she wasn't asking for that. In fact, she seemed to be going somewhere with this.

"You're not going to tell me you're getting married, are you?" I burst out, struck by the brain-freezing thought.

"No. Oh, no. No, it's too soon." She chewed on her thumbnail. "It's that . . ."

We all waited. When she didn't continue, CeeCee made motioning signals for her to get on with it.

"It's that he went to see his old girlfriend." She sat back.

"Heather?" I asked.

"No! His first real girlfriend. The one that mattered."

"What do you mean?" Jill demanded.

"Yeah, I'm not following," said CeeCee.

"Ditto," I put in.

"You know, your first real love. Not the first one you did it with, necessarily, or even got involved with. Your first *love*," she stressed.

"And so he went to see her? Why?" Jill asked.

"Because . . ." She shrugged. "Because we're getting closer. And it's important to clear things up."

"Did he have feelings for her still?" I asked.

"No, it was just to put it behind him." Her lips tightened and she glared at us all. "You're trying not to understand."

"No," I burst in and Jill and CeeCee made similar denials. "So, how did it work out for him?"

"Okay . . . ."

"Did he get things settled with her?" I asked, feeling my way. I wasn't sure what she wanted from us.

"You don't think he should have seen her." Daphne sounded mad at me.

"Lots of guys go see their old girlfriends," said Jill. "They have to. It's like they need to make sure they've made the right decision. That they didn't let the right one get away." I gave her a sharp look, wondering if she was referring somehow to Ian. But no, she appeared to just be trying to help Daphne along in the telling of the Saga of Leo.

"So, how was the ex?" CeeCee asked.

"Well . . . he said she'd gained some weight."

"Promising," I murmured.

"Watch out," CeeCee said. "If it gets really ugly, he'll do the same to you when it's over."

"If it's over," Daphne corrected.

"So, what happened?" Jill asked.

Daphne squirmed a bit. We all leaned in closer. "This was a girlfriend from high school. I don't know if he ever really got her out of his heart before now. She came through LA last week and they—saw each other," Daphne said. She'd grabbed her napkin and was systematically shredding it. Jill, CeeCee, and I exchanged glances.

"They slept together?" I asked, watching bits of napkin float to the floor.

"Yes."

A weighty pause ensued. Jill looked at Daphne as if she might be crazy. "And you're still with this loser . . . inc.?"

"They'd never slept together before," insisted Daphne. "It just didn't happen when they were together, so they did it now. That's all. Just to get it out of their systems."

"Oh, god . . ." Jill shot me a look that said, "Don't just sit there! Get in here!"

I reached a tentative toe into the water. "That isn't exactly a reason."

"Oh, go ahead, Blue. Act like my mother."

"Well, Jesus, somebody has to," CeeCee told her. "You make an excuse for this, you're making excuses all the way."

I was mildly surprised. CeeCee sometimes has an offbeat take on romance. You never know which way she's going to jump. This was a pretty conventional reaction for her.

Daphne apparently agreed with me. "I thought of all people that you'd be on my side!"

"Was it one time?" Jill asked, sounding like she felt this might matter. "With the ex?"

"One time is more than enough," I pointed out, surprised again that I seemed to be siding with CeeCee, not Jill.

"It was only once," Daphne assured.

"So he says." CeeCee murmured.

Jill asked, "You're in love with this guy?"

Daphne nodded curtly.

"Then, I don't know what I'd do. A few weeks ago, I would have said dump him. But it's hard."

CeeCee turned from staring disbelievingly at Jill, to gazing directly at Daphne. "Stop it now, before it gets worse."

"You're all just a wealth of advice, aren't you?" Daphne sniffed. She gazed toward the doors where Leo had departed.

"What do you want from us?" I asked. "We don't want you to get hurt."

"I just wanted you guys to meet him, to get to know him. Maybe even like him!"

"You may have to get new friends for that," CeeCee observed, just as the waitress finally came to take our order. "Because honestly, Daphne, from what I've seen and what you've said, what's there to like?"

Food. It strikes fear in the hearts of anorexics and bulimics alike. Since I was neither of these things, I tucked into my Monterey omelet with gusto. Shrimp, crab, and a sweet cheese I wouldn't even try to pronounce. My saliva glands went on overload while Daphne, silent and wounded, disinterestedly chased a tofu scramble around with her fork. Personally, if that were my diet, I'd probably quit eating, too. But Daphne wasn't the one with the serious problem. CeeCee didn't have an eating problem, unless you counted possible lung cancer as a side effect. Her answer to weight control was simple: substitute cigarettes if you gain a few pounds; smoke steadily in place of food until you lose weight. The idea makes me absolutely shudder. I find that I can't walk into a restaurant that still allows indoor smoking; smelling that permeating odor on all the fixtures and furniture makes me unable to eat ANYTHING. But, each to his own.

No, as I've said before, it's Jill with the anorexic/bulimic tendencies. One hell of a dilemma for a caterer. She's also one of those who likes to bake, cook, and create. It's apparently an odd kind of aromatherapy. But if she dares to imbibe, she makes a run for the bathroom. I've caught her a time or two but have yet to call her on it. She's an odd personality to have this problem. Every other anorexic I know—and in southern California there are more than a few of them—is a self-destructive, secretive pleaser churning with inner anxiety. But pugnacious Jill is one for the record books. She's so not the type to have an eating disorder, yet real food rarely passes her lips. Alcohol, yes. A dressingless salad here and again.

Today I tried hard to keep my eyes on my own plate and resisted the urge to smack my lips. Jill had ordered a parfait glass full of granola and yogurt. She kept sticking her spoon in and pretending to lick off the yogurt, all the while surreptitiously slipping the spoon back inside again.

Most of the time I ignore her habits, but lately I'm having more and more trouble. I don't know exactly what came over me, but one minute I was chewing my omelet, still feeling prickly about the Liam Engleston incident, wondering about

Jill's relationship with Ian, annoyed with Daphne for being so blind about Leo and currently sitting over there nursing her hurt, and worried about CeeCee and what was going on in her romantic world—and I guess you could say I just kind of lost it. Into the pall that had settled over our table I said suddenly, "Jill, eat something, for God's sake."

Three heads popped up, eyes full of surprise and/or horror at my bald statement. I didn't care. I bit into a piece of toast and chewed heartily.

"Well, thanks a lot, Blue." Jill looked torn between tears and fury. "I'm eating this granola parfait."

"I feel like we're all just lying to each other," I said, feeling something inside just boiling up. "Jill, you cook. You bake. You foist food on us sometimes, as if that gives you some kind of perverse pleasure. But you *pretend* to eat."

"By the way, I love those blueberry tart things you make," Daphne slipped in.

"You're not helping," I pointed out tautly.

"Sorry." She lapsed back into wounded mode.

"Why are you attacking me?" Jill demanded. "I'm not dating Leo."

"Wow." Daphne shoved her tofu aside, stunned.

I said, "I just want it all out on the table. You're torn up about Ian, and I know things aren't settled. And you don't eat. And Ian knows it. It's part of the problem."

"Oh, I'm a big problem. Thanks. Good."

CeeCee said, "I've got shit going at my job. Relationships and stuff."

"I've got problems, too," I said. "I just feel like we're all tiptoeing around everything and it's not helping any of us."

"What are your problems?" Jill demanded.

"Hey, I go to Dr. Dick, don't I? I don't do it for my health." I stopped, thought a second. "Actually, I guess I do."

"He said you were disgustingly normal, or something," Jill pointed out.

"Well, I'm not." I turned to CeeCee. "You've got a problem at work?"

"I hate everyone I work with."

"That's not a problem. That's the human condition," said Jill.

"I don't really hate them," CeeCee contradicted herself. "It's just . . . a mess."

Daphne said, "Well, you all think I pick the worst men. And you hate Leo."

"More like we're worried he isn't right for you," I clarified.

"Maybe I should make an appointment with Dr. Dick." She turned to me. "Would that bother you?"

"Hell, no."

"What about your crush on him, Blue?" Jill demanded. She was out for blood and I couldn't really blame her. I was the one who'd thrown out our tacit "what's okay to talk about; what's not" code of ethics.

"Like it's ever going to happen with him. Reality check. Dr. Dick's my therapist. Make an appointment, Daphne. Please."

"I don't think I have an eating disorder," Daphne said, as if we'd accused her of it instead of Jill. "But I don't like eating in front of people. It's so intimate."

Jill examined her granola parfait and swallowed hard. "Yeah."

"I don't really give a damn who sees me eat," I said.

"Me, neither," CeeCee agreed.

"I worry," Daphne confessed, as if it were a secret she'd just been waiting to unload. "Especially on a date. What if I get something caught in my teeth?"

"Your date will get over it," I said.

CeeCee looked off into space. "All that mouth action. Lips and teeth and smacking. It's so sexual."

"Food is fuel," I reminded. "Fu—el. That's all."

Jill proceeded to take a big bite of her granola parfait, crunching away. She then sat back, cradling her coffee cup, glaring at us.

"Why are we all over each other?" Daphne asked.

"Blue started it," Jill pointed out.

I threw up my hands. "It's not like I asked you to consume insect larvae. I just said eat something. Like, so you don't expire on us."

"We should face our problems," CeeCee added, as if from a distance.

"So, what's wrong with you, Blue?" Jill asked. "We all know what's wrong with me, thank you very much, but you've been a total bitch ever since you showed up today."

"Is it the job?" CeeCee asked, as if suddenly this were a bald fact rather than a matter of discussion. "I hear ya, there."

"No . . . ."

"We've all said what's wrong with us," Daphne said.

So, here they were, three of my closest friends, suddenly putting me under the microscope. Not that I hadn't asked for it, but it's tough to be in the hot seat. "I'm single," I said.

"We all are," CeeCee pointed out, but I'd grabbed her attention. "Tell us what's going on with you."

"Nothing . . . really."

"It took you awhile to tell us about the break up with Nate," Daphne reminded. "Why?"

"I don't know."

"You can do better than that," Jill said.

There was no way to fob them off. I wasn't even sure I wanted to. If we were going to be honest with each other instead of pussyfooting around certain topics, then we had to be completely honest. I couldn't put my finger on what my exact problems were, so I just started talking. I told them in detail about my problems with Liam Engleston, then I segued into a little bit about Sean, and I ended up launching into the tale of having Charlie and Hog show up at my door-step. My tale of Charlie and Hog grew stronger as I warmed to being the center of attention. I finished by relating my dis-cussion with Dr. Dick about the Ex-Files. "Shouldn't I have learned something after all those guys?" I questioned as a final button to my argument. I knew it was a mistake almost immediately, as I'd cracked opened the door to inviting their opinions.

"You said you felt good about seeing Charlie," Jill re-minded.

"Yeah. After he left." I twisted my cup of coffee around. "I wonder if it's all that helpful, taking a trip down the soured relationship road."

"We learn from our mistakes," said Daphne. "That's why we're supposed to talk about them. Can't bury them."

CeeCee said, "Kind of like a twelve-step program."

"An eight-step program," I said. "Starting with Charlie."

"Who you can cross off now," Jill pointed out. "You've seen him and dealt with him."

I nodded. She had a point. "Then there's Kane. Number Two." Crinkling my nose, I admitted reluctantly, "He's com-ing to LA Kane Reynolds. The motivational speaker?"

"Really?" Daphne was delighted. "We've got to all go!"

CeeCee was truly tuned in. "No kidding. You do have to see him. See them all. Get rid of the fascination."

"That's what Leo was doing. Getting rid of the fascina-tion," Daphne piped up. "Okay, he slept with her. But it was supposed to be that he would get over her, once and for all."

I had a mental image of Leo's shaggy-haired body getting "over" his old girlfriend, then shook it away. "I'm not sleep-ing with them."

"Hell, no. Of course not," CeeCee agreed. "Just find out what it was that attracted you in the first place. See what it is. Go through them systematically. Check them off, one by one."

"Who's number three?" Jill asked.

"Larry Stoddard. Hairy Larry."

Daphne made a face. "The guy with the matches? Oh, no."

CeeCee's head swiveled. "I guess I haven't heard this one."

"Hairy Larry's party trick was to set his chest hair on fire," I explained. "It would go up in a kind of *swoosh.* I don't know if he put anything on it or not. Like lighter fluid. But he'd fire it up whenever he drank too much tequila, which was all the time."

"Yuk," Jill said, "What about regrowth? Didn't he need some restoration time?"

"Oh. Yeah."

"Four?" Daphne asked.

"That would be John Langdon. You guys are making me count him."

"Ah, yes . . . Mr. Famous Actor," Jill said.

"Seeing him again might be a kick," said Daphne.

"Yeah. Right." I snorted. "Five is Don the Devout. Don't even go there. I don't think I could again."

"He lives here in LA, though doesn't he?" Jill was being entirely too helpful.

"San Francisco," I said.

"Six?" CeeCee asked.

"Six is Brad Knowles. Knowles-It-All. No, wait . . . he's Seven. Six is Mark McGruder," I said. "Black Mark. He's a director I was once involved with. Lives in San Diego now. Married, with a couple of kids." I grimaced to myself. Revisiting the Ex-Files might sound like a healthy idea, but it really made you wonder about yourself sometimes.

"So, Seven is Knowles-It-All," CeeCee said.

"A lawyer. You kinda get the idea."

"Eight?" Daphne asked.

"Nate the Nearly Normal."

"Oh, right," she said. "We're there already. That's all the men you've had relationships with?"

I nodded. "I've had a few minor skirmishes along the way. Like with Sean the other night. He wanted to have sex, but I just couldn't." I briefly explained about Sean's and my tryst and his night on my couch.

"I'm sure my count would be higher," Daphne said.

"It would?" I was amazed. She's always so vocal about how it's got to be "right," how love should always be part of everything.

CeeCee said, blowing us all away. "I've had three lovers."

"That's *it*?" I asked, shocked.

"I'd like to have more," she admitted. "But sex for me can be a little like eating for Daphne and Jill. Way too personal."

"Well, of course it's personal," said Daphne.

"God." Jill stared into her empty coffee cup. "I quit counting at ten. But none of them meant a damn thing. Except for Ian." She closed her eyes and drew a deep breath. Her lashes grew damp. "I know that's what's wrong with me and Ian. I don't eat enough."

"Has he said so?" I asked.

"No . . . but that's it."

"I'm going to straighten things out at work," CeeCee said with sudden determination. "I don't want to fuck up my job because of all this."

Daphne added, "Maybe I should tell Leo what I really think about him sleeping with his ex." She paused. "That it absolutely sucks!"

Jill brushed away her tears. "I'll talk to Ian. There are clinics all over this city. If he wants me to go to one, I'll do it."

I was amazed. "Is this what's happening? We're all facing our demons?" Everyone looked at one another and silently agreed. "Well, okay, then. I'll finish sorting through the Ex-Files and see if that'll help me find Mr. Right. Or, failing that, Mr. Okay for Right Now."

"It'd be better to find Mr. Right," Daphne said wistfully.

Unbidden, Jackson Wright's face crossed the screen of my mind. I looked down at the table quickly. No one seemed to notice.

But I noticed. And it worried me.

Chapter

11

Deciding to examine the Ex-Files was one thing—making it a full-time job was nowhere in the cards. Since I didn't feel it was a truly immediate problem, I pushed it aside and decided to concentrate on work instead. Even so, the Sedona job started before I was really ready. I found myself logging long hours at the office, embroiled in pre-production, working like an automaton. It was good, in a way, as it kept me from worrying about my personal life. However, it did not keep me away from Sean, who popped in and out of the office all day long every day, running errands as all good PAs should. I could feel his eyes on me, but coward that I am, I tried to ignore him. I should not, not, *not* have let things get as far as they had between us. My reputation as a production manager depends on my decision-making ability. And my decision to indulge some kind of relationship with Sean was, well . . . not good.

I said aloud to Tom, "Are you any good at casual sex?"

Tom sat up straighter. "Who's asking and why?"

"One of my friends outranks me in numbers, and she's the last person I would expect."

"Oh." He looked wise. "Now it's a competition."

"Hell, no."

"Oh, yeah." He bobbed his head up and down.

"I just want to meet someone and fall in lust, like, or love."

"The three L's . . . hmmmm . . ."

"I just have to face it: I'm not good at casual sex."

At that moment Sean blasted through the front door. He gave me a quick smile and said, "Hey, Gin Blue-san," then hurried out with new orders from the Holy Terror herself. The door banged shut loudly behind him.

Tom gazed thoughtfully at the closed door. "What's going on with you and the PA?"

"Who? Sean?"

"Yes, 'Gin Blue-san.' What the hell is that, anyway?"

I tried a diversion tactic, not certain I'd be able to explain even if I wanted him to know. "Toss me a Jolly Rancher." I turned toward him. "Green apple or fire."

"Grape?"

"No."

"Lemon?"

"Are you deaf?"

"Don't have any of those left. Watermelon? Oh, wait. One more fire." He suddenly hurled it at me. I instantly ducked to avoid putting out an eye. The candy pinged against the window and fell into my waste can. I fished it out. Luckily, they're individually wrapped so I wasn't too worried about mine coming in contact with anything icky.

"What are you two throwing around?" Holly demanded, throwing open her inner office door as I popped the candy into my mouth.

"Jolly Ranchers," I mumbled, sucking in air to cool my mouth. Hot cinnamon. Holy mama. Doesn't get any better than this.

"Want one?" Tom asked.

He looked ready to fire one her direction and she shook

her head and asked me, "Think Sean can drive a cargo van to the job?"

Jolly Rancher cinnamon juice slipped into my windpipe. I started choking. A cargo van to Sedona? Eight and a half hours away at a good clip? With Sean toking away for all he was worth?

"God no!" I rasped out.

The front door banged open and slammed against the wall as Sean, who entered a room about as softly as a jet engine, stuck his head inside. "Am I supposed to go get lunch?"

We all went dead quiet—except for my compressed coughing as I tried to fend off an all-out cinnamon attack.

Holly said, "In a while."

With a shrug of his shoulders Sean slammed the door shut behind him. A faint, familiar odor floated in his wake. Tom made a motion of drawing hard on a joint behind Holly's back. I studiously ignored him and said, "I think I might have somebody else already."

Holly nodded and returned to work. It really wasn't her job to hire the PAs. I don't even know why she mentioned Sean. Maybe she sensed something wasn't quite jake about him, that his responsibility level lay a little on the low side. Maybe, like Tom, she suspected something was up between us. I needed to squelch that idea, and fast.

"Who do you have in mind?" Tom asked curiously once Holly was out of earshot.

"Someone who doesn't smoke on the job."

"Aha." Tom smirked. "Sean's usefulness is over and you're ready to get rid of him."

"I can't risk him behind the wheel," I snapped.

"So, who are you gonna get?"

"Maybe no one."

"Come again?"

"I can drive the van myself."

He stared at me. "You?"

"Yeah, me."

I pretended that it was a normal choice. Just a Ginny-Blue kind of whim. The thing is, as production manager, it's understood that I should be flying with the Above-the-Liners. But the trip was on a commercial airline to Phoenix, and then a small hopper to Sedona. I'm not good with small hoppers. Circling my brain was the thought that I could drive the van myself and we could pick up an extra PA in Sedona to make up for Sean. It would save one day's PA pay and it would mean Sean wouldn't have to be on this job at all. I could live with that. My reasons were entirely selfish; I wanted Sean out of my sphere. Avoidance. One of my favorite answers to problem solving. Not exactly the kind of responsible decision making appropriate for a production manager.

But I was the production manager. So anybody who wanted to argue with me could just piss off.

"I have a friend who may go with me," I added, more to myself than Tom. Since our breakfast at Sammy's CeeCee had called several times, which was unusual as she only used the phone when absolutely necessary and her conversations were notoriously brief. I'd picked up that things at work were still messy and when I mentioned I was about to leave for Sedona, she'd said she might come with me—as if I'd invited her. Clearly, something was up at work.

"Who?" Tom asked.

"Someone who might PA for me."

This suddenly seemed like a great idea. Still, it didn't help my stress level to have Sean keep shooting me a smile when he dropped in the productions offices. I felt like a heel. This was really low.

"I'm a shit," I muttered under my breath.

"What?" Tom asked. He's so nosy.

I ignored him and called Dr. Dick. I don't like being a shit. By some strange and wonderful alignment of the stars, his usual receptionist was out of the office. The temp said,

"There's a cancellation this afternoon at three. Does that sound okay?"

"See you at three!"

It wasn't the most satisfactory of sessions. I'd come in all jazzed to tell him about what a terrible person I was and he hit me with, "Tell me about your friends," almost before we were settled in our client/doctor chairs.

I frowned at him. What was this all about? "You want to know about my friends?"

He gazed at me steadily. I was completely aware of the fact that he'd removed his jacket and rolled his shirt sleeves up his arms. I could see the hair on his arms and I liked the way his hands looked—capable and strong, no namby-pamby pink palms for our Dr. Dick. "You intimated that you'd made some kind of pact with them," he said. "That exploring your 'Ex-Files' is your part of a bargain with them."

I quickly reviewed my conversation since I'd walked in the door. Yes, I'd made some throwaway comment about the Ex-Files, but it had been said as a means to segue into what a horrible, deeply troubled soul I was. How I used and abused people. How selfish and egocentric I'd become. I felt (and maybe I was wrong here, okay; I'm willing to admit that I reach for cheap drama from time to time) that Dr. Dick would be more interested in me if I were truly a black hole of depression.

"That's not really the important part," I explained. "I don't even know why I mentioned it."

He was not deterred. "What are their parts of the bargain?"

Well, for crying out loud. This was my therapy time, not my friends'. But then I figured a straight answer might be the quickest way to move back to what was really important: me. "Okay, in a nutshell: Jill's going to try to stop stalking

Ian and start eating again. CeeCee's going to fix things at work. I don't know what that's all about as yet, but it's got to do with this guy who she calls Cheese-Dick. Personally, I'm kind of flattered that she's started naming her exes, too, although he isn't strictly an ex as he and she never got together." I hesitated, then added, "She burned him with a cigarette after he kept grabbing her ass."

"On purpose?" Dr. Dick asked.

"Well, yeah."

When he didn't offer further comment, I added, "And Daphne always picks the wrong guys. Her latest slept with his first real girlfriend after he and Daphne got together. He acted as if it was okay because he should have slept with her in the past but didn't because their relationship was in high school and it just didn't happen." I paused. "He's an actor. Up for a role in *Losers, Inc.* A new teevee show."

He seemed to absorb my recap. I added, "Daphne said she was going to make an appointment to see you. Has she?"

"I haven't looked at my schedule."

"I'm sure she used me as a reference. Oh, and my friend Kristl's leaving for Seattle. Already left, I think. She's getting married for the fourth time."

"You don't sound happy for her."

"I'm not." I was point blank. "I think she's making a huge mistake, but at least she'll have some experience to draw upon when it goes south."

I waited for him to say something else and when he didn't, I asked, "Are we ready to talk about me?"

He smiled. "Step right up."

"One more thing." Although I was desperate to go on and on about Ginny Blue, I said, "My mother called me right before I came here."

His brows lifted. I think all therapist types get excited when a patient mentions her mother. Moths to the flame.

Mom had caught me on the fly. I'd been distracted anyway, what with the job and my friends and thoughts of the

Ex-Files churning around in my head, so when she announced, "I'm coming to LA to get my eyes done. I hope you're going to be around. I'd love to stay with you," I was initially too blown away to do more than repeat, "You're coming to LA to get your eyes done?"

"Do you have room?" she asked.

I shook the cobwebs out of my head. "Yeah. Sure."

"Oh, good."

Lorraine Bluebell—she of the big-ass purses—was coming my way. I snapped to and asked, "Why aren't you getting this done in Portland?"

"I met the doctor on a plane trip. We sat by each other. One thing came to another, and I was signing up. You know, a lot of these new agents are younger and younger."

"Real estate agents?"

"The competition. I gotta stay in the game."

"And you think getting your eyes done will even the playing field?"

"Ginny . . ." Mom sighed as if I were extremely dense.

"Mom, you're good at what you do."

"Thanks, sweetie. So, what's your schedule?"

I heard myself telling her about my pending trip to Sedona. Since she wasn't due to visit until after the shoot, she was thrilled. Before I could really process everything, Mom had booked herself to stay with me for a week at the end of the month.

Then she dropped the bomb and asked, "Will Nate be around?"

At this point in my narrative Dr. Dick interrupted me to ask how long Nate and I had been apart. A few weeks, I answered back. He nodded and I continued:

I could feel the seconds tick by on the phone as Mom waited for an answer. I finally decided to bite the bullet. "Nate's not really spending a lot of time here anymore."

"Oh? Why not?"

"Well . . . he moved out. We're not together anymore."

I inwardly cringed. My mother really liked Nate. After Don the Devout, Nate was her favorite.

"What about Don?" she asked, right on cue.

"I haven't seen him in a while, Mom."

"I got a card from him at Christmas," she said.

Well, of course you did, I thought. Don the Devout loved Christmas. A salesman, he sent cards out at any given opportunity. He probably had my mother's birthday listed and sent her birthday cards, too. He was like that. Handy with a date book and a scripture. Though undiagnosed, he was one of the most obsessive/compulsive people I'd ever run across. It's a wonder I managed to stay sane when we were together, but I guess somebody had to.

"So . . . I guess Mom's coming to visit," I finished, tossing up my hands in surrender.

Dr. Dick said, "You get along fairly well with your mother."

"This is true. I'm just not sure how many days we're talking about. My next job's in Sedona and then Mom comes." I paused, then added, "CeeCee might go with me to Sedona."

"The one who burned a man with her cigarette?"

"It was a little burn," I defended. "A warning. If she'd had a can of mace, she would've used that. The cigarette was at hand, so to speak."

"You intimated this happened at her workplace."

"The radio station. Yeah."

"Do you think her way of dealing with sexual harassment was better than going to her employers?"

I gave Dr. Dick a sharp look. "How do you want me to answer that?"

"Try giving it your true feelings."

Funny man. Though he tried to hide it, I could hear the sarcasm beneath the quiet statement. Leaning forward, I said, "Here's the thing: though I'm kind of appalled, since, hey, there's enough violence out there already, I almost admire her. She's cool and collected and fearless. I mean, truthfully, the guy who grabbed her ass? What is he? A masochist? If you meet CeeCee just one time, you have a pretty good idea what she's about. And if you want to push her, you're going to feel it. Like, you don't piss off a three-hundred-pound bouncer at a fancy club. You just don't do it. The guy's a moron."

"Have you met him?"

"Yes, actually. He moonlighted at this restaurant where we all hang out. In fact, CeeCee thinks he took the job just to get in her face. I think she's right. But then he got his job back at the station, so he's gone now."

"What do you think she thinks of him?"

"Why ask me?"

"You seem to be struggling with this."

"No."

"They both work at the radio station?" I nodded. "How do you think that's working out?"

"Terrible. She can't stand him." Something must have showed on my face because Dr. Dick's brows lifted in expectation. I said heatedly, "Only an idiot wouldn't be able to read CeeCee. Maybe he wanted a reaction. Maybe he wanted her to notice him. Any way around it, he's seriously screwed-up."

"So, no blame goes to CeeCee?"

"Do you want me to say it was wrong? Okay, it was wrong. She verbally warned him and he ignored her. If he thought it was an okay mating ritual, he was wrong." My conscience twinged. What had CeeCee thought about it? "I don't know why we're talking about this. It's CeeCee's problem, not mine."

"I just wanted your opinion." He smiled.

"What?" I demanded.

"You gave it to me."

He was clearly happy with me. No dissembling this time. Right to the bottom line. "I know, I'm disgustingly normal, right?"

The smile widened. "Have fun in Sedona," he said, without even looking at the clock. The guy has a sixth sense about when a session is up. My eyes took in a last, lingering glance of him. Damn. The man was delicious, and I'm not even the kind who usually thinks in those kind of adjectives.

"Maybe you can suggest to your friend that secondhand smoke should be the extent of a cigarette's harm to others."

"I'm sure she'll be thrilled with the free advice," I said dryly.

It turned out CeeCee meant it when she said she wanted to accompany me to Sedona. I mentioned we could probably use another PA on the job, and she dropped everything to jump on board. Though the Holy Terror bitched mightily about the time it would take me to drive, I stuck to the plan and CeeCee and I took off early on a foggy Santa Monica morning after loading up the van with a mountain of camera equipment. The trunks of cameras, lenses, etc. weighed about forty pounds apiece and the van was stuffed to the gills with them. By the time we were heading toward the 10 east my arms ached from weariness—and we had eight and a half hours of driving ahead of us.

We made it to West Covina before CeeCee felt compelled to light up. I knew she was struggling not to smoke in the car because she knows it about asphyxiates me. I tried not to cough too much because I was glad for her company. Still, my eyes felt gritty, my arms dull, and I knew I was going to have to hit the ground running as soon as we got to Sedona.

We were traveling along in relative silence, desultorily bringing up thoughts as they occurred to us. I managed to tell her about my mother's impending visit and my feelings about Sean and how I'd taken the van in order to keep him off the job, and she returned with comments about the traffic, the music on the radio, and the weather.

My cell phone sang merrily and I answered to Daphne. She was barely coherent.

"He dumped me!" she cried when she finally got her voice beyond sobbing gasps. "Leo! He got the part and then he dumped me!"

"I'm sorry," I said, meaning it.

"Leo?" CeeCee asked quietly, and I nodded as Daphne raged on about what a loser he was and how she was just a stupid, stupid, stupid idiot to have possibly *believed* that he could actually *care* about her. I offered words of solace—the clucking of a mother hen—and she suddenly had to get off as another call was coming in on her phone.

I hung up and said, "Huge Waste of Time."

CeeCee half laughed. "You called that one.

"So, what's going on with you and work?"

CeeCee looked out the window, thinking over a response. After a long moment, she admitted, "I've fallen for a guy."

This was so not what I'd expected that I did a classic double-take and nearly missed my turn off for our In-N-Out burger, one of the last in California, though there are a few in Arizona, I think. There was only a slight squeal of tires and a whole helluva lot of honking behind me at my last-minute turn to the off ramp.

"Not Cheese-Dick?"

"Give me a break." She pulled out another cigarette and turned it end over end, tapping it against the pack on each rotation. "My boss."

"Your *boss?* Gerald something?"

She regarded me curiously. "Did I tell you his name?"

"Yep." I didn't want to add that Jackson had already told me that his client, the station manager, CeeCee's boss, was interested in her. I'd mistakenly believed she'd been interested in Cheese-Dick, but it had been Gerald all along. I should have been relieved, I guess, but it sounded like an even bigger, messier can of worms.

I waited for more information and as we headed into the In-N-Out, CeeCee said, "Okay, here it is . . ." and proceeded to give me the complete story as I ordered and sat down to eat my protein burger.

CeeCee's boss, Gerald Coopmoor, was in the throes of an ugly divorce with his soon-to-be ex, Pat. To hear Gerald tell it, Pat was a bitch *extraordinaire,* but CeeCee had met the woman and found her to be witty and decent. CeeCee had chalked Gerald up as a complete corporate loser bending over for the conglomerate bigwigs whenever they demanded. She silently cheered Pat's decision for the divorce.

But then, one night, when the usual DJ called in sick, Gerald asked CeeCee if she could take over. Naturally, she jumped at the chance. And Gerald stayed and helped and played general dogsbody to CeeCee, and during the broadcast CeeCee managed to get bleeped less than a half a dozen times so it was a big win all the way around. Gerald was so proud of her that he took her out for a few drinks later. He made no moves on her and listened intently when she told him the full story about Cheese-Dick. Gerald had been against hiring him back, but had been overridden by one of the station's investors—who just happened to be Cheese-Dick's uncle. Nepotism at its worst. Upon hearing CeeCee's side of the story, Gerald immediately planned to fire Cheese-Dick, but CeeCee waved that away.

"The truth is," CeeCee said to me as we threw our burger wrappers in the trash and headed back to the van, "I didn't actually mean to burn him with the cigarette."

I stopped short. "I thought you purposely got him."

"I turned around fast when he grabbed and was screaming in his face and I got him with the cigarette. It all happened at once. He thought I did it on purpose and I let him think it. Now, if I say I didn't mean to, it'll sound like an excuse."

"Yeah, but, this way he thinks you assaulted him."

"Let him think it. It keeps him in line. I've got bigger problems."

"Oh?"

We climbed in the van and CeeCee continued. Over the last couple of weeks her time on the air had quadrupled, then quadrupled again. The evening-shift DJ was pissed as hell, as he was being put in elsewhere. But the numbers were up on CeeCee's stint. Everyone was happy—except maybe the previous evening-shift DJ and Cheese-Dick, who seemed to be smoldering over CeeCee's sudden good fortune.

"Aren't you worried about him?" I asked. "You should really tell someone what really happened."

"I'd rather have him screw up on the job so Gerald can fire him without all the 'he said, she said' stuff." She lit another cigarette, inhaled, then released a slow, blue stream of smoke. "Gerald and I have started making a habit of staying late. The station goes to tape after midnight and there are a lot of hours till six A.M. when Koonst, the morning DJ, comes on. We've been having sex."

"You and Gerald."

"Well, it wasn't Koonst. He's into the coffee boy. Your Mr. Mane."

"Oh."

"Gerald's still not completely divorced."

"But he will be soon, right?"

"That's what he says."

"Uh-oh. You don't believe him."

CeeCee smoked silently for a little while. "I want to believe everything he says. Every word. I like to watch him talk. I like the way his teeth look. He has these stubby brown eyelashes but they're thick. I look at them and want to chew on them."

I couldn't recall ever wanting to chew anyone's eyelashes. "Really."

"We've been doing it on the floor, the chairs. Desks." She shrugged. "It's like animalistic. I've howled."

"Howled?"

"Like I'm screaming from inside. It's so damn good." She stubbed out the cigarette on the pack in vicious little jabs.

"Scares the shit outta me. And I don't want Pat to find out. She's seeing another guy, so it shouldn't matter. But it kinda does."

"I'm more concerned that this is all happening at the station," I said. "You love that job. And seeing the boss . . . let's face it. The death knell."

"I came on this trip to get some perspective, y'know? Told Gerald I needed a few days. I need more than that. I need to date some guys on this trip. Maybe sleep with 'em. It pissed me off that Daphne's had more men than I have. I'm too conservative."

I managed to keep a straight face. Just. And it wasn't like she didn't have a point when it came to sex. I surreptitiously studied her profile as I drove. CeeCee was extraordinarily attractive. Her pink tips were fading and her hair brushed her shoulders, not white-hot-blonde now, but more of an ashy color. With her pert nose, blue eyes with long-lashes (which I had no desire to chew on), and a stubborn chin, she could turn heads. Of course, the army fatigues, chains, and boots might turn off some, but sometimes they, too, worked as an aphrodisiac.

"Sleep away," I said. "Just stay away from the director and crew. It's an incestuous little group. I slept with an actor once. ONCE. Only because I really liked him. But it nearly ruined everything."

"Lang?"

I made the sign of the cross though I'm really not religious. "My first and last actor. He had his moments, though."

"Well, how about a Sedona local," CeeCee suggested. "There must be some bars around. I could probably pick up a one-nighter."

"You really want this? I mean, even with the lash-chewing and all?"

"That's exactly why," she stated emphatically. "I hate being in love. I want to be in lust."

"Sounds like you got that one covered."

"You know what I mean."

Her logic was, as ever, unique to CeeCee. She was taking fear of commitment to nuclear levels. Then I had a sudden thought. For a moment I kept it to myself. Carefully, I said, "Hairy Larry lives in Phoenix."

"An Ex-File?" CeeCee perked up. "And Phoenix is how far from Sedona?"

"Hour and a half?"

"This is the guy who burned off his chest hair?"

"That would be him."

"Interesting . . ."

We pulled into the Ramada about ten o'clock. Both of us got out and stretched. Red Rock towered over us to our right, though its beauty was disguised by the dark. I've been to Sedona a number of times. It's an artist's haven and the scenery is awe-inspiring, even to someone as unaware as myself. However, I am not in love, love, love with the place, which seems to be the prevailing feeling. Tourists arrive, swoon, and plunk down money on yet-to-be-built condos. Retirees flock to the area. Hikers, climbers, and outdoorspeople of all types hyperventilate just by looking. I know there's basically something wrong with me because I just don't get it. Give me the ocean and a Ketel One vodka martini. Spear the olive with a parasol for an added froufou factor. Now that's Eden.

CeeCee said, "The air feels so clear here."

I stared at her through the gloom. Like she could tell? As much as she smoked? Was she some closet nature girl? I grunted an acquiescence and we stepped into reception and checked in.

Later, we tried to hunt down a bar. The hotel was like a tomb. It was November and nothing much was happening besides our group. The air was chilly. High desert. Since we were in the van with hundreds of thousands of dollars of rental equipment, we really didn't want to be driving too far in search of alcohol.

We finally ran into Holly, who was walking along one of

the paths around the hotel carrying a bottle of vodka. Not Ketel One, but at this point I had no right to be picky. "We're meeting at Will's suite," she said, frowning at CeeCee.

"CeeCee's with me," I said. If director Will Torrance didn't want interlopers, I was more than happy to eschew the fun as well.

Holly, however, just shrugged. "It's twelve-oh-nine."

We were in jeans and puffy insulated jackets, so we went back to my room to change. Since CeeCee had come as my guest, she was either my roommate or paying her own way. I had two double beds and didn't mind sharing. PAs are generally hired at the location and therefore don't get their own rooms.

I changed into tan slacks and a clingy red shirt. Looking at my now-mostly-brown hair, I groaned. Long, slightly shaggy, and a pain in the ass at the best of times. I pulled it into a sleek ponytail, added lip gloss to my mouth. The height of fashion.

CeeCee changed from a snowboarder's shirt of dark blue to a snowboarder's shirt of dark green. The pants with their chains remained the same. She did throw on some whitish lip color, however, which shouldn't have worked but did.

"What are you doing?" I asked, standing by the door as she picked up a phone book.

"What's Hairy Larry's last name?"

"Stoddard. He lives in Phoenix, not Sedona."

"This is a Phoenix book." A moment later she found the number and dialed. I was shocked and couldn't hide it.

"You're just going to call him up?" I hissed. "And say what?"

"I'll think of something."

She apparently got an answering machine because she said in her CeeCee way, "This is Catherine Collingwood. My friends call me CeeCee. One of my friends is Ginny Bluebell. Her friends call her Blue. I'm with her right now and we're in Sedona. Ginny's cell phone number is—" I

started making frantic hand motions but CeeCee blithely ignored me and reeled off the digits. I glared in impotent fury.
I wanted to throttle her.

"I haven't spoken to him in years," I declared as she hung
up. "He's going to think I want to see him now!"

"Don't you?"

"NO."

"I do." She grabbed her coat and headed out the door.
"And he's an Ex-File. I haven't forgotten your pledge." She
grinned like a devil. "Some day you'll thank me."

Yeah, like *right*.

We went to the party.

Chapter

12

Will Torrance was staying in a two-bedroom suite with a full bar and a room full of loud people. I saw the "Agency" people for the *House About You?* commercial shoot first. They were grouped along the couch and several adjoining chairs, looking rather cold and feral. Sometimes Agency are pleasant and supportive, but lots of times their jobs are riding on how well a commercial is received so there's an undercurrent of tension throbbing around them. Agency are the people who decide which production company will produce their commercial. You might think it would be the client—in this case, *House About You?*— but the advertising agency is hired by the client and the production company is hired by the agency. Therefore production needs to suck up to Agency more than to the client to ensure future work. This doesn't mean we ignore the client; we just go out of our way to keep Agency happy. And sometimes Agency is okay. I've had good times with many an agency producer, art director, etc. Agency for the Waterstone Iced Tea shoot were a case in point. They were all polite, stayed out of the way, and wore smiles. The tenor of any location shoot all depends on who's powertripping at any given point.

As a production manager I report to the producer, which is, in the case of Wyatt Productions, Holly, though I'm really an independent, as all of us are to some degree. Producers generally connect with particular directors. Holly moves around a bit but sticks mostly with the tried and true. I float along with her more often than I'd like to admit. She might be the Holy Terror, but I know her ways and honestly, I'm not great about charging out and selling myself. I'm much happier just doing the work and having people get to know me on the job.

Holly has worked with Will Torrance several times and thinks fairly highly of him as a director. This, however, was to be my first job with him. My skeptical nature refuses to afford anyone high marks until after a shoot. I've been both pleasantly surprised and aggravated to the extreme. The jury was still out on Torrance and would be for a while.

Having CeeCee with me could be construed as an industry no-no, generally speaking: a production team never wants to appear as having "extra baggage" along—baggage that might pad the bill. But I was determined to have CeeCee be a production assistant. I just hadn't gotten it all straight yet. Therefore, CeeCee was in a kind of production work limbo. Though she technically wasn't working for us yet, we had to act as if she were already part of the crew for Agency's benefit. CeeCee definitely looked the part, and I told her to act as if she'd been on hundreds of jobs.

"No problemo," she assured me.

Will Torrance was at the bar as we moved into the room. He glanced up as we approached. The jury might still be out, but my heart did an uncomfortable little flip. The man possessed blue eyes. Oh, the trouble I've gotten into over a pair of blue eyes. Witness: Sean. Also Mr. Famous Actor, John Langdon. And, though not strictly an Ex-File, Jackson Wright. And if I ever get my chance, Dr. Dick . . . .

My second thought, irrationally, was the fear I might be too tall for him. At five feet nine, it's a consideration, espe-

cially around actors. But directors . . . . I watched as he
straightened to his full height in order to pull out the cork
from a bottle of Syrah. I calculated at least six feet. Hallelujah.

Why I was tracking this was something I didn't want to
examine too closely. My own EXCELLENT advice is to
stay away from liaisons on the job. But that didn't mean my
brain wasn't chalking up the man's pluses and minuses.
Just by the look of his lean, handsome frame, he was worth
breaking rules over.

"Thought you advised against getting involved with people in the biz. Too incestuous," CeeCee drawled, amused by
my cataloguing.

I pretended not to get her point, "I swore off Sean, didn't
I? And he was really too low in the pecking order to get me
into serious trouble."

"What about him?" She nodded toward Will.

"What about him?"

"Blue . . ." she chided softly, in a tone suggesting my attempt at deception was just plain sad. I thought about giving
it another try anyway, then shrugged and admitted defeat.

"He's nice to look at."

"Here, here," she muttered.

Since I was found out anyway, I stole another lingering
glance at Will. I was plagued by a *déjà vu* that wasn't entirely pleasant. Phantom memories circled. Carefully searching through the wreckage in my brain—carefully, because
sometimes you can be hurt by what you uncover, like a smoldering ember amongst cold ashes—I finally landed on the
source. Will Torrance bore a passing resemblance to Mark
McGruder, Ex-File Number Six, a gorgeous black Irishman
with long, wavy hair and a killer pair of electric blue eyes.
How had I forgotten his blue eyes? I asked myself, faintly
worried. Sometimes my ability to suppress history when
faced with a potential "current" File concerns me. But Mark

had a vile temper, which rose up whenever he drank, which was morning, noon, and night. These days I prefer to think of him as Black Mark, and the period of our relationship as the Black Death. Another Ex-File that had not ended well.

"Will Torrance looks like Ex-File Number Six," I related quietly to CeeCee.

"Which one's that?"

"Mark McGruder. Black Mark."

She grunted. "Well, if this starts to take off, you'd better look up Black Mark pronto to make peace with yourself."

"This isn't going to take off," I assured her, motioning between Will and myself. "And I'd never look up Black Mark."

"You said you were going to work your way through the Ex-Files. So far, Charlie's been it. Who was number two again?"

"Kane Reynolds."

"Oh, the motivational speaker. Right. We'll see him when he gets to LA."

"Like that's going to happen."

"Are you backing out of the deal?"

"No . . ."

She looked at me and silently asked, *Well?* I said, "Charlie's not the only Ex-File I've dealt with."

"Name another one." CeeCee bypassed the wine and examined the makings available for a mix-your-own rum drink. Several brightly colored bottles of different juices awaited the brave who might be into potpourri approach to mai-tais. Examining the array, CeeCee reached for a Heineken in a tub of ice.

I thought really, really hard and said, "Nate."

"That leaves six more," CeeCee pointed out.

My cell phone, silent for quite a long period, bleated at this point. I cringed at my current choice of ring. Too whiny. Note to self: change immediately after answering call. "Hello?"

"Ginny? Virginia?"

Virginia? I did a veritable double take. Memory hit with a bang. "Larry," I said, my voice undeniably dull though I strove for "unexpected delight." Ex-File Number Three, as if listening in on our conversation, had called right on time.

"I got this message on my phone—"

"Yeah, I know. My friend CeeCee called. And she's right here with me now." I thrust the phone into CeeCee's hands and walked away. *Virginia.* Jesus Christ. Now, I remembered the other irritating things about Hairy Larry that nearly drove me mad. Never mind the fact that he broke up with me. Sad as that is, it's true. My boyfriend who had a tendency to light his chest hair on fire had broken up with me. The reason? None, as far as I could tell. He'd been one of those relationships that I'd chased after, and I remembered one of those, "It's not you, it's me," kind of lines in the end, and then he was out of there. I recall wondering whether I was upset or not. Still would be hard pressed to answer that one.

CeeCee jumped into the fray with gusto. "Hi, there," she greeted brightly. "Blue's been reminiscing about old friends, so we thought we'd give you a call." I bristled a little at the "we" but kept my cool. Larry must have given her an earful, because she listened for quite a while. Feeling like an eavesdropper, I moved away. I avoided Will Torrance, I can't say quite why. Well, yes, I can. I didn't want to give CeeCee any ideas, and I also felt it was smart to keep my distance. Whenever my antennae start picking up vibes, and I sense myself inordinately aware of someone else's proximity, like knowing where they are in the room at any given moment, it's a potentially hot situation. These are the times I make bad judgment calls. I get too flirty, or too loud, or too something. I was very cautious these days about the dance with the opposite sex, and kind of out of practice. I'd been with Nate awhile and, let's face it, choosing Sean as my first foray into the dating world wasn't exactly inspired.

CeeCee clicked off my phone with a flourish and sent me

a sideways smile. Trouble, I thought instantly. Not CeeCee's usual approach.

"What?" I demanded.

"He's coming over."

"Who? Larry? *Here?*" I pointed to the walls, meaning the hotel. When CeeCee nodded, I said, "You're kidding."

"I invited him."

"This party is for people on the shoot! Only people on the shoot. That's why you have to keep your mouth shut about yourself and your 'job.' I thought you got that."

"Larry sounded like a kick." She shrugged. "We'll go to the bar."

"He's driving from Phoenix tonight? Where's he gonna stay?"

"He said he'd get a room."

Peachy. I turned away from her, uncertain whether I was mad or not. Was I ready to see Hairy Larry again? Especially with my senses on overload where our new director was concerned? I stole a look at Will. He was bent forward, listening, as one of the prettier women at the party—a petite blonde—whispered something in his ear. She grinned and giggled a little and he smiled appreciatively. *Nope*, I reminded myself. *You're not going to go there. No, no, no.*

While we waited the hour and a half it would take Larry to drive from Phoenix to Sedona, Will's party slowly drifted to the hotel bar. CeeCee and I trundled along with them, as we planned to meet Larry there anyway. I watched as many of the agency people became well and truly soused—a good thing, in my estimation. They'd be hung over tomorrow and either wouldn't come to the site, or if they did, they'd be too miserable to get in our way at the start of the shoot. Also, it showed they could be partyers and therefore possibly fun.

I was feeling edgy, contemplating a first sighting of Larry while being inordinately aware of Will. I really shouldn't have worried about Will, as he seemed to be an audacious flirt, and the blonde was working her mojo any which way she could—to seemingly little or no effect, however. The blonde was Agency, I'd learned. I wasn't sure what her actual function was.

CeeCee had found a soul mate in the first AD—that is, the assistant director. He was a bit of a player with a wife and two kids at home, but he was a really cute, outgoing guy. I'd given CeeCee all the particulars on him. She wasn't interested in him except as a smoking buddy. They kept heading outside even though I believe you can still smoke inside in Arizona. Apparently they'd both developed the California habit of heading immediately for the great outdoors. Either that or they just preferred each other's company and were lying to me.

I'd defaulted to my Ketel One vodka martini and was happy in a corner of the room, watching the action. It gave me time to think about Lawrence Stoddard, Ex-File Number 3, the infamous Hairy Larry. I'm ashamed to say it, but he'd started off as a one-night stand in my hometown of Portland. I'd somehow managed to drift through college without any serious attachments and at the time I met Larry, I was existing in a kind of post-upper-education limbo, still living at home with my mom. Call it having met my girlfriends at that time and not needing the sometimes downright claustrophobic relationship with a boyfriend. Or maybe it was just that after Charlie and then Kane, I'd become more cautious. In any event, Larry was the first guy who had seriously caught my interest since high school.

I was in that phase of wondering what the hell to do with the rest of my life. I'd finished school with a degree in liberal arts. Yes, I know: What the hell does that get you? I was certainly asking myself the same thing, so I figured I'd move back with Mom for a short stint while I put things together. A friend of my mother's had given her tickets to an NBA game, so one night I found myself with Mom at the Rose Garden, spending half my time telling her how the game was played, spending the other half in that blank space in my mind where I worried about my future.

Larry was seated directly in front of us and he was a Laker fan. His team was playing the Blazers and thumping them pretty badly. He was hooting, hollering, standing up and cheering. I thought he was a big galoot.

But then he turned around, smiled, and said, "I'm a problem. I know. I'll try to keep the decibel level down. I promise."

My mother sniffed. "I've heard about you Laker fans."

"Mom . . ." I said, worried about where this might be going. I'm never sure where my mother gets her information. I had a feeling we might be ready to fly off the rails into a crash zone. She's great at selling real estate, but other areas are definitely in question.

"Oh, have you?" Larry said, amused. "Well, it's all true. Hi, I'm Lawrence Stoddard. My friends call me Larry," he added, thrusting out a hand to my mother and then to me. My palm was swallowed within his.

"Ginny Blue," I said.

"Virginia Bluebell," my mom corrected. "And I'm Lorraine."

The introductions averted trouble for the moment. Mom kept one suspicious eye on Larry for a while. If I hadn't known better I would have sworn she was a rabid Trailblazer fan.

Then the ball was inbounded, someone fouled another player, swear words were exchanged on both sides, and the Lakers were slapped with a technical foul.

Larry booed loudly and the Portland fans looked ready to lynch him, my mother among them. I, meanwhile, had realized that he was rather attractive. Sure, he was noticeably hairy. I mean, his arms were like a grizzly bear's. And his eyebrows were fairly bushy. But the hair on his head was thick and lustrous, and as his crown was directly in my eyesight, I had the urge to run my hands through it in a way that gave me the shivers.

At halftime Larry headed out for a beer and surprised me by asking us if we wanted to join him and his friend, Jeff. Jeff was utterly silent. I was half-convinced he was a mute until he managed to ask for a round of Budweiser and we all stood in the beer room sipping out of clear plastic cups. Mom wrinkled her nose at the flavor but she valiantly kept on drinking. I was pretty sure it was her first beer. She favors white wine and iced tea.

Larry let it be known that he was visiting Jeff, a college friend, and, no surprise here, that he lived in southern California, as many Lakers fans do. (Larry was, in fact, the reason I decided to move to sunny SoCal in the first place.) My mother then embarrassed me by launching into a story of Jackson Wright, *über*-success, who'd moved to Los Angeles from Portland and made it big in the finance and film industry. Larry, a screenwriter, was intrigued. Mom didn't have Jackson's phone number, but Larry turned over his.

At the end of the evening, after the Lakers had pulled out a squeaker in the fourth quarter, Larry leapt into the air with a raised fist. His pleasure drew swordlike glances from the disappointed Portland fans, but Mom, true to her fickle nature, had switched allegiances. She was talking real estate to Jeff as we filed out of the arena. Jeff was apparently listening.

"I'm going to be in town for a few more days," Larry said to me. "I'm staying with Jeff. I don't know the city all that well. Can you recommend someplace to eat?"

"Well . . ." I paused. "There's Jake's. It's been here for a century or so."

"Century-old Jake's sounds fantastic." His eyes seemed focused on mine. "Care to join me?"

I love Jake's, but I didn't know Larry at all. Mom wasn't being a whole lot of help in this regard as she'd mentally adopted both Larry and Jeff, I could tell. I weighed the whole thing and suggested cautiously, "Could I meet you there?"

"Good enough," he said.

We made a date for the following night, and while I prepared for the evening ahead I suffered serious cold feet. But Mom was now a Larry champion. "Oh, for pete's sake." She eyed me as if I couldn't possibly have come from her gene pool. "Do something."

Well, now, that hurt. Mainly because I *wasn't* doing anything and she'd hit right on it. It was February and cold as the arctic. I wouldn't have worn a dress if my life depended on it, so I put on a pair of black slacks and a fuzzy red sweater that looked okay with my brown hair. Mom *tsk*ed and complained. I said, rather tartly, that Lawrence Stoddard could be a serial killer for all we knew. I'm sure I heard wrong, but I think she muttered something about "at least having a goal."

I was carless at this point, so I drove Mom's blue Ford sedan and parked just off Burnside around the corner from Jake's. I felt cold, odd, and conspicuous as I stepped through the door into the bar and waded through groups of people. I was twenty-two; I hadn't gotten into Ketel One vodka martinis yet. Besides, I had no job, so I cheaped out and bought myself the least expensive beer on the menu. Glancing around for Larry, I realized he was late. I'd give him a few minutes and if he didn't show, I'd vamoose. I would have gone right then but the thought of free food was enough to keep me rooted awhile. I took off my black leather jacket and draped it over my arm.

The guy who'd carded me on the way in kept looking at me. I found it flattering so I smiled at him, then worried that there might be something in my teeth. With that in mind, I headed to the bathroom, and found there that I looked fine. In fact, I looked better than fine. Stepping from the frigid outside to the body warmth inside had added a pink tint to my cheeks that made me seem prettier than I believed myself to be. I pinched my cheeks, Scarlett O'Hara style, to keep the illusion going and headed back to the bar.

Larry was there when I returned. I lifted a hand in greeting and the guy at the door thought I was signaling him. When he realized my date had arrived he pretended to be very, very sad. I laughed.

Larry grinned. "You got a great laugh."

Flattery. It always worries me. Nevertheless, Larry was looking good in a blue dress shirt, open at the throat, the sleeves rolled up his muscular arms. His black leather jacket was draped over his arm as well, a concession to the body heat inside Jake's.

"We must buy at the same discount leather shop," I remarked.

"I can't stand retail," he revealed.

"Me, neither."

"Makes me feel like I'm getting cheated."

"Amen," I agreed, deciding I liked Larry a little.

"You ready to eat?" He glanced around and found the maître d' at his desk. We were shown to our table, a small, boothlike affair that would've been too intimate to my liking except that Larry was relaxed wherever he went. He ordered scotch on the rocks for both of us.

"I don't drink scotch," I said.

"Give it a try," he suggested. "If you don't like it, we'll find you something else."

What I didn't like was his high-handed ways, but since he was buying—at least, I assumed he was buying—I acquiesced. I had a moment of fear and distress, then decided if he suddenly wanted to go Dutch I'd pull a Nancy Reagan and "just say no."

The bad news: after a couple of sips that burned down my throat like molten ore, I found the scotch was not too bad. I drank my drink, and a second, and suddenly I was very much in love with Lawrence Stoddard. I also became way too chatty, as alcohol was wont to make me become, and before long I was remarking on his luscious head of hair.

"Oh, yeah?" he said, pleased. "I got hair everywhere. Except my back. So far, anyway."

I was glad to hear about the nonfoliated back. That might've put me over the edge.

I scarcely remember what I ate. I just was having such a jolly old time that the next time I truly surfaced, we were heading toward Jeff's place, which was around the corner from Jake's in a fairly chichi area of northwest Portland.

It worked for me.

Jeff, as it turned out, was incredibly wealthy. He was an investor, or partner, in several going concerns. I pointed out, rather cleverly I thought, that he must be a silent partner. When we got to his place, Larry steered me to the guest cottage—his own private digs.

Before you could quote Nine Inch Nails and say, "Fuck me like an animal," we were all over each other. Larry was stripping off his clothes in between heavy panting kisses; I was doing it even faster. Since Kane, I hadn't made it with anyone past a few heavy petting sessions before I'd lost interest. I was going to score with Larry if it killed me.

He was true to his word about the back hair. Nothing there. But legs, arms, and definitely beard made up for it. I ran my fingers through his mane and practically purred with delight. We didn't spend a lot of time on preliminaries which was just fine with me as I was in the mood as I'd never been before.

And . . . I climaxed for the first time ever. It was so unexpected and fantastic that I wanted to cheer. Trust me, it was nothing special Larry did; he was all business. In, out, a couple of joyously raucous thumps and I was THERE. I could have kissed him. Actually, I did kiss him. Repeatedly. We ended up having three lusty go-arounds before I felt the need to find my mother's car and head home.

I was so delighted I almost told Mom about it the next day. This, of course, does not fit into the mother-daughter rule book of behavior, but I thought, "What the hell. I'm of age."

I fumbled around with how to divulge my girlish delight, but in the end I kept what happened to myself. However, my Cheshire-cat smile must have given me away anyway, because late that same afternoon Mom looked up from digging inside one of her big-ass purses—a purple one—and said dryly, "It looks like you'll be seeing him again."

I grinned even wider. I did see him again, at the fateful chest hair burning event. He called me that afternoon and invited me to a party. Jeff and some buds were getting together. He wanted me to join. Thrilled, I dressed myself carefully in a long black skirt, black boots, and a pale blue boat-necked top. Feeling ultrafashionable, I showed up about ten minutes late to the party—didn't want to seem too eager—just in time for Larry to be coaxed by a horde of beer-swillers into performing his famed trick. In slack-jawed shock I watched as he poured a liberal amount of lighter fluid onto the shaggy black hair of his chest, picked up an automatic lighter and WHOOSH! He went up in flames!

I think I screamed. If I did, no one heard as they were screaming with laughter themselves. Everyone instantly and frantically patted him down hard, making sure he didn't burn anything besides the chest hair. The odor of singed fur permeated the air. Unlike CeeCee's long-haired friend who'd accidentally fried his locks, this was apparently a regular gig for Hairy Larry. I was horrified.

But . . . I did have sex with Larry that night. I didn't quite reach the pinnacle of ecstacy as the night before, but it was pretty good. Almost a climax. He took a shower before the big event, but even so I had to work hard to train my nose from twitching at the scent of his now hairless, slightly redskinned chest. I left him with slightly less of that euphoric feeling I'd possessed from the night before, but after a serious talking-to with myself in my bedroom mirror, I decided I was still game for the long haul.

That is, until he didn't call. Ever. Again.

I waited around the next day but when it was five o'clock and no Larry, I grew a set of balls and made the call myself. Jeff answered the phone with a rather croaky, "Hello?" as if his vocal cords were as rusty as I believed them to be.

"Hi, it's Ginny. Is Larry there?"

"Oh. No. He had to go back to LA. You want his number there?"

I was shocked. Poleaxed. I managed to say, "Sure" and to sound fairly nonchalant but come on! Give me a break. I should have known right then and there that it was never going to work with Larry, but nope. Instead I finally found the career goal I'd been looking for: a move to Los Angeles. And why not? All my college friends were already there. When I told Jill, Daphne, and CeeCee that I was coming down their way they were thrilled. I didn't have the heart— or the new, now seriously shrinking, set of balls—to tell them what had driven my decision.

Now, sipping away at my martini, I cringed to remember how I'd looked Larry up in the land of everlasting sunshine. I'd called cheerily, blurting that I'd moved to the City of Angels myself, and wasn't that just the most amazing coincidence. The stars had just aligned themselves. He was pleasant. He actually sounded happy that I would be around, and when I showed up on his doorstep he enveloped me in a deep bear hug. My fears were allayed. My heart sang.

It's just that . . . he was really too busy for a girlfriend. Not that he came right out and said it, but it became crystal clear as I did all the calling, all the chasing, everything. Our relationship lasted a total of four months, on and off. Then, about the time I was ready to give up and call it off completely, he beat me to the punch.

Kind of like Nate.

Depressing.

The good thing was that my move to LA had been what it took for me to begin a career. While my relationship with

Larry stalled I jumped into the commercial production biz, starting out as a PA. When I'm feeling generous I recall that Larry's the reason I found the job that I love. Most of the time I don't think of him at all.

But now, joy of joys, I was going to get to see him again. Realizing that my martini was dry as a bone—and not from lack of vermouth—I got up from my chair. I took three steps toward the bar when the man of the hour himself strode into the room, big as life. Hairy Larry in the flesh. I did the proverbial double take. My jaw dropped almost as much as it had when I walked in on the pyrodefoliation. Hairy Larry was totally gray. A silver fox. And it looked damn good on him.

He spotted me and grinned. I raised a hand and smiled back. Well, hell. No use holding a grudge. "Hairy Larry, as I live and breathe."

"Virginia Bluebell. You're gorgeous, you know."

This was a blatant lie, but he made me feel gorgeous anyway. "I'm doing okay."

"Bullshit. You look like a million."

"So, CeeCee talked you into coming. I can't believe it."

"It's been awhile," he said, with just a trace of sheepishness.

"I hope you feel like dogmeat for breaking up with me."

"I was an idiot. I'm still an idiot, but that's okay."

"Yeah."

We smiled happily at each other again. CeeCee and the second AD returned at that moment. Spying me with Hairy Larry, CeeCee came right over. She sized him up. Will Torrance chose that exact moment to approach our group as well and instantly my concentration splintered. Larry was clearly taken with CeeCee's interesting look and they struck up a conversation like old friends. I turned to Will, feeling a tad breathless. This was more multitasking than I was ready for. I wasn't sure what he wanted, maybe just to meet and greet members of the production team. Since Holly had taken off to bed as soon as we left Will's room, I was the next person in charge.

He said, by way of greeting, "I understand you're a friend of Jack Wright's."

A moment passed while my brain stalled. "Jackson Wright?" I asked, though I knew who he meant. A blush flamed my cheeks. Good god, this industry is TOO SMALL.

"I saw Jack the other day," he said. "Told him I was on a shoot with Wyatt Productions and he mentioned that a friend of his was the production manager . . . Jenny Blue?"

"Ginny Blue." I stuck out my hand and he clasped it.

"How do you know Jack?"

I don't know Jack shit. I almost said it but managed to keep a civil tongue in my head, as they say. His palm was warm and strong. When he released my hand I found my attention still focused on my fingers, consummately aware of the lingering warmth. Dangerous. "We went to high school together, if you can believe it," I answered. "In Portland."

"Jack's been helping put together a deal for me," Will said. "We're drumming up financing for an indie."

"Great."

Independent films were a good way to break out of commercials and into the film business. Jackson was definitely someone to know.

Will and I might have gotten past the first tentative moves of introduction and progressed to more interesting fare, but that blond Agency woman appeared at that moment, staggering a bit on the tiny, tiny heels attached to her tiny, tiny feet. I felt like an elephant next to her. She had to be a size zero. Size zero. Can you stand it? Who comes up with these marketing ploys? In my mind, size zero is vapor. At least make the first size a one. Or a half. Or something.

Agency Blonde whined, "I've got to get to bed. We've got soooo much to do tomorrow."

As if Will, the director, wouldn't know. But he said kindly, "Want me to walk you back to your room?" It didn't sound like a come-on. I don't think it was. But the inebriated woman clearly hoped it was. They left together a few moments later. At the door Will looked back, searched me out, met my eye and lifted a hand to say good-bye.

I was in heaven.

CeeCee and Larry had moved to the center of the group that still remained. The place had grown raucous with noise, everyone shouting to be heard above thumping music and each other. CeeCee was sober, sipping a Heineken, maybe still her first, but Larry had joined the crew like a long-lost member and pounded back half a beer in the space of the five steps it took me to approach.

"Been writin' this college story," he said, wiping his mouth with the back of his hand. "These frat guys have this house that's fallin' down around 'em. Kinda like *Animal House*, y'know? But then the place is purchased by this do-gooder group who want to turn it into a rehab center for beauty freaks. The kind that have had too much plastic surgery. So, all these beautiful women are there. And they're needy and the guys don't leave and it kind of goes from there."

"High concept," someone murmured appreciatively.

I gave them a hard look. Who were these morons? I had to wonder what Larry's original screen ideas had been, back when I first met him. He'd had several scripts optioned, but nothing had made it to the screen.

CeeCee summed it up. "You're just doing this for the cold hard cash."

Larry fought a belch, gave it up, and let one rip. The group was too far gone to care. "Yep," he admitted freely. "My serious stuff is sitting on a shelf somewhere. Gets optioned now and again. My agent told me frat stories are hot."

This prompted a lively discussion on the merits of writing for the level of junior high school-age boys—the ultimate moneymaking group, as they tended to revisit a film several times if they liked it. Repeat ticket buyers were gold.

I pulled CeeCee aside and said I was heading to bed. She wasn't quite ready to leave yet, and, feeling a bit like a party pooper, I decided to hang in a few moments longer.

That's when it happened. Enough alcohol had been consumed for good behavior to lose out to stupidity. One guy showed off his personal body trick—a pretty good one: he could swallow his tongue and we could look up his nose and see it wiggling. I was, naturally, grossed out but compelled to look. The next thing you know, Larry was searching around for some lighter fluid—possessed, unfortunately by the rapt bartender, for some reason. His shirt came off and he liberally splashed on the lighter fluid like aftershave. His chest hair was magnificent, and I soon saw that he'd managed to begin a crop on his back as well. Time had taken over that broad expanse. He threw lighter fluid over his shoulder to catch those tender stalks and grabbed a lighter . . .

This whole process took about ten seconds and made me exceedingly nervous. I saw the bartender wasn't a complete idiot; he had a fire extinguisher in hand. But did anyone try to stop Larry? Not a chance. One moment he stood there in all his half-naked splendor, the next he went up in a *WHOOSH,* front and back. People screamed. Even CeeCee stepped back in shock. Larry yelled, "Youch!" and the bartender shot him down with foam. Moments later he was extinguished and dripping.

"Good God," someone murmured.

"Shit," Larry said. "Haven't done that in years. Think I took out some skin."

No kidding. There were red spots down his back. He gingerly put on his shirt, all the fun out of the moment.

The bartender said in awe to me, "I've heard about that trick. Never seen it, though."

"I've seen it twice," I told him. "Same guy." I turned to

CeeCee. "Somehow I feel I've answered any questions still left about Ex-File Number Three. I'm moving on."

She nodded.

We left Larry in the very capable hands of a rather heavy-set woman, who insisted Larry spend the night with her as she had a first aid kit in her room and wanted to make sure he was all right.

Chapter

13

The *House About You?* shoot wasn't anything to write home about. Everything went according to plan, even the weather, which remained utterly gorgeous throughout, and we finished up in two days instead of three. Agency left us alone, mostly, as they were hung over the first day, which kept them out of our bonding on the second. Will and the blonde seemed on warm terms, but not in that conspiratorial way reserved for lovers. Or maybe that was just me hoping. CeeCee, though she never got laid, worked out beautifully as a PA, managing to hold her tongue when Holly barked at her to make sure gawkers weren't parking too close to the shot. She stepped up to the job and scowled fiercely at anyone who slowed down as if to park. One look at CeeCee and without fail they quickly drove away.

We were shooting the last shot and my mind was drifting pleasantly onto thoughts of gorgeous Will Torrance when my walkie-talkie crackled to life. CeeCee's voice ordered, "Ginny, go to two." I immediately punched onto channel two—the channel reserved for production assistants, not directors or grips—and said, "Go for Ginny."

CeeCee revealed, "There's someone here who claims to

know Will. A woman. Arrived in a black town car. Says her name is Rhianna."

"Will's just finishing. I'll tell him."

"Looks like a possible girlfriend."

"Got it."

I clicked off, wondering about the new arrival. Deciding to learn more before I interrupted Will, I turned to Holly, who grimaced when I told her the news.

"Absolute pain in the ass," she said.

"Girlfriend?"

She nodded. So much for my pleasant thoughts. Of course he had a girlfriend. They all had girlfriends. And/or wives.

"Tell her to meet him at the hotel. He's busy," Holly said. "I'll give him the word that she's here."

"Happy to do it."

Holly gave me a faint smile. "You have no idea."

It sounded as if Rhianna might be even worse than the usual insecure, "it's all about me" women who seemed to bond like industrial glue to the directors. I was glad Holly made the executive decision to book her off-set. If Rhianna didn't like it, she couldn't go over someone's head and complain since Holly was the producer and therefore top woman on the totem pole. True, Wyatt Productions also had an Executive Producer, but DeAnn stayed in the office and spent most of her time bidding other jobs. She hated dealing with the problems of the shoot and anyone who had the bad judgment to try and go over Holly's head—or whatever producer was on the job at the time—learned *tout suite* that DeAnn would have none of it.

From the distance of the production trailer I watched Holly diffidently wait for a moment with Will as he peered through the camera, setting the shot. Red Rock was directly behind, eye-hurtingly bright against a blue, blue sky. The painted house with its actor/painter was a light, lemony yellow color. It was startling to look at. While I watched, the first AD took the shot with Will looking on. He bent an ear to

Holly, then swept an eye toward the perimeter of the shoot, as if expecting to see Rhianna, who was cooling her heels in CeeCee's quadrant. I watched him wave off Holly, clearly saying he'd see Rhianna later, and Holly returned to me and told me to send the woman on her way. I called CeeCee, who sounded quietly delighted to shoo the interloper to the hotel. I kept my eyes on the ridge where this was taking place and saw a black town car glide smoothly away.

I should have known better than to expect that would be the end of it. By the time the Above-the-Liners, Agency and I trudged back to the hotel (CeeCee and the other PAs and grips were still disassembling equipment) we were all dead tired, hungry, and thirsty. I wanted a shower and a Ketel One martini and maybe an exotic hors d'oeuvre or two at the hotel restaurant and then bed. It was scarcely six o'clock, but we'd put in a couple of twenty-hour days and I was at the end of my endurance. I figured Will would be taken up with Rhianna and decided I wanted to skedaddle before I had to think about it too much.

But my isolation was not to be, as Rhianna chose that moment to sashay from the lobby to the hotel parking lot as Will, Holly, various Agency people, and I tumbled out of a couple of the job's rented Suburbans. She was bristling with indignation. Her dyed red hair—closer to orange—was pulled back into a scarf and she wore huge black sunglasses. It was the Audrey Hepburn motif to the fullest. Didn't look half bad on her, actually, but she was fit to be tied and not bothering to conceal it.

"Will," she said imperiously. "I came to the set and was ordered by some creature to wait at the hotel."

I smiled. CeeCee was going to like being called a creature.

Will answered, "I told them to send you back."

This momentarily stumped her, as it kind of spoiled her simmering fury. The Agency blonde, who after two days' of solid work outside was looking as weatherbeaten and weary as the rest of us, couldn't muster up the kind of sidelong glares I expected from her kind. She passed by Rhianna without a look. I wondered if I could do the same. Taking my cue from Holly, I waited a moment to see if we needed to defend ourselves, but Will had Rhianna firmly in hand. Satisfied, Holly moved off. I followed, but was able to eavesdrop easily as Rhianna and Will fell in behind me.

"I came all this way. You could have told me yourself," she hissed.

"I'm going to take a shower." Will sounded almost bored, which only served to notch her up.

"You're not even going to answer me?"

"When I'm out of the shower you can list your complaints."

Bravo! I thought. Cool, terse Will with his deep blue eyes and sanguine smile was my new hero. But if this was the caliber of his girlfriends, I reminded myself, the man probably wasn't worth all the mental energy I'd already invested in him. And he was off-limits anyway.

I peeled off toward my room. Rhianna complained from down the hallway, "That woman was absolutely rude. Who is she? Chains and dungarees. Didn't anyone tell her you're not shooting an MTV video?"

I missed Will's response if there was one.

Three hours later I was showered and possessed of much-needed sleep when CeeCee came rolling in on a deep yawn. She stripped naked, ran herself through the shower, then redressed in a pair of surprisingly modest black pants. I peeked an eye out from under the covers. "You're not sleeping?"

"I can sleep when I'm dead."

"We're leaving at five A.M. tomorrow," I reminded. "We gotta turn the van in by around four."

"I'll be ready."

I watched her pull on a black sleeveless top, cut in at the shoulders, no bra. CeeCee boasts less in the breast department than I do, but the shirt clung in ways that made it not matter. She looked fantastic.

"What's going on?" I asked, pulling my weary bones out of bed and searching for something presentable. It was our last night. Agency might want to party on and if so, Holly, Will, and I should be there. It was an unspoken tradition that the production company pick up the tab for the last night's meal—a "thank you" for being awarded the job in the first place. Hopefully, everyone would make it an early night. We would reconvene for editing/ wrap in LA.

"All my good clothes are dirty," CeeCee said.

Ask a stupid question . . .

I threw on my only still-presentable pants—black jeans—and, after smelling the pits of my only still-presentable black shirt, I determined it was suitable for wearing. I tossed it on, mimicking CeeCee's all-black look. We joined Holly in the restaurant. Will and Rhianna were late, which was nice because it gave us a chance to talk about them. I asked Holly for details on their relationship.

She eyed me suspiciously. "Why do you want to know?"

"I was thinking of having his baby."

She snorted. "They've been dating awhile but I think it's pretty one-sided. She makes a point of coming to all his jobs, whether invited or not. I thought he might be with Kathy, but . . ." She shrugged.

"Kathy's the Agency blonde?"

"Yeah. Though Will doesn't often do bedtime calisthenics on the job," Holly revealed.

"Don't tell me he's saving it all for Rhianna."

"That would be a tragedy," CeeCee added, approaching us after ordering a Heineken at the bar. I'd placed my drink order with our waiter, but CeeCee had been too restless to bide her time. She'd drunk half the bottle by the time my Ketel One martini arrived. Holly, who was drinking club soda, looked kind of envious. She would have a glass of white wine now and again, but the Holy Terror wasn't a huge drinker.

"Oh, fuck it," she suddenly said and ordered the same. "This fucking diet can wait," she added, making her club soda motivation clear.

Since Holly is as lean and mean as a snake, I find her diet talk interesting. But Holly isn't one to give much away, so I let it be. Agency arrived en masse and Will and Rhianna trailed them to the table. We ordered wine and appetizers and luscious entrees. The hotel restaurant was pretty damn good, and as I drank I felt my bones loosen up—along with my inhibitions.

As luck would have it, Rhianna was seated directly across from me with Will on her left. She'd vacuum-packed herself into a royal blue dress that looked good but scarily painted on. I doubted she could breathe. The red hair was down and artfully tucked behind one ear. Enormous teardrop pearl earrings jiggled and bobbed along with her quick, darting movements, which made me grow slightly anxious over time.

I wished I'd brought jewelry to jazz up my own outfit, but I was lucky to have remembered a decent set of clothes, luckier still that they weren't covered in dust and/or general work grime. Rhianna apparently thought CeeCee and I were a matched pair because she asked with fake interest, "Are you two girlfriends?"

"Like in lesbians?" CeeCee asked, never one to worry she might be too direct.

Rhianna was a bit taken aback. She wasn't certain how to respond.

CeeCee forged right on, "Actually, we haven't tried that. What do you think, Blue? Want to make this trip more interesting than we'd planned?"

I could feel Will's intense interest. Actually, this was probably my own imagination. Suddenly I started feeling embarrassed. And with that embarrassment came a blush. I could feel it creep up my neck. To my horror, I was unable to stop it, so I feigned a contact lens attack—though I don't wear the things—and hurried off to the bathroom.

By the time I returned, the conversation had moved on. Why I sometimes have these strange attacks of self-consciousness is a mystery. They happen so rarely I forget I'm even susceptible. Most of the time my tongue is quick and sharp. It's humiliating really to find myself rattled and off-center. My defense is that Will Torrance had gotten under my skin in a way that defied rationality. Even Rhianna's presence hadn't dampened my feelings.

But he was off limits. Off, off, off.

I looked across the table and we clashed eyes. Was I crazy, or was I reading a question in their mysterious blue depths? I felt like I needed air.

CeeCee, in a scene-stealing moment said, "Anyone want to get laid? I'm looking for some experience and I'm not picky."

The men exchanged glances. Three hands shot into the air.

"I guess that counts me out," I drawled, recovering my aplomb most admirably, I felt.

CeeCee looked at the vying contenders. "Damn it," she muttered in self-disgust. "I can't do it. I can't work up the enthusiasm. I want to. But I can't."

"More alcohol," one of the contenders suggested.

"How about a walk in the night air to get you in the mood?" another suggested.

"I've got ribbed condoms," the third tried.

CeeCee sighed and shook her head. "I'm in love with the bastard and I can't cheat. Loyalty sucks."

Rhianna looked down her nose at CeeCee. "Loyalty is an admirable quality."

CeeCee eyed her carefully. I felt bad things brewing. "Maybe we should call it a night," I suggested.

"You haven't had dinner yet," Will pointed out. "Stay awhile."

Rhianna looked ready to explode. I pictured blue Lycra-infused fabric splattered around the room.

"Excuse me!" I called to our waiter. "We need to order."

"And bring us another round of drinks!" Holly added. For a moment I worried she was going to complain about CeeCee being part of our party as CeeCee was definitely below the line and causing a certain amount of dissension. But the Holy Terror was amused. I could see it around the corners of her eyes.

I stole a look at Will. He was watching me, evaluating me the way males evaluate females they're interested in. Rhianna caught our exchange. Her face blanched.

"Why don't you just fuck her and get it over with?" she declared.

"Why don't I?" he called her bluff.

She shot her chair back and stalked from the room. He shot his chair back and disappeared in another direction. Kathy, the Agency blonde, looked worried that he might have been talking about her. Conversation sprang up all around, fast, furious, and loud to cover the moment.

CeeCee looked at me. "I think it's rude you weren't asked first."

"Be careful," Holly warned softly.

"I'm not doing anything," I promised, but it turned out on that, I would be proven wrong.

I woke up in my own bed two days later, squinted an eye at the clock, groaned, then staggered to my feet, carrying a train of covers with me. I was vaguely worried about the taste in my mouth. Some morning breath is worse than others. As far as I remembered I hadn't done anything to create such an offensive smell—no drinking wildly into the night, eating spicy, garlicky food or smoking of any kind. Maybe it was just one of those mornings.

I made the colossal mistake of stepping onto the scales then damn near howled with disbelief. *Five pounds?* I'd gained five pounds over that trip to Sedona?

"Shit."

I'm not as nutty about weight gain as some, but come on . . . it's no fun thinking about days of future dieting and/or, God forbid, exercise. The thought of going to the gym just plain depresses me. A love affair with celery sours in mere days.

I opted for work instead. This would be my first day back to wrap. Wrapping a job takes about a week of office work, depending on the size of the job. Sometimes it takes both a production manager and a production coordinator to slog through all the paperwork. *House About You?* had a small budget, so I was wearing both hats and therefore putting in thirteen-hour days. This does NOT mean I was earning twice the salary, just doing twice the work. But to be competitive, production companies resort to minimizing staff when they can.

I was deep into the petty cash receipts when Sean sauntered into the room. He was onboard for basic gofer stuff while we wrapped, but I could tell he was still miffed about being left out of the shoot. I said, "Hey, there."

"Hi." He was cautious.

"Tom's got the order for lunch," I said. "Do you need more petty cash?"

"Yeah . . ."

Alarm bells sounded in my brain. "You're keeping your money to yourself," I reminded, feeling like his mother and hating the role.

"Yep." Surly, now.

I'd been hunched over a desk with papers sticking out at all angles, but now I gave him my full attention. "Sean," I said in a low voice, not wanting Tom to overhear. "The petty cash mess from the last job is hanging on like stink on shit. Neither you, nor I, nor anyone else can let that happen again."

"I sent Bettina to you with everything," he burst out. "She had the receipts and the money!"

"Yeah, Bettina had some of the stuff, but we work with cash and purchase orders," I explained patiently. "Lots and lots of greenbacks floating around. The only thing between us and total financial chaos is our accounting system."

"Jesus H. Christ," he muttered.

I said, "And about Bettina . . . she was working with Liam Engleston."

"Who?" He blinked, totally perplexed.

"The caterer? Apparently supplies lots of commercial shoots? They knew each other and it didn't help things."

"Oh . . ." He thought about that. "Yeah." On a note of discovery, he added, "Oh, yeah. That's how I met her."

"What do you mean?"

"She brought over some papers from him. The contracts, I think."

"She didn't give them to me."

"Oh."

We stared at each other. I saw now how Bettina had floated into the mix. I didn't know how to tell Sean that Bettina's association with Liam had created a political hot potato for me. Sean's brain just didn't work that way. He was utterly devoid of manipulation himself and didn't see it in others. Drifty Bettina hadn't brought me anything from Liam Engleston, but maybe he'd given her something to hand over. But I'd never seen it nor signed it, so who knew what the real case was? And what kind of company would trust someone like Bettina as their messenger?

It all served to remind me to keep personal relationships separate from business ones. I'd messed up with Sean and that had led to this mess with Bettina and Liam Engleston. I was done.

"Ginny, line one," said Laurie, Wyatt Productions' receptionist.

This surprised me as most everyone I know, business or personal, calls me on my cell. Sean got that I was busy and turned to Tom to finish the lunch order. I answered the office line crisply, "This is Ginny."

"This is Will. Holly not around? She's not answering her cell."

My heart skipped a little, then calmed down as I realized the call wasn't really for me. *And I didn't want it to be, right?* "That's strange. She's always hooked to her cell."

"Agency and *House About You?* are getting together again tonight. Name a good place to meet for dinner and drinks. We need to send them out happy."

With Holly unavailable, I was suddenly in charge. I grimaced. "How upscale do you want? Casa del Mar's nice, right on the water, overlooking the great Pacific. Or, I can name a great burger spot on Montana."

"Father's Office?"

"You know it."

"Good place," he agreed, but sounded like he wanted more options.

I racked my brain. Will lived in west LA and obviously knew quite a few Santa Monica spots himself. I could tell he wanted me to come up with something new, different, and perfect. Isn't that what we all want? And I sure as hell wanted to impress the hell out of him. For future work and . . . just because.

"There's the Love Shack," I said, more as a joke than a real option. I needed time. "The food's merely so-so, but they make a mean drink. I'm personally fond of the Amethyst."

"What kind of food?"

"Seafood. But up the street—"

"Let's try the Love Shack," he said, surprising me. I instantly worried my local hangout wasn't going to be good enough.

It's amazing how I can obsess over these things. Will told me to make the reservation for eleven people, counting Holly and myself. I fervently hoped Rhianna would not be one of the guests but it was highly likely she would be.

Holly appeared just as Sean brought back our lunch order. Since she hadn't ordered, she snacked on extra french fries and pickles and cole slaw that we cobbled together from our meals. I gave her the particulars about our evening ahead. I knew if she'd made other plans she would break them. With Holly, work came first. She merely asked, "Where's the Love Shack?" to which I gave her directions. She added, "I'm glad you're getting to know Will. He's directing the Tuaca commercial."

"He is?" I tried to hide my excitement. We'd been awarded the job for the liqueur company: *To You, To Me, Tuaca!* The shoot was slated for the following week and it was to film outside one of the houses on the Venice Canals. It was going to be a parking nightmare, but a fun shoot. Lots of people on the deck drinking Tuaca; others in replicas of gondolas floating on the canal beyond. Kind of your fake Italian/Spanish combo. Like fusion food. Mix 'em together and see what happens.

"I know you're wrapping, but we need to get deep into pre-pro on this one."

"I'm on it," I said, wondering where I'd find the extra hours.

I called Jill straight away and asked her to be the caterer. She said, "Thank God, you're back. I nearly went crazy with both you and CeeCee out of town. But I can't do it, Blue. I've got two jobs going at the same time. I'm crazed already."

"Bummer." I instantly told myself it was somebody else's problem from here on out. No more babying the crew. In fact, I decided to give the task to the woman Holly had hired as production coordinator for the next job. Let her come up with the caterer.

"I need to talk to you," Jill added.

I glanced around the office. "Make it quick. I'm buried here."

"I'm back with Ian."

"Really?" Hearing my surprised tone, Tom looked up questioningly. I waved him off. He's a gossipmonger of the worst kind, and though I sometimes try to feed his habit, Jill back with Ian would barely be a blip on his "interest" radar. Tom likes to find out if anyone slept with anyone they shouldn't have, that sort of thing. Jill and Ian reuniting was way too tame. From my point of view, however, it was pretty strong stuff.

"When did this happen?"

"I just broke down," she said. "Went over to his place, told him I missed him, that kind of thing. Told him . . ."

"I'm listening."

"We talked about the other thing. A little bit. He knows I'm trying."

"Well, good." She had serious trouble saying anorexia aloud. "What about the other woman?"

"Oh, he wasn't seeing anyone. He was just dating. It wasn't anything."

"So, you're back together again."

"Uh-huh. We haven't had sex yet, but we're getting there."

"Why?"

"Sex? Oh . . . because . . ." I waited. "You'll think it's really stupid. Ginny, I accepted the ring. Ian and I are engaged. We've decided to hold off having sex again till we're married."

I sat back in my chair. I really didn't know what to say. "Wow." Tom looked over again and I frowned at him and shook my head.

"Let's go out tonight, just the girls, and celebrate," she pleaded. She knew I was flummoxed.

"I can't. I've got a command performance for work tomorrow and for the next couple of weeks." I paused and asked quietly, "Y'sure you don't want to have sex 'til marriage? This isn't some kind of test, is it?"

"We're just trying to be romantic, all right? Is that so goddamn hard to get? And I'm eating like a PIG, if you want to know. Starches and sugar and crap. I've probably gained five pounds."

"I'm up five pounds after Sedona."

"Oh."

"We'll talk about it Saturday morning," I suggested.

"What's going on?" Tom asked as I hung up.

"Shut up and throw me a Jolly Rancher."

Dinner at the Love Shack started with appetizers of mussels and calamari. They were fairly tasty and no one complained, which I took as a personal compliment. I ordered Amethysts all around. The women were delighted. The men worried about the lavender color.

Rhianna was nowhere to be seen.

I'd managed to work things so I was seated next to Will. I don't know what I was hoping for, but he just looked so great. And he smelled good, too. A clean scent. Just a hint that nevertheless filled my head. Whenever I leaned in to say something I caught a whiff of it and inhaled deeply.

I had to be careful about my alcohol consumption because I had way too much work in my future. Normally a production manager gets to choose her/his production coordinator as the two jobs practically intermingle, but I'd left it to Holly in order to get the Tuaca commercial ball rolling. I'd managed to confer with the new coordinator exactly once while I was wrapping the Sedona job. It had not been an auspicious beginning. Holly's recruit wasn't doing the job at the usual breakneck speed commercial production required. Since I was bound and determined not to fall down in Will's eyes it meant I was going to have to be especially vigilant in my job—and that meant possibly riding my pokey new coordinator.

I lifted my Amethyst and said to Will, "Looks like we'll be drinking Tuaca soon instead of these."

"You're the production manager?" He slid me a look to which I nodded. "Good."

That warmed me from the inside out. I could feel the smile that wouldn't leave my lips. *Oh, Ginny, Ginny, Ginny . . .* I warned myself. My hormones, however, had clapped their hands over their ears, singing, "La, la, la, la, la," over my own objections.

"Where's your friend?" Will asked.

For a moment I wasn't sure whom he meant. "Oh. CeeCee. She was just helping out on the Sedona job. Actually, she works at KLAS. Total class alternative rock."

"An oxymoron," he observed.

"CeeCee's taken over the evening show. She was sort of in between it all when we were in Sedona."

"Still in love with 'the bastard'?"

"Her boss."

"Not a good idea," said Will.

I filed that away. Yes. Not a good idea. I asked boldly, "Where's your friend?"

He frowned. "Oh, Rhianna. She couldn't make it tonight."

Oh, what a terrible tragedy, I thought, my heart light.

"And she won't be at the Tuaca job," he stated with certainty. "It's going to be a tight fit. I don't want her there."

You and me both, Bucko. I nodded. Kathy, our Agency friend, suddenly called for Will's attention. I was glad we were dealing with a different agency group for the Tuaca commercial. I was tired of competing with Kathy whether she had any hold on Will or not.

Checking my watch, I begged off early. I really had to go home. Will, as it turned out, felt the same way and we walked into the cool evening together. He asked if I needed a ride as he'd called a cab. I shook my head, pointing out that I lived just down the block. I hoped he would take note, but he just said, "See you next week," leaving me a bit deflated as I hoofed it home alone.

I ended up working like a Trojan wrapping the Sedona job for the rest of the week. My attention was split because my new snail of a production coordinator wasn't exactly blazing through pre-pro on the Tuaca job. The truth was she wasn't worth shit, which put me in a bind. I was forced to complain to Holly, who told me to do whatever I wanted. Thanks a lot, I thought. I tried nicely to fire Barb the Snail but she broke down and cried and promised serious improvement. Softy that I am, I ended up giving her a second chance. By the time I moved my full attention to the Tuaca job, production was in such a state of chaos that it was still in shambles after several twenty-hour days. Barb the Snail turned out to also be Barb the Whiner. By the end of the week I was teetering on the verge of a breakdown.

When Saturday morning rolled around all I wanted to do was sleep. I didn't think I had the time and energy to meet with my friends. I tried to beg off on the phone but Jill yelled at me that I had promised. I yelled back that it was work, okay? Then, before things turned truly vicious I suddenly capitulated. What the hell. I needed the break. I'd make up the time some other way.

My phone rang just as I was leaving the condo. Debating answering it, I checked caller ID only to see an "out of state" message. I touched the green answer key and said cautiously, "Hello?"

"I caught you at home." Kristl's voice was full of happy disbelief. "I was just going to leave a message rather than bother you on your cell."

Since when had she gotten so solicitous? "How's life in the Emerald City?" I asked.

"Where? Oh. Seattle. Yeah, that's true. It always reminds me of *The Wizard of Oz.* It's going great. I'm working at a bar around the corner and Brandon's been really busy at the office."

"What does he do?"

"I don't know. His company makes widgets of some kind

for computers." She sounded inordinately bored. "I just wanted to check in."

"Nothing new here, really. Work. Oh. My mom's coming to stay with me. She's getting her eyes done in LA."

"Really? When?"

"Sometime next week, I think, but I'm on another job so I don't know what's going to happen."

We talked along in the same vein for a while, then Kristl said she had to go. I could tell she was wistful. I wanted to ask her about wedding plans but held my tongue. I did manage to tell her Jill and Ian were engaged. She rallied briefly. I think it made her feel good to have someone in the same boat as she was, but by the time we hung up I got the distinct impression things weren't going well up north.

I arrived at Sammy's to find Daphne was the only one of my friends already there. Before I could even greet her, she said, "I went to see Dr. Dick! You were right, Blue. He's sooooo fabulous."

Instantly I felt threatened. "Told you he was," I sniffed snottily.

"Oh, my God. He wears these pressed jeans. I've never been a really huge denim fan. I mean, apart from a Gap item or two. But then I saw Dr. Dick. Oh, my God," she said again.

I snatched up a menu and buried my nose in it. I know Sammy's menu backwards and forwards but I had to feign total absorption or scream. I hate these selfish moments. They're so juvenile. It seems so wrong to have to school myself into behaving like an adult, but the truth of the matter was I wanted to clap my hand over Daphne's mouth and stop her from saying one more nice thing about Dr. Dick.

"I'm following the plan," Daphne went on, oblivious. "No more loser guys. I'm through with Leo. You were all right. I can't be with someone who sleeps with an ex-girlfriend. It doesn't matter why. I told Dr. Dick all about it. How we all decided to attack and address some of our worst failings."

"I thought I was just reviewing the Ex-Files."

"And fixing them," Daphne declared, not to be dissuaded. "One by one, you said. How are you doing, by the way?"

"Just peachy."

"Doesn't really sound like it, from your tone," Daphne pointed out.

"It's going," I said repressively.

"Dr. Dick commended us for our 'group therapy' tactics. Keeping things bottled up or avoiding looking at them or generally running away from them—that's not healthy. We need to tell each other our true feelings. It's the basis of communication."

"Daphne," I said, leaning forward. "You're starting to piss me off."

She blinked her blue eyes.

"I've talked to Dr. Dick, too. Maybe we shouldn't discuss our sessions with him with each other."

"Oh, it's no problem," she said, relieved. "Everything I talked about—it's nothing you haven't heard. I told him that I always pick the wrong guys. But I told him I'm really paying attention to what's important in a partner now. In fact, I made a list to keep me focused." She suddenly snatched up her purse and started pawing through it. "Where is it . . ."

"It's okay," I said weakly.

"*Voilà!*" She yanked a slip of paper from her purse triumphantly and thrust it at me. I had no choice but to take it, but all this talk of Dr. Dick was making me feel uncomfortable and contrary. I could barely glance at the words, although a few jumped out at me: *emotionally mature, don't go for looks, hair is secondary to intelligence, kindness above attitude.*

She could have been describing Mr. Rogers.

Instantly I wanted to kick myself. Of course those attributes were important. Did I want her to find another Leo? I was saved from spiraling into a true well of self-loathing by the arrival of CeeCee, and then Jill and Ian.

Ian. The *fucking* asshole.

Is it wrong of me to admit that I've never been a fan? The guy's tall, decent-looking, intense and, to my mind, devoid of all humor. No, that's not true. He finds those stupid kind of guy-things funny, which seems weird, being that he's so narrow and sort of self-righteous. This isn't to say he doesn't have his moments. He does. It's just that he and I are polar opposites, and we never seem to find a middle ground.

Ian inclined his head of dark hair my direction. "Ginny."

I inclined my head back. "Ian."

He said hello to everyone else and I did a silent, surreptitious inventory of my friends' reactions. Daphne grinned wildly and said how happy she was to see him again and congratulations and wow, she was so excited for both of them. CeeCee shook Ian's hand and said, "Nice job," to which Jill beamed and Ian smiled. The guy does have nice teeth. His set rivals Daphne's for overall whiteness, which is saying something. Jill gave me a sharp look and I forced myself to lie lightly, "I'm really amazed and glad you're engaged."

Ian shot me a look. "Are you?"

The *fucking* asshole. He's nothing, if not perceptive, damn him. Well, I probably deserved that. I searched my feelings, thought about going for honesty over niceness, caught the thunderous, warning look on Jill's face and lied again, "You bet."

Daphne launched into tales about Dr. Dick, and CeeCee started tapping her fingers and looking around, ready for a smoke. The waiter took our order before she catapulted from her chair and headed outside. I wanted to follow and hear the latest on her affairs at the station, but abandoning Jill-Ian on their first public outing since the engagement wouldn't have gone over well.

So, I suffered. I wanted to be happy for Jill. I really did. And I don't think this was marriage-envy or anything like that on my part. God, I hoped not. I think I'd just lost the ability to believe that tying the knot will help a dicey relationship. Ninety-nine percent of the time it seems to ruin everything. But even couples who KNOW what their problems are still seem intent on getting to the altar. Marriage above all else.

We all made small talk instead of real conversation; a function of having Ian with us. I watched as Jill made a serious attempt to eat her breakfast of fruit, a poached egg, wheat toast, and black coffee. She managed the coffee and a teensy little bit of fruit. Feeling my eyes on her, she placed a big bite of egg and toast in her mouth and rolled it around awhile. I was afraid to think of what that bite of food looked like by the time she managed to choke it down. She glared at me in a way that said, "Happy now?" to which I started laughing.

"What?" she demanded.

"You know," I told her, and everyone at the table looked at us askance but neither of us explained.

I tried to engage CeeCee in some conversation about the radio station but she seemed as remote as a distant star. I didn't take her in-person absence personally; she clearly was just someplace else. I did ask in an aside if she still wanted to chew on her boss's eyelashes. She managed to engage long enough to state flatly, "No."

I didn't take it as a good sign.

I was thinking how Ian's appearance had taken the fun "girl" thing out of our meeting and wondering if I could vamoose anytime soon when Daphne launched into her session with Dr. Dick to the half-hearted listening pleasure of the whole group. I mumbled an excuse about getting ready for my mother's visit and lammed out. As much as I love my girlfriends, sometimes it's just plain hard to be social.

The Tuaca job started with a bang. Literally. I had barely gotten to set when one of the production trucks backfired so loudly some of the serious security people hit the deck as if we were being attacked. I was on the walkie to Will and froze midsyllable. "What the fuck was that?" he demanded. He was down on the canal, setting up a shot.

"Backfiring," I told him, though at that point I wasn't really too sure. My heart was doing a raging gallop across my chest.

"Huh," he responded and clicked off.

I checked to see that everyone was alive and well and then told one of the PAs to drive that truck back to the rental agency and get another. Nerves tended to get frayed on a job no matter what; I had no time for faulty equipment.

Barb treated me like Beelzebub incarnate though I was trying extra hard to make things work between us. She resented that I'd assigned her the catering duty and she'd hired a group who delivered great food but ran around like Keystone Cops, forgetting everything from plastic forks to cups to chairs. Their disorganization was a thing to behold. PAs were picking up paper plates and napkins all afternoon that swirled around in their wake.

By three o'clock the team was already frazzled and there were days and days of work still ahead of us. I got off about eleven that night and celebrated by cracking open a bottle of Tuaca as I walked to my front door. "To you, to me, Tuaca!" I declared as I took a gulp at the same moment I threaded my key in the door. I didn't have time for heavy drinking, but a sampling of the product definitely seemed in order.

To my shock the door suddenly flung open from the inside. "Jesus," I sputtered, the second before I realized it had to be my mother, arriving from the north. She's the only one who has the key.

A moment later my jaw dropped. Standing in front of me was not the smiling, real estate maven Lorraine Bluebell, but a man about my own age, whose lips were pulled into a smile of greeting behind his neat, reddish-gray beard.

It was Don the Devout. Ex-File Number Five.

"Good God," I said fervently.

Chapter

14

"Still taking the name of the Lord in vain?" Don chided me gently.

My initial surprise turned to irritation. Don clearly hadn't changed one iota since I'd bolted from our relationship, practically screaming. I wanted to point out that it had been *he* who'd howled out the Lord's name in frenzied, panting lust the last time we'd made love. If that's not in vain, what is? But I managed to hold my tongue. Barely. After a moment of silence while we sized each other up, I tipped up the Tuaca bottle and swallowed a long draft. Wiping the top of the bottle with my sleeve, I asked, "Want some?"

"No, thank you." Don was the picture of strained politeness.

Mom appeared from behind him at that moment. "Virginia!" she greeted me in delight, her eyes taking in my bottle of Tuaca and my generally scraggly appearance in one sweeping glance. But she was too happy to see me to comment on it.

She reached out and hugged me close. She smelled great, but she nearly bowled me over with her big-ass purse. A green one. Satiny. With a thick gold lock on the front that worked as its clasp. She explained, "I called Don and he said he was going to be in LA while I was here, so I invited him over."

"Oh. Goody."

Don added, "I bought a Jeep dealership in San José. I'm looking around down here, too."

I scrutinized him some more. The hair on his head had decidedly more gray in it than his beard. *Jesus, are all my exes going gray?* I thought in horror. This could seriously reflect on me. A moment later I dismissed the idea. The problem was more likely that I simply picked the wrong kind of man. Poor genes. Early aging.

Don's blue eyes regarded me as critically as I regarded him. I said, as an icebreaker, "You're a used car salesman?"

"Only you would make a comment like that," he responded on a sigh, turning to look at my mother. They had a pact, I saw. They were the adults; I, the errant child. Well, okay. If that was the game, I was up for it. I tipped up my bottle of Tuaca again, keeping one eye on the two of them as I chugalugged.

"I've invited Don to stay with us for a while," Mom said. "He can have the extra room and you and I can share your bed."

I choked, sputtered, and spit out half of my last gulp. Eyes tearing, I said in a faint rasp, "I'll take the couch."

"You don't mind?" Mom asked, concerned.

Mind? How could I possibly mind? My mother and one of my least favorite Ex-Files were moving in with me.

I said to Don, "God giveth and God taketh away."

"What is that supposed to mean?"

My mother, bless her soul, looked faintly amused. She coughed delicately into her fist to hide a smile. "I like your hair," I said. She'd cut it into a pageboy style. It was streaky blonde.

"What is that supposed to mean?" Don demanded again. He really had no sense of humor.

"I'm not the one who knows all about religion," I said, all innocence. "You tell me."

I thought it was a good exit line so I headed for the stairs.

Two days later I watched morosely as the camera arm tilted downward like a loose noodle over the faux Venetian gondola. Faulty equipment. One of our PAs was on his way to the camera rental store for a replacement, but we were already way behind schedule. And the time wasted had put Will in a dark mood, which made it impossible for anyone to talk to him.

This was too bad, as I'd developed a serious crush on him. While I worked in the makeshift trailer-office my thoughts were definitely X-rated when it came to Will. Like Dr. Dick, he wore jeans. They were tight enough across his derriere to warrant drooling; loose enough to allow for the bending and stretching he needed to film. He wore white shirts with sleeves rolled up the forearms and basic sneakers. His dark hair called to me. I ached to dig my fingers through it. I didn't have any desire to chew on his eyelashes but I had various other things in mind. *Lots* of various other things in mind.

None of it was a good idea, but I'd moved past my own lengthy list of reasons not to get involved with someone I worked with.

Tom was back at the main office and therefore I was short of Jolly Ranchers. I could have used something to occupy my mouth and tongue; watching Will without kissing, licking, and tasting him left me in an overall unsatisfied state that I really didn't have time for.

"What are you looking at?" Barb asked.

"My past," I said. I liked to keep our conversation to a minimum.

She frowned and went back to work. My comment had been the truth. Will really did hold a disturbing resemblance to Ex-File Number Six, Mark McGruder. Black Mark. Even though Lang, Mr. Famous Actor, was the Ex-File I didn't like to count; Black Mark was the one I never wanted to talk about. It was embarrassing for me to admit I'd stayed with him as long as I did. Maybe it was because he crossed my path directly after Don the Devout. Maybe that's why I needed to be with someone so totally wrong for me. Black Mark drank like a sailor and swore like one, too. He didn't beat me or threaten me or hurt me in any way, but he was damn scary when he was drunk, which, as I've said before, was all the time. I'd just come off a year and a half with Don the Devout, who was the first Ex-File after the Lang fiasco. At first Don had been fine. Like a Holiday Inn: no surprises. But toward the end all his genuflecting and "grateful to God on high" stuff wore me down. I can handle anything—almost—in moderation. But I'm the kind of person who thinks religion matters most when it's kept personal and private. Don was the polar opposite. He was all about religion all the time. No time off for good behavior. No time off for bad behavior. No time off, period. I found myself looking for excuses to break dates. One time I made an appointment to have my teeth cleaned, just to be busy, and it was well within my six months between visits. My dentist seriously worried I was developing a fetish. He still scrutinizes the dates of my appointments, making sure I'm not coming in too often. Go figure.

Anyway, one day I just broke.

It was while I was cooking dinner for Don and myself. Not that making the "family meal" was a regular occurrence for me. Far from it. But Don had gotten some kind of promotion at work, so it was something of a special occasion. I was using the Cutco knife my mother had bought me the Christmas before and let me tell you, those things are sharp. Early into the evening Don began watching the level of the wine bottle, as he'd become increasingly concerned about my intake. If anyone did that to me now, I'd kick his butt out the door, but at the time I was deeply committed to my dysfunctional relationship and I'd simply learned to circumvent his eagle-eyed observance. It was a game to me, and I learned to sneak extra drinks when his back was turned. Looking back, it's amazing to me that I didn't turn into a raging alcoholic during this period. So, while he carefully poured us glasses of wine from one of the two labels of Syrah he would deign to drink, I poured myself generous helpings from a secret, second bottle—one of the cheapest, most unsophisticated Cabernets that Sav-On had to offer—hidden in a lower cupboard. I would mix my Syrah and my Cabernet and smack my lips in satisfaction. Yes, I have no palate. Don and I did not live together, though he made noises to that effect—to the point of hinting of marriage—so I was able to keep up this strange double life for quite a while.

I was already mildly inebriated when he came over that fateful night. And with Cutco knife in hand, I was unprepared when Don suddenly came up behind me and began nuzzling my neck. One accidental swipe and I damn near sliced off my finger. I said, without the proper shock and concern, "I see a trip to the emergency room in my future."

Don gazed in horror at the blood welling from the tip of my middle finger. Then he looked me right in the face. "You're drunk!"

"Buzzed," I corrected.

"You're drunk. And you've nearly cut your finger off!" With rapid, angry movements he yanked off several sheets of paper towels and wrapped them around my hand. He hustled me out to the car. I felt very sheepish and small at first, and it didn't help when the nurses and staff at the ER gave me sidelong glances. Please note, this was not because they necessarily thought I was drunk. It was because Don *told* them I was drunk. But trust me on this, my little cleaving action had sobered me up like yesterday.

Anyway, the doctor came in, numbed my finger with Lidocaine and stitched me up. Don and I were back at my tiny apartment within the hour. I braced myself for further remonstrations as Don regarded me like a recalcitrant child. He said, "Virginia, what am I going to do with you?"

I don't know about you, but any man who wonders what he's going to do with me is asking to have his lights punched out.

I said, succinctly, "I just had a message from God. He thinks it's time for you to go home."

"That's not funny."

"It wasn't meant to be."

"I'm not leaving you alone."

I watched him settle himself on the couch, his jaw tight. I headed for my bedroom, threw some clothes in a suitcase, then marched to the door.

Don smiled patiently and said, "You're not leaving," as if I couldn't possibly walk out on him, great guy that he was.

I extended my bandaged middle finger toward him in the time-honored way, then slammed the door behind me. This created a bit of a problem, as I'd slammed out of my own apartment, but Don eventually vacated and I made certain he took all of his belongings with him.

For the briefest of periods I was alone. Boyfriendless. A little scared.

And then I met Mark.

Don had definitely left me questioning my alcohol intake. Was I drinking too much? It was definitely not a good sign to hide alcohol consumption. I mean, that must be rule number one on the deadly signs of alcoholism. Could I be on the path to ruination, so help me God?

Well, I'm here to tell you, after a few months with Mark McGruder I could probably apply for sainthood—in the matter of my alcohol consumption as compared to his—and at least be considered.

The night I met Mark I was out with Jill and Ian. This was maybe five or six years ago. We were kind of into that Lord of the Dance thing and we'd gone to a St. Patrick's Day party at a local bar that had dancers performing all weekend long.

Mark was there with some buddies, drinking Guinness. He made a few sneering comments about the dancers, more amusing than truly horrifying, and I was so happy to be around someone who possessed a sense of humor that I overlooked the fact that he was making fun of them. I took one look at Mark—his dark hair, brilliant blue eyes, and strong biceps— and thought, "Mine." He was the antithesis of Don. Wild. Sexy. Walking with the devil.

And Black Mark possessed a killer smile. I mean, killer.

Jill and I had started out with green beer; Ian, Irish coffee. It was nine o'clock in the morning. Someone said something about kegs and eggs, and we were suddenly having breakfast with huge glass mugs of Guinness. Jill was struggling with everything. I wasn't as keenly aware of her eating habits then, and I put her pickiness down to an overall fussiness about food. She was a fledgling caterer at the time, working for a big company that did megaevents. I was a production coordinator/production assistant, which means I was doing two jobs with minimal pay.

Mark squinched himself onto my barstool. We teetered precariously, but I was breathless. Jill-Ian left me alone, though Jill shot me interested looks from time to time. I was just enjoying the hell out of myself.

Mark said, "You have a boyfriend, don't you."

"Nope. Had. Over. Completely."

"Ahhh . . ." He picked up my tone and grinned like a satyr. I grinned back over the top of my Guinness. When I set it down he reached a thumb to my lip, wiped off a bit of foam, then sucked that thumb hard, all the time watching me. Overt? You bet. Effective? Darn-tootin'.

We were at his place by one-thirty. My hands were clawing at him as we ground together on his couch, first with all our clothes, and then finally with none. Mark growled and thrust and generally lived out some kind of primal mating ritual. I was right there, digging and yanking with my hands, pulling his lips with my teeth. It was wild. Unabashed.

Deeply satisfying. I came over and over again, and so did Mark.

So began our relationship.

So began the daily drinking on his part, the teetotaling on mine.

So began the yelling, shrieking, slamming of doors, and punching of walls.

We lasted five months, two days, and nine hours. It was about five months and two days too long. And maybe a few hours . . .

I came back to my apartment one night and fell into bed and slept and slept and slept. I slept all weekend. Then I slept all week. On a Saturday night I lifted my head to the sound of my blasting, ringing phone. Mark was on the other end of the line, drunk, querulous, and horny.

I hung up and slept some more.

Jill told me later that she had a dream about me the first night I met Mark. In the dream, she said, I looked her right in the eye and said, "Don't tell me. I already know. But I have to do this."

And maybe I did. Maybe I needed a complete exorcism of Don the Devout. Maybe Black Mark was my subconscious way to put that into effect. It sure as hell worked.

Now, I looked out the window of our trailer and watched Will at work, adjusting the cameras, looking through the viewfinder. I gazed past him to our gondolas and our wilting partiers. Idly I wondered why a drink with decidedly Spanish origins was being promoted with Italian accoutrements.

Barb broke into my thoughts. "Your mother called."

"Here?" I demanded, turning on her. Mom's eye surgery was scheduled for this morning. I'd called her cell phone several times but only reached her sunny, Real-Estate-Lady voice: "Hi, this is Lorraine. Please leave a message and I'll get back to you as soon as possible. Thank you!"

Barb nodded. "She said she was in good hands and not to worry."

"Well, I'm worried." I checked my watch. "Don's picking her up because I can't and it just pisses me off."

"You're lucky there's someone there to do it for you."

I gave her a long look. I absolutely hate it when people point out how 'lucky' I am about anything. She sensed my mood and turned away from me. I hoped, probably in vain, that she was actually going to do some work.

Holly swept in from outside, banging the trailer door against the wall, shaking the whole kit and caboodle. "What?" she demanded, picking up the vibes.

"I didn't say anything."

"You said you were worried about your mother," Barb corrected. "That you were pissed off that you couldn't be with her."

Holly frowned. "What's wrong with your mother?"

"She's having her eyes done," Barb put in. "A friend of Ginny's is picking her up."

"So, there's no problem?" Holly asked me.

"None at all."

Holly shot a glance at Barb, then me. I turned to my erstwhile coordinator and commented, "Way to be a suck-up."

"What do you mean?" Barb asked, but she subsided into injured silence, not as obtuse as she would have me believe.

"I hope Mom's on her way back to my house," I told Holly. "I just can't reach her on her cell."

"You don't want her to be alone." Holly's frown deepened. She wanted me at work, but it was hard to deny the "sick mother" card.

"No, I'm sure she's with Don the Devout. Everything's fine."

Relieved that I wasn't bailing, Holly swept into what she needed me to do to finish up the day. By the time we got through all the notes and checklists, an hour had passed. Holly headed out and I turned back to the myriad phone messages I needed to follow up on. Most of the rest of the day Barb ignored me, favoring me with her rigid back, but when I looked up suddenly, drawn by a kind of subliminal magnetic force—a sixth sense you don't even know you've engaged—I caught her laserlike gaze drilling into the back of my head. She dropped her eyes swiftly, but it was too late. I knew. But I didn't have the energy to be totally bugged. I reminded myself that we only had a couple of more days of working together. Then I could leave her to her own personal weirdness and move on.

Unfortunately, only a couple of more days with Barb meant only a couple of more days with Will.

"Who's Don the Devout?" Barb asked.

It was a rarity when she addressed me directly. She must really want to know. I punched out my mother's cell phone number again. "Ex-File Number Five," I said unhelpfully.

"Is he—religious—or something?"

"Yep."

"You say it so disparagingly."

"Do I?"

"Yes," she said primly.

As I counted the rings I noticed it then: the charm bracelet that swung from her wrist. It had been tinkling and chiming away for days, driving me crazy. With sudden insight, I zeroed in on the chatty jewelry and realized all the charms were religious icons of one kind or another.

"Don's a priggish, judgmental pain in the ass. It has nothing to do with religion and everything to do with him." I added pointedly, "Some people are just made that way."

It went sailing right over her head. She scolded, "Maybe you should call him something else, then."

I thought it over. "Like Don the Dickweed?"

Her neck flushed and she bent back over her work. I could tell by the pinch of her lips that I'd really pissed her off. This made me feel inordinately good as I gave up on my mom's cell number and called my condo.

I was relieved when Don picked up. "Virginia Bluebell's residence," he said in his careful way.

"Damn it, Don," I said without heat. "The name's Ginny. It's not that hard. Get it right. Is Mom there? How's she doing?"

"She's fine," he said coolly. "She's resting on your couch."

This was the couch I'd chosen as my new bed because as much as I love my mother, I didn't feel like sleeping with her. Unfortunately, the past couple of nights I'd been teetering on its edge. Maybe that's why I've been testier than usual.

"May I talk to her?" I asked through gritted teeth.

"I'll take her the phone."

Well, finally. Hallelujah. Don had clearly not improved with age. I probably should have been thankful that Don had stepped in as my mother's chauffeur when it became clear that I couldn't. But Don has a way of scraping my nerves raw. After Lang I was looking for stability and stoic strength, two qualities I prized to the exclusion of ones more in keeping with my nature: flexibility and the need to get the hell out of trouble first, ask questions later. Don definitely possessed stability and stoic strength. But I'd long since gotten over my need for those traits above all else.

Sometimes I wonder how I ended up with Don at all, but the truth is, I'd definitely been physically attracted to him in the early days. At that time his hair had been reddish-blonde—not gray—and he'd been as fit as a man could be: rock-hard muscles, taut skin, strong limbs. Not that Lang had been any slouch in that department, but Don was like Atlas.

And he was nice to me and showed me attention. He made me feel like I was first . . . something Mr. Famous Actor could never have done. So, I fell in lust/love with Don. And then I fell out. But it took a couple of years in between. And then five months, two days, and nine hours with Black Mark. Good God, this skipping along the Ex-File lane was enough to make me rethink my heterosexuality.

"Hello, Ginny?" Mom said into the phone, sounding a little shaky.

"Are you all right?" I said with concern.

"Oh, sure. Don's been taking great care of me. But my face is swollen."

"Kind of to be expected?"

"Thank God for pain pills, huh?" She laughed softly.

"You're going to look beautiful," I told her.

Sometimes I shock myself at what a liar I can be. Not that I was really lying. I was just soothing. But it's so out of character for me to be a caregiver that I marveled at how quickly I went into this mode. Zero to sixty in one second flat.

"Thanks," she said. "I'm sleeping on your couch. Will you be home soon?"

"As soon as I can make it," I promised, suddenly wanting to be with her with every fiber of my being.

I hung up, torn. I wanted to leave right then and there. This was irrational, as I knew Don would take better care of my mother than about anyone else on the planet could. But *I* needed it. I wanted it.

I was about an inch away from just running out on Barb and Holly and the whole commercial and damn the consequences when Barb, seeming to sense I was a flight risk, said quickly, "I'm sure your friend Don's taking great care of your mother. He sounds perfect for the job."

She only wanted me to stay because she was afraid of the pile of extra work. If it weren't for that I knew she'd be waving the flag in front of my face, urging me to tear out of there. She was the kind who would love to have me do something serious enough to jeopardize not only this job but my career. It gave me pause.

And that was just long enough for Holly to bang open the trailer door one more time and say, "That new PA got in a traffic accident. Fucked up the rented van and broke his leg."

Barb gasped. "Not Daniel!"

"Is he all right?" I asked.

"At the ER. He's such a moron. What is he, like fourteen?"

"Twenty," Barb assured. Then, "Maybe nineteen or eighteen."

"Call Sean," I said.

"Why wasn't he on this job, again?" Holly asked as she headed outside.

I shrugged, looking through my cell phone listing. Should I mention that Sean wasn't much older? That most PA's were young? That Sean had a tendency to smoke that devil weed?

"Hey, Sean," I said to his cell phone's voice mail. "It's Ginny. We could really use you on the Tuaca job. If you haven't already got another—" I heard a beep in my ear alerting me to a call coming in. Guessing it was Sean, I hung up and answered.

"Hey," Sean said, not bothering to hide his surprise. "You leaving me a message?"

I explained that we needed another PA, adding, "If you're not on another job, please, please . . . jump on board."

"You sure you want me?"

I made myself not be irked by his need for affirmation. After all, I'd been bobbing and weaving where he was concerned and he wanted to pin me down. "As sure as death and taxes."

"Yeah . . ." That confused him, but he said cheerily, "I'm ready to go. Tell me where and I'll be there tomorrow."

"Any chance you could be here today?" I glanced at the clock. It was five P.M.

"Will I get paid for a whole day?"

"I guarantee it."

He whooped with delight and clicked off.

Barb said, "Nobody seems all that concerned about Daniel."

"Oh, we are," I assured. "It's just that we don't have time right now."

I banged out of the trailer, too, glad, glad, glad to be away from the cloying atmosphere Barb created. If I had to direct and film the goddamn commercial myself, I was going to get things going.

"Let's get on with this," I told some grips and others hanging around smoking, watching Will and the first AD do their thing. They all gazed at me like I'd lost it. No one pushes the director.

"Must be PMS," one of them drawled and the rest snickered.

"It's my mother," I said.

"Same thing," one said dolefully, shooting me a look of commiseration.

I didn't succeed in speeding anything up. When I approached Will I lost my nerve. Also, I was distracted by his forearms, peeking out beneath rolled up taupe sleeves. There was just something muscular and male about him that called out to me. When he glanced around, saw me, and faintly smiled, I melted a bit. I stood on the periphery with Holly who endeared me to her when she said, "That Barb. She's got a rod up her butt. Why'd we hire her?" It was as close to a joke as Holly ever made.

"Lapse of judgment?"

"Serious lapse."

I was pleased that it looked like this would be my one and only assignment with Barb.

"So, you've got a thing for Will, huh?" she remarked.

"What? Where'd that come from?" I studiously plucked a piece of lint off my sleeve, struggling for nonchalance.

"The drool in the corner of your mouth."

"That's not drool," I said. Then a moment later, "My mouth's too dry for drool."

"He is good-looking," she agreed. "But beware."

"Of what? The dreaded girlfriend? Temporary liaisons destined to fail?"

"His temper," she said.

Once more, Black Mark came to mind. With a strength of determination I normally failed to draw up when thoughts touched on Mark, I decided I was going to look him up in San Diego *tout suite*, possibly this weekend, and put the ghost of Ex-File Number Six to rest once and for all.

By the time I got home it was after nine P.M. I let myself in softly, lest I wake my mother, who had sounded as if she planned to park it on the couch for the entire night. I was tip-toeing near her, as she was indeed asleep, when my condo phone started ringing, sounding like a series of raging Christmas bells, loud and insistent with false cheer. I snatched up the receiver and whispered, "Hello?" inordinately angry with the caller on the other end—as if they could know my mother was recuperating from surgery.

"Blue?"

It was Daphne. I wanted to kill her. My mother made a sighing noise as I carried the handset toward the stairway, whispering harshly, "My mom just had her surgery. I'm taking this upstairs."

"Oh. Sorry! How is she?"

"I haven't had a chance to find out. I just walked in."

"You want to call me back?"

No, I didn't want to call her back. I didn't want to hear about another session with Dr. Dick. "No, go ahead. What's up?"

"Virginia? Ginny?" Mom called softly from the living room.

I instantly backtracked from the stairs as Daphne said, "I was having coffee with Dr. Dick and you'll never guess who I saw. Carmen Watkins! Has she seen a surgeon? She looks ten years younger!"

"Uh . . . yeah . . . I think so," I sputtered. My mind wasn't on our old college buddy's plastic surgery. But buzzing around inside my skull was the comment that she was *having coffee with Dr. Dick*!

I didn't realize I was making faces until my mother, her face puffy and discolored—she was going to have a couple of beautiful shiners, I could tell—asked, "Why are you squinching up your face like that and sticking out your tongue?"

"Tourette's," I said, placing my hand over the receiver.

Mom sighed and looked away.

That brought me up short. She wasn't finding me amusing. Normally I can scare a smile out of her. But she was hurting and nothing was funny, I guess.

"Daphne, I can't talk right now. Mom needs me."

"No, go ahead," Mom said, giving me a dismissive wave.

"Okay." Daphne was contrite, which made me feel like a heel. "I just wanted to say that Carmen was talking about you. She had nice things to say."

"Uh-huh." I'll just bet. Carmen was the master of saying "nice" things while stabbing you in the back. Like that line from *The Best Little Whorehouse in Texas:* she was the kind of person who'd piss on your shoe and tell you it was raining. Well, if she were a guy, that is. A bit tougher, given the female anatomy, but you get the idea.

"She brought up Kane Reynolds. We've got to go see him! He's going to be here next week."

"Kane Reynolds is here next week?" I repeated.

"You forgot."

"No," I lied. Actually, it wasn't a total lie. I hadn't completely forgotten Kane was coming. I'd just put it way, way out of my mind. Issues like Daphne growing cozy with Dr. Dick took precedence. And I was still working through Don and Mark, Ex-Files Five and Six, respectively.

"Carmen said she really wants to see him, especially since you went to high school with him."

I had a sudden bad feeling about this. Something I couldn't quite place inside my head.

"I'll call Jill and CeeCee, see if they want to go, then I'll get tickets. He's got a weekend workshop, I think."

"No weekend workshop. Count me out. I'll do the initial presentation, and that's it," I stated firmly. No way was I going to lock myself into one of those "Finding Yourself" weekends. I had visions of being locked up without bathroom rights. Peeing on the floor in front of people? No, thank you.

"I didn't mean we would go to that," Daphne said. "I was just getting the dates. The initial presentation is Thursday night."

"I'll be there unless I have another job that gets in the way." I had nothing scheduled but it's always good to give yourself an out. "Is Dr. Dick going?"

"Oh. Should I ask him?"

"Well, I—"

"That's a great idea, Blue. I'll invite him to join us. I'd better let you go. Bye."

I was left holding the phone. From behind closed lids, Mom said, "You're going to 'Getting Able with Kane'?"

I blinked. "What? *That's* what it's called?"

"That's what it's called," she said.

I wondered if dope smoking was part of getting able.

"Maybe Jackson will be there," Mom said. "He knew Kane in high school."

It was shaping up to be one hell of a fun evening.

I went out for a few drinks with CeeCee a few hours later. Mom had fallen asleep for the night and since I didn't want to disturb her that meant I was relegated to my bedroom. This was fine except for the fact that Don returned from his Jeep business and wanted to engage me in conversation. This meant we were stuck in either my bedroom or his and I've got to say, there's nothing more uncomfortable than sitting around alone in a bedroom with an Ex-File in whom you have no interest. And I had no interest in Don—although I'm not sure the same could be said for him. He had that way of gazing at me appreciatively. Normally I might be susceptible to this kind of behavior. (Hey, it beats having someone angry, annoyed, or generally tired of you.) But there was something about Don . . . a fingernails-scraping-on-a-blackboard kind of thing. And it was weird, because he was really better-looking now. Even trimmer. Tougher. Fitter. And, actually, the graying hair really worked for him. His complexion seemed less the fair-freckled redhead; it was now a warmer tannish color.

Yet . . . yet . . .

He made me want to run rip out my hair by the roots and shriek. I managed to keep those shrieks from being voiced—barely—as a I snatched up my purse and blasted out of the condo.

At the door, Mom mumbled, "Virginia, why don't you buy this condo? It would be a wonderful investment."

Always the real estate agent. "It's a matter of economics," I reminded her.

"I could give you the down payment," she said.

"Mom." I stalked over to her, staring down at her swollen eyes. "They gave you some valium derivative, didn't they?"

"I have the money, Ginny. If you're going to marry someone like Don, let me help you."

I don't know what surprised me more: that she was throwing her life savings at me, or that she'd called me Ginny. The Don part was expected. "You need rest," I told her roughly. I could feel emotion scarily taking me over. I'm not usually prone to waterworks, but the sting behind my eyes was real. Damn it, but I hate it when people are nice to me! I mean, no, not really. But yeah . . . sometimes. My mom was killing me. And she looked so damn pathetic!

"Have a nice time," she murmured, and I bolted to meet CeeCee.

Chapter

15

". . . and she told me she'd loan me the money for the down payment," I said, swilling down the last drops of my second Ketel One martini. I had to shake the reluctant liquid into my mouth. I was definitely feeling very teary. Not a good sign. Not a good idea to knock back a depressant when one is feeling exceptionally low.

"Is the condo for sale?" CeeCee asked.

I focused in on her. She'd about knocked me over when she strode into the Love Shack. This was not the CeeCee I knew. This CeeCee wore a business suit with a very short skirt which showed off attractive, muscular legs. Beneath the gray pinstripe peeked an orange V-necked T-shirt. Her hair was all one length and one color, a light brown, one side tucked behind her ear. Her shoes were black flats. Her only concession to the CeeCee I knew was the the absence of stockings and the whiff of cigarette smoke that lingered.

I'd said, upon first viewing, "Oh . . . my . . . God."

Her answer: "I hate these fucking clothes."

"Then what's it all about?"

"Role playing."

I should have guessed. What was shocking was how utterly wonderful she looked in the outfit. "This get-up's for the boss?"

"He likes to do it on his desk whenever we're alone. I can't tell you how many times I've been lying on my back with my legs in the air, this stupid little skirt hiked up to my armpits. On the corner of his desk is this wide metal frame surrounding a picture of his ex-wife and the kids. I watch my reflection in the metal frame."

"Oh."

"I think I'm about done with him."

"And give up eyelash chewing?" I asked, surprised.

"That's long over. We're into—something else. I don't know what I was thinking." She snorted and asked again, "Your condo's for sale?"

"The owner said something about it once or twice. But I'm not taking my mother's money."

"Could you swing it on your own?"

I shook my head. "Do you know what a down payment would be on property in Santa Monica? On *any* property?"

"I've got an idea. It's good to own real estate."

"If you can afford it."

She abruptly changed the subject, "Tell me about Don."

"Not a chance. I haven't forgotten what happened with Hairy Larry. I mentioned him, and you called him up."

"I like Hairy," she said.

"It's Larry," I reminded.

She looked thoughtful "I should've gone for him myself that night, instead of letting that Agency chick go after him."

"You were in love."

"Well, I'm not any more," she stated grimly. "I'm going to have to quit my job," she revealed. "Cheese-Dick wins the prize after all."

"That sucks."

"Yep."

A moment passed between us, then I asked, "Should I have another drink?"

"Have ten," she suggested.

"Nope. Gotta get back to Mom. I left her in Don's care and even though he's close to goodliness, er, Godliness . . ." I hiccupped. "I can't be gone long. He's wormed his way into her affections and it really bugs me."

CeeCee fiddled with her pack of cigarettes, examining the little circular cigarette ends longingly. "He's still doing all that bowing, scraping, and genuflecting?"

"Oh, yeah." I stared at my empty glass morosely. "But he's got money."

"Whoop-dee-do."

"Mom seems to think it matters. She'd like to see me settled."

"All moms want to see their daughters settled. Though your friend Kristl's mother might be over that by now."

"Kristl's not married yet," I defended, as if this somehow meant something, which I wasn't really sure it did.

"Jill's close."

"Jill and Ian . . . Jill-Ian . . ."

"One of us was bound to go first," CeeCee said fatalistically. "I always thought it would be Daphne, despite how long Jill and Ian have been living unhappily ever after. But since Leo took off for *Losers, Inc.* and she decided he was a loser in real life . . ."

"She's been hanging out with Dr. Dick." I didn't want to think about Daphne. I was having a hard time with the whole Dr. Dick thing.

CeeCee waved that away. "That doesn't mean anything."

"Daphne's ordering us tickets to 'Getting Able with Kane.'"

CeeCee gave me a sharp look. "Jesus."

I lifted a hand in surrender. "I wouldn't even go except I made that stupid promise to you guys about putting all my

Ex-Files to bed, or something like that. At least I can see Kane and get it over with all at once." I paused. "Charlie and Hog sent me a postcard from Tijuana. I saw it on the counter. I almost wanted to . . ."

"What?"

"I don't know. Run away, I guess."

"To Mexico?"

"From my life."

"Have you seen Black Mark yet?"

"Lemme see . . ." I held up one hand and started counting. "Saw Charlie again, saw Hairy Larry, thanks to you—"

"My pleasure," CeeCee murmured. One of the cocktail waiters looked anxious about CeeCee holding her pack of cigarettes. She waved him over and ordered me another vodka martini and scotch on the rocks for herself.

I touched my third finger, "I'm in the middle of *seeing* Don the Devout . . . whatever that means. That's three down. When we get to 'Getting Able' that'll be four. Oh, and there's Nate. He's way done with, so that's five."

"Who's left?"

"Six'll be Black Mark. I'm planning to go to San Diego this weekend."

"And?"

I sighed heavily and thought hard. Our waiter placed my drink in front of me. I watched the way the clear liquid sloshed lightly in the triangular glass. "The last two are Lang and Knowles-It-All. And I'm tellin' ya, right now, I'm not gonna look up Mr. Famous Actor."

She ignored that and asked, "What's the deal with Knowles-It-All?"

"You don't want to Knowles." I laughed at my little joke. Kinda surprised I could pull it off as I was definitely feeling the effects. I couldn't touch my third drink. A little voice inside my head reminded me of WORK tomorrow.

"Did I tell you I'm on a job with Will?" I asked her. "To you, to me, TUACA!"

She nodded, smiling faintly. "How's that going?"

"He reminds me an awful lot of Black Mark. And I've got sex on the brain, just like I did with him. It doesn't bode well."

"You haven't slept with him yet?"

"Hell, no. We've just been workin', workin', workin'." I carefully lifted the martini glass, trying to look through the liquid. "He's got that girlfriend."

CeeCee grunted.

"A girlfriend is a girlfriend," I said. This somehow sounded sage and profound to my ears. CeeCee must have thought so, too, because she sighed and said, "And wives are worse."

"Gerald's ex in the pitcher . . . um . . . picture . . . again?"

"Right in the center of the frame," she said.

It took me until the next day to really get her point.

I never touched that third martini, and CeeCee and I separated at the Love Shack's front door. I half-staggered, half-walked back to my condo. CeeCee had offered me a ride, as she was remarkably clear and sober, but I needed to clear my head so I hoofed it. The night was coolish; November in southern California definitely has a bite.

As I approached my complex I saw a small crowd gathered near the door to the garage. Feeling far more sober and filled with curiosity, I stepped forward. One of my neighbors, a burly guy with a belly laugh who nodded at me cheerily whenever I saw him, had his shoulder against the garage gate and was manually pushing it aside. Apparently the mechanism had broken. This happens sometimes. I was glad that burly guy was there to get it open as I didn't want to be locked inside tomorrow morning, late for work and hung over, as I was bound to be.

It was then I realized Don was on the ground, his right leg splayed out in front, his foot caught between the gate and the wall. Another neighbor, a young woman, was inside the garage, attempting to take Don's shoe off. Her ministrations weren't entirely gentle as I heard Don suck air sharply through gritted teeth.

"Jesus," I murmured in awe, staring. "Schematic Man actually got someone."

"Don't swear," Don muttered fiercely.

Everyone turned to look at me. I smiled meekly. It was all I could do to keep from cracking up.

I had an epiphany right there, a serious religious realization: *God possesses a sense of humor.*

At work the next day I found myself nearly chirping from my good mood. There was no way to explain how I felt about what had happened to Don without coming off as a sadist. He was on crutches now, and he seemed to have no real explanation about how the accident occurred. I asked if the gate had suddenly sped up and slammed into his foot, but Don muttered a sharp, "No," and left it at that. His ankle was torn up a bit, and swollen. A bad sprain, I guess. He wasn't in a cast but he was wrapped up halfway to his knee. I knew it hurt, and I should have felt some empathy and remorse, but I've got to admit, all I really felt was glee.

His injury had turned my mother from a patient to a caretaker in no time flat. With what looked like two black eyes, she buzzed around and happily took care of Don, who now was on the couch. Mom had taken over his room, a game of musical bedrooms that was working for me. I liked this arrangement much better as Mom was down the hall from me, not Don. It is mind-boggling how done I am with Don. Don the Done. Hmmm . . .

On set I managed a few flirtatious moments with Will. Sean, now on the job, witnessed these incidents but he'd forgiven me entirely for everything that had transpired since I'd added him onto the job and paid him for an extra half day. I didn't care what Holly thought of my actions; they could take the money from my check, for all I cared. It was just worth it having peace reign again; Sean was a pretty decent PA, considering all. And I hadn't caught the scent of any funny cigarettes around. He seemed to understand how I felt, and we left it at that. I learned that he and Bettina had become a more serious item. Since the catering was taken care of and there was no Liam Engleston to worry about, Bettina was off my shit list. I did warn Sean not to have her, or anyone else not connected with the job, turn in the petty cash receipts. "Not good business," I pointed out, meaning it could affect my job, his, and any other PAs carelessly tossing cash around.

"Got it," Sean said, and I hoped he did.

Toward the end of the day I was watching Will and the first AD attempting to catch the last rays of the dying sun. They were working hard, hurrying to push things a little farther before the light waned, when Holly sidled up to me, looking inordinately shaken. This was a new view of the Holy Terror and I hardly knew how to ask what was wrong. I did manage "You all right?" to which she nodded abruptly and moved off. Mystified, I checked my watch. I wanted to wrap this damn thing up and fast. Tomorrow was our last shoot day and I might not be seeing Will again anytime soon unless I made a move.

To my everlasting joy he suddenly shut everything down. They just couldn't get the shot. As the grips and assistants starting packing up for the night, Will headed my way. Or, at least in my general direction.

"Hey," I said.

"Let's get the hell outta here," he said to me. "You wanna?"

"Yep."

When the director says "jump," you jump. I walked out with Will and left Holly and Barb and everyone else to clean up. The great thing was, I wouldn't even hear about it. The director is God on the set. Holly merely mouthed, "Careful" to me, and I nodded, though it burst my bubble a little. Pissed me off, too. I didn't ask her to be my mother.

Will sent me a sidelong look. "I want a shower and then a hot tub. I've got both at my place."

I asked, "Where's your place?"

"Follow me."

No more doing the getting-to-know-you dance. We were apparently on our way. My thoughts flew to the girlfriend, but maybe Rhianna was history. Jumping behind the wheel of my Explorer, I trailed after his Ferrari. This was standard issue for directors of any note. Expensive cars were a must. If the shoot was anywhere near their home, they'd drive themselves in their most upscale vehicle; out-of-town jobs most often meant the director had his or her own driver.

It took an hour to get to Will's place in the Hollywood Hills, fast by Los Angeles commuting standards. True to his word he headed straight for the shower, telling me to fix myself a drink. I glanced around. He didn't have bad taste: sage chenille couch, sea grass area rug, antiqued maple tables, and indirect lighting. I suspected some decorator had made a huge order to Pottery Barn and Restoration Hardware. My eye caught on a cherry-red club chair. I sat down in it and realized it was a recliner. I LOVED it. Instantly I got up and headed for the mirrored bar, recoiling a bit at my own reflection. I was still in work garb: short-sleeved tan T-shirt, muddy-colored cargo capris, my hair pulled back into a makeshift ponytail-bun thing, more function than form. Did I look too not-beautiful? When you live in LA, with beauties everywhere you look, you have to seriously worry about these things.

I worried for a moment, then shut my brain down hard, like a trap door. Too late for that now.

The idea of mixing a drink sounded too hard, and let's face it, I wasn't all that eager to swill down more vodka after last night. Though I hadn't suffered the expected hangover, I was more interested in keeping a clear head tonight. But I didn't want to appear to be a sudden teetotaler. It might jar the mood. So, thinking, I examined the array of wine. Mostly unrecognizable to my untutored eye. I searched for something I knew wasn't going to break the bank and found a bottle of Merlot with a California label I recognized from Sav-On. I uncorked it, waited a good three seconds for it to breathe, then poured myself a balloon goblet nearly to the brim. Uncool. I hadn't meant to look like an amateur. I quickly grabbed another goblet and sloshed half my Merlot into a glass for Will. I accidently rained red drops on a snow globe which sat on the bar. It was one of those promotional ones from the film *Fargo*, with a dead body, blood, and a police car in its snowy little tableau. I quickly wiped off the wine.

Sex, I thought. *I'm going to have sex tonight!*

"Thank you, God," I said, squelching a thought of Don.

Will returned in black terrycloth robe. I'd been thinking of nicknaming him Will Power, but it looked like we were ready to rock and roll, so I was thinking Willing and Able might be more apt.

He went out to the back deck. His house was on a hillside and he had a hot tub built right into the back deck. Through a glass partition, the lights of the city winked and undulated against an inky black sky. Will removed the tub's cover and I heard, saw, and smelled the chlorinated water bubbling and frothing. For a moment my Seinfeld-ish self lifted its head and worried about the bacteria that live in warm water. If the hot tub isn't hot enough, or chlorinated enough, or *something* enough, the pesky pseudomonas bacteria attacks with a vengeance. I've seen torso skin covered in huge red bumps, the product of poorly attended hot tubs. Ug–ly. Not good. Scary. A huge, seething rash.

I shuddered. However, fear of bacteria is not a turn-on by anyone's standards. Gritting my teeth into a smile, I handed Will his balloon of Merlot. He took a healthy swallow then set the glass on the deck beside the tub, slipped out of his robe and stepped into the turgid water.

I got a good clear view of his equipment. Not as impressive as Black Mark's had been, but hey, it's not what you've got, it's how you use it, right? Besides, I've never been one of those who swooned over the length and breadth of the male member. It seems so . . . wrong, somehow. Like guys who pass over a woman because her breasts aren't big enough.

This thought made me look down at my own chest. Adequate. Just.

"Come on in," Will invited.

Deliberately I removed my shoes and socks, worrying that my body wouldn't measure up. And what if I crashed and burned during sex? What if he remembered me in the same way I remembered Charlie?

Fear coursed through my veins. I'm rarely plagued by serious doubts about my sexual ability, but apart from Nate and what had become a kind of rote lovemaking, it had been awhile. Will was someone I really didn't want to disappoint.

I managed to take off my tee-shirt and cargo pants, but I had an attack of shyness I couldn't quite get over, so I slipped into the water wearing a matching black bra and panties, glad I had purged from my closet all manner of holey underwear about two weeks earlier. That would have been too embarrassing. If I happen to throw on some holey underwear and catch a glimpse of myself in a mirror, I even embarrass myself.

Will didn't waste a lot of time. He drew me to him. We began kissing and I have to say it was really nice. I don't know about other people but a hot tub, even if chlorinated correctly, is really not a venue for me to get all worked up and lusting for sex. Too much noise and heat and worry. Water's great, but sorry, I'm a traditionalist: I like a bed. Still, I relaxed enough to enjoy the foreplay. And somewhere in our make-out session I managed, with Will's help, to slip out of bra and panties. Unfortunately, both pieces kept bobbing around just outside my peripheral vision and for the life of me I couldn't get in the mood. My mouth kept curving into a smile. Again, Will didn't seem to mind even though he was sort of all business.

The next thing I knew he'd grabbed a condom and we were engaged in actual sex. One moment we were making out, the next he was feeling around between my legs and attempting entry. I could feel the jets of water rushing around the outside of my thighs. God help me, I suddenly heard this imaginary air traffic controller's litany inside my head. "Approaching for landing . . . runway clear . . . you're right on target . . . no, veer to the left . . . left . . . *left!* . . . That's right . . . easy, easy . . . touchdown!"

Okay, maybe that's not exactly how they talk, but it worked for me. Next thing we were bumping and grinding and I was worried I might scrape my back against one of the jets or the rough tile edge of the hot tub. I certainly was going to have a bruise somewhere around my shoulder blades as the upper part of my body kept flinging upward, half out of the water, only to be hauled back down.

My discomfort didn't last long. We were about to launch skyward again when Will gave a shudder and a short, bitten off howl, then collapsed against me. "Sorry," he gasped softly. "It just came over me."

"No problem," I answered lightly. Actually, there was a niggling worry running around inside my brain. This encounter had shades of Charlie's wham, bam, thank you, ma'am. On the other hand, I try very hard not to let my own high expectations run amok and ruin something before it's got a chance to start.

But . . . but . . .

I snatched up my gaily bobbing undergarments and dragged them on, wet, which wasn't exactly an exercise in grace itself. Will managed to climb out of the water, shrug into his bathrobe and head inside, dripping water, undoubtedly to peel off the used condom and dispose of it. This left me to scramble into my clothes. Of course my wet underwear soaked through immediately but I didn't care. I was just glad to be covered and have my armor on. I wasn't sure how to feel. It might have been a first union of body but it sure wasn't a union of spirit. I sometimes wonder if there's something wrong with me. I worry too much. I know I do. Something to take up with Dr. Dick, I guess.

"Hey," Will called from somewhere inside the depths of his house. "Come in here and listen to this."

I carried my shoes and socks and found him in the recesses of a den that was through an archway off the initial living room. The walls and ceiling were formed from wood. It looked like fir. Having come from Oregon I know a thing or two about wood. Not much. Just enough to impress guys. I mentioned the fir but Will wasn't one of those types who pay any attention to anything that isn't in their immediate vision. And in his immediate vision was a music system to end all music systems: amps, speakers, tuners, etc. He hit a few switches and we were blasted with sound. I feigned an interested expression. Now, I like a good rock song, but that's about where my taste begins and ends. This was something jazzy and cool, I guess. The only thing about it I liked was that it reminded me of martinis.

"How's that?" he screamed above the noise.

"Wow," I yelled back.

What is it about guys and electronics? I swear, ninety percent of them have a hard-on for anything that sends radio, television, or cyber messages across space. Ear-bleeding, penetrating volume is the mark of a good sound system.

Because of the noise we didn't hear anything else. But I must have felt a change in the air pressure, because I turned from inspection of the knobs, dials, and pulsating lines of light to see Rhianna standing in the archway. Her face was white with shock.

"You fucker!" she screamed, but because she was a few paces away it came out small, tinny, and fake. But the fury exploding across her face was real enough.

She suddenly turned and bolted. I looked at Will, whose head was cocked as if he were waiting to hear an explosion. His hand reached for a dial on his system and the volume decreased slightly.

Then Rhianna was back in the archway. In her fist was the *Fargo* snow globe. Her hand was cocked back, ready to throw.

I stood there in disbelief. I thought, *She won't do it.* Then, *She's probably a terrible shot.* And all of a sudden, she wound up and hurled the damn thing at ME! I ducked instinctively, self-preservation taking over in the nick of time. The snow globe smashed into the wall of electronic equipment behind me. Metal and glass and water and fake snow and tiny plastic figures and a teensy police car scattered and splashed. Will roared in fury and went for her in a rush. I pressed myself to the wall, heart accelerating madly. He grabbed Rhianna's arms. She glared at him, unrepentant. I felt like I was witnessing a scene from a movie. I could only see the back of his head, but her face was illuminated. Her eyes snapped with fury.

"Bitch."

"Fucker."

"Whore."

"Asshole."

Suddenly her face crumpled, her lips turning into an ugly crying mess. If I'd had any idea how I would have turned down the noise some more, but there were too many buttons. Besides, I didn't dare take my eyes off Will and the Rocket. Another missile could sail my way.

Note to self: Remember to ask about girlfriend status before lovemaking next time.

Now she was pointing at me and wailing. I would have eased out of the room but she blocked my exit.

Will, apparently realizing my dilemma, led her away. I took the cue and scurried through the archway across the living room and out the front door. I wanted to run, run, run. As soon as I jumped in the Explorer and jabbed the key in the ignition I was revving the engine. My wheels cried out a little *eech* as I tore away.

Good . . . God.

There was a lot of traffic on the road and I was only about halfway home when my cell phone sang. I glanced at the caller ID. Will.

Coward that I am, I almost didn't answer it. Swearing softly beneath my breath, I pressed the green button. "Hello?"

"Sorry about that. Rhianna and I are long over, but she knows the code to get into my house. I'm changing it tonight."

"Good idea."

"Can I see you tomorrow?"

"We're still on the job. Our last day together," I reminded.

"Not if you don't want it to be."

This sort of warmed me inside. I glanced out at the sea of red taillights ahead of me. LA. The Lonely City. I did want to see him, didn't I? I did want to be with him.

"Okay," I said.

He sounded relieved. "See you tomorrow."

I dressed with extra care the next day: good jeans, fresh red T-shirt. I even worked on my hair some. I actually used hair products and blew it dry into some kind of style. Barb remarked on my appearance.

"You look . . . different."

"Better?" I asked, pushing the envelope.

"Yeah . . ."

Her affirmation, reluctantly given as it was, buoyed my spirits. It was a good start, and the day actually kept going pretty well. Will was in good humor, too, which both baffled and touched me, as I credited his mood to myself. It was over with Rhianna. The girlfriend was now an ex-girlfriend— a necessary distinction. And though I didn't appreciate having anything tossed at me, I did like moving into first place.

Maybe, from this shaky beginning, something good could develop.

"Where's Holly?" I asked Barb. She'd been on the job when I arrived but I'd hardly seen her.

"Hiding from Will, I suppose," Barb answered with a sniff.

"Will?" My antennae lifted.

"He really tore into her yesterday. It was gruesome. Someone forgot to put the cream out with the coffee and he ripped into Holly as if she'd personally attacked him. In front of everybody. I mean, it was ugly."

"You saw this?" A cold feeling developed in the pit of my stomach.

"I *heard* it," she said, dropping the file she was looking at and turning toward me, all resentment toward me vanishing in this moment of supreme gossiping. "Ug—ly."

I recalled Holly's quiet yesterday. I also recalled how she'd mentioned Will's temper. And the way she'd mouthed, "Careful."

I wanted to defend Will. We'd slept together. He was my guy. Before I had a chance to, Holly entered the trailer, all business. I didn't have a chance to get to personal business as we all dug in to finish the job. We did manage to wrap the shoot around six P.M.—a triumph of sorts—but it was pitch-black outside. Will breezed into the trailer. Holly was absent, but Barb came to spine-straight attention, smiling like an idiot, ingratiating rat that she is. I just sort of waited for whatever would happen next.

"Let's get out of here," he said to me. I nodded. Barb's brows lifted so high they nearly soared right off her forehead. Luckily, Will added, "We need to take Agency out to dinner. Most of them are flying out tomorrow. Let's meet at Shutters."

This safely put me back into work-mode. "Want me to tell Holly?" I asked.

"No." Will was firm.

This was so out of protocol that Barb actually gasped. The producer was always there to schmooze Agency.

But Will was gone. Holly appeared a few moments later. She stated flatly, "Will doesn't want me around tonight. I'd tell him to fuck off but I've got to work with him next month on that cellular phone job. Agency's going to wonder where I am. Ginny, you need to tell them I had a flight to catch tonight, or something. Make up some excuse."

"All right."

"I hate bastards," she added and slammed out.

That was one the Rocket left out last night.

Barb gave me a long look. I smiled weakly and headed for the Santa Monica waterfront and Shutters Hotel.

The actual dinner was kind of a letdown. The Agency people wanted to talk to Will almost exclusively and once I'd explained Holly's absence—her imaginary daughter's car trouble—they let it slide. I managed to get into a fairly decent conversation with the agency art director, but I spent a majority of my time stealing glances at my wristwatch.

"What's up?" Will asked, catching me in the act and frowning. I should have been hanging on every scintillating word from my oh, so boring tablemate.

"I've got house guests," I said, not wanting to go into my mother's surgery and Don the Devout's ankle injury. I also didn't know how to say that I just wanted to leave and go home and think about things.

Will didn't like the sound of that. I hung around a little bit longer, then excused myself to place a call to Mom. She sounded cheery as a robin in spring. "Don's doing so much better," she enthused. "He might have a bone chip, though. They're still checking. His tendons definitely were stretched."

"Did you ever learn how it happened?" I questioned.

"What?"

"The accident. How he got his foot stuck in Schematic Man's gate."

"What?" she repeated, lost.

"That gate moves so slowly," I explained. "Did he fall asleep? What?"

"I think he tried to slip through and it just came at him."

"At snail speed? He couldn't get out of the way?"

"Did you want to talk to him?"

Before I could say no, she called, "Don! Telephone!"

"Mom?" I waited. "Mom?"

Don picked up. "Hello."

"Hey . . ." I said. "How are you?"

"You really want to know?" He sounded pissed. "That machinery is a menace. I'm surprised there haven't been more accidents."

"I just don't see it, Don. I mean, were your feet super-glued down?"

"What does it matter?" he demanded. "It shouldn't hit like that no matter what you do!"

I heard some kind of guilt in there somewhere. "Oh, come on, tell me."

Virginia," he said through his teeth. I waited, half-expecting him to scream at me. But finally, tightly, he bit out, "I tried to squeeze through as it was closing and it caught my ankle."

You must be the slowest person on the planet, I thought in disbelief. Aloud, I said, "I'm sorry you got hurt."

"You'd better report this to your homeowners association. Someone might sue."

I didn't feel I needed to point out that even Mrs. Farley, she of the poor eyesight and slow steps, had never been re-motely threatened by Schematic Man's gate. "Someone like yourself?" I suggested.

"I should," he agreed eagerly, as if he'd just been waiting for an opening. "The gate company should know."

"I know a good personal injury lawyer," I said, playing along.

"You do?"

I gazed through the doorway into the private dining room I'd just vacated. Will was in deep conversation with one of the agency men. I said, thinking maybe I shouldn't have baited Don after all, "Brad Knowles." Ex-File Number Seven. Knowles-It-All.

"Maybe I'll give him a call," Don said. "I'll get the number from you later."

"Oh, I don't know if that's such a good idea."

"You're the one who brought it up," he said, then hung up with a sharp click.

I slowly clicked off my cell phone, feeling bone weary. What had I been thinking?

Sometimes I really piss myself off.

Chapter
16

I met my friends for our usual Saturday morning breakfast at Sammy's full of new information, only to learn I couldn't get a word in edgewise. Jill brought Ian again, which I'd determined would not quell my tongue, but I didn't get a chance to say anything anyway because Daphne was a-bubble over Dr. Dick and blathering on about her self-professed "new best friend" in a way that made me want to pound my head against a wall. I chose instead to clamp my jaw shut like a vise. Once in a while I would wedge my teeth open with some ice from my water glass and crunch down hard and loud. This was less than effective as Daphne had the floor. I couldn't even comment on the big surprise of the morning, which was CeeCee's mode of dress. She was back to her cargo pants with chains and a wrinkled red T-shirt that said simply, "NO." Her hair was still sans pink tips, but I sensed it was only a matter of time until they, or something equally interesting, returned. I managed to mouth, "What happened?" to her around my ice chips, but she merely shrugged. No more role playing, apparently. Maybe Gerald, the boss, went back to his ex permanently.

Daphne leaned forward as the waiter brought our orders

and said in a conspiratorial tone, "It's all set. Thursday's the night we're going to 'Getting Able With Kane.' I bought us all tickets."

"Jesus," I murmured.

"What?" Ian asked. He gazed at Daphne as if she were speaking Martian.

I couldn't contain my snort of derision. Ian gave me a look. I explained, "Kane's one of my Ex-Files. He's a motivational speaker now." His lips parted in query, but I said, "Don't ask. Really."

He closed his mouth and looked amused. I smiled. Ian and I shared a rare moment of understanding. *Maybe it would be okay if he married Jill,* I thought. He was actually tolerable when he wasn't being an asshole.

"I didn't actually get a ticket for you," Daphne admitted. "But I can get another, I'm pretty sure."

"No. It's okay," he said immediately. "Jill, honey, I think this is one of those events where you can represent both of us."

Jill-honey gave him a long-suffering look that was nevertheless full of love. I suddenly wanted to tell them both— and everyone else—about my evening with Will. I opened my mouth to commandeer the conversation, but Daphne barreled on.

"It starts at seven and I think we should get there a few minutes early. That'll give Blue enough time to reconnect before the program starts."

"Oh, whoa." I held up my hands. "I don't want to talk to Kane 'till afterwards. Actually, I don't want to talk to him at all, but I can see I'm doomed."

Jill pointed out, "You said you would."

"I know what I said," I answered testily. "And I will. But not till afterwards. Hey, I'm going to see Black Mark as soon as breakfast is over. Rome wasn't built in a day, as far as I know. Give me a break."

"Black Mark?" Ian questioned.

"Again, don't ask." I glared at all my friends, then turned to Ian, relenting. "My friends feel the need to torture me about my past mistakes. Why I agreed to this, I can't remember."

"So Jill would eat, Daphne would stop picking losers, and I would straighten things out at work," CeeCee reminded in that distant way she sometimes had that members of the opposite sex seemed to find so attractive. CeeCee had the attitude down. I often tried for it, but I couldn't quite manage the 'cool' of it. For CeeCee, it appeared effortless. Even Ian gave her a reflective look, as if he, too, were trying to figure it all out.

"Carmen Watkins will be there," Daphne said.

"This has something to do with us?" CeeCee asked.

Jill leaned toward me. "We weren't friends with her, right?"

"She was a college acquaintance. Nothing more."

"Then why do we care?" CeeCee asked.

"She just came into Starbucks and we started talking," Daphne said with a shrug. "She brought up going to see Kane Reynolds." She turned to me. "Did you know she knows Jack Wright?"

"Jackson Wright," I corrected. "Yes, we all know Jackson. How did his name come up?"

"She said she had drinks with him."

"She's not dating him, is she?" CeeCee asked, slightly horrified.

"Oh, I don't think so." Daphne gave me a sidelong glance.

"What?" I demanded.

"You and Jackson are friends."

Was it my imagination or was Daphne purposely needling me? Maybe she and Dr. Dick had indulged in a gabfest all about Ginny Blue and her many, many problems. Ginny might be frightfully well adjusted, but she was fodder, grist for the grist mill, nevertheless. I could picture Daphne and

Dr. Dick, heads bent together, laughing in that raspy way of dirty old men over what to do about poor Ginny.

Paranoia. Not my usual problem. I shook myself out of it. It wasn't always all about me . . . was it?

"Okay, I'm in." Jill glanced at Ian fondly. "And you don't have to go. But you'll owe me."

He smiled, conceding the point. They'd definitely reached a new acme in their relationship. Maybe the upcoming wedding wouldn't be the disaster I'd envisioned.

"As long as we have you both here," I said, finally grabbing the floor. "When's the big day scheduled?"

"The second Saturday in December," Jill answered promptly.

My jaw dropped. I hadn't really expected an answer. CeeCee and Daphne looked as poleaxed as I felt. "What?" I said, my voice sounding distant and tinny to my ears. "*What?*"

"So soon?" Daphne asked.

"We set a date," Jill explained calmly. She knew the bomb she'd dropped but was determined to act like it was no big deal.

I nearly choked on a bite of toast. Tears filled my eyes as I reached for my water glass. I quickly tossed back several large gulps. It didn't help. I coughed as if I were intent on hacking up a lung. Tears streamed down my face. I squeaked out, "It's really happening?"

"It's really happening," Jill repeated, happy.

Ian sometimes had that effect on her: rounding out her sharp edges. Sometimes I appreciated it; sometimes I loathed it. He said to the group as a whole, "She's eating better. We weren't going to get married unless there was some improvement there."

"Ian . . ." Jill murmured, uncomfortable.

"I guess I have you guys to thank." He gave me a slight smile. "And the purging of the Ex-Files."

I stared at Ian in shock and surprise. Was the world com-

ing to an end? Ian? Being sensitive? Actually acting as if
Jill's friends had value and worth? Actually *thanking* us? I
sure as hell wouldn't want my boyfriend bringing up my
faults, problems and weaknesses to my girlfriends who knew
them backwards and forwards anyway, but he'd done it so
nicely. I stammered, "Um . . . yeah . . . weird . . . who'd'a thunk
it?"

"Wow." CeeCee gazed at Ian as if considering him a new
species. Maybe he was.

Daphne regarded Ian with a kind of female adoration
only seen when the human male does something so rare, re-
markable, and wonderful that they drop all their feminine
defenses. The words "about to swoon" crossed my mind. I
instantly felt real fear. But she snapped herself out of it and
breathed, "I can't wait for the wedding. It's going to be fabulous. You're really doing it."

"And you're all bridesmaids," Jill said.

"God, NO!" I flipped out. "I don't do bridesmaid dresses."

"I won't do bridesmaid dresses," CeeCee added calmly.

"The wedding's black and white," Jill told her. "You're all
wearing straight black dresses."

CeeCee rolled that over in her mind. I envisioned myself
in a straight black dress. It wasn't a terrible picture, but I was
sure there was a pitfall in there somewhere. Jill simply
shrugged her acceptance. Straight black dress. The best one
could hope for. Daphne nodded eagerly.

"I need you to make some appointments pronto," Jill said,
acting as if we'd all acquiesced though the silence was
deadly. She pulled out a card with the name of a shop where
we were to go try them on. I glanced down at the pink and
cream business card and swallowed hard. A wedding. Jill's
wedding. White lace and promises.

But a straight black dress, I reminded myself like a litany.

Jill suddenly turned into an animated Bride from Hell,
pulling out samples of items from her own big-ass purse—a
new addition my mother would be proud of—and showing

off satin and vellum and even pastel mints in cool wedding-like shapes. "And check this out," she said, stabbing a snapshot with one fingernail. It was a chocolate truffle dressed up in a frosting/gel tuxedo.

"Too cute," Daphne said.

"No shit." CeeCee stared at the photo and absentmindedly ate one of the mints.

I murmured something appropriate, I think. In truth, I was kind of deflated. Here, I thought I'd had all this big news about myself and Will. My friends had trumped me with bigger, better stuff at every turn.

Daphne regarded me with sudden concern. "You okay, Blue?"

"Just fine."

"How's it going with Don the Devout and your mom?"

"Mom's great. Don's tolerable."

"Do you think you've worked things out with him?" Daphne asked seriously. "I mean, so that he can be put to rest?"

"Amen," CeeCee murmured.

I was in a bitchy mood. In truth, it wasn't Daphne's fault. Her liaison with Dr. Dick definitely pissed me off but it was my problem, not hers. With an effort I shook off my bad feelings and launched into the tale of Don and Schematic Man. By the time I was finished the waiter had cleared our plates. The mood had definitely lightened. Daphne actually leaned over and hugged me. "You are so funny," she said, which made me feel like a worse heel for being so annoyed with her.

"So, Dr. Dick's going to be at 'Getting Able'?"

"With his wife," Daphne revealed on a sigh.

"Ex-wife," I reminded.

"Are you sure they're divorced, Blue?"

"Positive," I responded promptly, but I could feel my certainty eroding even as I spoke the words.

"I just get the feeling . . . I don't know."

"God, maybe you're right." I felt like I'd been hit with a low blow. Was it true? Not that Dr. Dick had lied to me. I'd just assumed by the snippets of conversation I'd overheard now and again whenever I barreled into his office a bit early— as I'd been wont to do before I was nicely, but pointedly, asked to wait for my appointment. That was from Dr. Dick himself, not the snotty Janice. But I'd been so sure he was well and truly divorced. Now, I couldn't say why I'd been so certain.

"I'm pretty sure she'll be there with him," Daphne said.

"Along with Carmen . . . and maybe Jackson." Did my voice really sound as depressed as it did to my ears? I was dreading this Kane event more and more. The only good news was it was making my forthcoming trip down to San Diego to see Black Mark seem like less of a chore.

"You're not going to back out, are you?" Jill demanded, surfacing from her coma of wedding bliss long enough to snap at me.

"Did I say I was?"

"It'll be okay," Daphne soothed.

"Yeah." CeeCee was ironic.

I got up from my chair, throwing down my part of the meal cost and a healthy tip. "Love to stay and chat, but I've got an Ex-File to see. Number Six. Wish me luck."

"Luck," Ian said, sounding totally serious.

I saluted them all on my way out.

I headed down the 405 to San Diego, leaving early enough to *almost* make the freeway a breeze to drive. My mind drifted to my burgeoning romantic relationship with Will, the one I didn't get to tell my friends about. Since the Rocket had nearly taken my head off he'd phoned me a number of times. He didn't offer any more information about his supposedly ex-girlfriend and I didn't ask. I had my hands full with my own Ex-Files; I didn't need the aggravation of his.

Our conversations went like this:

"Hey," Will would greet me.

"Hey," I'd respond.

"Are we getting together tonight?"

"I can't. I'm getting off late and I have house guests."

"When are they leaving, again?"

"I'm not sure."

"I'll call later."

"Okay."

This left me to figure out what to do at home with Don, as he'd extended his trip indefinitely. He'd been needling me for Brad Knowles' number—my own fault for being a smart mouth—and I'd finally given it to him, hoping he would just vamoose. But it didn't happen that way. If anything, Don seemed more ensconced in my place than before. He explained that he really just couldn't get around like he should and therefore couldn't meet with his prospective dealership sellers. It sounded like an excuse for a free vacation to me, but hey, I'd gotten past caring. I had enough balls in the air with wrapping the Tuaca job, trying to scare up future work, and obsessing over what Will Torrance and I were becoming. Whenever I was home I chose to hole up in the sanctuary of my room rather than deal with Don. Mom checked on me every now and then, to make sure I wasn't sick, but whenever I complained about Don she *tsk-tsk*ed me and said he would be leaving soon enough, as would she. I could tell she was disappointed in me. She wanted to see me in a committed relationship. *I* wanted to see me in a committed relationship—but not with Don.

But was Will the one?

I recalled Holly mouthing "careful," to me, and her tail-between-her-legs attitude after the missing cream incident. If Will could reduce the Holy Terror to a quivering mass of jelly, I was in deep trouble.

And truthfully, whenever I picked through my brain to my real feelings, I would land on that synapse that said "wham, bam, thank you, ma'am" was nothing I ever wanted to experience again. Charlie had cured me of that forever. But Will . . . was this the way it was always destined to be? I really needed more field testing with him to be sure. Maybe, in a different venue, with a different set of circumstances and a—my evil mind stepped in here and suggested 'different partner,' but I swept right past that to 'different mood'— maybe then sex with Will could be stimulating and exhilarating and something to damn well think about morning, noon, and night. That's the way it should be at the beginning of a relationship, right?

"Right," I said aloud, stepping on the accelerator. The Explorer jumped forward toward San Diego and I chased my doubts away with steely determination.

Time to put thoughts of Will aside and concentrate on Black Mark.

I hadn't called Mark and warned him of my imminent arrival. I hadn't wanted to tip my hat, so to speak. Meeting the Ex-Files is stressful enough anyway, for crying out loud . . . and probably for both sides, come to think of it. But I really didn't give a rat's ass about how THEY felt. I was only concerned with how *I* felt, and with this thoroughly selfish frame of mind, I'd set out for San Diego on this gray November morning, glad that I lied to Don and my mother by telling them I had to work. Mom seemed okay with the working through the weekend thing; she did it all the time herself. Don, too, probably, in his business, but he seemed more perturbed by my flitting away than he had any right to. I had this weird feeling he was actually trying to reconnect with me. I'd done nothing to reveal that I might actually be interested, even less to behave like someone he might want to be with (I'd taken to belching loudly in front of him rather than discreetly hiding behind a few girlish hiccups, and I'd been gratified to see the strain on his face at my distinct lack of couth). I'd also studiously avoided any serious conversation or intimate moment with him. Did this make me more desirable? Possibly. If so, he was a true Rat-Man. I'd known girls who were the ultimate Rat-Women, but not that many men. Don seemed to be one. The more distant and unlovable I became, the better he seemed to like me.

Good . . . God.

A worry niggled. How would I ever get rid of him? Maybe I should have told him about Will, or would that have boomeranged on me, as well?

My brain suddenly jumped—in that irritating way it seems wont to do—straight to Jackson Wright. Why, I didn't want to look at too closely. Maybe it was because Jackson never showed interest in anyone and hence had women fawning all over him. I'd been one of the few who'd remained aloof in high school, although it was out of self-preservation rather than lack of interest. I'd known instinctively that he wouldn't want anyone who wanted him. Very, very high school. Ridiculous. But true.

But back to Black Mark: my purpose in heading to San Diego. He was the next Ex-File to meet, greet, and delete. I knew where he lived and where he worked. Sometime alcoholic that he was, he'd managed to buy into a restaurant/bar that was more about the drinks than the food. He was one of those types who periodically make a drunken phone call to an ex-lover, only to call the next day and apologize. I've had a few of his drunken calls over the years, and I've chatted on the phone with him after the requisite "I'm sorry" on several morning-afters. This is how I know more about him than I really want to. He makes a point of keeping ex-girlfriends informed.

So, the key points about Black Mark are: 1) he is currently married; 2) it is a tempestuous relationship at best, and 3) he has one son with said wife, another with the girlfriend before me, and I think there was a child conceived during his high school years who must be a teenager by now. Prolific sire, he is. Stellar Dad, he is not.

But my memory is sharp: Black Mark was one hell of a

lover. I ran screaming from Don the Devout straight into the heat of Mark's incendiary passion. Not that Don was a bad lover; heavens, no. It's just that Don's less-than-perfect other traits drove me to the edge of insanity. It's like some wild, cosmic joke that I'm dealing with both Black Mark and Don the Devout in my life again at the same moment in time.

Wonder what Dr. Dick would make of that.

Anyway, Mark was great in bed. Pure fact. He made me nuts over sex. Obsessed and out of control. I'd pretty much always enjoyed lovemaking with the right partner. But Mark . . . I hate to admit it, but the guy knew how to do things to me that made me claw, and howl, and turned my cheeks red with embarrassment whenever I thought back on our lovemaking. I shocked myself with my abandonment. After a love bout with Mark, I would find myself staring at my reflection in the mirror, cataloguing my flushed face, wild hair, and sparkling eyes. I saw what I'd hitherto only heard about: the "freshly fucked" look. I'm ashamed to say it looked damn good on me.

And then I would look over at Mark, still tangled in the sheets and catch his smile. He had this lazy amusement about him right after sex that only made me want to do it all over again. We spent a lot of our time together in the bedroom. A lot of it.

However.

Mark also had one doozy of a temper. What time was not spent howling between the sheets was spent screaming at each other everywhere else. He made me INSANE!!!

I took up nail biting during the Black Death. Nearly took those nails down to the quick. To this day I fight the compulsion.

So thinking I glanced down at my nails. Nicely trimmed and just over the edge of my fingertips. No polish. I can't be bothered while on the job. I had a sudden urge to grab onto a nail with my teeth and rip away for all I'm worth. Curbing the impulse took real willpower.

This did not bode well for my upcoming meeting.

There was the chance he wouldn't be at work or home, I reminded myself hopefully. The last time he'd called me had been nearly a year earlier, anything could have happened since then. But earlier this week I'd phoned the number for his bar—the Pot O'Gold Saloon—and been treated to a recording in his raspy voice that invited all and sundry to come in and enjoy Guinness and Irish stew. On St. Patrick's Day drinks were on the house until noon. I could just imagine what that meant for the afternoon and evening of that holiday. Hopefully, this revelry was saved for just once a year.

The second to last time Mark had called me he'd been roaring drunk and bound and determined to drive up to Santa Monica right then to see me. I'd managed to convince him otherwise—although he probably depressed the receiver just long enough to get another dial tone for the next ex-girlfriend after he hung up on me. He phoned me two days later, contrite, sober, and full of promises that he definitely would stay sober from now on. These promises were for himself, apparently, as I had no stake in the deal. Bitch that I am, I suggested maybe he should find some other line of work. I explained that owning a bar seemed to create inherent problems for alcoholics. Mark quickly informed me that he was not an alcoholic; he just mistreated alcohol. Though I failed to catch the distinction, I let it pass.

So, now, approaching the city limits of San Diego, I checked my watch to realize that it was only about ten-thirty in the morning. As it wasn't St. Patrick's Day, it was a wee bit early to appear at the Pot O'Gold. I was just debating on what to do when my cell phone started singing. Glancing at the Caller ID, I realized it was my home number.

"Mom?" I answered.

"It's me," Don said.

I swore silently and pungently to myself. I did not want to talk to Don for any reason.

"What time do you get off today? Do you know yet?"

My lie about working had apparently already taken on a life of its own. "Um . . . not sure."

"Sounds like you're driving."

"I am. Had to make a run for stuff."

"I thought you had PAs for that."

"Don, was there something specific?" I asked. As ever, a good offense is the best defense.

"I've had some time to think while I've been down here," he said, as if he'd just been waiting for me to cue him. "I've been working hard a long time, and it's paid off, financially speaking. I've bought several dealerships. It hasn't been that long ago that I was just trying to buy my first. You remember."

My mind drifted. I yanked it back with an effort. "Huh?"

"I sold you your Explorer from my first one. Remember? The dealership in Venice? The first one . . . before I moved to the Bay Area?"

Oh, yes. Did I mention that that's how I met Don? My car of the time—an old, old Chevy—had crapped out on me and left me stranded on Pico during rush hour. I could barely coax the damn thing over to the side of the road but the anxious drivers were furious with me for delaying them nonetheless. A lot of horns honked. I love LA but never get between a driver and his destination for any reason. Drive-by's do happen.

I managed to call a tow truck and we'd ended up at a repair service place near Don's first Jeep dealership. The mechanics at the repair place shook their heads and told me basically that the patient had died. I walked over to Don's place and saw the Explorer in the used car lot. It was only a year old with low mileage and it was black. I was in love. With the car.

And then there was Don.

Now, I dragged my thoughts back to the present. Don was still waiting for a response. "The Explorer's still great," I said. I hadn't had a problem with it outside of regular maintenance.

Don instantly went into car salesman mode. "I could get you a good deal on a Jeep. You should see the new ones."

I yawned. "You mean the ones with the round headlights that look like C-3PO?"

"You think they look like C-3PO?"

"You didn't call me to talk about cars."

"No . . ." He sighed. "You sure as hell don't make it easy, do you?"

"Make what easy?"

"Anything!" he said, exasperated. "Virginia—Ginny— I've been trying to have a few moments alone with you. I think we need to talk."

"Do we?" I asked, sounding as wearing as I felt. I was pulling into the parking lot of the Pot O'Gold. Surprisingly, there were more than a few cars around. "Talking's not good, Don. I can't talk now. I'm busy and I'm not sure where you're heading with this, but it doesn't sound good to me." There. Dr. Dick would be proud. I'd said what was on my mind. Maybe I am frightfully well adjusted. Wouldn't that just be a joke.

"When you get back tonight, give me a few minutes, okay?" he said. "We'll talk then."

"Don—"

He hung up. His words had sounded more like an order than a plea. They fueled my never-far-below-the-surface automatic, knee-jerk fury at anyone in authority.

"Asshole," I said, clicking off with gusto.

The phone rang in my hand. I glared at the number, but it was Daphne, not a repeat of Don. "Hey, there," I greeted her cautiously, still fuming over Don's high-handedness.

"Oh, Blue! I got a commercial! My God! We're shooting next week. Can you stand it? A real live job. Now, I'll be able to pay for those new Diesel jeans I bought!"

"That's great, Daphne," I said, meaning it. Commercials paid well. "Who's it for?"

"It's a pharmaceutical company," she said, her voice dampening a bit.

"And?"

"It's for Soft & Soothing."

"Sounds familiar. Is that some kind of skin cream?"

Daphne cleared her throat. "It's a vaginal itch remedy."

"Oh. Fun."

"But it's okay. I don't have to do anything embarrassing, or anything."

"That's good," I said. I'd had a momentary vision of Daphne digging away furiously at her crotch for realism's sake.

"It's one of those commercials where I talk to the camera. Y'know, girl-to-girl."

"Like these are the kind of things we talk about."

"Yeah." She laughed.

"Is it national?" I asked, getting back to the important thing: money.

"Yes, it is." There was a smile in her voice.

"Fantastic."

"Oh, and Blue? I hope you're not mad at me about seeing Dr. Dick. He's really helped me."

"Oh, forget about it." I am such a shit sometimes. I really am. She'd picked up on my vibes and now I was acting as if it were all in her head. I overrate myself sometimes. I really do. I'm just not that great.

"I just got the feeling you were kind of upset. If you want me to quit seeing him, I will. We don't really talk about you, y'know. It wouldn't be ethical. It's just afterwards, as I'm leaving I say something about you because you're my friend. Something nice."

Now I really felt like a heel.

"Daphne, when I get back, let's go out for a drink, just you and me," I said suddenly. Guilt. But I really did want to get together.

"Get back? Where are you?"

"San Diego."

"Oh, God, yes! I forgot."

I looked over at Black Mark's bar: dusty, shuttered, and tired-looking in the unforgiving midmorning sun. Without neon lights, bars are notoriously uninviting. This one looked worn down.

"Good luck, Blue," she said with feeling.

What was it with everyone feeling I needed luck to deal with Black Mark? They seemed to possess a collective sixth sense, knowing this Ex-File would be worse than others. I hoped they were wrong.

Drawing a deep breath I locked up the Explorer and headed toward the Pot O'Gold Saloon.

Chapter
17

I pushed open the front door, a heavy plank affair that looked as if it had been formed from the trunk of a mighty oak. An eerie *creeeaaakkkk* followed me inside. I glanced at the door handle. It was fashioned from some fake gold metal and was made to look like an elongated leprechaun wearing an evil smirk.

Classy.

I half-expected a few seedy looking regulars glued to bar stools, seeming to have been there for eons. Actually, the chairs were upside down atop the tables and the only body in the place was of a woman around my age with a thick tangle of red curls, and biceps showing beneath a sleeveless black top that made me do a double take. Clearly a workout maven. I felt instantly weak and worthless. I was going to have to do something serious about exercise soon or risk my mother's thickening waistline.

The woman was bent over a mop, swabbing the wooden floor down with repressed energy. She moved the mop in quick, hard strokes, her chin set. I could smell beer but the odor was surprisingly pleasant. Not stale and sour but inviting and fresh.

She stopped swabbing and gave me a hard look. "We're not open."

"I . . . was just looking for someone. Mark McGruder?"

"You want my husband?"

She said it like a challenge. "Not really," I stated matter-of-factly, an automatic response. "I just . . ." I paused, thinking how to explain. She waited, and I forged on, "Mark and I dated about a hundred years ago and I'm just kind of reconnecting—checking in—with my exes. He's not expecting me. Don't ask me why I'm doing this because I've already forgotten."

She leaned on the end of the mop. "Easy to forget things when it's been a hundred years."

I laughed. She took me completely by surprise. My initial impression had been that she was seething with anger or jealousy or something. Being with Mark could foster any number of unwelcome emotions.

"I'm Colleen," she introduced herself. "The fool that married the man."

"I'm Ginny Bluebell."

"Oh, you're that one."

She sounded so knowing that I was instantly on alert. "That one?" I repeated.

"Better than most."

"Well . . . good."

"What'll it be?" Colleen turned the 'closed' sign I hadn't noticed in the window to 'open.'

I couldn't imagine drinking at this hour. I glanced at the array of bottles behind the bar. Sunlight slanted through wooden blinds. Both the blinds and the bottles were dust-free. I was impressed. Product of Colleen's work, not Mark's, if I were any judge. "Irish coffee?"

She snorted, which could have meant anything, and circled to the back of the bar. With an economy of movement that signified long hours as a barkeep, she grabbed a clear glass cup in one hand, a bottle of Irish whiskey in another, poured the shot, set down the bottle and picked up the coffee pot. I decided not to comment that I preferred a little sugar in my drink as she topped off the coffee with a spurt of whipped cream and then drew a thin green line of creme de menthe across the top. She slid the cup my way. I glanced around for some sugar packets. None. Carefully, I dipped my tongue in the whipped cream. All I could think about were the calories. If I could catch about 10 percent of anorexia, just a mild case . . . But being a little anorexic is kind of like being a little pregnant.

I was encouraged to see that Colleen was pouring herself a beer. It came out of the tap fresh and bright amber. Seeing my gaze, she asked, "Want one?"

"I think I'd better wait till eleven. I've got this to finish." I hefted my Irish coffee.

"He's still sleeping," she said. I watched her press a cigarette between her lips and light it with a Bic. I decided not to point out California's no smoking law. What the hell. It was her place. "Tell me about this checking off the exes thing."

I shrugged. "My friends and I had this . . . meeting, I guess, and somehow we all said we'd try to improve our lives. Deal with the biggest problems that are affecting us. I have a friend who's basically anorexic."

"Basically?" She exhaled with authority.

"Sometimes bulimic, I think. Not that she's been diagnosed by a professional. And another friend has problems at work." Note to self: ask CeeCee what's up with the boss. "And another one's trying to quit dating losers. She seems to be closest to realizing her goal."

"How're you doing?"

"I'm getting through the list. Like a purge."

"Hmmm . . ." She exhaled long and thoughtfully. "Mark and I have a son. He stays the weekends with my mother."

I wasn't sure what she wanted me to make of that. I examined her surreptitiously. She had a killer body but lines of weariness framed her rather full mouth, and her large brown eyes seemed dulled by time and disappointment. More signs of life with Mark? I felt a rush of relief that was purely self-ish. I had dodged this particular bullet. The single life never looked better.

"Mark is unbearable before four o'clock," she said. "If you want to risk it, I'll go get him."

"I do have a time constraint," I admitted.

She drank half her glass, set it down, stubbed out her smoke, then pushed herself away from the bar. I gulped the rest of my Irish coffee, my eyes trained on the swinging doors through which she departed to the bar's interior. I heard footsteps on stairs and realized she was heading to the second floor. When she returned a few minutes later, she looked a bit more grim. A moment later I heard a loud thunk behind her and Mark staggered into view.

"Jesus fucking Christ!" he cried upon seeing me, lurch-ing my way.

Now I smelled the stale beer scent. He wrapped long arms around me and hugged me for all he was worth. I couldn't breathe, which was just as well since the odor of his breath could have asphyxiated me on the spot. Colleen left quickly. So much for thinking she might have jealous thoughts. She seemed more than happy to let me carry the load.

"Hi, Mark," I said a bit weakly.

"God . . ." He let go of me to swing his way around the back of the bar. He poured himself a huge mug of beer and gulped it as if it were life-giving elixir. In the end he wiped his mouth with the back of his hand. I don't know why, but it was kind of sexy. Slob that he was rapidly becoming, he still had that charm. I felt its tug and was a bit dumbstruck. Maybe there *is* something wrong with me. Most women would think twice about being with a man who was coming off a drunk and thinking about starting a new one.

But he had that Viggo Mortensen, *Lord of the Rings* thing going for him: long dark hair, scruffy yet trimmed, short beard, blue eyes, sly smile . . .

"Ya came down to see me, huh?" He grinned like a devil.

"Yep."

"I'm married, y'know."

"You don't deserve her."

He threw back his head with laughter. "She's lucky to have me."

It flooded back against my will: the reasons I'd run madly into his arms, away from Don and his rules. If I'd been in the market for lovemaking for the sake of lovemaking—which actually, I was, if you thought about it that way—Mark would be the kind of guy I'd want. But not married Mark. And well, not Mark anymore, either. I hadn't forgotten the Black Death and I resisted the urge to cross myself in some way in an effort to ward off evil. I had survived my relationship with Mark with only a few scars. I'd run screaming into his arms, then screaming out of them. It had been a long, quiet period between Black Mark and Knowles-It-All, and an even longer one between Knowles-It-All and Nate the Nearly Normal. After Mark, I really thought I'd learned my lesson. Well, I'd learned *a* lesson, at any rate. No matter how attractive they may seem, men like Mark McGruder were to be avoided at all cost. It's part of the female survivor guide. A part of me wanted to go after Colleen and try an intervention.

"Wanna beer?" Mark asked, pouring me one and himself another.

I took the glass mug and tentatively sipped. Beer, though it appeals in ways that defy explanation, has never been my drink. But a Ketel One vodka martini at eleven-thirty in the morning was a bad idea. So, I drank the beer and chatted with Mark, telling him why I'd come to see him.

At noon I switched to Ketel One. At four I was in the bag

and I'd made a whole host of new best friends: Mark's regulars, who had scattered in over the course of the afternoon.

"You can't drive home," Colleen told me. She'd reappeared at some point but by that time my vision was a little fuzzy.

"No shit," I said. Vaguely, I recalled there might be something I was supposed to do. The thought slipped into my head and flew out.

"She's staying with us," Mark told his wife. Colleen seemed slightly perturbed. I mumbled that I couldn't impose on them. Mark belched, then grinned. He had beautiful white teeth he didn't deserve. I told him so and he reached across the bar, grabbed my face and kissed me full on the mouth.

The bar erupted in shouts and catcalls. Colleen gave me a pitying look and disappeared again. She had a tendency to swim in and out of the picture.

I said to the room at large, "I think I'm drunk."

More hooting and hollering. I grinned. They loved me!

One of Mark's burliest friends suddenly growled, "What's that fucking noise?"

We all cocked an ear to listen. My cell phone was singing away in my purse. "Oh, shit," I said, giggling, picking up my purse. "It's my phone."

Mr. Burly grabbed my purse, yanked out the still cheerily ringing phone, eyed it malevolently, punched the green button and stated grimly, "Shut the fuck up."

I grabbed for it, suddenly alarmed. "That could be my mother!" Burly gave it up with a shrug and I said urgently, "Hello? Hello?"

"Virginia?" It was Don.

A jolt of sobriety hit me like a hammer. Not enough to totally kill the buzz, but enough to make me anxious. "It's Ginny, Don. *Ginny*. Please. It's not that hard."

"Where are you?"

"I'm at a bar."

"I thought you were at work."

"Believe me, this is work." I was proud of myself. Scarcely a slur in there. "You rang?"

"Are you going to be home soon?" He sounded prissy, pissed, and skeptical.

"Is my mom there?" I retorted, sounding equally prissy, pissed, and skeptical.

"Lorraine's at the movies. She wore dark glasses."

"Did she smuggle in popcorn in one of her big-ass purses?" I asked, delighted that Mom was doing something without Don.

"I don't know." He bit off the words.

I looked around. I didn't want to lose my new friendships because I'd been yanked back to another time and place. Mark caught my eye and signaled *who is that?*. I said aloud, "You wouldn't believe it."

"What?" asked Don.

"I'm not coming back tonight. I've had too much to drink."

"I'll come get you . . . Ginny."

"Nope."

"Just tell me where you are."

"San Diego."

A long, long pause. I listened hard. I could tell he was about to explode. "Fine," he snapped out. "Let me know when you're sober." He hung up.

"What happened?" Mark asked.

I focused in on him. He was beginning to look better and better. It was a damn good thing he was married or I might have found myself doing something totally stupid. I scooped up my purse and asked, "Is there a motel within walking distance?"

Mark put his arm around my shoulders and led me through the swinging doors to the narrow stairway to the second floor. "I spend a lot of nights here," he said.

"I'm not sleeping with you."

"I know."

"Do you?"

"Colleen will break a bottle over my head if I even try. She likes you. So, you stay here, and I'll go home with my lovely wife tonight." He opened the door to a plain room with a sofa and a big-ass television. "Pity," he said.

I collapsed on the sofa, my head spinning.

I woke up at three A.M., dying of thirst. It was as if all the cells in my body suddenly collapsed on themselves, crying out: WATER.

I could still hear noise from the bar below. Sure, it was after closing. The doors were undoubtedly locked. But a few hearty souls were still awake and undoubtedly imbibing. I determined I, too, would never be able to own a bar. The hours would shorten my life.

I stumbled downstairs and pushed through the swinging doors. Mark, Colleen, and a couple of gentlemen I couldn't remember were drinking coffee. Well, Colleen was drinking coffee; the others were drinking coffee and whiskey. Mark was glassy-eyed and grabbing at his wife. She sidled away but he managed to get a piece of her shirt, dragging her back. She full on slapped him and he roared with outrage. Colleen started shrieking like a banshee and Mark yelled at the top of his lungs. Sexual tension thickened the air. I could almost smell a feral, primitive, lusty scent that seemed to pour out of them like pheromones.

I remembered being with Mark. The terrible dangerousness of it all.

I decided dying of thirst was better than being part of that scene. I snuck back up the stairs.

The next morning I left at the crack of dawn, writing a letter of thanks on a cocktail napkin for Colleen. I was momentarily stumped by the deadbolt. I could open it from the inside, but then I wouldn't be able to relock the door. My answer was to climb out a window in the kitchen, which was through a door behind the bar. I slammed the window shut behind me and walked to my car through the sharp, unforgiving light.

I felt like hell. As I started the engine, I considered my drunken day with Black Mark. Had anything positive gotten accomplished? I sat in the growing heat of the morning, smelling dust and the faint leathery scent of the Explorer's interior. Maybe something had gotten accomplished: I knew I was totally cured of Black Mark. I'd suspected it before; been glad I'd run from the disaster of his life. But I was completely, utterly sure now. Mark McGruder was a piece of my history, much like Charlie and Larry. If I saw them on the street I'd say hello; if they passed without seeing me, too far out of range to holler to, I wouldn't care.

Progress.

I searched all over my car for my Altoids, finally settling for a group of little red Tic Tacs that were hiding in a corner of my door pocket.

"God," I said, tentatively sticking them in my mouth. Their cinnamon flavor instantly masked the leftover whiskey, beer, and whatever else which made my mouth taste so godawful. Somewhere in the evening I recalled eating french fries, potato chips and some deep fried vegetable that I suspect may have come from another planet.

"And here you were worried about the whipped cream," I muttered, heading up the freeway to Santa Monica.

The Ginny Blue All-Carb diet.

I made it almost all the way up the 405 to Santa Monica in nearly two hours of seventy-miles-per-hour driving before traffic slowed me down. And the reason traffic slowed me down was that it had started to rain. And in southern California a) it never rains; b) when it rains it runs like gushing rivulets through parched, hard land and pours onto the freeways and causes all the drivers to freak out, slam on their brakes, skid wildly, then creep along at less than ten miles per hour.

So, I drummed my fingers on the steering wheel and fumed. Glancing around at the nearby cars, I wistfully longed for the couple who'd engaged in car-bouncing sex. It would have been a nice diversion. And a diversion I needed, as I was feeling a little odd. Say what you will, Mark and Colleen had that sexual thing going—something I hadn't felt in a long while—something I wasn't getting with Will. Was sex really something I had to work on with Will? That's not the way it was with Mark, or even with Don, for that matter.

And even if I got there, I doubted I could sustain a long-term relationship and a happening sex life. Colleen and Mark could, albeit in a dysfunctional, edge-of-violence kind of way. I easily recalled that feeling: fight to your last breath, no holds barred, then collapse into bed and make love as if you could bring the dead back to life.

My cell phone started chiming. Since I was at a dead stop I took both hands off the wheel to dig into my purse. I found it, clicked the green button and said, "Hello," while the neighbor on my left lit a cigarette and the one on my right began applying eyeliner in the rearview mirror. As this was a man, I gave him a second look. He glanced my way and smiled. Dyed black hair. Pale skin. Very Gothic. Not the usual LA look.

"Virginia?"

Oh, Christ. Don. "Sorry, I haven't called. Although I am sober now."

"I'm heading out today. I was hoping I could see you before I left, but since you took off for San Diego . . ."

"I'm back in Santa Monica. Well, nearly. I'm getting off the 405 to the 10 as soon as the traffic moves. Rain," I added.

"Oh." He thought that over.

"Is my mom around?"

"She's getting ready to leave, too."

"What? Is she still there?"

"Here . . ." He handed off the phone and mom came on, "Hi, Virginia. I hate to leave without seeing you."

"I'll be there in a few minutes. Don't leave yet."

"I'll be here for a few more minutes. I've got to get back to work."

"Are you ready? How are the eyes?"

"Oh, no change since yesterday. Ugly as sin. Dark and battered. Thank God for sunglasses. I bought a new purse. On Montana. A really great shop. I love Montana."

I nodded, though she couldn't see me. Montana was the street in Santa Monica for boutiques with the most outrageous price tags. Cool stuff, but scary to shop there if you're on any kind of budget. I was glad I didn't know what my mother paid for her latest big-ass purse.

"I have time for lunch if you can get here. Then can I catch a ride to the airport?"

"Sure." I felt a pang. I was going to miss my mother. I hadn't spent enough time with her because of Don. I wished she would stay and Don would go.

I managed to squeak past a few cars and was actually on the off ramp when my phone chirped again. This time I wasn't taking my eyes off the rain-slicked pavement and I kept my left hand firmly clamped on the steering wheel as I dug blindly through my purse for the phone I had just put back in there. I snatched it up on about the fifth ring and said somewhat impatiently, "Yeah?"

"Hi, Ginny. It's Jackson."

I dropped the phone. It slipped out of nerveless fingers and found its way somewhere near my feet, wedging under the accelerator. "Fuck," I said through gritted teeth. "Jackson!" I yelled. "I dropped the phone! Call me back in ten minutes!"

It actually took me nearly twenty minutes to get on the 10 and then off at Cloverfield, my exit. I swore the whole way. Worse than a truck driver. By the time I got my hand on my phone I was on Olympic and nearly home. Jackson had not called back.

I pulled into my underground lot and dejectedly watched Schematic Man slide past me as the gate opened. I knew my disappointment was way out of line for the circumstances. If I hadn't been so disappointed I would have berated myself for acting like an idiot. What was it with Jackson Wright?

But then my brain started whirling. Why was he calling me? How did he get my number? Did he *have* my number? Did he ask someone for it? Why, why, why didn't he call back!

My Caller ID couldn't pick up his number so I was stuck. I entered my condo, lost in thought. Mom and Don were in the kitchen, chatting away about my mother's favorite topic: real estate.

"Oh, Ginny," she said. "There you are. I've gotta run. I just called and got an earlier flight. The Samuelsons are buying that house on Lake Chinook. It's that dilapidated monstrosity on that beautiful piece of property."

"Okay."

"And if this deal goes through, we're getting a proposal together for this condo. Your landlord called, by the way. Mr. Norell? I told him you were interested in buying."

"Mom . . ."

"He's one of those," she said with a shake of her head. "Thinks it's worth tons more than it is. I think I straightened him out."

"Mom . . . ."

"What do you think it's worth?" Don asked my mother curiously.

"A lot more than Oregon prices, that's for sure. It's mind-boggling, really," she said, sounding as if it wasn't at all. In the world of real estate, possibilities were endless.

"I can't afford it," I said.

She smiled sweetly, deaf to my words. "Would you get my bag?" she asked Don, and he sprinted off to do her bidding. Fifteen minutes later we were all in my Explorer, heading to LAX. I knew Don had joined so he could have that talk with me.

I lingered at the departure point until my mother practically yanked her bag away from me and waved good-bye. Her dull, mustard-yellow purse was nearly as large as her one piece of roller luggage.

"Alone at last," Don said.

I gave him a look as I climbed behind the wheel and maneuvered my way back to the 405. "Okay, hit me," I said as we merged onto the freeway. Traffic wasn't too bad for a Sunday afternoon.

"Don't worry," Don said, chiding me. "I know you want me out of here. I'm going. I'm not interested in starting up something between us again."

"I didn't say you were."

"You thought it." He sniffed in amusement. "Thanks for putting up with me for so long. Oh, and I called your friend Bradley Knowles."

"You got hold of Brad?" I have to admit, I was kind of bugged at Don for his sudden "you had me all wrong, Virginia, I was never interested in starting up with you again" act. Call me egotistical, but it seemed a little false. Or maybe that was just me, trying to make myself better than I am.

"It's Bradley," Don informed me.

His teaching tone scraped my nerves, reminding me of all the reasons I was glad he wanted NOTHING TO DO WITH ME. I snorted. "Since when."

"It's what his receptionist said when I asked for Brad Knowles."

"Well . . . great. Did he take your case?"

"I haven't talked to him directly yet. I'll let you know."

"Do that," I said, not meaning it.

"I left the card you gave me with his number on the kitchen counter."

"Thanks."

We returned to the condo and Don, who'd already packed up, added, "One thing about the rain, huh? It'll dampen things up."

I nodded. Rain was a natural deterrent to the Santa Ana winds that fanned the slightest ember in the tinder-dry southern California hills and created firestorms. Though it was November, everything was bone dry.

"Good-bye . . . Ginny," Don said with a smile.

We hugged and I felt a pang. This was new for me. Don, though he wasn't for me, was a decent guy. I watched him walk to his car from my living room window. He'd parked on the street, having to remember to move his car every Monday morning for the street cleaners. Parking was a battle out there. Don hadn't complained or expected special treatment.

I wondered how Will would fare if he were to come visit me.

I felt kind of down. Maybe going through the Ex-Files wasn't good for my psyche; I seemed to be feeling oddly vulnerable and alone. And this feeling had progressed from Nate to Charlie to Larry to Don and through Mark. I only had Kane, Lang, and Brad*ley* Knowles left. And then what? Something new with Will?

"Damn," I muttered softly.

I sure as hell wished I hadn't missed Jackson's call.

Chapter
18

The following Thursday I stared at myself in the Cheval mirror of the ultracool dressing room at Charisma, THE wedding store on Montana. I said through the wall to Daphne who was in the room next to me, "I thought black would save me but I look like a zombie."

"Shhh! Jill will hear you."

"Bridesmaid dresses? These are Vegas cocktail gowns. My thighs are scary."

"Mine's too short, too."

"Is CeeCee here yet?"

"I don't think so."

"We need her to be our spokesperson."

"Don't you think Jill will notice herself? She doesn't want her bridesmaids looking like streetwalkers."

I examined my thighs critically, turning from side to side. Not good. And Jill? Who knew what she would do. She was as unstable as I'd ever seen her. Planning a wedding had killed her sense of humor, such as it was. I was hoping to pull her aside and try to jolly her out of it a bit, but I was actually a bit preoccupied.

Tonight we were all going to "Getting Able with Kane."

"We still haven't had our drink, just you and me," Daphne reminded.

"You're the one that's busy," I said. "Tomorrow's the shoot?"

She sighed heavily. "I just wish the commercial weren't about vaginal itching. It was hard to tell my mother. She was thrilled until she found out what it was about. She actually hung up on me. Made an excuse to change the subject, then she was gone."

"Hard to have bragging rights over a vaginal itchy commercial."

CeeCee said, loudly, from another cubicle. "What are these things? Shirts?"

"Shhhh!" Daphne shushed. "Jill's in the store."

"Glad you're here," I called. "We need someone to explain the situation to Jill. She's kind of—wound up."

"I could use some Soft & Soothing for the pain in my ass caused by these stupid dresses."

Daphne groaned and I pointed out, "Not exactly the right part of the anatomy," I said. "Close, though."

"Damn it . . ." Daphne said in frustration. I heard a little scream, a rending of material, then silence.

"Dare I ask what happened?" I said after a few moments of silence.

"No."

"Is the dress still in one piece?" CeeCee asked.

". . . no . . ."

"Is it fixable?" I waited, frozen, glad Jill was still apparently out of earshot, lost in a plethora of wedding dresses, veils, and doodads in another part of the store.

"The fabric's ruined! It just tore! Right in the center of the bodice. No seam or anything! What do you think?"

"Are you guys in here?" Jill's voice yelled from outside the dressing room cells.

I jumped and listened hard. There was ominous silence from Daphne's room.

"We're here," CeeCee answered.

"Come out and model," Jill ordered.

Like hell. I wriggled out of my minigown and threw on my jeans and black tee. Unlatching the lock on my door, I stepped into the hallway and beheld CeeCee just exiting her cubicle. Her hair was cropped and bleached white. She'd also pulled on her own clothes: a wife-beater in khaki and olive camouflage and a pair of cargo pants whose pockets bulged with items that looked like hard pieces of plastic. She pulled out these treasures, which resolved into a cell phone, iPod, Game Boy, and little discs and widgets whose purpose I could only guess at.

Jill demanded, "Why aren't you in your dresses?"

"Mine needs a little altering," I said, still aware of the silence of Daphne's tomblike room.

"Yeah. It needs a SKIRT." Still holding her bits of gear, CeeCee hitched a thumb toward the dressing room she'd just exited. "I'm not wearing it."

"They're too short?" Jill looked anxious enough to cry. "Daphne? Have you still got yours on."

"Sort of . . ."

"Open the door. Let me see."

CeeCee and I gave each other a look. I glanced momentarily at the paraphernalia in her hands. "Been hanging out with a gamer," she explained.

Daphne opened her door. The black sheath had a rip in the center. The material frayed around an opening, which revealed Daphne's belly button. An inny. She actually looked rather good.

Jill suddenly burst into tears. None of us moved. "I didn't mean to," Daphne said.

"Oh, fuck," Jill muttered around tears. She walked out of the dressing room and right out of the store. Daphne looked as if she might cry, too, so I helped her out of the disaster of a dress and we all vamoosed as quickly as possible. The salesgirl looked shell-shocked. I felt for her. I'd seen the prices on the would-be bridesmaid dresses.

There was no talking to Jill. She'd swiped away the tears and was angry in that deep, hurt, miserable way. We tried to be supportive about the dresses but she slapped a hand in the air. "It's all just a mess," she declared. "I'll see you tonight." She ran across the street to where her car was parked.

Daphne whispered, "It's all my fault."

"Oh, it is not," I said, annoyed. "There's something going on."

"I wouldn't count on this wedding taking place," CeeCee muttered, pulling out a cigarette.

We all tacitly agreed. Daphne left us, but I stuck around while CeeCee lit up.

"Do weddings have to make you crazy?" she asked, exhaling blue smoke from the side of her mouth.

"Yes," I said.

We pondered this fact in silence for a few moments, then I said, "So, I get it that you and the boss are totally done."

She shrugged. "He went back to his wife. I got pissed. Thought about sleeping with Cheese-Dick for about a nanosecond, just to make him as pissed. Found a better way to get even."

"I don't think I want to know."

"Demanded more money."

"Oh." I was pleasantly surprised. "Way to capitalize."

"Talked him into letting his son work at the station."

"His son?"

"A cool kid."

"The gamer?" I asked, my heart sinking with dread.

"We're not doing it," she said calmly. "He's eighteen, so legally we could, but that's not it. It just scares Gerald that we're friends. He thinks I might talk."

"Be careful," I warned.

"Uh-huh."

A terrible thought crossed my mind. "The son isn't in that picture on his desk, is he?"

CeeCee cocked her head thoughtfully. "He might be. What do you think that means?"

"Nothing good," I stated firmly.

"Blue, the kid's just my friend. And if it drives a knife in Gerald's heart, all the better. I cared about that asshole." She swallowed hard and narrowed her eyes against the smoke.

CeeCee being hurt was a new one on me. I thought briefly about Will. My little fling seemed unimportant and uninteresting next to her heartbreak. I said, "I slept with Will Torrance. And then Rhianna showed up and threw a *Fargo* snow globe at me. I haven't slept with him since."

"A *Fargo* snow globe? Did it break?"

"Uh-huh."

CeeCee shook her head at the waste of it all. "Are you going to sleep with him again?"

"No," I said.

A rawhide-thin woman with a snazzy, small blue case hurried past us to the door of Charisma. She stopped at the last moment. "Are you here for the fitting?"

We gazed at her, not sure how to answer. She took our hesitation as a yes and held the door, practically shooing us inside. CeeCee stubbed out her cigarette and frowned. I said, "Ummmm . . . we may have to delay."

"I don't have time." She stood at the door.

CeeCee and I shared a look. With a shrug CeeCee headed inside and I followed dutifully. The salesgirl's mouth dropped open.

"Where's Jill?" the woman asked impatiently. I realized she was the designer as she set her blue case on the counter and opened it. It was full of sewing supplies—a veritable torture chamber of needles, scissors, pins, and unidentifiable tiny little pieces of hardware that looked as if it could become a part of a Stephen King book in short order.

CeeCee said, "She had to leave."

The designer's nostrils flared so wide I marveled at the elasticity of human skin. "We had an appointment."

"There may be problems with the wedding," I offered cautiously. I didn't know what was going on, but I sensed this woman better be alerted *tout suite* that the dresses were probably not going to work.

"I need to get the dresses fitted," she insisted.

"Well, you can stand here and wait," CeeCee said. "But Jill's not coming back and one of your gowns has a rip right down the center and all of them don't have enough material to cover our asses."

It was a good exit line. And exiting seemed like a good idea as the designer's expression turned thunderous. I said, breathlessly, as CeeCee and I skedaddled, "I'm going to find Jill and see what's going on."

"I'll see you tonight."

I jumped into the Explorer and grabbed my cell phone. It rang in my hand. Impatiently I checked the Caller ID. I didn't want to talk to anyone but Jill. Surprised, I realized it *was* Jill.

"Hey," I answered. "Where are you?"

"The Coffee Bean on Wilshire."

"I'll be right there."

I grimaced as I clicked off. She sounded miserable. I prayed to the parking gods that I would find a nearby spot and was rewarded. As I walked past the open fire pit in the front courtyard I spotted Jill sitting dispiritedly at a small table for two. I sat down across from her. She looked like death. No expression. Hollow eyes. Sunken cheeks. Pasty skin. The works.

"What?" I asked quietly.

"He called it off." She drew a breath, her lips quivering faintly. "It's over."

"Ian called the wedding off?" I repeated, trying to hide my shock. Things were worse than I'd imagined. Further along than I'd imagined.

"He called everything off. He thinks I'm sick. He wants out. It's over. Over."

She closed her eyes and looked about to pass out. Gently I reached across and clasped her hand. For a few moments neither of us said anything then she inhaled shakily and said, "the *fucking* bastard."

I nodded in silent agreement. My heart went out to her. No more Jill-Ian? I couldn't wrap my brain around it.

Tears starred her lashes but her pugnacious jaw was set hard. I said, "Is it selfish of me to be relieved my thighs won't be wedged into that black dress?"

"Yes." But something softened in her expression.

"It's always about me, you know."

"They were too short anyway."

"You gonna be okay?" I searched her face.

Her chin trembled. She tried to hang onto her hard jaw and couldn't. "I don't want to talk about it," she said in a teary voice. "I want to go to your thing tonight."

"Getting Able?"

She nodded.

"Jill, for pete's sake . . ."

"No, I'm going. I'm not thinking about this. I want to think about your problems, not mine. How are you doing on the Ex-Files? I haven't asked in a while."

"Fine."

"How many are left?"

"Ummm . . . three, I guess. I haven't quite dealt with Lang. And there's Kane, of course. And Knowles-It-All."

"You're done with Charlie and that hairy guy?" Jill's brow was furrowed. She seemed to be putting a ton of energy into this task.

"Hairy Larry," I agreed.

"And Don the Devout?"

"Done with Don."

"And the next one?"

"Black Mark," I said. "Done with him, too."

"Tonight's Kane."

"Looks like it."

She drew a long, shuddering breath. "How long does it take, Blue? To get over them?"

She wanted answers. She wanted to know when she would be as frightfully well adjusted as I was supposed to be. I shook my head. "Eons," I said depressingly.

Too late I realized that sounded a lot like "Ians."

I am so not good at commiserating . . . unless maybe alcohol is involved.

To say that the nixed wedding plans affected our mood as we dutifully headed to the Kane Reynolds extravaganza was putting it mildly indeed. I expected Jill to change her mind and beg off, but she was determined to go to the motivational session. This didn't mean she was a barrel of laughs. She was so silent and removed that we all felt unsettled. Daphne and I chattered away to fill the gaps and CeeCee just lowered the Explorer's window and smoked. Jill, always so vocal, opinionated, and tough was the proverbial shadow of her former self. The *fucking* bastard had really done her in.

"I could kill him," Daphne declared through tight lips as she and I walked ahead of Jill and CeeCee on our way to the entry doors of the auditorium. "Getting Able With Kane" was being held at a rent-a-room in the business district of downtown LA, not far from Liam Engleston's restaurant. I recalled how Jill had dressed him down, much to my horror at the time, and my mouth curved at the memory.

"Why are you smiling?" Daphne demanded.

"Ian's going to miss her."

She reared back and gave me a look of horror. "Do you want them to get back together?"

"I have no idea," I said truthfully.

"Well, I don't. He's hurt her so much. Talk about a loser. He's at the top of the list."

"I can't decide whether he called it off over her eating disorder, or if he's just saying that's the reason. He's known she's had food issues all along. Maybe he just got scared. The responsibility of marriage, and all that."

"I hope he really, *really* misses her."

"At least we don't have to wear the dresses."

"Thank God." She darted a glance back at Jill. "Who'll pay for them, do you think?"

"Let's hope it's Ian."

Daphne checked her watch. I knew she was thinking ahead to tomorrow's shoot. Though she'd been the one who'd pushed hardest for this event, she was fighting the clock.

"We don't have to stay for the whole thing," I pointed out.

"*You* do," Daphne stressed, shaking a finger playfully at my nose. "Come on, Blue. You're not going to let this derail you, are you?"

"I'll use any excuse I can get," I answered honestly.

Daphne chuckled. "And I'm here to save you from yourself."

"Like Kane?"

"Exactly."

Inside we were met by several fresh-faced young women in dark blue shirts and slacks with bright red "Time To Get Able" stickers affixed above their breasts. I suddenly felt very strange. I'd been so wrapped up in Jill's problems—and CeeCee's, and come to think of it, my own—that I really hadn't thought ahead to what this meeting would be like.

Jill and CeeCee met us at the entry door and we all nodded to the greeters. I declined a name tag, though the pressure was pretty damn intense. Free will seemed to be something Kane & his Able company didn't believe in. I had to be firm, as firm as I am to the people who try to get me to switch long-distance service. Thanks, but no thanks. I'm not interested. I'm getting off the phone now. Click.

Unfortunately, I couldn't just hang up on these kids. CeeCee gazed down her nose, looking fierce and alternative.

But the kids were spunky, giddy, and kind of spaced out in that natural high way only religion, mind-altering drugs— and, I guess, Kane Reynolds—seemed to provide. Nothing could get them down. I had a feeling we were all going to join in with *Kumbaya* or *We Are The World*.

Jill let them stick a name tag on her—a clear indication that the real Jill wasn't inhabiting her body just now. She followed me to a seat about halfway to the front and left of the main aisle. I gave the people sitting front and center a hard look. Who are these people who have to be right up in front?

"Let's move closer," Daphne said.

Oh.

"I don't want to miss anything," she continued.

"I do," I said, planting myself in a chair.

"This Kane is the guy you smoked dope with in high school?" CeeCee, still exhibiting her just-dare-to-speak-to-me body language, asked without looking at me. She perched on the edge of her chair, ready to shoot out of there at a moment's notice. I glanced around the gathering crowd. There were several middle-aged women in knitted sweaters; one displayed Persian cats; another, baskets of fruit. The men were in suits and ties that were about eight years past the current fashion trend.

"This is . . . frightening," I said.

"It hasn't even started yet," Daphne shushed me. "You should tell someone that you know Kane. Warn him, so that you can have some time afterwards without all the wannabes around."

"I'll take my chances."

I was having a hard time remembering that Dr. Dick had professed some interest in Kane's inspirational self-awareness shtick, but as we got closer to the actual start time more young professionals began to fill in the seats. I thought about Kane and the other nerds from high school, those evenings spent sucking smoke from a water pipe and the stoned hours afterward.

"Cool," I said aloud.

CeeCee gave me a sideways look. Before I could explain, there was a sudden change of air pressure in the room. Everyone looked up expectantly as a side door opened and Kane strode to the front of the room.

People in the first few rows actually stood up and clapped. Kane held up a hand, all modesty, and announced, "Welcome, one and all. So glad you could make it. I've been learning the LA freeway system. In the time it took to get here from the airport, I learned all the names and numbers. I hit the 405—the San Diego Freeway; the 10—the Santa Monica Freeway; and the 110—the Harbor Freeway; and I might've caught a bit of the 101—the Ventura Freeway. And wow. Traffic's a bitch, huh?"

The sweater ladies shifted in their seats and giggled as another wave of thunderous clapping ensued. I stared at Kane. This was my one-time lover? Ex-File Number Two, who'd gotten my mind off Charlie, then expanded it with drugs, alcohol, and rock and roll? If anyone had ever decided to become a Tony Robbins clone, Kane was it.

"He's really good-looking," Daphne said, sounding surprised.

"At least he's not gray," I said, examining Kane's cool, dark looks. "Or bald."

"I like bald," remarked CeeCee.

"I like it, too," I said. "But not with Kane. He's too . . ."

"Perfect."

This was from Jill, about the first thing she'd said all night. We all looked at her. "It's an act, a show, a Barnum & Bailey circus. He dyes that hair. It's too dark, too monochrome. And those teeth? They've been shined and buffed."

"That's what we do in LA," Daphne reminded her. I just shrugged, happy Jill had joined the living again.

"He's a Ken doll," Jill said. And then her eyes suddenly filled with tears. "God damn it," she whispered, bending her head.

"It's okay," I murmured.

"There aren't any decent men left! They're all fakes."

"That's not true," Daphne tried to soothe, but Jill wasn't having any of it.

"They're all about the big show. The big *fucking* show. And you'd better be a part of it, 'cause if you're not, you're history. A broken toy. Shit to throw away!"

"I don't think that's strictly true." Daphne couldn't help arguing. She wanted things to be rosy. She lived for the silver lining. I put my hand on her shoulder to hold back anything else. Let Jill rant.

"Have you dated anyone since Leo?" Jill demanded in a harsh whisper. By this time Kane was in full swing, talking about self-awareness, goals, picturing yourself in the future . . . pretty much the usual stuff.

"Do you mind?" a voice hissed from the row behind us.

"No," Daphne whispered quietly to Jill, a little hurt that she was suddenly under attack.

"Shut the fuck up," the voice behind us said.

I suddenly felt very self-aware, very motivated. I pictured myself in the near future turning to clock the guy behind me. But Jill came alive with all the fury and hurt she'd been nursing toward Ian. She twisted sharply, giving our annoyed friend the full benefit of her blotchy, furious, tear-stained face.

"Don't worry. I'm leaving," she told him coldly.

"Good." He made one of those male sneers and glanced around, seeking supporters. I'd seen that sneer and glance technique before. It was used when some guy wanted to point out what a horror story the girl talking to him was.

Jill pushed out her chair and stood right in front of him. Several of the fresh-faced crew glanced over, alarmed at the developing scene. Most of the room laughed at some other amusing Kane remark.

"What do you want, bitch?" he said deliberately.

CeeCee suddenly swiveled sharply and karate-chopped

him in the knee, like a doctor checking reflexes. Sure enough, his leg flew forward and banged into my chair. It was so comical it broke the tension. I think we would have burst into laughter if he'd relaxed a little. Instead, his face drew back into a grimace of fury and I swear twin streams of vapor shot from his nostrils. El Toro seemed to be pawing the floor, ready to charge CeeCee.

She warned coldly, "The last guy who touched me got a cigarette burn in the back of his hand."

"Fuck you," he said decisively.

"Excuse me?" a fresh-face interrupted. "Is there a problem?"

"These cunts can't stop talking," El Toro spewed. "Get rid of 'em."

Her face whitened. She glanced around helplessly.

Kane seemed to wake up to the fact that there was a disturbance in the southwest quadrant. He glanced our way and I saw him zero in on me. There was no mistaking the flicker of surprise that crossed his face. I didn't respond in any way. I couldn't. Not while CeeCee was now nose-to-nose with El Toro. I thought she might get scorched by the fumes. I held my breath. He was a rhino-necked guy with close-set eyes and sausage-shaped fingers. I pegged him for either a hit man or an actor specializing in Mafioso parts.

Jill threw gasoline on the fire. "You're making my point," she told him. "The big show. All muscle-head bullshit."

He threw back his head. I winced, certain he was about to bellow his fury and charge. More fresh-faced followers appeared. I expected no more than their collective wringing of hands but anything's possible.

"Let's go," I urged harshly.

Daphne didn't waste time. She practically yanked Jill out of her chair. That left me with CeeCee, who was keeping up a cool matador staring contest with our furious Taurus. She did let me drag her away; she's not suicidal. But she kept her eyes on him all the way out. He, in turn, glared back, sneeringly triumphant. CeeCee gave him the classic "up-yours" gesture before we hit the cool night air outside.

"Well, that was fun," I said.

"He called us the 'c' word," Daphne whispered.

CeeCee snorted. "That was meant for me."

"I think I can safely say that was meant for all of us," I rejoined.

"My fault," Jill said. But she didn't sound repentant.

"Asshole," CeeCee muttered. She was still focused, laser-like, on the auditorium doors.

"What are we going to do now?" Daphne looked shattered. "Ginny can't meet with Kane."

Since this seemed like the least important aspect of the situation, I pointed out, "We're all still alive."

"But this is your chance."

I wasn't sure if this was the right time to mention that Kane and I had briefly locked eyes during the skirmish. This wasn't how I wanted to meet up with him again.

A door pushed open behind us. All four of us whipped around, wondering if El Toro had broken from the ring. But it was one of the fresh-faced blue shirts, a young man with an earnest face. "Is one of you Virginia Bluebell?" he asked.

I lifted a hand. Wearily, I said, "That would be me."

Chapter

19

If there is a hell, I'm in it.

I sat primly in one of the straight-backed, auditorium chairs in an anteroom off to one side of the meeting room. Where my friends were I had no idea. After locking eyes with me, Kane had apparently asked one of his minions to fetch me. So, here I was. Waiting. For Ex-File Number Two.

I examined my fingernails, lifted my arms over my head several times and stretched. A refrain from a song kept running through my head, and I realized it was a song from my time with Kane. We'd been together, what? Two months? It was a far more distant memory than even Charlie, though it had been relatively soon after my first sexual experience. Funny, I had trouble remembering having sex with Kane, except for the fact that he liked to refer to it as 'making love,' as if that made it better somehow. I certainly believed it did at the time. Still, my memory of my efforts to smoke dope, and my lung-hacking afterwards, were far more indelibly etched in the wrinkles and folds of my brain. Was that all there really was to our relationship? Experimentation with marijuana? What I recalled most were the images of the basement of his parents' house and the couch where we'd "done it," and not much about Kane himself. It was high school, for God's sake. *High school.*

I didn't see how meeting with Kane could make any difference to my life now.

The good news was I had neither fears nor anticipation. It sort of felt like I was on a job interview for a position I didn't want.

My cell phone, which I had turned to vibrate, suddenly went off in my pants pocket. So far, this was my only thrill of the day. "Hello?"

"Hi, it's me," said Holly. "We've got a job for Trash Athletics in Seattle. I'm booking flights for a week from Sunday."

"I'm in." What a relief. The working world. The real world.

"We're picking up a coordinator up there unless you have someone in mind."

"Sounds good." As long as it wasn't Barb, I was happy.

Trash Athletics. A snowboard/skateboard/grunge-type outfit. CeeCee's style to the max. I wondered if there was any chance she could come with along as a PA. I'd be happy to buy her airline ticket. Wishful thinking on my part, as she seemed to have her job at the radio station—and her nonrelationship with Gerald—thoroughly under control.

I'd barely hung up when the phone vibrated again, this time in my hand. I nearly dropped it and went through a juggling act for a second or two. "Yeah?" I answered.

"I'm naked and waiting for you."

It was Will. I thought of Holly, her warnings, my future employment. I realized I had zero sex drive when it came to Will. Maybe seeing Black Mark, whom Will reminded me of, had some play in that as well.

I said, "I'm at 'Getting Able with Kane'."

"Where? Who?"

I was actually gratified that he didn't know what it meant, until he said, "Oh, that self-help guru?"

"I wouldn't call him a guru." I was firm. This distinction

mattered, though if asked I wouldn't have been able to quite say why.

"Can you leave and get over here? I'm going to grill some steaks on the barbeque."

"Naked?"

"I'll be wearing a chef's hat."

I smiled to myself. This was more like it but it still wasn't quite enough. "Promise I won't get any more snow globes thrown at me."

"Oh, for God's sake." He sounded pissed.

"We've got a logistics problem," I said, stalling. "I'm not even close to your place." *And I've still got to meet with Kane.* "Can we delay a couple of hours?"

"No, Ginny," he said with extreme patience. "Hard-ons don't last that long."

I almost said, "Ever thought about Viagra?" but decided it wasn't the right call. Instead I said, "If I walked out the door now, I'd still be forty-five minutes from the barbeque."

"Fuck it, then." He hung up.

I stared at my phone as if it were a Judas. He *hung up* on me? Because I was across town? It's not like anybody's ever near anyone else in LA! What a pain in the ass!

I ground my teeth. Hadn't I warned myself about directors? They weren't any better than actors. It was all about me, me, me, and there was no room for anything else. Didn't I know this. *Hadn't I learned?*

I heard a faint cheer go up and I checked my watch. It sounded like Kane was finally done motivating. Hopefully, this was the end of the event. I wondered if my friends were still hanging around outside or if they'd taken off in a cab. I phoned Daphne's cell as she was the most reliable about answering but was instantly put through to voice mail.

"Still here," I said to her chirpy direction to leave a message. "But it looks like the Dr. Feel Good is almost done."

I was in the process of dialing CeeCee when the door opened and a couple of minions appeared, wearing their patented bright, white smiles, blue shirts, black slacks and red "Time To Get Able" stickers.

"Kane is almost ready for you," one of the female ones said. The reverential way her mouth caressed "Kane" kind of gave me pause.

"But am I ready for him?" I asked.

They smiled knowingly at one another, completely missing the irony. "We'll be back when the auditorium's empty."

"Go tend the flock. I'll just wait here in my cell," I said agreeably. Tiny frown lines briefly appeared between their brows, but then they must have spied their leader because they flew through the doors as if greeting a returning king.

It still was a good fifteen minutes before Kane entered the room. I used the time to stew about Will and his childish ways. I'd sensed a maturity in him that apparently was just a veneer. The good news was, I didn't think Will could be considered an Ex-File. One sexual encounter does not an Ex-File make. Okay, maybe it had with Charlie, but not with Will. Charlie had been my first and that gave it more weight. This thing with Will was more like checking to see if we had things in common. And I was discovering that I didn't really want to be with him or see him any more.

And besides, I reminded myself with new conviction, I hadn't told anyone about Will except CeeCee. Jill and Daphne didn't even know. So Will didn't count. The fewer Ex-Files, the better.

Kane burst through the door at that moment, arms outstretched. A bevy of fresh-faced acolytes hovered by the door, their eyes adoring. He said simply, "Ginny," and gathered me to him like a long lost sheep.

I let him hug me. I felt like crossing my eyes over his shoulder for the minions' benefit. I held myself back at the last minute. Immaturity might not behoove me amongst the saved.

"You asked for Virginia," I said to Kane. "Since when? I've never gone by Virginia."

He laughed. "I always liked the name Virginia Bluebell."

"You and no one else. Possibly my mother," I conceded. "I didn't even know you knew it."

"When Mr. Tanlesky called roll, he asked for Virginia."

Kane's memory surprised and somewhat awed me. Mr. Tanlesky had been head of study hall, which I'd continually skipped, which had merely added more study halls on, which accumulated to a point where the threat of *you will not graduate if you don't attend study hall* hung over my head. However, my grades had improved so drastically during my last semester in school, as I'd finally decided to be a student, that my mother marched into the school and suggested we rethink this whole graduation thing, pronto. Lorraine had made veiled threats about writing letters to the local paper about the lockdown policies Carriage Hill High pressed on the academically solid students of the school while truants with juvenile, nay, adult criminal records ran wild in the streets. Or something like that. Anyway, the school had relented and I'd managed to walk to the podium on graduation night. But it was testament to my rejection of authority that I'd been to Tanlesky's study hall so few times he hadn't even known my name.

"So, you actually made study hall?" I said, impressed.

"I had a tendency to stare silently into space just to bother the man. It was a highlight for me." He released me and smiled benevolently down on me. I thought maybe he'd had his eyes done, too. After Mom, I was becoming an expert.

"But as you can see," he went on. "I've learned a lot on my journey of life. That kind of passive–aggressive behavior merely drags you down." For emphasis, he pulled his clenched fists toward himself. I copied the gesture, careful to keep my expression neutral so he would have to guess whether I was poking a bit of fun at him. He took me at face value. There was a roteness to his being, a staleness. He'd been at this game way, way too long. I silently mourned the maverick nerd of his youth. It looked like he was due for a little self-help shake-up himself.

"Ever been to Tony Robbins?" I asked curiously.

He sidestepped adroitly. "What are you doing now, Ginny? Are you happy? Feel productive? Useful to yourself and others?"

"I work in commercials as a production manager. Productive is what I am."

"You look well," he said.

"Well . . . thanks."

"What happened in the auditorium? I understand there was a miscommunication."

I paused. "Actually, I think we were communicating all right."

"I understand you and your group were asked to leave?"

"We thought the guy behind us was an asshole and he thought we were . . ." I couldn't make myself use the "c" word. "He thought we were the problem."

"You had a disagreement?"

I gazed at him in wonder. Did he seriously make money at this? "It was kind of a hearing issue," I explained. "Some could hear, some couldn't."

"The acoustics weren't effective?"

"My friends and I were talking and the guy behind us wanted us to stop. Tension grew. Ugly names were called. Luckily, one of your blue-clad assistants took care of the situation before it got out of hand."

He gazed at me with, I swear, disappointment. "Do you need your money refunded?"

"You do that?" I asked in surprise.

"Well, of course."

"We were all thrown out. My friends could use being reimbursed, too."

"Thrown out is a hostile term. How many friends do you have?"

"Three came with me tonight."

"Excuse me." Kane left the room abruptly.

Well, now what was I supposed to do? Wait while Kane

cut us a check? Or would we be getting vouchers for future Getting Able sessions? Somehow I didn't think this meeting was really helping me in any meaningful way. It hadn't even brushed on what reconnecting with the Ex-Files was all about. Sad to say, but the only one of my exes who seemed to really want to get to a touchy-feely reconnection stage had been Don.

To my surprise I heard familiar voices: Daphne, CeeCee, and Jill. They entered the room with Kane following. All of them had their eyes on him, really checking him out. He glowed under the attention.

Daphne sported a faint blush. "I didn't expect a one-on-one. Especially after what happened."

"It's a one-on-four," CeeCee pointed out. She was turning an unlit cigarette end-on-end on a pack, assessing Kane through narrowed eyes.

Jill said, "Are we ready to go?"

For his part, Kane couldn't take his eyes off Daphne. At first I thought he'd chosen our weakest link, so to speak. Daphne was niceness personified. But then I realized our weakest link was currently Jill, as she was so shattered. The look on her face, though she sought hard to hide it, was pure misery.

"So, you're all friends who live in LA together," Kane remarked.

"Makes the lonely city a little less lonely," Daphne said, smiling prettily.

CeeCee shot me a look. "I've got to leave."

"How long are your sessions?" Jill asked him.

"They're tailored for the individual."

"How long to get over a really, really bad breakup?"

"It takes a while, but you come out the other side. It does happen."

"But how long?" Jill was raw.

For an answer, Kane slipped her a card. As an afterthought he gave one to Daphne, pressing it into her palm. "I'm going back to my hotel in a few minutes. Why don't you join me in the lobby bar?"

"That'd be great," Daphne said a bit breathlessly. She didn't even bother checking to see if it would be "great" for the rest of us.

"I have someplace I have to be," I told them even though I had no intention of going over to Will's now.

Daphne grabbed me by the arm, hard. "Later," she said cheerily, then practically propelled me out of the room.

If I'd thought my night couldn't get much worse, I was dead wrong. Jill and CeeCee let it be known that they did NOT want to meet up with Kane at his lobby bar or anywhere else. But Daphne insisted that *I* needed to talk to Kane, and that we weren't being fair if we didn't help make that happen. I tried to say that I felt Kane and I had talked enough, but I was overridden. The voices of my friends swelled so loudly that my ears were ringing as we walked into the lobby bar of the Beverly Westside Hotel, straight into Jackson Wright and his date. Carmen Watkins.

"Peachy," I muttered under my breath. Whatever his reason had been for calling me could scarcely matter now. If he was dating Carmen, I wasn't interested in keeping up on the friendship.

Carmen, as pulled and stretched as I remembered from my view of her in her convertible, looked at me as if she hadn't the faintest idea who I was. I chose to ignore her as Jackson detached himself from her arm—which was quite a task, as she was wrapped around his arm like a boa constrictor—and walked toward me. He gave me a quick hug, which sent the needle of my anxiety into the red. What was this? Instantly I thought of my fat thighs, my flat hair, my red stretchy shirt that really should have been thrown away months, maybe years ago. I actually leaned backward a bit, but he folded me into the warmth of his hard chest, sending my heartbeat into the stratosphere. I prayed fervently that he wouldn't notice and that this message wouldn't be sent to my sweat glands.

Sometimes the human body just wants to ruin things for you, you know?

"I'm glad you're here," he said, sounding like he really meant it. "I called you, but I didn't get through."

"I know. I heard you." My voice was a squeak. I cleared my throat and added, "I would have called you back but I didn't have your number."

"I thought I might see you at Kane's meeting. I remember you dated in high school."

That stopped me. I cringed a bit inside. Sometimes I forget that Jackson went to Carriage Hill with Charlie, me, and yes, Kane. "Kind of like an old home revival meeting."

"No kidding." Jackson smiled. I could tell he thought the whole thing was bogus, which warmed the cockles of my heart, whatever they are.

"Are you here to meet him, too?" I asked.

"Actually . . . no. I was already leaving by the time you got thrown out. I wondered what happened to you. Carmen and I crossed the street and got something to eat, and then you all came out and I heard you say you were meeting here. I decided to take a chance on catching up with you."

I was struggling to process. "You . . . came to see me?"

Carmen was hovering so close that her breath stirred my hair. Jackson smiled at her and said, "I need to talk to Ginny for a sec, okay?"

He stepped away and I went with him. Carmen might have ignored his tacit rejection but Jill suddenly said loudly, "Carmen Watkins! Good grief, girl. What have you been doing since college?"

Bless my friends. They came through at the most unexpected times.

Jackson guided me over to a corner where we sat on a loveseat-like affair situated in a quiet corner of the bar, hidden behind a black Baby Grand currently not in use.

"I've written a screenplay," he revealed. "I've already got the financing. It's all in place. I'm the executive producer and I want you on the production team. Truthfully, I need your help."

My jaw dropped. "You wrote a screenplay?"

"Yeah. Weird, huh?" He shook his head in wonder. "We're making a film!"

He was as excited as a little boy. I couldn't blame him. "Good God," I said.

"So . . . ?"

"So, yeah. Yeah. No kidding. I'll do it. Of course, I'll do it. When?"

"In about a month."

I calculated quickly, my brain spinning wildly. "Perfect. I've got a commercial in Seattle and then I'm free."

He suddenly hugged me again. It took my breath away. I couldn't help inhaling his scent. The musky cologne was just right. My cell phone vibrated silently in my pant pocket, next to Jackson's thigh.

He said, "Is someone calling you . . . or are you just happy to see me?"

You have no idea, I thought, as I checked the Caller ID. It was Will. Now, what?

"I gotta take this," I said.

Jackson released me to give me some privacy. I was sorry to lose the warmth of his arms. Carmen, however, had edged away from Jill, who'd determinedly followed her and kept up a fast conversation. They both noticed me take the call and Carmen instantly pounced on Jackson. I turned my back to them, but my attention was diverted.

"Hey . . ." Will's voice was full of apology and he'd only uttered one syllable.

"Hey, yourself," I said cautiously. "I'm kind of involved in something here."

"I've got a surprise for you," he said.

"That's great."

Jackson had shifted closer to me to make room for Carmen, who was trying to get close to him. I could tell he was being merely polite, however, and it put a smile on my face.

"Are you coming over?" Will asked.

"Um . . . well, actually, I had a change of plans."

My mind was on Jackson, the screenplay and ten other things. I didn't have time for Will, his relationship with Rhianna, and the sexual coaxing I suspected might be involved with giving him an erection—which didn't have to last much more than a few minutes, let alone an hour. I wondered, suddenly, with a freezing of my blood, if Will was involved in the Trash Athletics commercial. Surely not. Not the way he'd treated Holly.

"You know Jackson Wright?" he demanded, sounding like my cavalier attitude had started his temper simmering.

That snapped me back. "You know I do," I stalled, remembering we'd had the Jackson Wright conversation in Sedona. Could he know Jackson was right here, next to me? *How?*

"He's got all the investors lined up for a film he's putting together. I'm directing it. I suggested having you on the team."

I closed my eyes. I'd never been so deflated over such ostensibly good news. "Really?"

"I thought Jackson would have gotten hold of you by now. Don't worry. I'll make sure he does."

My ears started buzzing. Will talked on but I heard nothing else. I must have made the appropriate responses because pretty soon I'd clicked off. He'd made another attempt to get me over to his place, but I'd politely refused and he ended up hanging up on me a second time, though I sensed he was more perplexed by my attitude than infuriated. I must have sounded like a zombie because that's how I felt. Not alive. Running by brain stem alone.

"You okay?" Jill asked, perching on the arm of the couch and peering at me closely.

Jackson and Carmen were still at my back. "I'm fine."

She nodded in a way that said she didn't believe me. Was I acting so strangely?

"CeeCee's outside smoking and Daphne's flirting with Kane, who's definitely flirting back. At least he's not a loser, by the usual standards anyway. You think we could go home now?"

"I'd love to," I said, standing.

"Are you leaving?" Jackson turned to us, also rising. This forced Carmen to climb to her four-inch heels, smooth her skirt, and shoot me a venomous glance.

"I have to," I said. My voice sounded odd. Kind of echoey. Like it was down in the bottom of a barrel.

"I asked Will Torrance to be our director. You know him, don't you?"

"Yessirree."

"Do you need a ride back?"

"Jackson . . ." Carmen plucked at his sleeve.

I said, "I drove. I brought my friends. But thanks."

He seemed disappointed. "I'll call you tomorrow. And here . . ." He pulled out a business card and scratched out a number on the back. "My cell."

"Thanks."

I walked off with Jill, who looked as if she thought she might have to catch me should I fall. That would be a riot. All five feet nine inches of me toppling onto her five feet one frame.

"How does Jackson know Carmen?" she asked as we stepped outside to meet CeeCee.

"I think I introduced them. At college." I handed my hotel parking ticket to the valet.

"You introduced him to everybody," she observed.

"I didn't mean to," I said with a strange kind of miserable candor.

Jill said, "It has not been a good day."

"No."

CeeCee joined us and asked, "Daphne coming with us?"

"You want to ask her, be my guest." Jill jerked her head in the general direction where Daphne and Kane had last been seen. About twenty of Kane's disciples had walked in with him, but he'd gently shooed them away as he'd tucked Daphne's hand through his arm and led her toward the far end of the bar. They milled around in anxious circles, worried their leader had chosen someone above them. I guessed they were still milling.

At this point Jackson and Carmen came outside. Jackson sent the valet for his car and Carmen leaned on tiptoe to whisper something into Jackson's ear. She was so eager she was bent like a bow string. I reminded myself that Jackson was off-limits. It was like a mantra. If I was really going to work with him, I had to remember that.

"He is attractive," Jill observed. "In a less pretty way than Kane. He's got more natural charm. Less bullshit."

"And he's all Blue's," CeeCee said.

"The hell he is." I surfaced from my self-induced coma.

"He always has been," Jill agreed.

"Oh, give me a break."

Luckily, one of the valets squealed out of the underground lot with my car at that moment. I tipped him and quickly climbed inside. Jill slammed into the back and CeeCee ran inside to see if Daphne was ready to go or if she was still getting able.

Jackson caught my eye as his dark Lexus was delivered and he helped Carmen into the passenger side. To my surprise he suddenly walked briskly to my car. He said, "You haven't changed your mind, have you?"

"What do you mean?"

"I got the feeling something happened."

"No. I'm in."

"Will Torrance is all right with you?" he asked.

"He's a great director."

"Okay." He shot Jill a quick smile. "See you later."

"Oh, he's yours," Jill said, as soon as Jackson was out of earshot. I could hear the smile in her voice.

Because she was going through hell I didn't argue with her.

But it didn't mean she was right.

Chapter
20

I left for Seattle on the first day of December, exactly ten days after the Kane Reynolds revival meeting. Nothing much had changed in my world in that time, other than a few calls from Jackson about our scheduled mid-December production start and a lot of calls from Holly, who was obsessing over the setup for the Trash Athletics shoot.

Suffice it to say, I was sort of let down. I don't know what I'd expected of Jackson, but I'd gotten my hopes up. Yes. It had happened. I'd been one of the idiots that wanted something *more* from him than friendship. I'd believed my friends. I'd pretended not to—even to myself—but in the end I'd heard what I'd wanted to hear: *He's all Blue's.*

It was really better for me when they'd all professed to hate him.

Before I left the state I managed to squeeze in a quick session with Dr. Dick. Evil Janice hadn't found a way to squelch my appointment, apparently, but I could feel her seething as I sat in the waiting room, toying with my cell phone. I didn't have to make a call; just holding the offending item was enough to keep her perturbed and off-balance. Oh, the small joys of immaturity. Sometimes I revel in them.

I didn't give Dr. Dick a chance to ask any questions. As soon as I crossed his office threshold I launched into a diatribe about my friends and all the events that had led up to this moment. To wit: Daphne had survived both a) her vaginal itch commercial, which I'd seen already and in which she'd looked fresh-faced and beautiful as she conspiratorially whispered that Soft & Soothing had been a lifesaver for her, and b) her pseudorelationship with Kane, who'd apparently been more interested in turning her into a fresh-faced and beautiful acolyte than into a girlfriend. (Secretly I believe Kane couldn't have a girlfriend with a vaginal itching problem, real or imagined, who broadcast the problem over national television. Bad for the "Getting Able" image.) CeeCee, I reported, had cemented her job by fair means or foul, and she'd even cleaned up her act on the air; she was only bleeped fourteen times the last time I'd listened to her program. Jill had asked me to speak to Ian about their relationship, which I had. A mistake, as it turned out, because Ian was quite voluble about how Jill had fallen into her bulimic habits one too many times. He loved her and always would, but it was over. Ian was now somewhere in Mexico with his friend Worth—I still don't know his last name so we'll stick with Worth Less—and Jill was absolutely convinced this was all a huge lie and that Ian was once again with his ex-girlfriend of over five years earlier. I seriously doubted this. I mean, come on! But being the frightfully well-adjusted friend that I am, I guess I can't be trusted, or listened to, or expected to know anything that might actually be the truth.

". . . of course, none of it matters anyway," I finished up. "Jill and Ian are no longer Jill-Ian. But then, that's kind of what they do. Ian's paying for the unused bridesmaid dresses. I guess that's something."

"How do you think Jill's doing?" Dr. Dick asked.

"Better than I expected," I admitted. "Unless it's all an act. She's thrown herself into work. The weird thing is she got offered a job at Ian's restaurant. Ian's half-owner, but the partner asked her to come on board as one of their chefs. It's really a coup, but she turned it down for obvious reasons. Ian stayed noncommital during the whole thing. That's kind of his usual middle-of-the-road approach."

"You don't like Ian."

"I don't like him hurting Jill. But if he wasn't ready to get married . . ." I shrugged. "Truthfully, they both struggle with commitment. I'm surprised their engagement got as far as it did."

"How are you with commitment?"

I almost yelled, *this isn't about me*, but decided, well . . . yes, it was, actually. It was my session with my shrink. I paused for thought, wondering why I so wanted to avoid talking about myself. "I'm not exactly a poster child for commitment. The difference is that Jill and Ian are actively *trying* to commit. I'm not. I'm . . . not even really dating right now."

"Are you still examining your past relationships?"

Dr. Dick was lightly tapping his pen against a desk pad, not impatiently, more as if his mind were elsewhere. The motion distracted me as well. I suddenly had a few questions of my own for Dr. Dick. "Daphne says you're back with your wife."

"Daphne says?" He sounded surprised to be a topic of conversation.

"Mmm-hmmm. She acted like you were going to be at 'Getting Able with Kane,' but I didn't see you."

"We were there." He gave me a direct look with those blue eyes. I hadn't been feeling the heat, so to speak, but now I remembered that I found him very attractive. Well, sort of. In the deep recesses of my soul I knew some sort of threshold had been crossed in my relationship with Jackson, such as it was. Nothing concrete in the real world. Just my own evaluation of myself. A sort of recognition that I'd been lying to myself for a long, long time. And that it colored how I perceived any other male.

"You and your wife were there?" I asked.

"Anna and I were never officially apart. I'm surprised Daphne thought so."

We both thought so. Or, maybe it was just a hope Daphne and I had shared, both knowing we couldn't get involved with our analyst—even if he wanted to, which he didn't.

"Anna and I saw you," Dr. Dick informed me, his expression carefully neutral.

"Me? Or, me and my friends?"

"You and your friends."

"Go ahead and say it. You saw us get thrown out."

He didn't deny it. "What happened?"

I thought about it a moment, running my fingers over the edge of the chair's arm. It all seemed distant and childish now, but there had been real emotions at work that night. I drew a breath and said, "Ian had just broken up with Jill, so she was upset. I didn't think she would even go, but there she was. And she was spoiling for a fight. Maybe we all were. And this guy told her to shut up and sit down and Jill wasn't in the mood to hear it, and then CeeCee karate-chopped his knee to take the heat off Jill, and then . . . things deteriorated from there."

"Did you play peacemaker?"

I frowned at him. "No. I was there to see Kane. Why? Did you expect me to play peacemaker? Oh, right." I answered my own question. "I'm so 'frightfully well adjusted,' I just can't help myself."

"You don't like conflict," he said.

Well, duh. I started calculating how much I paid him an hour and wondered if I was getting my money's worth. With a distinct shock I realized I wasn't interested in seeing Dr. Dick for a while. Maybe ever again. Was that progress? It was certainly something.

That thought pretty much blew my concentration for the rest of our hour. I went right to that place in my head where I fret and stew and toil over problems. I even went so far as to ask myself why I'd ever started with Dr. Dick, apart from the obvious fact that I'd found him attractive. Sifting through the ashes of my own suspect motives, I suddenly turned over a scorching ember: *I wanted a therapist, just like all my friends!*

"Good God," I said aloud. I was back in the moment, big-time. And I wanted out.

Dr. Dick lifted his brows as I hurriedly slung the strap of my purse over my shoulder.

"I just realized I've never left junior high," I said, then ran for the door before he could ask the question forming on his lips.

I spent Thanksgiving alone and was totally thankful for it. Jill flew to Colorado to be with her parents, Daphne met with actor friends, and CeeCee went snowboarding at Mammoth with Sonny Boy. I actually baked a turkey breast and made myself sandwiches. Mom called. She was sharing a Thanksgiving meal with some friends of hers and said she'd spoken to Mr. Norell, my landlord, again. She was hot on the idea of buying me the condo. I'd thought this might be a passing fancy, but I should have known better because my mother isn't like that. She's more like a piranha when she decides on a plan—she bites in and hangs on for all she's worth.

I told her again that I would love to own my place but I couldn't afford the down payment. She told me again that it was under control. I found myself torn by feelings of inadequacy. My mother didn't owe me anything. I tried to say as much to her and she made her *tsk-tsk* noises and said I was making everything harder than it had to be.

Was that true? I always think of myself as such a facilitator. But then, I'd thought I wasn't judgmental and learned that I might be a teensy bit wrong on that, too.

Hmmmm . . .

I packed for Seattle like it was a time test, throwing items in my roller bag with minimum thought, maximum speed. I caught a nine A.M. flight, barely making it through all the airport rigamarole to get to the gate on time. I was speed-walking down the concourse when I caught sight of Holly, seated at a sports bar, drinking a bloody Mary. She hollered at me as I sped by and I practically ran in place, one eye on my watch, as I gazed at her in surprise.

"We're late!" I pointed out.

She waved me to a seat. "They've got issues with a drunk and disorderly deplaning passenger. We're going to be here awhile."

"Oh." I tentatively perched on the edge of the chair across from hers. Inside, I felt as if a clock were ticking off the seconds, counting down my life, I guess. I'm always in such a hurry.

"Relax," Holly said on a yawn.

"I am relaxed." I am such a liar.

I'd left a message on Kristl's voice mail. I hadn't heard from her since her last, somewhat wistful call, and I had no idea how she and Brandon were getting along. There had also been no call about a wedding, however; I looked on that as a good sign.

Holly ordered another bloody Mary, and before I could stop her, one for me. I'm not a huge bloody Mary fan, but it's made with vodka so I can go there if I choose. I just wasn't sure I chose this morning. I realized, sort of indistinctly, that I wanted to just get through this job in Seattle and get to the film with Jackson.

"I have an opportunity to produce," I said carefully. I knew Holly saw me as a production manager and it's where she wanted me to be. It's where she felt safe. Many times producers don't want you snapping at their heels, so to speak, and so I was fairly certain my elevation in job status wouldn't be cause for celebration.

"Yeah?" The drinks came. She lifted her glass and sucked

down a hefty slug of spicy tomato juice and alcohol. "What's the job?"

"A small-budget film. I know the screenwriter. He's the exec producer and he got the financing together."

"Good for you," Holly said and actually sounded like she meant it.

"Will Torrance is directing."

She snorted and half-choked, which caused her to reach quickly for her glass and gulp some more. "Did you sleep with him?"

I'm terrible with direct questions. It's one facet of my lying I can't seem to get down. My hesitation was answer enough. She gave me a sorrowful look, so I admitted, "Only once." I looked at my drink but didn't touch it. I really needed breakfast, though the idea of a leathery bagel and/or box of sugary cereal on the plane didn't exactly appeal.

"Once was enough, huh?" She checked her own watch. As if on cue, several security men hauled a handcuffed man past the open door of the concourse bar. The man wore a rumpled suit and a red face. He looked as if he could barely manage putting one foot in front of the other. Blotto. Silent, but steaming.

"A case for anger management," I said.

"I'm glad you figured that out early. He may be an *artiste*, but his temper makes him a thug."

I realized she meant Will. I nodded and let it go at that. They called our flight over the loudspeakers and we went to the gate.

Trash Athletics was a small-budget job, and I mean small. We filmed it in one afternoon on a set with cute, prepubescent teenage girls who pranced around in the raw-edged, army-lettered sweats in green, gray, and camouflage and tried to look tough. The makeup and hair woman had ratted their hair and put fake nose rings on them. I guess the idea was "urban chic" but they looked like suburban kids who were playacting. Agency would have been better off coming up with a slut theme. I could see these girls wearing black lace bras with their sweats and getting into some of that sick baby stuff, like sucking their thumbs or licking a pacifier: Seattle Grunge meets Frederick's of Hollywood meets Babes "R" Us. I pointed this out to Holly, who grunted and said maybe I should air my views to Agency. As this would be professional suicide, I kept my idea to myself.

I met Kristl for dinner my second night in Seattle. I wanted to do something totally touristy like eat at the Space Needle, but she took me to a hole-in-the-wall bar where everyone dressed as if they were the inspiration for Trash Athletics. I swear there wasn't one item of clothing on the customers that wasn't ripped, faded, shrunk, or stained. In my ubiquitous jeans and cotton T-shirt—and a black leather coat purchased the first day on the job as it was patootie-freezing cold in the Emerald City—I was several tiers classier than the mainstay crowd.

"Grunge came back in style?"

"It never left this place," Kristl observed. "I used to work here."

I gave her a once-over. She was in a deep purple-blue long-sleeved top, tight black cords, and a massive pair of black boots that added at least three inches to her slender frame. With the added elevation, she almost looked me in the eye. Everything was skintight and her red hair glowed under the dimmed lights. Male eyes followed her body's every movement.

"You're not dressing the part anymore," I said. I was getting a few looks myself. Glancing over the crowd, I wondered if this was a good thing.

"Yeah, it's changed." She sighed and lit up a cigarette. Here, you could still smoke if the establishment deemed it okay. "Kind of grunge, but different. Nothing's the same."

"How're the wedding plans?"

"Well, let's see . . ." Her lips tightened. "Brandon's whole family has gotten into the act. I caught his mother field-testing several types of ribbon—satin, velvet, grosgrain—to see which would be best to tie on the knife that cuts the cake. None of them worked. It took hours."

I made sympathetic noises. What could you say about wedding day obsessions?

"And his sister, whom he insists I have in the wedding party, is a crier. I can't talk to her without her eyes welling with tears. I can't even tell anymore if she's happy or sad or something else. I think she secretly hates me." She sucked on her cigarette as if it had life-giving powers. "Brandon's father's a lech. He brushed his hand across my breasts twice before I caught on. Every time he hugs me he pushes his crotch against mine. The day he starts thrusting he's getting bitch-slapped and I don't care who sees."

I made a face. Father-in-Law lechers? A new deterrent to my already lukewarm wedding desires. "Have you told Brandon?"

"Oh, sure. Like he's listening to anything I have to say." Kristl squinted through the smoke. "I'm not going through with it. I can't. This is the worst one yet."

I wanted to say *I told you so* and possibly point at her and say *nanny, nanny, nanny*, but I kept my juvenile reactions to myself. I didn't want to chance it that I could spoil things. I was just happy she'd come to her senses.

She shot me a look. "What? You have nothing to add?"

"I'm trying to be adult."

"Difficult, huh?"

"You have no idea."

That scared a smile out of her. "I miss you, Blue. And your friends, too."

"Come back to LA."

"I just might."

"Excuse me . . ."

I jumped in my chair, the male voice coming from somewhere behind my left shoulder. I turned to find a Kurt Cobain wannabe circa 1992 hovering nearby. He looked scraggly and emaciated, and his blondish hair fell in front of his eyes and curled toward his stubbly chin. His gaze was fixed on me, not Kristl, which definitely made me worry.

"Oh," he said, unable to hide his disappointment as we gazed at each other full on. "You're not who I thought you were."

"Sorry," I said, not sure what my response should be.

Kristl eyed him critically as he sort of stumbled, shuffled away. "Major drugs," she decreed.

I shrugged. The incident kind of depressed me for some reason. Though it fell into my 'there aren't any good men out there' theory, it also seemed like the Cobain clone had experienced the reverse: there aren't any good women.

"What a pisser," I said on a sigh.

We left the bar and shivered down the street to Kristl's car. She saved me a cab ride and on the way to my hotel, I said thoughtfully, "If you leave, Brandon's going to think I had something to do with it."

"Let him," she sniffed.

"Maybe you ought to have it out with him. All the problems."

"You're kidding!" She gazed at me as if I were Benedict Arnold. "You gave me the lecture on staying single. Now, you're playing marriage counselor?"

"Hardly. I'm just saying you need your day in court, metaphorically speaking. Tell him why you're out of the deal."

"Yeah, maybe." She didn't sound convinced. "So, tell me about you and your friends. I'm sick of talking about me. How's the job going?"

"Not bad." I caught her up on what was going on with Daphne, CeeCee, and Jill, and I even touched on my own problems. It was really great to get it all out there—especially without having to pay someone to listen. I finished up with a quick review of my kinda-relationship with Will and the news that he, Jackson, and I were the core of the production team for Jackson's script, which I'd read on the plane and found incredibly good.

She listened carefully; I think she was dying for news outside of her own life. When I wound down, she said, "Are you happy to be working with Jackson?"

"Happy? I guess. Why? It's Will I'm worried about. We're in relationship limbo, which is just a less-involved version of relationship hell. I swear, neither of us really knows what to do with the other."

"You and Will are through," she stated. "You know it. He knows it."

"Well, yeah . . ."

"I could tell when I met Jackson that there was something going on with you and him."

"Oh, bullshit. You only saw *him* that night—and the blonde who stepped all over your game."

"At first," she agreed congenially. "But you guys have got something unresolved going on. That kind of deep-down shit that never goes away."

"You're full of it." My hand scrabbled for the door handle.

"Chicken."

"Everybody acts like I have some secret thing going with Jackson," I said hotly. "It just isn't true."

"Everybody?" She pulled out a tube of lipstick and drew a luscious red coat upon her lips. We were double-parked in front of my hotel and getting dirty looks. Kristl just didn't care.

"Good-bye." I stepped onto the sidewalk. I wasn't really mad at Kristl. I was secretly pleased that she'd said what she had. Junior high reaction again. Deny, deny, deny.

"Let's just say, *aloha, au revoir, adieu.* Until we meet again. Maybe sooner than either of us knows."

"Come back to LA," I urged. "Come live with me. We were good roommates."

"Yeah?"

"Yeah." I gently shut the door and waved. Kristl put on her left blinker and edged into traffic, then pushed the button for the passenger window and yelled, "Bet you get married before I do again!"

She quickly rolled up her window. I managed to give her a loud raspberry before she succeeded.

I landed in LA two days later at nine P.M. Bleary-eyed, I turned on my cell phone as I waited to deplane. The landing had caused a baby in the rear to wake up and begin an ear-splitting howl. His screeching created a dull headache. I realized I had one missed call. My heart jerked painfully upon seeing it was Will. I'd added his name into my phone directory under Will Power. Now it was more like giving me the Willies.

I called him back, preparing all kinds of things to say to his voice mail, as Will never answered his phone. But he proved me wrong this time, surprising me into blurting, "Well, hi, there. You called?"

"Did you listen to the message?"

"Haven't had a chance. I'm just getting off a flight."

"I wanted you to know, since we're going to be working together, that I'm back with Rhianna."

That caught me up. Really. Huh. I couldn't find anything appropriate to say, so I just said, "Oh?"

"It wasn't working with you and me. Might as well just get it out there."

His voice was terse and practiced. He was delivering bad news and he wanted it out. I realized I was being broken up with, sort of. This pissed me off some.

"Keep her away from snow globes," I suggested, but I forced a smile as I spoke. Didn't want to give away the fact that I was infuriated. I don't take breakups well. Any kind of breakup. And really, who does?

"I don't have a problem with you being the producer of Jackson's film," he said, as if I'd asked.

Big of him. "I don't have a problem with you being the director."

"Good."

"Good."

"See ya soon, then. Jackson wants to get together at Someplace Else, probably tomorrow."

"I'd rather go to The Other Place."

"Take it up with him," Will said, completely missing the point. He was that anxious to get off the phone. I wasn't exactly dying to hang on the line. At least he'd broken up with me so I hadn't had to do the dirty deed myself. Had that been the case, I might have received the brunt of his notorious temper.

I walked to baggage claim, reminding myself that this was all a good thing. Never mind that I wanted to bite someone's head off. Into this cheery mood, my cell phone trilled again. Blocked call. I debated answering it. If someone wasn't in my phone's address book, chances were it wasn't anyone I wanted to talk to. And I didn't feel like talking to anyone right now anyway.

But curiosity won out over seething anger. "Hello," I answered tautly.

"Ginny?" a male voice inquired.

It took me a moment. Two syllables just isn't enough to place a voice. Struggling, I said, "Brad?"

"It's Bradley, yes. Hi. How are you?"

I thought it apropos that Knowles-It-All had found me, not the other way around. I said, "I'm okay. How about yourself?"

"I'm buying a house in Santa Monica."

I fell into immediate panic. Brad . . . ley in Santa Monica again? That was way too close. When he and I had been together we'd lived in Pasadena, which was straight east on the 10. Close enough to drive to, but far enough to count as *someplace else*, and I didn't mean the bar.

"A friend of yours called me. An old boyfriend, I think."

"Ah, yes. Don's looking for a good personal injury lawyer."

Brad had a good memory. I could give him that. I winced, wondering how much I'd told him about all of the Ex-Files. He'd been Ex-File Number Seven, second to last; the one before Nate. I'd been circumspect about discussing my past relationships with Nate, but I think I might have been a blabbermouth with Brad . . . ley.

"Mr. Delaney wants to sue your landlord over a faulty automatic garage gate."

"Who? Oh. Don." I'd begun to think "the Devout" was his last name.

"Can you tell me something about this accident? Honestly, Gin, it doesn't sound like something I want to bother with. How dangerous is this gate?"

"On a scale of one to a hundred? Two."

"It doesn't bear down on you?"

"Sure it does . . . at a rollicking snail's pace."

"Any warning notices?" I could hear him taking notes.

"Schematic Man is doing the doubled-over in pain dance in black and white."

He went right past that. I don't think Brad*ley* ever really appreciated me. "Would you say there's any case, there?"

"No." I was bluntly honest. "I don't even know how Don did it. Did he fall into a temporary coma? Did he just forget to move? It's one of life's great mysteries."

"Can I see you tonight? I'll show you the house and you can buy me a drink."

I drew in a breath of remembrance. Knowles-It-All at his finest. Push fast to capture what you want—then bore the hell out of whomever you trap.

"*I* can buy *you* a drink? I don't think so."

"I'll treat," he said, as if that answered it. "Give me your address. I'll pick you up in an hour."

I hesitated. Although this was a golden opportunity to meet and greet Ex-File Number Seven, was I really ready to spend some time with him? Being with Brad*ley* could be excruciating. And he was moving back to Santa Monica? Good God.

"Ginny?"

I must have capitulated because before he hung up he said he was looking forward to seeing me and he gave me his new cell phone number. That woke me up enough to remind him that I was starting a job the next morning—although that was a fib—because I suspected I might need an out if he either put me to sleep with his myriad political facts that I DON'T GIVE A DAMN ABOUT, or if he pushed me into an argument where he ended up having all the answers and I had none.

You can see why our relationship didn't last.

Give me time . . . I might remember how it got started.

Chapter

21

Okay, I'm kidding. I remember. Knowles-It-All was the Ex-File right before Nate, so it would be hard for me to really forget. But sometimes it's a struggle. I have to get past the locks and keys on my own recall, and believe me, that can be a job. I'm pretty good at actively forgetting, which is kind of scary. It's like wishing yourself short-term memory loss. A truly effective defense mechanism against the God-awful breakup.

But I could remember Brad Knowles, all right. As I unpacked from my Seattle trip, I forced myself to review our relationship. Oh, yes. What a peachy time we'd had. Recalling my time with Knowles-It-All was not conducive to raising the mercury on my enthusiasm meter. I had to try very, very hard not to dread our upcoming meeting.

Brad had been forty-one when we started dating. I was twenty-seven at the time. It wasn't a huge gap; it wasn't even as huge as mine and Lang's had been. But Brad and I were light years apart in experience, whereas Lang and I had been about on par. This was because thirty-eight-year-old Lang suffered from a self-professed ten-year-old mind-set: he was basically a kid who happened to possess his own place and a boatload of money. Lang wasn't far off in his assessment of himself. I was a green, twenty-one-year-old production assistant and yet I was way ahead of him in maturity and worldliness. This worked for us basically because I never lived with Lang. We just had fun together.

Not so with Brad*ley* Knowles. He and I made the colossal mistake of cohabitation soon after we met. But that was only part of the problem. A bigger slice was that Knowles was an expert in all ways. I mean, he really was. There was hardly a topic he didn't know something—a whole *lot* of something— about. The Ex-File directly before Brad was Black Mark. It goes without saying that meeting intelligent, calm, and worldly Brad Knowles was, timing-wise, just what the doctor ordered. (I'd used this phrase referring to Brad in Dr. Dick's office one time, and he made a face. I guess Brad wouldn't have been Dr. Dick's particular prescription.)

Anyway, Brad and I met at a party. Friends of friends of friends, and at a time when I hadn't been my usual scintillating self. In fact, I'd pretty damn well become a wallflower. It had been quite some time since I'd run from Black Mark, and I was feeling parched for male companionship and somehow letting it erode my self-esteem. All I could think was I might never be with a real live man again—which is such a crock of shit for any able-bodied young woman to think. I mean, come on! But nevertheless I was wallowing in self-pity, nursing my dating disappointments over a Ketel One vodka martini and sucking on one of the olives, when Brad walked straight up to me.

At first I didn't believe he was really interested in me. Brad Knowles, tall, gray-haired (his was already way gone before the start of our relationship, so I'm not blaming myself on that one) and handsome, with a devastating crooked smile and gray-blue eyes that matched his mane, seemed out of my league. He truly was head-turningly attractive, but my first thought was that he was way past his pull date. (That gray hair and aura of maturity . . .) I automatically figured I was too young for him. Maybe I was.

"Could I get you another one of those?" he asked, indicating my nearly empty glass.

"I've had three already."

"You know what Dorothy Parker says about that?"

I almost said, "Who's Dorothy Parker?" but wisely decided to keep my ignorance in this matter a still-to-be-discovered characteristic. Instead I raised inquiring brows.

Brad quoted: "*I love martinis, one or two at the most, three you're under the table, four you're under the host.* A woman's point of view, obviously," he added, grinning.

I gave him a once over. It was an unusual come-on line. "As far as I know, our host is married. Not really my style."

"If I bring you a drink, I'll consider myself a very hopeful host," he said lightly.

Bold, but not crossing the line into crass. I smiled and allowed him to order me another Ketel One martini. While I slowly sipped it, he informed me that Dorothy Parker was a famous New York writer from the thirties who spent time with fellow writers at the Algonquin Hotel—which became the meeting place of their group, the equally famous Algonquin Club—drinking martinis and creating witticisms and swapping stories and generally bullshitting. I was pretty buzzed by the time I got all this information. Well, to be frank, I was out-and-out drunk, and that's how I ended up at Brad's place, both under the table and under the host.

I remember finding this the height of hilarity, laughing myself silly until I bonked my head on the underside of the table and developed a rabid case of the hiccups. After that we moved to his sumptuous king-sized bed and I crashed into a pillowy loveliness that basically sealed the deal. I moved in within two weeks.

Brad lived in Pasadena in a bungalow that was cuteness

personified and undoubtedly cost an absolute fortune. He wasn't far off Colorado Boulevard, made famous in the Jan and Dean song, *The Little Old Lady From Pasadena,* as she "drives real fast and drives real hard/She's the terror of Colorado Boulevard."

I decided I loved, loved, *loved* Pasadena. I was moving away from production assistant status and into production management/ coordination. I was happier than I'd ever been. This was absolutely great. Brad made me feel like a grown-up, something that had pretty much eluded me until this time. I hate to admit it, but I was feeling inwardly superior to my girlfriends as CeeCee was tearing through jobs like a race car; Daphne was dating her perennial losers; and Jill and Ian were already into the first stages of their dysfunctional "he loves me, he loves me not" thing. But I, Ginny Blue, was with Brad Knowles, successful personal injury attorney. I liked to call him Brad Knowles, Esquire, which he seemed to enjoy. There was something British about him though he was born in the Bronx. Somewhere over the years he'd lost his New York accent and developed this sort of polished diction that totally turned me on.

We set up house together, my first attempt at actually living with the object of my affection. I tried cooking. Started out with a basic Betty Crocker cookbook and built from there. Brad was hopeless in the kitchen, but hey, we were doing fine in the bedroom. Life was wonderful. I actually entertained fleeting ideas—scenarios, if you will—of us as a married couple.

Then Brad let me in on the big secret: he'd been married before. This did not bother me. In fact, it kind of put my mind at ease. A guy who's reached his forties without even one marriage behind him is kind of a red flag. Maybe he's the swinging single type who's never been interested (*uh huh, yeah,* read "gay" for that) or maybe he's just been so focused on a career (read "pathologically self-involved" here) or maybe he's simply been unmarriageable and therefore rejected by any woman with any worth (read "loser").

So, I was initially happy to hear about the ex. Brad said they were on amicable terms, so okay, even better. I had this unformed notion that she and I might actually get along and share Brad stories, or something.

Then he told me that he had a child. Children. Three, to be exact. And they weren't babies. One was actually fifteen. A boy. With a surly expression and a monosyllabic delivery that became like the sound of fingernails scraping on a blackboard to me. His name was Tremaine and he started spending more and more time with his dad, which Brad professed to love, but which left me teensitting him whenever I wasn't on a job, which was most of the time since Brad really resented my work and its long hours.

Thus, I found myself in the role of wicked stepmother, even before any serious thought of a wedding. I also found myself racking my brain, struggling for some kind of meaningful communication between us. With a Stepford-wife smile, I asked, "Tremaine, would you like me to order a pizza?"

"Nah."

"I could make lasagna. I'm good at that one."

"Nah."

"Chicken?"

"Nah."

"Hamburgers?" *Ha, ha, ho, ho. Oh, Ginny Blue, trying to jolly the unjollyable, miserable teenager sprawled on the sofa, watching television and playing video games.*

"Nah."

"Cioppino?"

"Huh?"

"Never mind." I gave up any interest in culinary skills at that juncture in my life. Tremaine just sucked the joy out of anything domestic. Brad sensed that I was unhappy and he knew the cause but rather than face the fact that his lovely offspring and I weren't getting along, he chose to break into long dissertations on the law and his latest case rather than talk about anything personal, interesting or relevant.

Brad's other two kids weren't much better. The middle daughter, twelve, surly, and possessed of huge mascaraed eyes which she constantly rolled, was a teensy-weensy little bitch. She hated me thoroughly. I could tell she went straight home to Mumsy and laid out all my faults. I used to obsess about this until I stopped loving Brad; then I scrutinized my own faults as well, chief among them being the fact that I'd gotten myself into this trap in the first place.

The youngest boy was simply rude. Wouldn't talk to me. Wouldn't look at me. And as for Mumsy herself, she was all sweetness and sugar to my face but a real rattlesnake behind my back. I read that one straight off. My illusions were shattered upon first meeting, thank God, so I didn't have to feel like an idiot for ever believing in her.

So, what did this all say about Brad?

The way I saw it, he helped create these little monsters by marrying one.

Still, I hung in there. Some kind of sick desperation on my part, I guess. Me, trying to do something I can't: tolerate bad behavior for the sake of a boyfriend. How pathetic can you get!

Then, the *coup de grace*. And this is where it gets really ugly. Knowles-It-All decided it was time to change *me*! His screwed-up family wasn't enough. He needed fresh meat to pound down.

"Ginny, who's your stylist?"

He caught me as I was digging into my favorite dish: pizza casserole. It was one I'd learned to make during the failed get-close-to-Tremaine era: ground Italian sausage sauteed with sliced mushrooms added into spaghetti sauce and olives then poured over pasta and baked with a crust of mozzarella cheese. Yum! Even Tremaine ate it and grunted "good," which was high praise indeed. Brad wouldn't eat it, however, as he was fashionably "no carb" long before it became the rage.

"My stylist?" I repeated, gulping down a bite before speaking. Brad didn't like me talking with my mouth full. My hair was always stick straight and sometimes I curled it and sometimes I didn't. There was no stylist, as he well knew.

"You need something more around your face. Go to Sylvia's on Fairfax." He opened his wallet and peeled off some bills. Well.

I couldn't decide whether I was totally pissed or marginally amused. I chose amused, for the time being, and went to Sylvia who chopped, sheared, scissored, and prattled and pretty much ruined me in one sitting. My hair was supposed to feather around my face but it simply got in my eyes. Brad professed to love my new look, but Brad was never wrong about anything, or so he liked to believe.

I left Brad after about a year of this torture and scoured the ads for someplace to live. The Santa Monica condo was available for lease and I threw down the first and last month's rent with a gulp as I hadn't been working as steadily—owing to Brad—and it was highway robbery, what they wanted to charge.

My friends were thrilled that I was a) living closer to them, and b) through with Knowles-It-All, but none of them could move in with me and help out with rent as they were all deep into their own leases. I advertised for a roommate and got Nate. Nate and I lived together for two months before we became a couple. I realize, somewhat belatedly, that it was nice of Nate to just up and move out without creating a problem for me. The trauma of trying to find another place around Santa Monica—my preferred choice of location but where the rents jump astronomically once you move—might have sent me around the bend.

My trip down this Knowles-It-All Memory Lane ended in an epiphany so strong it sounded like a *bang* to my ears.

My mother wanted to help me buy my condo.

"What the hell's wrong with you?" I practically yelled at myself. The empty walls were the only ones who heard. Good God. What was I waiting for?

In a frenzy of sudden decision, appreciation, love, and gratitude, I called Mom.

"This is Lorraine," she said in her bright realtor's voice.

"Are you serious about the down payment for the condo?"

"Virginia! Er . . . Ginny. Yes, of course I'm serious."

"And you've talked to Mr. Norrell about it?"

"Yes. If you've had a change of heart, just say so." I could hear the smile in her voice.

"I have," I said humbly. "I'll pay you back. I need some kind of security in my life."

"Darling, if it's not going to be a wedding ring, it sure as hell better be real estate."

Words of wisdom from Lorraine Bluebell, she of the big-ass purses and vast knowledge of the residential market. I said, "I love you."

She said, "I'm calling your landlord right now."

My meeting with Brad wasn't the trial I imagined. I never got the hang of calling him Brad*ley*, but I did check out his Santa Monica purchase and was a little surprised that it wasn't as nice as mine, although it made up for it in square footage. I asked about his kids—just to be polite—and learned that Tremaine was a senior and would be graduating in the spring. The daughter (He called her Kate. I never would have remembered that) was about to get her driving permit, and the youngest boy was into snowboarding in a huge, huge way. As Brad prattled on, I wondered if CeeCee and her boy-toy would meet this *wunderkind* on the mountain, but I kept my thoughts to myself.

I asked Brad about his work and he started talking in theory. Memories swirled. I felt my energy level sink like a deflating balloon. My mind wandered. For some reason I remembered sex with Brad. What it had been like.

While he rambled, punctuating the air with a finger now and again to make a point, I thought about his nighttime calisthenics. Brad was the distracting sort. Always moving and grunting and generally turning lovemaking into a noisefest. Just when I was close to that elusive "feel-good," the first hint that a dozing climax, the kind sleeping just out of reach, might be about to stretch and awaken, Brad would do something like blow in my ear and bite my earlobe. This sounded like the surf at Diamond Head and felt like a sand crab grabbing hold. Or, maybe he would squeeze a breast too hard, or shift position and *take away* the pressure from the only thing that was working: the penis. Sometimes, you just gotta wonder.

Hurried attempts on my part to put things right made the nearly waking climax slip into a huge yawn. This was followed by a loss of sensation, where all the parts of my body suddenly slipped into a nap. I wanted to cry out from frustration, but that would give Brad the wrong idea. Any sound during sex was a turn-on to him. If I wanted any hope of regaining what was lost I had to remain utterly silent and damn near immobile. Unfortunately passivity only increased Brad's need to stir me up and I would be vigorously bounced, bitten, and rubbed.

Nothing worked.

Now, true, any one of these little tricks can be an enticement, something to jolt the sleeping climax to full alertness. But with Brad it never quite happened that way. He'd always do something that would send everything sideways. My own frustration would build and build and build until I wanted to explode—and not from sexual release. To this day, Brad is the only man I faked an orgasm with. Sometimes out of sheer necessity to get him to GET ON WITH IT ALREADY.

"What are you thinking about?" he asked suddenly.

We were seated at a little bar off Third Street Promenade. I'd scarcely touched my martini. I'd almost forgotten where I was.

"I was actually thinking about us," I admitted.

He grinned. I didn't have the heart to tell him the gist of my thoughts. "I was thinking about us, too."

In a moment of pure reaction, I swept my hand over his and said, "No, Brad."

We sat that way a moment. For once in his life Brad didn't talk, he listened.

And he heard.

And that was the end of my evening with Brad.

I was still inwardly marveling about this moment of pure communication that had never happened before, with me and *anyone,* as I pulled up to the valet at Someplace Else the following night. I watched my Explorer disappear and forced myself not to worry about theft.

Drawing a breath, I crossed to the door. I'd dressed for success. A tight blue dress. Bare legs. Strappy black heels. A black jacket.

I actually got a whistle as I strode inside. Calves. My best asset. Cover up most of the thighs and the nonexistent boobs and I wasn't half bad.

My confidence was definitely hitting the upper reaches. A little more whistling and I might hit the red zone.

Good. It was how I needed to feel to face both Jackson and Will.

My gaze fell on them the next moment. They were seated at CeeCee's birthday booth. They were sitting fairly close to each other for two men in such a large space, which led me to believe someone out of my range of vision was seated across from them. Jackson was wearing a white shirt, open at the throat, exposing a vee of tanned skin. His sleeves were rolled up his forearms. There was something wonderfully masculine about him.

I had a moment of pure clarity: *I want him.*

I managed to keep my tongue from hanging out as I approached their booth. I told myself I was feeling great. And why not? So I'd slept with Will? So he'd ended things first? So Jackson and I were in some kind of strange dance that would probably never be resolved? I'd seen Brad*ley* Knowles-It-All and had gotten the last word! That was worth celebrating in itself.

"Come here often?" I said to both of them, my smile wide. My gaze swept around to the other side of the booth.

Oh. God. Shit. No.

My jaw slackened. John Langdon sat there, grinning at me like an oaf. And beside him was a very young, very blonde girl, of the Nate's Tara ilk, who blinked and smiled and gazed from one man to the other as if waiting for her cue.

"Well, hello," I said, finding my voice. I tried to pretend it didn't squeak like a mouse on helium.

One Ex-File and two near misses all at one table? There oughtta be a law.

"Could I get you something?" The approaching barmaid looked at me expectantly.

"Ketel One vodka martini. Lightning speed or sooner."

Jackson was looking me over appreciatively. I tried hard to concentrate on that and feel good as he said, "John's agreed to be in the film. He's investing in it."

"Jackson's my financial manager," said Lang. "He tried to talk me out of it. Said I should stick to more 'sure things.' I say bullshit to that."

My breath, which had been caught in my throat, came out

in a rush. I said, forcing a normality I didn't feel, "You're playing Boone?" Lang nodded and I added, "You're perfect for it."

"Thanks." He was surprised, I could tell. I was, too, come to think of it. Sometimes manners take over to save the day. *Thank you, Lorraine Bluebell.*

Will stated flatly, "Let's all stop congratulating ourselves and really talk about this project. We don't have a lot of time."

Trust Will to be the wet blanket. What had I found attractive about him? For the life of me, I couldn't remember.

The girl bubbled, "John said I might have a small part. I can't wait! I'm so excited!"

Lang gave her a hug, as if he were trying to squeeze her lips closed. She gazed up at him adoringly. I excused myself for a moment. Time to catch my bearings. I was halfway to the ladies' room when a hand touched my shoulder. I turned around, half-expecting and half-hoping it was Jackson.

I stared into Lang's famous face.

"You're the one that got away," he said.

A feeling of joy swept over me. Then a vague memory. Jackson telling me at CeeCee's party that Lang had said that about me. Another woman might have believed it to be true, but I knew Lang. I said dryly, "Bet you say that to all the girls."

He grinned.

Bullseye, Ginny Blue.

"I love you," he said.

"The feeling's mutual," I said. Not really. But Lang was basically harmless as long as you stayed detached.

Like you should do with Jackson.

"We're going to have a good time," Lang predicted.

"I think you're right," I said, not sure if I believed it or not.

I left him and headed for the restroom. When I returned

to the table, Jackson had made room for me. I sat down beside him and there was just enough space to perch on the edge, as long as my thigh was pressed tightly against his. The warmth split my attention throughout the meeting. Later, all I remembered was Jackson's heat, his blue eyes, Lang's gift of cowboyish bonhomie, and Will's dourness.

But Jackson's heat was foremost in my mind.

Maybe we were going to have a good time.

I hope so, I thought, meeting his gaze.

His fingers lightly grazed my arm.

Dial it back, I told myself, plastering on a smile for the others at the table. Dial it back.

A week later I met the girls at Sammy's. Jill arrived sans Ian, but looking healthier. I gazed at her expectantly and she said, "So, I'm eating better. I'm trying to change."

"Good."

"I took the job at Ian's restaurant," she added.

I was blown away. Trust my friends to always have more interesting stories than I did, even when mine were *good.* "What about the catering?"

"I'm still doing some jobs. But I needed a little more stability. Ian and I are working things out."

"Meaning?"

"We're not dating—but we're not *not* dating."

Which, in Jill-Ian speak, meant status quo.

Daphne arrived in a bright pink blouse and tight faded blue jeans. She said, scooting into her chair, "I've met a great guy."

"An actor?" I asked. I'm sorry. I can't help myself sometimes.

"An acting coach." She dimpled. "He's teaching me things I never knew."

"Better than 'Getting Able'?"

She sniffed. "Don't talk to me about Kane. He couldn't handle a relationship."

"He couldn't handle vaginal itching," Jill pointed out.

"Oh, I don't think that was it. He really has no time for anything but his work."

Denial, I thought. Maybe it's how we all live.

CeeCee came last. Her hair was a tad longer; her once-pink tips now a virulent shade of orange. She said, "Yes, I'm sleeping with him. He's young. He's quick. He doesn't ever say anything meaningful. I like that in a man."

"A boy," I corrected.

"He's eighteen," she reminded.

"How are things going with you, Blue?" Jill asked.

"Passable." I waited a moment, savoring the spotlight. All three of my friends waited expectantly. "We're starting the film next week. John Langdon's starring."

Daphne actually gasped aloud. Maybe they all did. "Mr. Famous Actor?"

"In the flesh. I have completed my mission," I informed them all. Counting on my fingers, I stated with a flourish, "Nate, Charlie, Kane, Hairy Larry, Don the Devout, Black Mark, Knowles-It-All—yes, it's true, I've dealt with Brad*ley*—and last but not least, John Langdon, Mr. Famous Actor."

"And?" Jill asked, looking decidedly impressed.

"Are you cured?" CeeCee put in.

"Cured?"

"Of bad relationships," Daphne stated impatiently.

"That's the point, isn't it?" Jill put in. "You seem about to swear off men forever."

"Really?"

They all nodded in unison. The three of them acted as if they'd been talking this out behind my back. I could gain a serious complex. I swear, sometimes I think it's a conspiracy: Fix Ginny Blue.

Why is it I think *they're* the ones with the problems?

"Swear off men forever?" I repeated.

Jackson Wright's face swam in front of my vision. My inner eyes focused on the curve of his lips, the strength of his jaw. His humor. His intelligence.

I knew I was going to sleep with him. It was in the stars.

I looked at my three friends and grinned like a devil.

"Nah."

Please turn the page for an
exciting sneak peek at
Nancy Bush's
CANDY APPLE RED
the first Jane Kelly mystery
Now available in paperback!

Chapter

1

If I'd known they were about to find a body at the bottom of Lake Chinook, I never would have gotten myself into the whole mess. The lake's deep in places and the Lake Corporation only drains it every couple of years to check the sewer lines running along its muddy bottom. The thought of the little fishy things trolling the waters, chewing off teensy nibbles of human flesh, would have been enough for me to say, "*Hasta la vista*, baby" and I would have exerted great haste in making tracks.

But I didn't know. And I also didn't know my whole life was about to change. The day I spoke with *uber*-bitch/lawyer Marta Cornell I was blissfully ignorant of the events in store for me which was just as well. Don't ever tell yourself you're happy with the way things are because that's when everything changes in seconds flat. And not necessarily for the better.

That particular morning—let's call it "The Day Jane Kelly's Life Changed, Not Necessarily For The Better"—I walked through the front door of the Coffee Nook, breathing hard from the two-and-a-half mile run from my bungalow. I had nothing more in mind than a cup of coffee and maybe a little conversation with friends. I slid onto my usual stool and Billy Leonard sat down next to me.

He said, "How ya doin'?"

I nodded. "Good."

"Me, too."

"Good."

We both ordered basic black coffee. Billy, an ex-I.R.S. man and current C.P.A. whom I turn to for advice about my modest finances, seemed a bit preoccupied. I assumed it was over his kids. Billy has this theory about why there seems to be less ambition and direction among young people in general, and his boys in particular.

As I blew across the top of my cup, Billy said, "I'm a fisherman, y'know? I mean, I fish." He pretended to cast out a line with an imaginary fishing pole.

Maybe I was wrong as Billy appeared to be heading onto a new topic. I carefully tested my drink. Steaming coffee. Sometimes the damn stuff is so hot it burns off the taste buds and a few layers of tongue underneath.

"When you've got a wild salmon, a Coho, on your line, it's like *zziinnnggg!*" He cast again, this time with more body English.

I watched his invisible line grab an equally invisible Coho. Billy rocked and twisted and generally acted as if Moby Dick himself had swallowed the bait.

My eye traveled past him to a newcomer to the Nook, a woman I didn't recognize. She was thin and small and her hair was completely wrapped in a virulent pink scarf. Wide, round sunglasses covered much of her face which was perched upon a long, white neck. She was a passable Audrey Hepburn. She stood to one side and pretended interest in the glass case of pastries, but I could tell her mind was on something else. I could swear she was playacting, pretending to be thinking over a purchase.

Billy continued, "I mean you *know* it, y'know? It's fightin' and fightin' and you're rockin' and rollin'." He twisted to and fro and nearly fell off his stool. "Those fish are tough. Really tough. But sometimes you cast out . . ." He reeled in again. Actually reeled in. And for just a moment I almost forgot it was all illusion. Once more the imaginary line sailed toward the heads of the other customers whose blank oblivion said more about the hour of the morning than any disinterest in Billy's story. "You get a bite and it's kinda like . . . ugh." His shoulders drooped. He jiggled the line with a slack wrist. "He's on, y'know? Grabbed it big time. But there's just no *zzziinnnggg*." He grimaced and nodded. "Hatchery fish."

Julie, the Coffee Nook's proprietress, asked "Audrey" what she would like. I realized with a jolt that Audrey seemed to be staring across the room at *me*. She saw that I noticed and quickly murmured something to Julie, then hurriedly walked out of the Nook. Julie shrugged.

I sipped my black coffee. It's a shame, but I struggle with both caffeine and lactose. I'm determined to give up neither. If I ever have to give up alcohol I'll start smoking or doing drugs or indulging in weird sex acts. If I can't have a vice I just don't want to live.

Billy continued, "They don't quite have that survival instinct, y'know?" He sighed and wagged his head slowly, side to side. "Just can't really make it out there. And that's the problem with our kids. They're hatchery fish."

Aha . . . he'd managed to pull the allegory back to his favorite subject. Billy's boys were in college, taking a jumble of courses with no clear career path in sight. Most of their friends were in the same boat. I grimaced. Even though I hit the big 3-0 this year and consider myself long finished with higher education, I'm not convinced that I won't be tossed in with these shiftless souls Billy seems to know so much about. My job situation alone might drop me into the loser bin.

"But they'll—they'll figure it out," Billy added. He nodded jerkily as if to convince himself, then ran his hands through his hair, making it stand straight off his head. Billy always looks like he just woke up after a two-week bender.

He's so *not* the three-piece-suit type that his choice of profession almost awes me. But then, I've changed professions so many times that sometimes I think I should tack Misc. after my name. Jane Kelly, Misc.

I asked Julie, "Do you know who that woman was? The one dressed like Audrey Hepburn?"

She shook her head. "Never seen her before. She didn't want anything."

I decided to forget about her. If I started thinking people were watching me, I would become as paranoid as the rest of the world. I turned to Billy and said with conviction, "My brother's a hatchery fish."

"Booth?"

"Yep." I hoped this deflection would take the light off me since I definitely preferred the idea of being a wild Coho to a hatchery fish.

Billy considered. "Booth's all right."

I snorted. My twin was a source of irritation to me. Path of least resistance, that was Booth. Christened Richard Booth Kelly, Junior after my shiftless, deadbeat father. Mom, in a moment of belated clarity, decided she couldn't have her children be Dick and Jane and so Booth became Booth.

"Hey, the guy's got a job," Billy remarked.

Yes, Booth was part of the Portland Police Department. I, on the other hand, felt like a poser. I pointed out dampeningly, "The L.A.P.D. breathed a sigh of relief when he left."

"Nah . . ." Billy smiled and clapped me on the shoulder. He loves it when I'm grumpy.

My brother did choose a career path while I've seesawed around the whole issue for years. But Booth's reasons are so wily that I can't trust anything he does. During his stint in L.A. I'm sure he spent most of his time patrolling the area around the University of Southern California and hitting on the sorority chicks on 28th Street. I don't think he ever got lucky, but it wasn't for lack of trying. I suppose I should look on his following me out of So-Cal north to Portland, Oregon, as a move in the right direction, but with Booth, you just never know. This isn't to say I don't love him. Family is just a pain in the ass. Ask anyone.

Billy said, "You're a process server, Jane."

I just managed to keep myself from saying, "You call that a job?"

Billy shrugged. A friend of mine Dwayne Durbin, an "information specialist" (current buzzwords for private investigator) fervently believes I have all the earmarks of a top investigator, which means he thinks I'm a snoop. He wants me to hone these skills while learning the biz through him. The idea makes a certain amount of sense as I took criminology courses at a Southern California community college with just that thought in mind. Well, okay, there were other reasons, too—reasons that had everything to do with blindly following after a guy who had a serious interest in police work and whom I was nuts over and who subsequently dumped me. But regardless, I've done a fair amount of classroom training.

As I sat at the counter, I truly believed—at least in that moment—that I could become an information specialist. I had training and a mentor who would guide me into that world. Why not just go for it? I'd been resisting the full-on private investigator gig all the while I'd been in Portland. I'm not sure why. Self-preservation, I guess.

However, for the last six months I'd been working as general dogsbody to Dwayne who sometimes needs to be in two places at the same time. The fact that Dwayne thinks I have the makings of a first-class information specialist worries—and yes, flatters—me. Dwayne's cute in that kind of slow-talkin' cowboy way, but I'm not sure he's really on the level sometimes. Half the time I get the feeling he's putting me on. Sometimes he's enough to make me want to rip out my hair, scream and stamp my feet. (I also have a problem with a name that begins with *Dw*. I mean . . . *Dwayne, dwindle, dweeb* . . . None of those words conjure up an image of a guy I want to hook up with, even professionally.)

But between doing background checks for Dwayne and process serving for some of the people he knows—mainly landlords—I've kept my head above water financially speaking. I keep toying with the idea of selling the Venice four-unit I own with my mother, but that would mean dealing with her in close contact and I've already voiced my feelings on family. Mom lives in one of the upstairs units, and though I love her dearly she's not exactly on my wavelength about a lot of things. Sometimes we struggle just getting through to each other. She's talked about selling the units, but selling entails moving, and she's dropped more than a few hints about making a move from So-Cal to Portland, and I'm damn sure I don't want her to be the next member of my family to follow me north. Booth's bad enough. I'm just not good with either of them. (I'm very self-aware, especially about my failings. Not that this has helped me much, but if pushed to the wall, I'll pull it out as some kind of badge of honor.) I've reminded my mother of this fact many a time. She always looks at me half-puzzled, as if she can't understand how she could have given birth to me. Luckily, she seems to feel the same way about Booth so I've never worried that he was her favorite.

"You were a bartender in Santa Monica, right?" Billy said on a note of discovery. "What was the name of that place?"

"Sting Ray's. Ray being the owner."

"My old man owned a bar. Did I tell you?"

I nodded. On numerous occasions. About as many times as I've told him I used to bartend. Neither Billy nor I worry that we recycle conversations. I also never have to worry that he'll get pissy over my inherent lack of attentiveness. Hey, I was ADD before it was even popular.

"Evict anyone I know lately?" he asked, grinning.

"Probably."

This was a long-standing joke between us. The scary part was that his question might one day become reality as Billy knew a wide, wide range of people around the greater Portland area.

He slid off the stool and turned toward the door. At the last moment he said, "Hey, I ran into Marta last night at Millennium Park. She wants you to do some work for her."

"What kind of work?"

Billy shrugged. "Said she had a job that required tact. You any good at tact?"

"About as good as you are," I said.

"You hear about that kid fell in the lake? He's in a coma in the hospital."

Billy's good at shifting subjects faster than warp speed. I may be ADD but he takes the cake. "What happened?"

"Buncha kids screwing around in a boat." He shrugged. "He fell somewhere and was trying to get back in the boat. Think it happened on the island."

There is one island in Lake Chinook. Circling it is a footpath and guarding this footpath is a black chain-link fence. Enterprising teenagers make a habit of leaping the fence and racing the perimeter, trying to speed all the way around before the island's Dobermans catch their scent.

"He was running around the island?"

"Probably. Mighta tried to jump in the boat from the island. There are a lot of big rocks around that one side. But kids are tough. Don't know what his name is. Julie . . . you know?"

"What?" Julie was deep into the whir of a latte, staring into a fat silver cylinder where foam lifted and fell in white waves.

"What the Coma Kid's name is?"

She shook her head. "Everyone's been talking about it this morning. I hope he's okay."

Billy nodded, then waved a good-bye as he headed out. I sent a silent wish that the Coma Kid would be all right. Hadn't we all done something dangerous and stupid in our youth that might have killed us?

I drank some more coffee and my thoughts turned to Marta Cornell. She was the best and baddest divorce lawyer in the city of Portland and probably the entire state. Come to that, she could probably rival anyone in the region. Dwayne was her information specialist of choice, and I'd done a bit of work for her through him. Not pretty stuff. Divorces were messy and ugly and, personally, I'd rather be a process server and evict crack dealers armed with semiautomatic weapons than deal with one of Marta's jobs. (This is a lie as guns generally worry me, but you get the idea.)

But Marta pays well. Dwayne says he'd put her first for money alone. This makes him sound mercenary and maybe he is a little, but you'd never be able to tell by his minuscule cabana off North Shore which makes my bungalow on West Bay look like a palace. Dwayne wants me to move my business to his cabana, but I fear for my independence and my soul. Not to mention I can't see myself working cheek-to-jowl inside Dwayne's living space. This is where the guy resides, after all, and Dwayne just doesn't strike me as the kind of guy I want to get that close to. I have this sneaking suspicion I will turn into his cleaning woman/coffee maker/receptionist and God knows what else.

I finished the rest of my coffee. Every muscle felt stretched out of whack from my run. I don't think exercise can seriously be good for you, but I sure as hell have to keep up with it. The last time I process-served, the woman opened her door, reluctantly accepted the eviction notice I thrust into her hands, gave it one look and howled as if I'd hit her. She then grabbed a broom and whacked me once, hard. I left with one shin smarting and my pride bruised even worse. Talk about killing the messenger. I don't plan on being taken by surprise again.

I wondered what Marta had in store for me. Her jobs tend to be a little more involved than mere process serving. I'd once been asked to drive to Baker—a city plopped way off in eastern Oregon and miles and miles from *anything* else—and question the locals about the habits of a Portland businessman who'd suddenly grown a hankering for ranch life out in this remote windblown part of the state. His wife wanted to know whom he was ranching with and what she looked like. It turned out the lady in question was surprisingly plump, sweet and homegrown, and I didn't blame the guy one bit when I met the real wife, Marta's client, who was thin, grim, long-nailed and tense. It sorta bothered me to be on her side, so to speak. But, once again, it paid well.

With a last gulp of now cold coffee I gathered up my energy and jogged the three miles back to my rundown 1930s bungalow on West Bay, the small body of water on Lake Chinook's westernmost tip. Once upon a time wealthy Portlanders owned summer homes on the man-made lake. Lake Chinook was created by Chinese laborers who dug a canal in the late 1800s and connected the sluggish nearby river to what was by all accounts little more than a large pond, beautifully named Sucker Lake. Now the town thinks it's beyond upscale, and though Lake Chinook is a nice community, I think it's good to remember one's roots.

My cottage is a ramshackle remnant, built a few decades after the lake became a desirable locale for summering. It's Craftsman style, which means there's a lot of wood trim, a wraparound porch and the exterior is composed of shingles. The inside must have been utter crap because my landlord, Mr. Ogilvy, updated the place before I moved in. Ogilvy's known for his pecuniary ways, so the improvements—new kitchen appliances and a low-water pressure toilet which requires two or three good flushes to work properly—are a complete and utter gift. The cottage sits on a flag lot, encroached on each side by huge new homes whose builders fought city ordinances against the setbacks and succeeded. Ogilvy is about sixty-five and hates government, especially city government, so he cheerfully okays every variance sent his way. Along the way he's chopped off chunks of his own property and sold them for a premium price so now I have a teensy line of sight and strip of land that leads to the water. Still, there's enough room for a boathouse, also ramshackle, which matches the taupe, shingle siding of the cottage. This matching color scheme exists because last year I talked Ogilvy into painting the place. This is saying a lot for my skills of persuasion as Ogilvy bitched, moaned and side-stepped until we were both beyond exasperation. Eventually, he just bellowed, "Fine!" and signed on the painters. Now the place looks semi-presentable and if I had any serious cash I'd try to buy it. On my own dime I'd cleaned out everything on the inside—some of the items in the storage shed had been left over since the cottage was built, I swear—ripped up the carpet and had the old hardwood floors stripped, sanded and generally redone. I possess a modicum of furniture, all of it castoffs that, for some reason or other, I can't seem to cast off as well. Except my bed, which is new, springy and a dou-ble—nothing bigger fits in the bedroom—and covered with a solid red, quilted cover—a splurge at Pottery Barn.

As I jogged up to my front door, catching my breath and slipping the key in the lock, I mentally congratulated myself on my industrious fitness program. Self-affirmation is all that stands between me and the depression of reality so I keep a steady "Atta, girl!" going in my head at every given opportunity.

Stripping off my In-N-Out Burger T-shirt (which I brought back with me from my last trip to California) I walked into the bathroom and reminded myself I had to buy groceries or die. My desktop computer—years old and a real electronic grinder—sits cold, blank and silent in the little desk/nook I've arranged next to my bed. Though mainly used for writ-ing up short reports for Dwayne, invoices for my process serving services, e-mail, and the occasional resume, I worry its life is close to ending and whenever I hit the switch, I fear its little green "on" light might sputter and slowly fade out forever. I'm not only afraid of the cost of replacing it, I'm afraid of new technology, period. I keep a laptop in a case nearby, just in case. It's far newer, though given how quickly computers grow obsolete, it's definitely in its twilight years. I'm attached to both of them in a way that defies description, especially for a loner like myself. And what's really amazing is although they both have this nagging quality about them— their very silence a stern reminder for me to get to work—I would be completely bereft without them.

I took a quick shower, toweled off, threw on a robe, then pushed the play button on my answering machine. Marta's voice loudly told me to phone her A.S.A.P. I made a face, sensing I should avoid the call. Then Billy's hatchery fish comment skimmed across my mind and propelled me into action.

"Jane Kelly returning Marta's call," I snapped out to the receptionist. This particular woman has one of the snottiest voices on record and I always try to cut her off as fast as possible.

She smoothly responded, "Ms. Cornell's in a meeting."

Though I should have felt relief that I could delay my talk with Marta, I was consumed with impatience. There's a whiff of smugness to the receptionist's tone which calls me to battle in spite of myself. "Tell her I'm on my cell phone," I said, then reeled off the number as fast as humanly possible.

"Could you repeat that, please?" she asked, not bothering to hide her scorn.

"Oh, sure." This time I spoke clearly and slowly. Even while I was running through this mini-drama I asked myself why I do such things. Call it my low tolerance for frosty self-importance.

"I'll give her the message," she said and abruptly clicked off.

I sat back in my chair and surveyed my domain. Pretty much a desk, chair, phone, notepad, pen and stapler. And computer, of course. I switched it on and waited while it went through its beeps, whirs and flashing screens. I know others grow annoyed if their computer doesn't jump to attention like a military cadet but I don't mind the wait. It's like a cat stretching awake.

Sometimes, there's a moment of perfect synergy when what you're thinking suddenly comes into the moment of your life. As I waited for my computer to finish its wake-up routine, my mind drifted to thoughts of Murphy. Tim Murphy, to be exact, though no one called him by his first name. He was the guy who'd walked into Sting Ray's one night and bowled me over with quick repartee, wicked sarcasm, innate politeness and one dimple in an otherwise masculine jaw. I'd fallen in lust with him right there and then. When I learned he was taking criminology courses, I'd signed up at the first opportunity. And when he'd finally left L.A. for his native Oregon, I'd followed him blindly to Lake Chinook as soon as I could. I'd wanted to live with him, soak him into my system, wrap our lives together, but Murphy had resisted. He'd sworn he loved me, but it turned out his love hadn't been quite as real as mine. His was the kind that disappeared like fairy dust as soon as I grabbed for it. And though it lasted a while, it had already faded some by the time a horrific tragedy involving his best friend from high school placed us on opposite sides of the law. Murphy never forgave me for believing the worst of his friend, despite overwhelming evidence. He chose to run away from me and all things related to Lake Chinook. I, however, have remained. A part of me I don't often face knows that although Murphy was devastated by his friend's tragedy, he also used that event as an excuse to end our faltering relationship.

These thoughts flashed across my mind in quick succession, about three seconds in real time. At the end of those three seconds my cell phone buzzed, splintering the images and memories.

"Hello?"

"Jane!" Marta boomed over the phone. The woman was

over six-feet-tall with a voice to match. She could deafen with one word. I yanked the phone from my ear and hoped I still possessed my hearing.

"Jane?" Marta demanded, her voice now tinny and far-away as my arm was stretched straight out from my torso. I carefully placed the receiver to my ear.

"I hear you."

"I have a client who has an unusual request and I think you're just the person to help."

I opened and closed my mouth several times, seeing if I could pop my ears. They seemed okay but there was an alarming little creaking sound at the corner of my jaw. I thought about TMJ. Temporal . . . mandibular . . . jaw thing. Whatever. It was bad and sometimes it takes an operation where your jaw's wired shut for six weeks. I don't normally worry about such things, but the thought of all food coming through a straw for six weeks was enough to scare me straight. No more caramels? No more Red Vines? I'd *never* be able to eat beef jerky again?

"What unusual request?" I asked.

"It's about Cotton Reynolds."

My heart leapt. Christ, I thought a bit shakily. Had thoughts of Murphy actually triggered the past? "What about him?" I asked, trying to hold my voice steady.

"My client wants some follow-up on . . . Bobby Reynolds." Marta hesitated, unlike her to the extreme. "She wants you to interview Cotton."

I stared at my office door and instead of its scarred, paneled wood saw the white-haired man who happened to be one of the wealthiest in the state of Oregon. Cotton Reynolds lived on the island—the site of the Coma Kid's accident— and it was less than a mile from my bungalow. By boat, I could be there in ten minutes, if I wanted to. By car, it would be trickier. The island was private and Cotton's was the only house on its three acres. If I dropped in to say hello, I wouldn't get past the huge wrought iron gate nor the Dobermans.

But interviewing Cotton wasn't what was on my mind. Following up on Bobby Reynolds was. Murphy's close, high school friend. His best buddy. The cause of the horrific tragedy my mind had briefly touched on.

I almost hung up right then. I probably should have. A shiver slid coldly down my spine; someone walking on my grave.

Bobby Reynolds had murdered his family and left their bodies lined up in a row—wife, Laura; Aaron, 8; Jenny, 3; and infant, Kit—somewhere in the Tillamook State Forest, just off the Oregon coast. Bobby Reynolds was a "family annihilator": a man apparently overwhelmed with the responsibility of his family so he chose to send them to a "better place." He shot them each once in the back of the head, then drove away. He dumped his Dodge Caravan on a turnout off Highway 101 which meanders along the West Coast throughout Washington, Oregon and into California, then disappeared without a trace, though he'd been rumored to have been seen as far north as the Canadian border, and as far south as Puerto Vallarta. To date, after four years, he was still very much a fugitive. The murders—disputed by Murphy who simply could not believe his friend capable of cold-blooded homicide—had driven Murphy away from Lake Chinook, the tragedy and me.

I cleared my throat and asked, "Who is this client?"

"Tess Reynolds Bradbury."

"Bobby's *mother?*"

"Cotton won't talk to her about Bobby or anything else. They haven't spoken civilly in years. When it was all over the news they had words, but it wasn't exactly what I would call communication."

"I remember," I said, recalling how Cotton's ex, with her blond bob, hard eyes and angry mouth had been bleeped out by the local news, time and again. Cotton had been silent and stony, although my impression was that it was a mask for deep, deep pain and shock. I'd tried to talk to Murphy but he'd gone to a place inside himself, as distant as a cold moon, before he'd left for good.

"Why does she want me to talk to him?" I asked, baffled. "The police and F.B.I. and every news channel around has been on this since it happened. What could I learn? I don't even know Cotton."

"You've met. You were Tim Murphy's girlfriend."

"I wouldn't call myself his girlfriend," I said succinctly. "I knew him." Not as well as I thought I did, as it turned out.

"Murphy was close to Bobby and Cotton. Tess thinks you can use that connection—"

"*No*," I said again, with more force. "I'm outta this. I'd be useless."

"She stopped by my office the other day, and we started talking about Bobby a little. She never could before. But it's like she's suddenly gotta get it out."

"You're a divorce attorney," I reminded Marta tonelessly. I couldn't keep up with this. My head reeled. I felt ill.

"I'm her divorce attorney," Marta agreed. "But I'm also a friend. After she started talking, your name came up. She remembered you."

If I hadn't been so overwhelmed I would have been surprised. Tess had barely seen me. She'd been divorced from Cotton in those few months before Bobby's deadly deed was discovered. I hadn't known Bobby very well, as he and his family had moved to Astoria. I mostly knew about them through Murphy. I'd only met Bobby and his wife Laura a few times, so when their pictures were in the papers they'd looked like the strangers they were to me. I said, "It would be a miracle if Cotton remembered me."

"He knows Murphy. That's all that matters."

I didn't like it. It was sneaky and wrong. Oh, sure, I can be a snoop, but this tragedy was epic. I felt small and mean even talking about it with Marta. "What kind of information does she expect?" I asked. "I don't get it."

"Whether she's right or wrong, she thinks Cotton's been

in touch with Bobby. I know the police and F.B.I. have wrung him dry, and he's been more than cooperative. I'm just telling you what she wants. And she's willing to pay well."

"I'm not a private investigator." *Or information services specialist.*

"As good as," Marta dismissed, but then she was always saying things like that when she wanted something.

"How much is she willing to pay?" I asked cautiously, lured in spite of myself. I inwardly shuddered. It was like dipping a toe in cold, cold water.

"An initial five hundred dollars and then whatever you work out. She wants you to develop some kind of relationship, Jane," Marta went on. "She says Cotton always admired you when you were there with Murphy. She thinks you could . . . have some sway."

"I doubt it."

"Are you saying you won't do it?"

I didn't know what I was saying. I was out of my depth and I knew it. I'm not all that hot at self-delusion. If I were really thinking about taking the jump to information specialist, I'd sure as hell like to start with something smaller. Like grand larceny. Or . . . corporate tax fraud. Or that Erin Brockovich deadly chemical thing. I did not want to be personally involved in the investigation, no matter how distantly, as I was in this one.

"Cotton remembers you," Marta insisted. "Bobby told Tess how his dad liked you."

"Bobby told his mother that his dad liked me? That's just great. When was that, Marta? I was only here for a few months before it happened."

Marta sighed at my obstinance. "Are you going to do it, or not?"

"All signs point to *not*." I paused, belatedly hearing some innuendo between the lines. Why did Tess want me to get close to Cotton? My thoughts took a turn toward the salacious. "I'm not going to sleep with him."

"Oh, for God's sake, Jane. Tess just wants you to suck up to him a little, show some interest in the guy. He's been living like a hermit with his young wife ever since Bobby slaughtered his family and ran." I cringed at her words. "Tess thinks this is the perfect time to lend a sympathetic ear."

"I won't get any results the police haven't."

"Five hundred dollars plus, whether you learn anything or not," Marta coerced.

Five hundred dollars plus. My brain started calculating, taking a trip of its own, as I wondered how many "sessions" I could squeeze out of the deal. It's hard to turn down pure, cold cash. Dwayne would be proud of my way of thinking.

"Cotton's having a party next Saturday night." Marta sweetened the pot. "I can get you an invitation."

"How?"

"Well . . . Murphy's been invited. He's coming into town this week."

I swore beneath my breath, loud enough for Marta to hear. *Murphy?* "What a setup. I'm not interested, Marta. Not one little bit."

"He knows you might be there. He wants to see you."

"Not a chance." Marta knows what she's doing at all times. She's an operator, someone who sees what she wants and goes after it, no matter how many souls she grinds into the pavement along the way. I almost admired her.

"Murphy still talks to Tess," Marta went on. "He mentioned you the other day. That's what got Tess thinking."

"Murphy and I don't talk."

"Jane, Tess is going to be in my office at three today. She'd really like to meet you."

"You're railroading me. I can hear the train whistle."

"I thought you might want to see him."

"Bullshit. You thought of a new way to squeeze money out of a client. How much is Tess paying you for this setup?"

"Plenty," was her equable answer. "Tess is a grateful client."

I almost laughed. I could imagine how well Marta had

put the squeeze on Cotton as Tess's representative in the divorce. Her unabashed greed appealed to me, maybe because deep inside I'm a kindred spirit. Okay, maybe it's just that I'm not that deep inside.

She seemed to sense my lessening fury. "Is that a yes?"

Distantly, I heard the sound of a buzzing boat's engine. I walked toward the rear windows for my peek-a-boo view of the water. It was a beautiful, 75-ish afternoon in late July. The weatherman had said the temperatures were going to rise through the weekend, peaking at about 88 degrees late afternoon Saturday. The night of Cotton's party. Great boating weather.

I had an instant memory of a hot midnight on Murphy's boat, illegally docked in the shelter of Phantom's Cove, two hundred feet beneath the houses perched on the bluff above, hidden by the canopies of oaks and firs which kept the cove under shadow most of the time. I remembered fevered bodies wrapped tightly together, sweat and silent laughter that remained caught in the back of my throat. And pleasure.

An ache filled me inside. I'd fallen in love once in college, but Murphy was the next, and last, man who'd ever filled my senses so completely. I half-believed now that it would never happen to me again. Maybe it would, but right now it felt impossible.

The thought that he might actually be at this party was enough to send me into the kind of female panic I loathed seeing in others. I couldn't go. Even if I met with Cotton, I couldn't go to this party if Murphy was going to be there.

I said as much to Marta. At least I think did. But she responded with a quick overview of how much income this could provide me. I turned her down over and over again, I swear. Yes, dollar signs danced in front of my eyes, but the thought of clapping eyes on Tim Murphy again was something my system couldn't take. I told myself I would rather live in destitution for a thousand lifetimes than go another round with Murphy.

". . . we'll see you at three, then," Marta said happily and hung up.

I was left staring into space, my jaw hanging open. Slowly, I brought my lips together again and clicked off my cell phone. There was no memory in my mind of an agreement to meet with Tess, but somehow I'd managed to say yes.

Some days are just weird city.

Take today, Jane Kelly, thirtysomething ex-bartender, current process server, and owner of The Binkster, a pug, is dutifully putting in slave-labor hours working for Dwayne Durbin, local "information specialist" (i.e., private investigator), and on the road to becoming a P.I. herself. Next thing she knows she's socializing with the Purcells, an eccentric rich family with a penchant for going crazy and/or dying in spectacularly mysterious ways.

From what Jane can tell, the Purcells all want Orchid Purcell's money. And when Orchid turns up in a pool of blood, the free-for-all has just begun. Then when Jane finds a second body, it seems weird city is about to get even weirder . . . and a lot more deadly . . .

In her second smash outing, Nancy Bush's wickedly funny heroine, Jane Kelly, proves herself a worthy successor to Stephanie Plum, but with a wit, style, and dog that are definitely all her own.

"Smart, sexy, and sassy. I loved ELECTRIC BLUE!"
—Lisa Jackson, *New York Times* bestselling author

"With her clever ability to handle the zaniest of life's circumstances, Jane won't disappoint readers."
—*Publishers Weekly*

**Please turn the page for a
sneak peek at Nancy Bush's
ELECTRIC BLUE
coming next month in paperback
wherever mysteries are sold!**

Chapter

1

Mental illness runs in the Purcell family.

I'd diligently typed this conclusion at the top of the report written on my word-processing program. I'd been so full of myself, so pleased with my thorough research and keen detecting skills that I'd smiled a Cheshire Cat smile for weeks on end. That smug grin hung around just like the cat's. It was on my face when I woke in the morning and it was there on my lips as I closed my eyes at night.

I spent hours in self-congratulation:

Oh, Jane Kelly, private investigator extraordinaire. *How easy it is for you to be a detective. How good you are at your job. How exceptional you are in your field!*

However . . .

I wasn't smiling now.

Directly in front of me was a knife-wielding, delusional, growling, schizophrenic—the situation a direct result of my investigation into the Purcells. In disbelief I danced left and right, frantic to avoid serious injury. I looked into the rolling eyes of my attacker and felt doomed. Doomed and downright *FURIOUS* at Dwayne Durbin. It was his fault I was here! It was his ridiculous belief in my abilities that had put me in harm's way! Hadn't I told him I'm no good at confrontation? Hadn't I made it clear that I'm damn near a chickenheart? Doesn't he *ever* listen to me?

His fervent belief in me was going to get me killed!

Gritting my teeth, I thought: *I hope I live long enough to kill Dwayne first. . . .*

I was deep into the grunt work necessary to earn my license as a private investigator. Dwayne Durbin, my mentor, had finally convinced me I would be good at the job. His cheerleading on my behalf was not entirely altruistic: he wanted me to come and work for him.

I'd resisted for a while but circumstances had arisen over the summer that had persuaded me Dwayne just might be right. So, in September I became Dwayne Durbin's apprentice—and then I became his slave, spending my time putting in the hours, digging through records, doing all his dog work—which really irritates me, more at myself than him, because I'd *known* this was going to happen.

And though I resented all the crap-work thrown my way, Dwayne wasn't really around enough for me to work up a head of steam and vent my feelings. He was embroiled in a messy divorce case for Camellia "Cammie" Purcell Denton. His association with the Purcell family was why I'd delved into the Purcell family history in the first place. I admit this was more for my own edification than any true need on Dwayne's part, but I figured it couldn't hurt.

That particular September afternoon—the afternoon I wrote my conclusion on the report—was sunny and warm and lazy. It was a pleasure to sit on Dwayne's couch, a piece of furniture I'd angled toward his sliding glass door for a view of the shining waters of Lake Chinook. I could look over the top of my laptop as I wirelessly searched databases and historical archives and catch a glimpse of sunlight bouncing like diamonds against green water.

Resentment faded. Contentment returned. After all, it's difficult to hold a grudge when, apart from some tedium, life was pretty darn good. My rent was paid, my mother's impending visit had yet to materialize, my brother was too involved with his fiancée to pay me much attention, and I had a dog who thought I was . . . well . . . the cat's meow.

I finished the report and typed my name on the first page, mentally patting myself on the back for a job well done. Reluctantly, I climbed to my feet and went to check out Dwayne's refrigerator. If he possessed anything more than beer and a suspect jar of half-eaten, orange-colored chili con queso dip, life would pass from pretty darn good to sublime. My gaze settled on a lone can of diet A&W root beer. Not bad. Popping the top, I returned to the couch and my laptop.

Intending to concentrate, my eyes kept wandering to the scene outside the sliding glass door. Dwayne, who'd been lounging in a deck chair, was now making desultory calls on his cell phone. He stepped in and out of my line of vision as I hit the print button, wirelessly sending information to Dwayne's printer. Nirvana. I'm technologically challenged, but Dwayne has a knack for keeping things running smoothly and efficiently despite my best efforts. Since I'd acquired my newest laptop—a gift from an ex-boyfriend—I'd slowly weaned myself from my old grinder of a desktop. This new, eager slimmed-down version had leapfrogged me into a new era of computers. It fired up and slammed me onto the Internet faster than you can say, "Olly olly Oxenfree." (I have no idea what this means but it was a favorite taunt from my brother Booth who was always crowing it when we were kids, gloating and laughing and skipping away, delighted that he'd somehow "got" me. Which, when I think about it, still has the power to piss me off.)

The new laptop untethered me from my old computer's roosting spot on the desk in my bedroom. Now, I'm mobile. I bring my work over to Dwayne's, which he highly encourages. I'm fairly certain Dwayne hopes I'll suddenly whirl into a female frenzy of cleaning and make his place spotlessly clean. Like, oh, sure, *that's* going to happen.

Still, I enjoy my newfound freedom and so Dwayne's cabana has become a sort of office for me. I claimed my spot on his well-used but extremely comfortable one-time blue, now dusty gray, sofa early. Being more of a phone guy, Dwayne spends his time on his back deck/dock and conducts business outdoors as long as it isn't raining or hailing and sometimes even if it is.

Feeling absurdly content (always a bad sign for me, one I choose to ignore) I checked my e-mail. Nothing besides a note from someone named Trixie which I instantly deleted. One day I made the mistake of opening one of those spam e-mails about super hot sex and ever since I've been blessed with a barrage of Viagra, Cialis and penis enlargement ads and/or promises. If I didn't have penis envy before, I sure as hell do now. Eighteen inches? Where would you park that thing on a daily basis? There are a lot of hours when it's not in use . . . unless you count the fact that it functions as some guys' brains. I have met these sorts, but I try not to date them. Makes for uncomfortable dinners out where I talk and they just stare at my breasts. If I had serious cleavage I could almost understand, but my fear is that it simply means my conversation is really boring.

My cell phone rang with a whiny, persistent ring. I am going to have to figure out how to change it. A James Bond theme would be nice. I snatched it up without looking at Caller ID. An error. Marta Cornell, one of Portland's most voracious divorce lawyers, was on the line.

"Jane!" Marta's voice shouted into my ear. Her voice lies at sonic-boom level. I feared this time she may have shot one of my inner ear bones—the hammer, the anvil or the stirrup—into the center of my brain. Who names those things, anyway?

"You know Dwayne was working for Cammie Purcell,"

Marta charged ahead without waiting for my response. "Jane? Are you there?"

"Yes." I was cautious. Marta was Cammie's divorce lawyer and Dwayne had been following Cammie's husband Chris around for several weeks, intent on obtaining proof that he possessed a second family. Said family was apparently sucking up some Purcell money. Chris Denton wasn't exactly a bigamist. He'd never actually married his other "wife." But he had children with her and he divided his time between them and Cammie. Stunted as he was maturity-wise, I was impressed he could juggle two relationships. Sometimes I find it difficult just taking care of my dog.

"That job's pretty much finished, isn't it?" Marta asked.

"I think so." Actually, I wasn't completely sure. Cases like Cammie's seemed to undulate: sometimes the work lasted days on end; other times it nearly died. When Dwayne had first discovered the dirt on Chris, he'd disclosed it to Cammie and Marta. With divorce in the offing, Marta must have seen greenbacks floating around her head, but weirdly, Cammie's only remark had been a question: "What are the childrens' names?"

Later I'd learned this query had some merit after all: Chris's two girls—with his almost wife—were Jasmine and Blossom. When Dwayne told Cammie their names her face crumpled as if she were going to cry. But then she fought off the tears and went into a quiet rage instead.

"Her eyes looked like they were going to bug out of her head," Dwayne told me later. "I took a step backward. Her hands were clenching and unclenching. She wanted to kill me for telling her. A part of my brain was searching the room for a weapon. But then she kinda pulled herself together." Dwayne gave me a long look. "I don't ever want to be in a room alone with her again. No wonder the bastard left her."

Camellia's strange behavior was explained when it surfaced that many of the female members of the Purcell family were named after flowers. Apparently Chris's non-Purcell "wife" had fallen for this weird obsession as well, and since it was a decidedly Purcell quirk, Cammie appeared ready to kill over it.

This was about the time I decided to indulge in some Purcell family history. Hence, my report.

"Jasper Purcell would like to meet with you," Marta said, bringing me back to the present with a bang. "He needs a P.I."

"You mean, meet with Dwayne?" I asked, puzzled. I was the research person, not the A-list investigator.

"Nope." Her voice sounded as if she were trying to tamp down her excitement. Must be more money involved. "He called this morning and asked me for the name of a private investigator. It's something of a personal nature, to do with his family."

"This is Dwayne's case," I reminded her. I didn't add that Dwayne wanted to wash his hands of the whole thing.

"Jasper wants someone else to tackle this one. Says it's sensitive."

I glanced through the sliding glass door to where Dwayne, who'd removed his shirt in the unseasonably hot, early October sunshine, was standing on the dock. His back was hard, tan and smooth. Someone who knew him drove by in a speedboat and shouted good-natured obscenities. Dwayne turned his head, grinned and gave the guy the finger.

"How sensitive?" I asked.

"He said he wants a woman."

I wasn't sure what I thought of that. Just how many private investigators did the Purcell family need? "I'll have to make sure this is okay with Dwayne."

"I talked to Dwayne this morning," Marta revealed. "He said he's had his fill of the Purcells but if you wanted to step in, he was all for it."

Nice of Marta to keep that tidbit of information back

while she felt me out on the subject. I didn't like being ma-nipulated, and I was pretty sure that was what she was doing.

Also, I knew Dwayne's feelings about Cammie, but this sounded suspicious. Dwayne likes to cherry-pick assign-ments. That's why I'd been relegated to grinding research and drudge work. I narrowed my eyes at his back until he glanced around. His brows lifted at my dark look and he stuck his head inside the gap in the sliding glass door. "What?"

"I'm talking to Marta Cornell about the Purcells."

"They pay well, darlin', and that's the only goddamn good thing about 'em." He went back to the sunshine, turn-ing his face skyward like a sybarite.

Marta persisted, "Our client wants you to meet him at Foster's around four. Get a table. He'll buy dinner."

Free food. I'm a sucker for it and Marta knows my weak-ness.

And Foster's On The Lake is just about my favorite restau-rant in the whole world. I seesawed, thinking I might be get-ting into something I really shouldn't. In the end, I agreed to go. How bad could the Purcells be?

Two hours later I found a parking spot about a block from Foster's On The Lake—no small feat—then walked through the restaurant to the back patio, snagging a table beneath one of the plastic, faux-grass umbrellas that sported a command-ing view of Lake Chinook. Most of the umbrellas are green canvas, but sometimes Jeff Foster, owner and manager of Foster's On The Lake, adds a bit of fun to the mix, hence the plastic-party-ones. He didn't notice my arrival or he would have steered me toward a less well-placed table. He knows how cheap I am and tries to give the paying customers the best seats. I was all ready to explain that I was being treated by one of the Purcells but a member of the wait staff I didn't know let me choose my table. Maybe it was because I'd taken a little extra care with my appearance. I'd unsnapped my ponytail, brushed and briefly hot-curled my hair, tossed on a tan, loosely flowing skirt and black tank top. I'd even done the mascara/eyeliner bit, topping the whole look off with some frosted lip gloss.

The Binkster, my pug, had cocked her head at me and slowly wagged her tail. I took this to mean I looked hot.

I'd forgotten to ask Marta what Jasper looked like. He was a Purcell and the Purcells were wealthy and notorious, so apparently that was supposed to be enough. From my research I knew he was in his mid-thirties. I settled back and ordered a Sparkling Cyanide, my new favorite drink, a bright blue martini that draws envious eyes from the people who've ordered your basic rum and Cokes.

I was sipping away when a man in the right age bracket strode onto the patio. He stopped short to look around. I nearly dropped my cocktail. I say nearly, because I'd paid a whopping eight bucks for it and I wasn't going to lose one drop unless Mt. St. Helen's erupted again and spewed ash and lava to rain down on Foster's patio, sending us all diving for cover. Even then I might be able to balance it.

I felt my lips part. Marta must have guessed what my reaction would be when I clapped eyes on him. She probably was fighting back a huge *hardy-har-har* all the while we were on the phone. This guy was flat-out gorgeous. Women seated around me took notice: smoothing their hair, sitting up straighter, looking interested and attentive. His gaze settled on me. I gulped against a dry throat. He had it all. Movie star good looks. Electric blue eyes and thick lashes. Chiseled jaw. Smooth, naturally dark skin and blinding white teeth. And a strong physique—taut and muscular with that kind of sinewy grace that belongs to jungle cats. I should have known this was going to turn out badly. I should have heard the "too handsome" alarm clang in my brain. But, honestly, I just stared.

He flashed me a smile, then scraped back the chair opposite me. The sun's rays sent a shaft of gold light over his left arm. His gray shirt was one of those suede-ish fabrics that moves like a second skin.

"Jane Kelly?" he asked.

Great voice. Warm and mellow. He smelled good, too. Musky and citrusy at the same time. And his dark hair had the faintest, and I mean faintest, of an auburn tint, a shade women pay big, big, HUGE, bucks for.

I nodded, wondering if I should check for drool on my chin. You can never be too careful.

"I'm Jasper Purcell."

"Hello."

"Thanks for meeting me. I know I didn't give you a lot of time."

I cleared my throat. "No problem. Marta Cornell said you wanted to see me about your family. She wasn't specific."

"I wasn't specific with her." He hesitated, his eyes squinting a bit as if he were wrestling with confiding in me. After a moment, he said, "It's about my grandmother, Orchid Purcell."

I looked interested, waiting for him to continue.

"She named all her girls after flowers. But it's the only crazy thing she's done until now."

Mental illness runs in the Purcell family. . . . "What's happened?" I asked cautiously, but Jasper Purcell didn't answer me. He appeared to be lost to some inner world.

Eventually he surfaced, glancing around, seeming to notice his surroundings for the first time. "Nice place. I've never been here."

Since Foster's was a Lake Chinook institution I was kind of surprised. The Dunthorpe area—where the Purcell mansion had been for the last century—was just north of the lake. If Jasper Purcell grew up there, the restaurant seemed like a natural.

"How can I help you, Mr. Purcell?"

"Sorry." He leaned across the table and shook my hand. The heat of his fingers ran right up my arm. I was dazzled by that incredible face so close to mine. "Call me Jazz."

"Jazz?"

"Short for Jasper. My cousin Cammie could never pronounce it."

Nowhere in my research had anything been said about this man's extraordinary good looks. Was Cammie as beautiful as Jasper—Jazz—was handsome? I made a mental note to ask Dwayne.

Instinctively, I knew I should stay out of whatever he had in store for me. But I really wanted to help him. Really, *really* wanted to help him. Call it temporary insanity. But every cell in my body seemed to be magnetically attracted to him.

Jazz looked down at the table, then across the patio toward the lake. Light refracted off the water's green depths, glittering in soft squares of illumination across his cheek and jaw. I lifted my glass and nearly missed my mouth. My gaze was riveted on his face.

"Do you know anything about my grandmother?"

"I know she's a philanthropist, active on all kinds of boards."

"Was. Her health's been failing her. It could be anything from simple forgetfulness to Alzheimer's to another form of dementia, to—according to my aunt—a nasty trick she's playing on all of us." He gave me a look. "Between you and me, that's just not possible. My grandmother isn't made that way."

"So, what do you think?"

"She's definitely not as sharp as she once was. She doesn't drive anymore. We have someone taking care of her during the day who Nana likes, but it's tricky."

I thought carefully and said, "I'm not sure what you'd like me to do. I'm certainly no expert on that kind of thing."

Missy, Foster's most generously endowed waitress, hovered nearby. Jazz smiled, but shook his head at her. She cast a lingering look over her shoulder as she swayed off. "I'd just like someone else's opinion."

"How about a doctor's?"

He smiled, briefly and bitterly. "If you can figure out how to get Nana to see a doctor, that would be fantastic. She's afraid we're trying to railroad her. Wrest the family fortune out of her hands."

I could hear the beginnings of a very loud inheritance squabble revving up. "Is it what you're trying to do?"

"Not unless it comes to that," Jazz said grimly. He lightly drummed his fingers on the table, frowning. "I just want you to meet her. Someone outside the family who has no ax to grind. A woman. My mother doesn't really trust strange men."

"You mean your grandmother."

His head snapped up. "Yes, grandmother. What did I say?"

"Mother."

I swear his skin paled a bit. "How Freudian," he murmured. "My mother's dead. Died not long after I was born. Nana gave me Purcell as a last name, and she raised me." He sighed. "Guess I'm throwing all the skeletons out of the closet. Feels easier than holding back, although other members of my family wouldn't agree."

"What caused—your mother's death?" In my research, I'd learned that Lily Purcell had died in a sanitarium when she was still in her teens. She'd had Jazz at a very tender age indeed.

Jazz's eyes met mine again. I felt slightly breathless under their solemn regard. He said, "She died in a mental hospital of complications that arose when the staff tried to restrain her. The whole thing was hushed up."

Not sure how to respond, I took a sip from my Sparkling Cyanide. The color of my martini was very close to the shade of Jazz's eyes.

"There have been all kinds of rumors over the years. My grandmother even thinks my mother was deliberately murdered."

"Murdered?" Disbelief rang in my voice. "At the sanitarium?"

"So, Nana believes. She says my mother was one of the meekest women on earth. Not a resistant bone in her body. Having to restrain her doesn't fit."

"Drugs can make people act like maniacs, sometimes."

Jazz inclined his head. "Nana believes there's more to that story, though frankly, I'm not so sure. But that's all past history. What matters now is Nana. Will you meet her? Just get an overall impression? That's all I'm looking for," he said, his gaze turning toward the lake. A sleek, black-and-white Master Craft pulled up to the dock outside Foster's patio.

I didn't talk about the cost. I didn't mention that I was barely an apprentice. I didn't say anything to jeopardize the moment. Under Jasper Purcell's spell I could only give one answer: "Yes."

That brought a brilliant smile to his lips. He gave me his full attention again and clasped my hands between his own. My knuckles tingled. "Thank you," he said, his gaze so warm my internal temperature shot skyward. *Whew.* I was going to have to order another drink . . . and pour it over my head to cool off.

Marry in haste, repent in leisure. One of my mother's favorite axioms slipped across my mind. So, okay, I wasn't marrying the guy. It wasn't like he was even interested. But I sure ended up with a lot of time wishing I hadn't been so hasty.

Every time I say "yes" it gets me in a shitload of trouble.